Christmas Revels IV

FOUR REGENCY NOVELLAS

Kate Parker

Louisa Cornell

Anna D. Allen

Hannah Meredith

SS

Singing Spring Press

CHRISTMAS REVELS IV : FOUR REGENCY NOVELLAS

The Sergeant's Christmas Bride copyright © 2017 by Anna D. Allen
Home for Christmas copyright © 2017 by Meredith Simmons
A Memorable Christmas Season copyright © 2017 by Kate Parker
A Perfectly Unforgettable Christmas copyright © 2017 by Pamela Bolton-Holifield

ISBN: 978-1-942470-07-6 (Print)
ISBN: 978-1-942470-06-9 (E-book)

Published by Singing Spring Press

Table of Contents

The Sergeant's Christmas Bride

by

Anna D. Allen

The Sergeant's Christmas Bride

6 December 1815

An ominous click instantly brought Sergeant Jacob Burrows out of his shallow sleep. In the full expectation of a fight, he opened his eyes, and found himself, not in Spain or Toulouse or even the wilds of America, but in a cold, dark stable in Gloucestershire. In the shadows before him stood a cloaked figure with a lantern in one hand and a fully-cocked pistol in the other.

Heart racing, Jacob jumped up, his paltry blanket falling to the straw bed he had made for himself in the empty stall. The nearby horses sounded agitated as well, stirring up the straw and shaking their manes with equine grumbles. Now on his feet and at his full height, he realized the figure was much smaller than he first believed, and he *almost* relaxed, just a bit, knowing he could easily overpower whoever it was. And as so many others did when made aware of his true size, the figure cautiously moved back a few steps toward the open stable door, light from the house beyond piercing the night and reflecting off the sparse, falling snowflakes.

"Keep your hands where I can see them." The voice surprised Jacob—soft and feminine but keenly edged. He took a half-step forward. "No. Not another step," the female said, "I *will* shoot you."

Jacob stopped and tried to figure out how to play this. He did not like having a pistol pointed at him, but this wasn't the enemy. It was an Englishwoman who had just discovered a strange soldier sleeping in her stable.

When shipped to fight in America after the Battle of Toulouse, Jacob had been warned about poisonous snakes. He never saw one, but he heard tales around the campfires, someone always claiming to have known someone who had been bitten and died. One such snake gave a warning by rattling, as if to ward off its victim. But another snake blended in with the leaves. One never knew it was even there until it was trod upon; it struck in a flash, with death quickly following.

Jacob did not know which this woman was. Was the pistol her warning, her rattle to alert her victim—or was it already too late? She was trod upon and would shoot? He feared her calm demeanor suggested the latter.

"I doubt that's loaded," he lied with a deceptive shrug.

"I'm willing to find out. Are you?"

He might have dismissed her detached tone, but she held the pistol steady, properly, not with her finger curled about the trigger like some novice first handling a weapon but pointed down the barrel to prevent a misfire. That told him everything he needed to know. She knew how to shoot, and she would kill him, if necessary.

He decided to play it nonchalantly, as a matter of course.

"Ah, but then you'd have a body on your hands and end up hanged for murder." He slowly reached down and picked up his blanket. The night was bitter cold, his red coat doing little to keep him warm, and he deliberately draped the blanket about his shoulders. It was one of his few remaining possessions, everything else sold off to pay for his passage back to England.

"Murder?" she said. He thought he heard a small snort. "Hardly. I'd give a performance worthy of Mrs. Siddons." Her voice went up an octave as she demonstrated feigned distress. "'I didn't know the gun was loaded. After all, what would a mere female know of such things?'" Her voice returned to its previous cadence. "And you, some thief come to murder us in our beds."

As she spoke, she moved the lantern oh so slightly, and Jacob saw her face. His heart skipped a beat at the sight— young, smooth-skinned, beautiful with classical features, but as frigid as the night air without the least hint of emotion. Only, he *knew* that face. No, they had never met before this moment, but Jacob knew that face as well as he knew his own, if not better. And he realized he'd made a mistake when he chose this stable to bed down for the night.

"A thief?" Jacob asked. He looked down at the straw beneath his feet. "Then why the body in the stable and not the house?"

For a moment, he thought he had her with that one, but she replied without hesitation, "Oh, I'll just drag you into the house." He could tell she had considered this potential situation long before tonight. He couldn't decide if he thought such a calculation unnerving or quite prudent and clever on her part. Admirable, even.

However, she was diminutive compared to him. If standing toe to toe, she would be eye level with his mid-chest and was probably a foot shorter than he. He was also solid muscle; God had created him in the image of a blacksmith, not a common soldier.

"By yourself?" He pointed out the obvious difficulty of dragging someone his size all the way to the house. "Unlikely."

"What makes you think I'm alone?"

The time had come, Jacob realized, to lay his cards on the table. "I suppose Mrs. Howard could help you...." He saw her look of surprise—mixed with something else. "...But with her rheumatism, I don't know how much help she'd really be. And Mr. Howard's been dead now for what? Two years?" As he finished speaking, he realized what else he recognized in her face—fear.

"Who are you? What do you want?"

"My name is Jacob Burrows." For a moment, recognition flickered in her eyes, and the pistol lowered fractionally. "I'm sorry," he continued, wishing he had been forthright with her from the start. "I didn't know this was Worthing House. I thought I still had several miles to go. I merely chose the first place I found as darkness fell. Just some place to bed down for the night. If I'd known where I was, I would have come to the kitchen door." When she didn't respond, he asked, "You're Miss FitzWalter... I mean, the new Lady Worthing, right?"

She simply nodded. She was the very image of her late brother, Major Matthew FitzWalter—for a short time also Viscount Worthing. Theirs was that rare aristocratic title that could pass through the female line in the absence of an immediate male successor. In this case, upon the major's death, the title had passed to his only surviving sibling, the lady now standing before Jacob.

He motioned to his pack leaning against the post. "I have something for you. From your brother."

"He died at Toulouse more than a year and a half ago."

"I know. I was with him."

In an instant, she stepped back and rapidly raised the pistol level with his chest again. This time, Jacob saw the flash of anger in her eyes. And he suddenly feared he'd played this all wrong, that even with honesty he might still get shot.

"Wait. I really do have something from him. He told me to bring it to you. I would have come sooner, but they shipped me to America." Again, he motioned to his pack.

"Careful."

"Yes. I know. You *will* shoot me." Cautiously, watching her as much as paying attention to what he was doing, Jacob opened his pack, reached in, and pulled out the sealed letter. He held it up to her so she could see the direction written upon it. "You know his hand?"

She raised the lantern and leaned in a bit to get a closer look. Then a small gasp escaped from her mouth, her eyes widening simultaneously.

"Here," she said, handing him the lantern. Once he took it from her, she snatched the letter from his other hand. Staring down at the folded paper, she slowly lowered the pistol, relief washing over Jacob. For a long while she just gazed at the letter, until finally clutching it to her chest. Then, with great deliberation, she lifted her eyes and looked at him.

"I'm sorry," she said, "There are many soldiers

wandering the countryside these days, some with nefarious intentions. We can't be too careful."

"Perfectly understandable."

Holding the lantern, Jacob could see her better. She adjusted her cloak, partially parting the folds. Beneath it, she wore a man's jacket, a belt buckled about it just below her bust and mimicking the current high-waisted fashion. She tucked the pistol awkwardly into the belt.

"Well then," she said, taking back the lantern, "there's no point in staying out here. We can at least offer you a place by the fire in the kitchen and a hot meal."

Jacob accepted the invitation without hesitation. He grabbed his pack and trailed her out of the stable, only pausing to close and secure the stable door. She waited for him before continuing across the winter-white yard to the house, Jacob just a couple steps behind her as the snow intensified. She walked with an inelegant gait, picking her way over frozen ruts and icy patches toward the broken stone steps leading into, he presumed, the kitchen.

But as she mounted the first step, she suddenly gave a slight cry, her foot slipping, the lantern dropping, and her arms flying outward in a vain attempt to catch herself in the midst of a fall. Instantly, without any thought, Jacob dropped his pack, and caught her about the waist before she could hit the ground.

Only, to his astonishment, she had no waist. Her swollen belly told him all he needed to know.

"You're with child!"

"How very perceptive of you."

Elizabeth FitzWalter clung to the soldier's arm about her

for a moment, amazed by the size and strength of it, until she felt steady on her feet again. Despite that, her heart still raced frantically from the fright she'd had upon losing her footing on the slick ice. She could have so easily fallen and broken her neck or, worse, injured her child. She was grateful to this Jacob Burrows—she had recognized his name the moment she heard it, as Matthew had often mentioned his sergeant in his letters—but now a third person after Mrs. Howard and the midwife knew of the condition she desperately wanted kept secret.

"You may let me go now," she said. He cautiously released her, his hand hovering near her as if she might slip again. She picked up the now-extinguished lantern, and still clutching the letter in her bare hand, she hurried up the few steps and into the kitchen, the massive soldier following her. She half expected him to duck his head as he came inside. Despite what he said—he wasn't the first man to say he was with her brother when he died—Elizabeth still wondered if she should allow him into the house, even just into the darkened kitchen, especially with only Mrs. Howard and her there. Of course, she assured herself, she could just shoot him, if need be. But somehow, she doubted it would come to that. Regardless of everything that had happened, her instincts had generally been right, and now, something told her this man was a good man. That didn't mean, however, she would throw caution to the wind. Instincts were all well and good, but her suspicious nature served her just as well—except when she chose to ignore it, a mistake she would not make again.

Sergeant Burrows, with his gray blanket still wrapped around him, immediately headed toward the kitchen fire and stood there warming his hands. From Matthew's letters, she had imagined the sergeant older, gruff, with a belly from too much drinking. Instead, he was tall and broad with unfashionably long blond hair just touching his wide shoulders, some of it pulled back in an untidy queue.

As Elizabeth hung up her cloak on a peg by the door and set aside the lantern, Mrs. Howard entered from the hall and hesitated at the sight of the soldier before the kitchen fire. She glanced at her mistress.

"Sergeant Burrows," Elizabeth said to her housekeeper, "Claims he was with Matthew when he died." She caught the glare he gave her. "You're in luck," she said to him, "we had a bit of beef, and Mrs. Howard made a stew of it. Pears. Cheese. Bread. Cider to wash it all down. And apple tart with cream for dessert." She said all this not to whet Sergeant Burrow's appetite but as instructions to Mrs. Howard. All they had planned for their dinner was the stew, bread, and the tart, but with a man here, Elizabeth wanted more on the table, primarily because she feared he'd eat all the stew, which she wanted to last at least two days.

"When did you last eat?" she asked him as Mrs. Howard set about getting dinner on the table.

He appeared reluctant to answer. "I had a bit of bread early this morning," he replied. Elizabeth suspected he'd had little to eat before that.

"In that case," she said, "just wash up in the scullery for now. You can take a proper bath after dinner."

"A bath?"

There was no polite way around it. "You smell. And you need to shave."

A slow, small laugh rumbled up in him, and he seemed

quite amused by her comment. "As you wish, my lady." He pulled the blanket from about him, dropped it onto the settle by the fire, and followed Elizabeth's finger pointing to the scullery. As soon as he was gone, Mrs. Howard hurried over to Elizabeth.

"Do you think it's safe having him in the house?" she asked in a rushed whisper.

"I don't know." Elizabeth showed her the letter.

"What's that?" The housekeeper squinted her eyes trying to read the writing in the glow of firelight.

"A letter from Matthew. Sergeant Burrows brought it."

"Gracious. After all this time."

"Go ahead and serve the sergeant his dinner." Elizabeth looked down at the letter in her hands and studied the familiar script. "I want to be alone for a little while."

"Of course, my lady. I'll see to the sergeant."

Elizabeth traversed the darkened hall and ascended the stairs to her chamber where a fire burned in the hearth. Other than the kitchen, it was the only room in the house where the fire was kept lit all day, as she spent so much time here.

She took the magnifying glass from her escritoire, laid the pistol down, and took her place in the overstuffed chair by the fire. She examined the red wax seal through the magnifying glass. It had been impressed with her brother's signet ring bearing the FitzWalter family crest. That ring, delivered to her with word of his death, now sat with her stationary. The wax seal was unbroken, and she saw no evidence suggesting the wax might have come away intact from the paper and been resealed at a later date.

Elizabeth broke the seal and unfolded the paper with

trembling fingers and tightening throat to see her brother's final words to her.

Toulouse, France - 12 April 1814

My dear Elizabeth,

I am sorry to leave you alone in this world, but it is not of my choosing. Know that I would give anything to be there with you. But you will make an exceptional Viscountess Worthing, have no fear.

The bearer of this letter should be Sergeant Burrows—exceptionally tall, strength of an ox, blond like a Norseman but with the beauty of Aphrodite. Most likely, he needs to shave. He served faithfully alongside me and saved my life countless times. You can trust him implicitly in all things.

I promised Sergeant Burrows work at Worthing House when the war ended. Please do not make a liar of me. He comes from a long line of farmers in Yorkshire, but he inherited nothing and his wife is dead. Find some occupation for him, if not there, then a situation with a neighbor who will treat him respectably. He is a good man and deserves nothing less. But I would rest easier knowing a man such as he were there to keep you safe. He is quite resourceful and can do almost anything. He can read and write and is good with numbers.

I love you, dear sister, and await the day when we will be reunited.

Your devoted brother,

Maj. Matthew FitzWalter — whom some have called Viscount Worthing.

Elizabeth wiped the tears from her cheeks with her fingertips, refolded the page, and crushed the letter against her chest above her pounding heart. "Oh, Matthew," she whispered and then let the tears flow unabated. The pain of her loss hurt just as much now as it did the day *that man* came to inform her of her brother's death in France—a slow, drawn out death from a stomach wound. It took nine days for him to die. Elizabeth remembered thinking, with that amount of time, he could have come home to die, if someone had just brought him. Rationally, she knew such a journey would have simply hastened his death, but her heart still couldn't understand it. So instead of awaiting the resurrection in the family vault, Matthew lay in an unmarked grave somewhere across the Channel. They couldn't even bring his body home, yet they managed to bring Lord Nelson back.

She put her head back and tried to calm herself. She needed to be sensible and find something for Sergeant Burrows to do. Matthew was right; the son of a farmer could be very useful, especially as she had quietly let go of most of the servants and found them better positions when she realized her condition last spring. He already knew of the imminent arrival she expected in about a month, perhaps even by Twelfth Night, and Matthew did claim the man could be trusted in all things.

It was so warm there by the fire, with her feet resting on the little cushioned stool and the pillow supporting her lower back, that she couldn't help but close her eyes. She had no idea how long she sat there like that, but at length, she found herself waking up. She felt especially hungry. As she rose, she realized she still held the letter, now quite crumpled, in her hand. Matthew's words lingered in her head—to find some occupation for Sergeant Burrows.

Still drowsy from her nap, her thoughts not yet clear,

Elizabeth picked up her pistol, tucked it back into its place in her belt, and followed the scent of cinnamon and spices down the stairs. Mrs. Howard's apple tart with cream, she recalled, suddenly fearing the strange man in her kitchen might have eaten it all, not to mention the beef stew. And as she crossed the hall to the kitchen, the oddest idea occurred to her, to the point she paused for a moment, now fully awake, to mull it over, there in the middle of the ancient hall. At first, she dismissed it as an utterly ridiculous notion, before taking a deep breath and continuing on to claim her portion of dinner. But then, after just a few steps, she stopped again, her mind considering the possibilities further, despite the oddity of it all. Even on deeper reflection, she still found it a ludicrous idea..., yet something about it made perfect sense. And Matthew would certainly rest easier, given everything.

As she entered the darkened kitchen bathed only in the light of the fire, her mind contemplating how best to broach the subject with her house guest, Elizabeth looked up to see the man himself standing there before the hearth... naked from the waist up... completely naked, in fact, except for the towel he held tightly wrapped about his waist.

Elizabeth let out a shriek—like some common schoolgirl—and quickly turned her back to the sergeant, part of her wanting to turn back—not to see him again but to confirm the spectacle behind her.

"I'm so... so terribly..." she swallowed hard, completely mortified, "...sorry." The sight of Sergeant Burrows burned in her mind—the tub filled and waiting for... but no, he was *finished* with his bath; his hair hung wet and limp, blond now temporarily turned dark, his face still unshaved, water clinging to his skin and dripping to the stone floor. *How long had she slept?*

She thought she heard him laugh, and when he spoke, amusement accompanied his words. "I don't mind if you don't. No privacy in an army camp. And I suspect, given your present state, I'm not the first naked man you've seen." Elizabeth was not about to tell him, but as a matter of fact, he *was* the first naked man she'd seen. And she doubted she could have found a better specimen, all lean, well-sculpted muscle. With such intense blue eyes. It made the proposition she contemplated all the more uncomfortable.

"I didn't realize the hour, Sergeant." She attempted to sound conversational. "I didn't know how late it had gotten."

"Mrs. Howard said she wouldn't let me sleep on her clean sheets until I bathed. She's looking for something for me to wear."

"Well, you'll never fit into any of Matthew's old clothes. Nor my late uncle's clothing. He was very short."

"Mrs. Howard said something about her husband. Said he was a large man."

"Fat is a more apt description."

Even as she finished speaking, Mrs. Howard came striding in, a stack of folded clothing in her arms, while she held up one particular garment, an immense nightshirt. "I think this will do for now." She looked up and stopped abruptly at the sight of Elizabeth. "Oh. My lady. I thought you were still asleep. You must be famished."

"Quite." But as much as her stomach rumbled, Elizabeth contemplated fleeing the room, despite the deceptive calm of her voice. At least, she hoped she seemed calm. She could not understand how Mrs. Howard could act so nonchalantly, as if a naked man—a disturbingly attractive man at that… *Heaven above*, she did not know God made such beings—weren't standing in the midst of her kitchen.

Mrs. Howard moved past her, Elizabeth resisting the urge to turn and watch the housekeeper as she approached their wet guest. "This should fit," Mrs. Howard said, "although it might be a bit tight across the chest. Don't worry if you tear it. And I found a dressing gown as well."

Out of the corner of her eye, Elizabeth saw Mrs. Howard going to the scullery with an armful of clothing, most notably a red coat with sergeant stripes. "We should burn these, they're so threadbare," the housekeeper said, "but I'll see what I can do with them tomorrow." She emerged from the scullery a moment later and headed toward the larder, but not before adding, "Don't doddle, Sergeant. My lady needs her supper."

Elizabeth heard movement behind her—the sound of heavy, wet cloth flopping onto the stone floor, the softer purr of clean muslin gliding over clean skin, the unfurling of cheap brocade. Again, as she saw in her mind's eye this naked man dressing behind her, Elizabeth considered leaving the room. But then he spoke.

"It's safe to turn around now, my lady."

Elizabeth turned to see him tying the tapes of the dressing gown, bits of the creamy night shirt peaking out at the neck and wrists. Mrs. Howard was wrong, at least about the dressing gown. It fit well across the shoulders. Everywhere else was a different matter entirely; the arms were too short, excess material bunched about the waist where the dressing gown tied, and the hem just skimmed his shins. His bare, wet feet stood in a puddle of water.

"You need some stockings," Elizabeth said.

"That's one thing I have extra of," he replied.

Strolling out of the larder, Mrs. Howard carried a breadboard with half a loaf of round bread and a crock of butter. "And are those stockings clean?" she asked, "Wouldn't do to be putting on dirty stockings after a bath, now would it?"

"They're clean," Sergeant Burrows assured her, "I've been saving them for a moment such as this."

As the housekeeper returned to the larder, the sergeant retrieved the folded stockings from his pack, and Elizabeth — carefully adjusting the pistol tucked into her belt — sat down at the table where Mrs. Howard had laid out a place for her earlier. She immediately sliced some bread and slathered it in butter. She couldn't wait for the rest of her dinner, especially as she needed to speak to this strange man in her house, and she didn't want the distraction of hunger.

As he sat down on the settle and pulled on his stockings, Elizabeth asked, "Did you have enough to eat?"

"Plenty. Thank you," he replied, "but Mrs. Howard would not serve any of the apple tart until you ate."

"Oh, that won't do." Elizabeth quickly devoured her bit of bread and cut another slice. "She should have served you a slice first. Once I get to it, there might not be anything left for you." Sergeant Burrows laughed, but Elizabeth was completely serious. When Mrs. Howard returned with the cheese and fruit, Elizabeth said, "Bring the tart, as well. Sergeant Burrows can join me." He looked up at her, the surprise on his face matching the housekeeper's. Elizabeth motioned him to a chair at the table — not too close to her place. Mrs. Howard hurried to do as she was bid, and the sergeant slowly took the offered seat at the table several chairs down from Elizabeth. The housekeeper returned with the tart and a jug of cream and then served up the stew still by the fire for her mistress. She then left Elizabeth alone with the sergeant.

Elizabeth ate in silence as she contemplated her plan. How did a lady ask a man such a thing? A stranger at that. She had no choice, and she couldn't very well let this chance pass her by. She merely had to find her courage. Considering the man before her didn't help. Sergeant Burrows was the largest man she'd ever encountered. His arms were massive. His hands—now engaged in cutting a slice of tart—could easily wrap around her head and crush her skull. With a single hand, he could snap her neck. Yet she didn't fear him. She felt safe with him, safer than she'd felt in a long while. Not that she would give up her pistol.

"My brother wrote in his letter that he promised you work," she managed to say, as she watched him eat. To her relief, his table manners were well-above his station. "I suppose that is why you're here, to find work. Your time in the army is over?"

"I came to deliver Major FitzWalter's letter," he replied succinctly, "but yes, I also hoped to find work now that my service is ended." She heard the trace of disappointment in his voice as he glanced about the room. "I suppose that won't be possible now. This isn't the first house I've come upon since my return that has fallen on hard times."

"Do not mistake the economy of this household for poverty," Elizabeth said lightly without any suggestion of a scold. "Given my current state, the fewer people about the better. Old Joe brings anything we need from the village, and the Clayton boys from the farm manage the horses and stable and anything else that might need doing. But rest assured, there is plenty of work to be found here, and you are welcome to stay as long as you wish."

"Thank you, my lady."

"And beyond finding work here, do you have any plans?" Her brother's letter was nearly two years old, and the sergeant could have found another wife in the meantime. No need to make a fool of herself if a family anxiously awaited his return home.

"I want to go back to America," he replied, "Once I have the money, that is. A man can buy land there. Make something of himself."

For a moment, Elizabeth felt a pang of disappointment, but as she considered it further, she realized this might work to her advantage. Given his state—he appeared little better off than a beggar—he clearly had nothing and would have to work for years, perhaps even a decade, to earn enough money to do as he proposed.

Elizabeth set her spoon down and took a deep breath. Even in that ridiculous dressing gown, Sergeant Burrows was disturbingly handsome with now-dry strands of blond hair falling across his face. She wasn't immune to such beauty, and she wondered if it made her question all that more difficult to ask.

"What is it, my lady?" he asked, catching her staring at him. Elizabeth felt heat rise to her cheeks as she flushed with embarrassment.

"I have a problem." She met his gaze without flinching. After all, she told herself, this was easy compared to what she had already endured.

His face softened and he inclined his head toward her. "If there is anything I can do, please, do not hesitate to ask."

"Perhaps...," but then she hesitated and reconsidered her words. "Perhaps we could agree to an arrangement that might suit both our needs."

"How so?"

"Sergeant Burrows... I need a husband."

Jacob never expected those words to come from those exquisite lips. He suspected Lady Worthing was unmarried—she wore no ring—and he knew all too well the realities of the world. Such things, while uncommon, did happen, even among high-born, respectable ladies of the ton. But those ladies did not suggest marriage to base-born soldiers with nary a penny to their name. Perhaps he misunderstood.

"I beg your pardon, my lady?" he asked without hiding the astonishment from his voice, "Are you proposing marriage? To me?"

"I know it's not the thing to do but...." She pulled back, a look of horror on her face. "Oh, dear. I've given you a terrible shock. Should I find some brandy?" She started to rise, but he motioned her to stop, and she gradually sank back down to her chair.

"No, no. It's just that...."

"You're not already married, are you? Promised, perhaps? I assumed...."

"No." His firm tone silenced her mad rush of words. After a deep breath, he gently added, "My wife died some years ago in Spain."

A soft blush graced her cheek, and she quietly asked after a long silence, "Then you are free to marry again?"

"Yes." He couldn't help but smile. Still, this lady's proposal, to him, of all people, completely baffled him, and it took the wind right of out his sails. He felt disarmed and strangely defenseless. "But tell me why?" he asked.

Lady Worthing looked down at her swollen belly and splayed her hand protectively over it. "This child," she said without looking at him, "regardless of its sex, will be my heir..." She looked up at him, her brown eyes full of fear. "...Provided he or she is legitimate." Jacob understood, and he felt a strange glimmer of hope, a chance to redeem himself for the sins of his own past. She continued, and he heard the hint of pleading in her voice. "Legally, a woman's husband is her child's father. So I just need to be married in time for the birth. Which will be soon."

Jacob looked down at his plate—a bit of blue and white china imported from the other side of the world, a half-eaten piece of apple tart smothered in cream, his now immaculately clean hand holding a sterling silver fork worth more money than a month's wages. He had spent the day before helping a baker, in the heat and aroma of a kitchen, all in exchange for a crust of bread and a place to sleep. And tonight, this great lady, a peeress of the realm, invited him into her home, fed him better than he'd eaten in years, and saw to his needs, when many another would have sent him back to the stables without any concern for his comfort.

And now this. A chance to make up for the past.

He gazed over at her belly, her hand still resting there, the pistol tucked neatly in her belt, and he wondered about the father of her child. What sort of man would get her with child and leave them both defenseless in this world, to the point she would feel no choice but to ask a poor, begging soldier to marry her? And while he understood her reasons and her need... he found it all so difficult to fathom.

"I know this is all so ridiculous," Lady Worthing continued, trying to explain, "But I'm the last of my family, and finding a husband in the usual manner just won't be possible given.... And I could never trick someone into marriage." It was, Jacob knew, an all too common practice among some women, and he had seen many a brother-in-arms fall for it. It reassured him that she did not believe in such trickery.

"I understand why you need a husband," he said at last and looked over at her, "but you don't know me."

"I know enough."

"I'm not a gentleman."

Lady Worthing smiled and almost laughed. "Yes. Well. There is that. But in my experience, gentlemen are rarely gentlemen."

That pained him, despite the fact she said it in jest. It matched much of his experience as well, and he did not want to know how she, too, had reached such a conclusion. He couldn't help but wonder....

Bemused, he shook his head. "Why me?"

She gave him a small, unladylike shrug. "Men are themselves around other men. I'm certain my brother saw you at your worst, and still he called you a good man. He said he would rest better knowing you were here with me. Although, I doubt this is what he meant."

Jacob let out a sigh and knew it didn't matter what she asked of him; he would do it. She was Major FitzWalter's sister. That alone sufficed. But she was so lovely, this fierce little thing, and her predicament brought out long dormant instincts in him. Besides, she wanted the one thing he could so easily give her—the protection of his name, for what it was worth. And for him to be a father to another man's child. Perhaps justice did exist in this world.

But then she added, "We wouldn't have to stay married. You could still have your dream of going to America. I would be happy to help you in any way." He knew she meant financially. "And a divorce would be less difficult to obtain in America. I promise not to be a problem."

He should have been offended—for all intents and purposes, she wished to buy him—but he wasn't. Her proposal was imminently practical, for both of them. She would have a name for her child, he would have money for land in America.

"That's how you want this...," he asked, "this *arrangement?*"

"Sergeant Burrows... I don't have much of a choice in the matter."

No, she didn't, Jacob realized. And her situation forced her to put all her trust in him, a man she knew little of beyond his name and the recommendation of her brother. *What courage she possessed!* A family trait, he knew from long experience.

"There's one more thing," she added, her voice filled with apprehension. "If you married me, you would be Viscount Worthing *jure uxoris*. It means..."

"'By right of his wife.' Yes. I know what it means." He caught the surprised expression on her face—a response he'd grown long accustomed to—and he gave his standard account for the uncommon ability. "My grandfather was a vicar. He taught me to read Latin. He wanted me to be a minister. Go to Oxford. That sort of thing."

"Why didn't you?"

Jacob took a deep breath. "At 16, I was caught poaching. The judge took pity on me and gave me a choice. The hangman's noose or the king's shilling."

Lady Worthing grew even more somber, if that were possible.

"I see," she said.

"Now that you know I'm a criminal, do you wish to take back your proposal?"

"Not at all." She replied quite forcefully, only to look away from him and continue speaking as if the subject had never changed. "The fourth Viscount Worthing was killed without a male heir during the Civil War, and as reward for his sacrifice, the title was conferred on his eldest daughter during the Restoration... but the patent of nobility stipulated her husband would also hold the title for his lifetime."

What an amazing woman to take such a risk, Jacob thought. Not just with a stranger—an admitted criminal at that—but to risk everything for her child? He realized that while her husband would never own this house or her lands or her money outright, that man would have absolute control of them, and for all intents and purposes, control of her. The law would give him the right to all she owned, including her person, to do with as he pleased. She was willing to give up everything she had, all her independence, just so her child would have a name.

"Please, Sergeant Burrows, consider my proposal. Take some time...."

"I don't have to consider it, my lady."

"Oh, please... if only you...."

"I will marry you."

Her whole body seemed to breathe a sigh of relief.

Yes, he would marry her, but it would be on his own terms. For his own reasons.

Elizabeth woke quite angry with herself. While she was greatly relieved Sergeant Burrows had agreed to marry her, she felt humiliated, having spent the previous evening practically begging the man to be her husband. And afterwards, she had grown so shy and wondered if most newly betrothed ladies, as a rule, reacted similarly while contemplating the wisdom of joining their lives to another person.

Despite the still, small voice inside her—along with her brother's words—assuring her that she could, indeed, trust Sergeant Burrows, Elizabeth doubted her own judgment. He now held her life and that of her child in his hands, as little more than property, to do with as he pleased. And what if it didn't *please* him to abide by their agreement and seek divorce in America? He might very well grow too fond of his title and enjoy being master of all he surveyed.

Yet she realized she had no right to condemn him. She was using him, even if to his advantage. But if she didn't and bore this child without a father's name, no respectable man, once he learned the truth, would ever accept her as a wife. She would never have another chance to bear a child, only this one. The eventual loss of all her family's lands and property to some unknown distant cousin paled in comparison to that.

Perhaps she overstepped the bounds of propriety and upset the social order by proposing marriage to a man deemed beneath her. But then, she never would have found the courage had he been a gentleman and if he had not been in such need. She suspected she proposed only because she recognized he was in no position to refuse.

Before retiring for the night, however, they had managed to concoct a story to explain their rapid courtship and hasty marriage. An infant appearing within weeks of a wedding was not unheard of but it would cause tongues to wag. Best they wag with the tale of their choosing rather than with the unsubstantiated speculation of ignorant but inventive gossipmongers. Mrs. Howard would conveniently relay the relevant information to the butcher, and that would suffice to spread the account throughout the village and countryside... of how Lady Worthing met a member of her brother's regiment in London last winter and wished to marry him, only cruel fate intervened, sending her lover to fight in America instead of to his intended destination before the altar. But now, he had returned to be reunited at long last—and none too soon—with Lady Worthing. There would be no need to mention his rank in that regiment, and anyone hearing the tale would naturally assume Sergeant Burrows was an officer, and neither he nor Elizabeth saw any reason to dissuade them with facts.

Yes, that would do nicely, a romantic tale to placate and satisfy the curious. Sergeant Burrows seemed especially concerned that no questions of paternity arise. Male pride, Elizabeth supposed, but she agreed it was most prudent.

As usual in recent months, Elizabeth slept poorly and rose late. She didn't know whether to blame the pain in her back or the little fellow kicking her in the ribs half the night. It occurred to her that a long, hot soak in a tub by the fire might relieve some of her discomfort. After all, a man like Sergeant Burrows would have no difficulty helping her out of the tub when she finished. But after last night, she had no wish to impose on him further—if only for the sake of her pride.

Despite that, she decided she would not dress before going down to breakfast. If she had a house full of servants, she would simply ring for breakfast in her room. With just Mrs. Howard, such an indulgence was impossible. But with the advantage of an empty house, Elizabeth could go about as she pleased, and Sergeant Burrows' presence would not stop her from doing as she wished, especially when she suffered such discomfort.

She put on her dressing gown and slippers, tidied her plaited hair, and went down to the kitchen—pistol in hand as always. The house chilled her, but she welcomed the warmth of the kitchen, and as she entered, Elizabeth saw Sergeant Burrows having breakfast at the table. He immediately stood when she shuffled in. To her surprise, he was dressed in his own clothes, now clean, if a bit frayed about the edges, and he still looked disturbingly handsome, with his hair in a tidy queue.

"You are unwell?" he asked, sincere concern on his face. His reaction surprised her. She expected shock over the fact that she would present herself thus dressed—deemed a state of *undressed* by polite society—at breakfast and before a virtual stranger... albeit one whom she would soon marry. Instead, she discovered a genuine concern for her health.

"I'm as well as can be expected," she replied, feeling tired and ready to return to bed. She set the pistol on the table and noticed the wary look he gave it. "I'm not giving it up," she said.

"I'm not asking you to, my lady," he said with a shrug. He remained standing until she sat down—although, Elizabeth felt as if she plopped down in a most unladylike manner. Only as he took up his spoon again did she notice this morning's breakfast consisted of porridge liberally embellished with honey and sultanas.

"Where is Mrs. Howard?" Elizabeth asked as Sergeant Burrows—much to her surprise—poured her a cup of tea.

"Some boys brought milk and eggs. She's seeing to that."

As Elizabeth accepted the warm cup from him, she asked, "Would you prefer coffee with your breakfast?"

Sergeant Burrows appeared to blush, and then the corner of his mouth turned upward. "I'm just happy to have breakfast."

"Oh." That pained her. And while she wished to know more about his past, she refused to pry, ever so grateful he never queried her about matters she preferred remain private.

"Shall I...?" He motioned to the pot of porridge by the fire.

"No. Thank you. Tea will suffice for now."

They sat in uncomfortable silence, the sergeant slowly eating his breakfast, Elizabeth sipping her tea and hoping Mrs. Howard would return soon to break the stillness of the room. When Sergeant Burrows spoke again, it startled Elizabeth, his voice rumbling and reminding her of a lion she once saw at the Tower of London menagerie.

"Will a bishop's license do?" he asked, "I'd rather not ride to London for a special license, and you're in no condition for a journey to Gretna Green."

For the briefest moment, she experienced utter confusion as visions of lions and bishops vied for dominance in her mind.

"Yes. Yes, of course," she replied, imagining herself in a curricle racing down a rutty road toward Gretna Green, her hand clutched at her belly while Sergeant Burrows cracked the whip. She suspected many a lady arrived there in such a state.

"Gloucester it is, then," he said decisively.

"You should go as soon as possible." The sooner, the better. Elizabeth didn't think this child would wait much longer. She was of two minds on the matter; she needed more time, but she wanted it all over and done with. She glanced over at the sergeant in his fraying red jacket and wondered what had become of his overcoat. Probably sold it to another soldier, she suspected.

"I can leave after breakfast," he said.

"You can visit a tailor as well." While not a gentleman, he could dress the part, Elizabeth thought and then realized he needed money for such an undertaking. Sadly, she doubted a tradesman would take the sergeant's word and send her the bill as the butcher did with Old Joe. With some effort, she stood up, the sergeant standing as well, a look of concern on his face.

"I'll return in a moment," she said and waddled away, back to her bedchamber. Such a strange thing, she contemplated as she retrieved a purse of coins, for a woman to provide a man with funds for his needs. She hoped it did not hurt Sergeant Burrows' pride too much, living in such reduced circumstances with no alternative but to accept money from a female. Some men might find it humiliating, but Elizabeth reminded herself that Sergeant Burrows agreed to their arrangement. He understood what it entailed.

As she ambled back to the kitchen, the weight of the coin purse heavy in her hand, a fear crept through her. She was about to give a total stranger a large amount of money. He could easily abscond away, never to return. She shook her head. She had never been so suspicious of people before.... Now, she sometimes believed everyone had nefarious motives.

She passed the bedchamber Mrs. Howard had made up last night for their unexpected guest. The door stood ajar, and Elizabeth glanced in, to the bed where Sergeant Burrows had slept the night, cold sunlight now filling the room. The sight which greeted her almost made her smile.

She returned to the kitchen in a more optimistic mood and found the sergeant finished with his breakfast and preparing to depart for Gloucester. She handed him the coin purse. He hefted it, as if feeling its weight, and put it inside his jacket.

"This may take a number of days," he said.

"I know."

Elizabeth sat down... and saw, there on the table, her pistol. With a start, as if her heart jumped into her throat, she glanced up, just as Mrs. Howard came in from the yard with the older Clayton boy carrying firewood. Sergeant Burrows hurried to help them, his back turned away from Elizabeth, much to her relief. She could not believe she had forgotten her pistol. She kept it with her always. And now to have left it on the table....

The younger Clayton boy came rushing in, proudly announcing he had prepared Elizabeth's best horse for the sergeant's ride to Gloucester. A cacophony of male voices—both young and older, boasting and congratulatory—followed, before the sergeant, good-heartedly, tousled the would-be groomsman's hair and sent both boys back out to finish their work.

Within a moment, Sergeant Burrows stood ready to depart. And as he fixed the late Mr. Howard's old broad hat atop his head—which clashed with his red coat—Elizabeth said, "Find a barber." Really, she thought, how could a military man be so lax; he still needed a shave.

A warm, rich laugh rumbled up from him, as if he knew some secret joke, and with a smile, he tipped his hat to her.

"My lady."

And with that, he left.

Mrs. Howard stood before the fire with her fists on her hips.

"We won't see the likes of him again," the housekeeper said.

"Oh, Mrs. Howard, have faith," Elizabeth chided with a faint smile, "After all, he made his bed this morning."

Mrs. Howard raised her eyebrows in surprise. "Did he, indeed? Well, then, it only goes to follow that he intends to lie in it."

"Exactly," Elizabeth replied. But then Mrs. Howard gave her a knowing look. *Oh, dear.* Elizabeth had not thought of *that.*

The morning of Elizabeth's wedding broke cold and bitter, much to her relief. Even on the best of days, the grim, damp, village church chilled her to the bone. Today, she had no doubt the holy water would be ice. So no one would question her cloak and the many layers hiding her figure.

Despite her words of assurance to Mrs. Howard, Elizabeth was surprised on the previous day to see Sergeant Burrows return after only a two-day's absence. He rode up, wearing a new suit, a new great coat, with new top boots, all spit and polished, looking every bit a gentleman, with promises that the rest of his wardrobe would follow by week's end... except he clearly never visited a barber. He still needed a good shave. But no matter. With the bishop's license in hand, he would pass nicely for an ardent, eager bridegroom.

The vicar expected them at half-past nine, and the couple duly arrived before the altar, alone, without a wedding party, or bridal veil, or any of the usual accoutrements of such a joyous occasion. Not even a bouquet. Instead, Elizabeth clutched her gloves in one hand as the vicar's wife and their cook stood witness to the solemn rite. It all felt so perfunctory, with no real meaning behind the sacred vows. And when the vicar pronounced them man and wife, Elizabeth felt no different—not a bride, not a wife. But at least her unborn child now had a name, come what may.

The moment the vicar closed his prayer book, the bridegroom turned to her and took Elizabeth's gloves. He handed them to the vicar's wife and then clasped both of Elizabeth's icy hands in his. One at a time, he lifted each of them to his lips and placed a kiss on her knuckles, his eyes boring intensely into hers. As Elizabeth stared up at him, into those deep blue eyes, she realized Sergeant Burrows—her husband—was now Viscount Worthing *jure uxoris*.

"My lord," she whispered.

The corner of his mouth turned upward, and Elizabeth

saw a spark of amusement in those eyes as he replied, "Mrs. Burrows."

She may have saved her family's title, she may have assured her child a legal father, but her family name, FitzWalter, died with this marriage. And she offered up a silent prayer that she had done the right thing, because now, with the deed done, doubt filled her.

Jacob couldn't read his new wife, Elizabeth—no surprise given the duration of their acquaintance. She wanted this marriage, but as soon as the echo of their vows faded in the grim church, she turned silent, cold. She neither refused nor rebuffed his assistance up to or down from the gig he drove, while the small courtesy of *thank you* barely escaped her lips. Even after they returned to Worthing House, she acted indifferently toward him, with hardly a glance in his direction during their silent *celebratory* wedding breakfast for two.

He imagined she already regretted her actions. But too late. They would both have to live with their decision, whether they liked it or not. Jacob, however, suspected he would find much to relish about his new position. He had consulted a solicitor in Gloucester and well-understood his legal rights as Elizabeth's husband... and as the new Lord Worthing, no matter how *jure uxoris* the title might be. In the eyes of the law, all he surveyed belonged to him—if only for his lifetime. Her land, her money, even her body, all to do with as he wished.

It felt so very wrong, like a kind of theft, and he promised himself he would never abuse any new-found right. Well, maybe other than hunting. He could hunt to his heart's content, with no one to drag him before a magistrate simply for wanting to feed his family. Other than that... he was no pleasure-seeking wastrel. He would not shirk his responsibilities or leave them to Elizabeth. She had enough to deal with now, and he could easily carry some of her burdens.

Such a strange thing, he thought, his marriage vows—not a proclamation of a love he didn't feel right now, but a vow he *would* love her. In the future. And he fully intended to keep that vow, regardless of her plans.

After breakfast, Elizabeth disappeared, and when Jacob asked, Mrs. Howard informed him she was resting in her room. His wife—*his wife?* How strange that sounded, especially referring to Elizabeth and not Maria, dead these many years—had left her door slightly ajar, and when Jacob glanced into the room, he saw her dozing by the fire, the ever-present pistol lying on the table beside her. He remembered Maria, as her time grew near, sleeping whenever she could.

He quietly closed the door and set about exploring the house—his house now, as far as the world was concerned. After all, as *lord and master*, he should have some idea of exactly what he *surveyed*. Much to his liking, he found the house small as country manors went—in other words, large but manageable—with dark wood and great windows indicative of the Elizabethan era. And he found it well-maintained, surprising given only the one servant currently employed by Lady Worthing. Most of the rooms were closed off, the furniture draped in Holland cloths and coated in dust, but nothing a spring cleaning and a few more servants could not fix in a day or two of hard work.

The thought of that led Jacob to wonder about the household accounts. Elizabeth had said she dismissed the servants to conceal her growing condition. But that could have simply been something to tell a stranger on her doorstep, a diversion to distract him from the truth. He knew she had secrets.

But when he examined the household ledgers in the library, he found them up-to-date, neat and tidy, with the estate lucrative well-beyond his modest expectations. A series of maps laid out the entire estate, and Jacob decided—with nothing more pressing—to ride out and see for himself.

By late afternoon, he had visited half a dozen tenants, with a dozen still remaining, and had consumed enough congratulatory tea, cakes, and biscuits to feed a temperance society meeting. Without a word from Jacob, everyone greeted him as *my lord*, the nuptial news—and the concocted story—travelling faster than he had expected, despite his long-experience with village gossip.

He soon discovered the Claytons lived at the estate's dairy. He considered hiring several of the older sons and daughters to serve at Worthing House, but on further thought, Jacob realized why Elizabeth kept just the two boys on; they were young enough not to recognize her condition. With that in mind, he promised them positions some time after the New Year. After Elizabeth delivered her child. *Their child*, he reminded himself. *Best to start thinking that way now*.

He arrived home just before dinner. Mrs. Howard informed him the fire had been laid in the dining room where Lady Worthing would join him within the hour. Jacob quickly bathed and dressed for dinner and managed to return to the dining room before Elizabeth. Two places were laid out on the long table—each at opposite ends, with a dozen chairs between them, bringing a chill to the room that the fire could not drive away. Rather than bother Mrs. Howard with it, Jacob simply moved one place setting to the place beside the other. Theirs might not be a love match, but they could sit together like a normal, congenial pair and share a civil meal.

When Elizabeth entered the dining room, her stride faltered upon seeing the rearranged place setting. Jacob witnessed the flicker of fear in her brown eyes, her body tensing, but when he held out the chair at the head of the table for her, she noticeably relaxed. She removed her pistol from the belt beneath her bust—this evening, she wore a gentleman's dark blue, silk jacket with embroidered lapels—and she placed the pistol on the table beside her setting. She sat down, and Jacob took the adjacent chair.

"You should be sitting here," she pointed out.

"I'm not that particular," he replied, thinking a place at table preferable to his more accustomed experience on the cold, hard ground. "When we have company and all these chairs are filled, I'll sit in my appropriate place."

Mrs. Howard served them a stewed hen and potatoes with all the accompaniments. As they ate, Elizabeth seemed to relax even more, and while she said little, she listened to Jacob's recounting of his day visiting her—their—tenants. Still, he couldn't help but wonder about her pistol and her need to keep it close at all times. He understood perfectly the incessant desire for a weapon within arm's reach for protection, but he wondered what she feared. He hoped it wasn't him.

When she finished eating—well before Jacob finished—

she pushed back her chair and announced she was retiring for the night. Only, she struggled to rise. Jacob stood and reached out to help her, but she refused his assistance, and eventually managed to stand, before bidding him goodnight. It sounded very much like a dismissal.

Jacob lingered over his port for too long, and it was quite late when he retired for the night. To his surprise, he found the door open and the fire lit in the room he had previously occupied—a spare bedroom, not Viscount Worthing's chamber. It pricked his pride, to see his few possessions, along with the new clothes he brought from Gloucester, here, in a guest's room rather than in the master's chamber where they belonged.

This could not wait, Jacob decided. Elizabeth needed to understand now, from the start. She might think this but a marriage of convenience, but he certainly did not.

Jacob quickly packed up his belongings and, with candlestick in hand, went in search of the rooms adjoining his wife's rooms—the chambers of Lord and Lady Worthing. He noticed the light from under Elizabeth's door, and proceeded to the next bedchamber. He found it dark and dusty and suspected it had not been aired since Elizabeth's uncle had died—the last Viscount Worthing in residence. Jacob lit a few candles, all the while wondering if he should return to the warmth of the guest room where a good fire burned. But no, he had endured worse on many a night, usually under the open sky. He simply needed to build a fire.

Contemplating the cold hearth, Jacob noted the smoky smell of damp ash permeating the room, and he wondered when a chimney sweep last visited. He knelt down to examine the fireplace and realized he did not feel any draft.

He held the candle up to get a better look, the flame never flickering but ever steady. Immediately, he noticed something blocking the flue. He reached up and pulled a large bundle loose, the candle flame fluttering as cold air began to draw up the chimney.

Uncertain of what he'd found, Jacob moved over to the bed to examine the dusty, brown bundle tied together with something akin to a filthy neck cloth. Unraveling it all, he revealed what appeared to be a complete set of clothes, albeit it for a beggar, from a worn, threadbare jacket to leather shoes full of holes, and even a grimy, well-used handkerchief stuffed into a pocket. The presence of such a kit, up a chimney no less, baffled Jacob. He could think of no reason for it to be in the house, let alone blocking the flue. And given that the late Viscount Worthing had occupied these rooms a little over two years ago and required a fire, someone had hidden the bundle since then, possibly even Elizabeth.

Jacob sat on the edge of the bed for a long while in deep thought and carefully considered his next actions, the new cold draft from the chimney growing more noticeable. He needed a fire, but whoever hid the bundle would be aware of its discovery by tomorrow if he lit one. Jacob glanced over to the door separating the bedchamber from the viscountess's. A warm light still glowed beneath the door, and he wondered if Elizabeth were awake.

And then it occurred to Jacob he could kill two birds with one stone.

He retied the bundled and returned it to its smoky hiding place.

Elizabeth sat up, reading in bed by a single candle flame.

She could not decide which was worse—the damp cold of the sheets or the pain piercing her lower back. She had hoped the slim volume would lull her to sleep, but her mind refused to still and settle, too many thoughts—and feelings—clamoring for her attention.

Seeing the place settings rearranged at dinner with Sergeant... *Jacob*... standing there had frightened her. As her husband, he had every right to sit at the head of the table, but Elizabeth felt like she had lost all control of her life, like he usurped her authority in her own house. Only then, he held out the chair for her and took the lesser position for himself. It surprised her, his act of generosity, so strangely humble and unassuming.

This small concession toward maintaining her dignity and reconfirming her place in the house went far to soften her dark mood. While not enough to move her to engage in loquacious conversation, it caused her to listen with renewed interest. For all Elizabeth's doubts regarding the wisdom of this marriage, Jacob's actions since their first meeting demonstrated he deserved her respect. And respect so often went hand in hand with trust.

After returning from the church and having their *wedding breakfast*, Elizabeth had retired to her chamber to rest. She neither knew nor cared what Jacob did at the time. Only at dinner did she learn he had put that time to excellent use, calling upon her tenants—now his tenants, as well—something she certainly could not manage in her present state. He even remembered their names and spoke of hiring people after her confinement. Elizabeth knew she had nothing to fear from Jacob. Matthew said as much in his letter. She simply had to trust her instincts once again.

A small, quiet tap at the door startled Elizabeth. It took a moment for her to realize the sound did not come from the door to the corridor but from the connecting door to the next room—the *unoccupied* bedchamber of the Viscount Worthing.

Before she could respond, the door creaked open, just a bit, but enough to allow a hand through the gap to wave a fluttering white handkerchief. The door opened a fraction more, and Jacob peered in. He motioned toward her side table, and Elizabeth followed his gaze to her pistol lying there alongside the candle.

"I'd rather not get shot." He flashed a quick, lopsided grin. Then he furrowed his brow and said in a serious but sarcastic tone, "You do realize you could kill someone with that thing?"

"That is the idea." As nonchalantly as she could muster, Elizabeth returned her gaze to her book and endeavored to feign an indifference she hardly felt—quite the opposite in fact, her heart pounding fiercely, not with fear but with anger, as Jacob now stood in her bedchamber. And then he closed the door.

"Whatever are you doing?" she demanded, outraged by his audacity.

"I'm coming to bed, Mrs. Burrows." He casually traversed the room to the opposite side of her bed where he proceeded to remove his jacket. He glanced over at her and added, "Have no fear. It is not my custom to ravish expectant women. Or any woman, for that matter. But if you wish to consummate our marriage, I'm quite willing to oblige you."

"That won't be necessary," Elizabeth grumbled, trying to ignore his smirk. "And you have a bed of your own."

"The adjoining chamber has not been properly aired and lacks a fire." He unraveled his neck cloth and raised his eyebrows. "Besides, we common men sleep with our wives. Or didn't you know that?"

Much to her annoyance, Elizabeth distinctly felt he was enjoying this, despite her discomfort, made worse as he now stood there in his shirtsleeves and waistcoat. The firelight bathed him bronze, and the sight of him—her husband—unbuttoning his waistcoat disturbed her even more. His blond hair hung long and loose, barely brushing against his shoulders. He still needed a shave, but Elizabeth was growing accustomed to the scruff and almost liked it. The thought alone shocked her, and she attempted to ignore it.

"You look like a pirate," she said, trying not to stare as he undressed.

"You know a lot of pirates, do you?" He turned his back—much to her relief—only to pull his shirt over his head, thereby revealing his broad, muscular back. And then, before she could look away, his knee breeches were gone. She closed her eyes and wished she could slump down beneath the bedcovers, but her present girth would never allow such ease of movement.

She felt the bed sink beneath his weight as he settled in, and with a stab of pain in her back, Elizabeth's body slumped toward his. Her hands reached out to catch herself, and instead of touching naked flesh, she found she clutched the linen of a nightshirt. She opened her eyes, mere inches from the solid muscle of his chest, her belly pressed against his side. *How strange.* She thought she should be frightened or angry. Instead, she marveled at the warmth beneath her fingers and the steady beat of another's heart.

"Are you all right?" Jacob asked softly, his voice filled with concern.

"Yes, of course," Elizabeth replied, realizing she had cried out with the pain. She tried to right herself, to little avail. "It's just my back."

"Allow me." His words—and tone—stilled her efforts. He reached down between them and retrieved her now-forgotten book. He closed it—careful to mark her place first—and stretched over her to set it on the bedside table. Then, before she even realized his intent, he gently eased her over onto her side, her back now to him.

"Here," he said, reaching down beneath the covers. Suddenly, she felt his hand slip between her bare knees as he parted them. But just as she squawked in protest, he shoved a pillow between her knees and thighs.

"That should help some," he assured her, his voice strangely soothing in the wake of her brief moment of panic. "This should help, too," and he handed her a flattened pillow. "Put it under your stomach." With difficulty—and with Jacob's help—she raised herself up and placed the pillow underneath her swollen belly.

"As for your back," he said, placing his hand on the small of her back, "is this the spot?" The mere pressure of his hand drove much of the pain away, leaving a dull but bearable ache in its wake.

"Yes, that's it exactly." She wondered how he knew. And then he began to rub the spot. Elizabeth closed her eyes and struggled to keep from sighing with contentment.

"I would prefer your side of the bed," Jacob abruptly said in a matter-of-fact way.

It took Elizabeth's mind a moment to understand what

he meant. "This is my bed," she eventually said. He might have the audacity to climb into it without her consent, but she was staying on *her side.*

"A man should sleep closest to the door," Jacob explained, his hand never ceasing in its ministration, "so that he may protect his wife in the event of danger."

Incredulous, she asked, "In your nightshirt? With your bare hands?"

Jacob laughed. "Put that way, it does sound ridiculous. Still, we do have your pistol." The humor in his voice faded away, and silence fell over them as he continued to rub her lower back. But then Jacob broke the stillness.

"Are you going to tell me about your child's father?" he asked.

Without the slightest hesitation, Elizabeth replied, "You are my child's father."

"I mean his real father."

"*You* are his *real* father."

"My lady, don't be coy. It doesn't become you." She could hear the hint of annoyance in his voice. "As your husband and as the father of your child, I have some right to know who fathered your child, don't you think? Or in the very least, know why he isn't here."

As much as Elizabeth wished never to speak of the matter, she supposed Jacob had a point. He had *some* right to know. After all, the blackguard could show up at any moment and demand his parental rights. That was, if he ever learned of her condition.

"Let me guess," Jacob continued, "Killed at Waterloo?"

Jacob's question indicated he assumed she had a lover. *What a lovely lie that would be.* One she never considered.

The timing was right, of course; Lieutenant Harris had departed for Waterloo shortly thereafter. She had but to fabricate a tale of lovers torn apart by war. But she knew she could never lie to Jacob. Deny the truth, conveniently forget pertinent facts, obfuscate, deliberately mislead, *yes*, but never outright lie.

"Oh, no," Elizabeth said, "He's alive and well. Somewhere." And she hoped to God never to see him again.

"But why marry me and not him?"

"He doesn't know."

"You never told him?"

"I've never told anyone. Mrs. Howard eventually came to her own conclusions. She informed the mid-wife. Other than you, no one else knows."

"Don't you think he has a right...?"

"He has no rights in this matter." She spoke more harshly than she intended, but she wished to end the discussion before it went any further. "I was compromised." Such a polite word to hide a myriad of sins. "I haven't seen him since." She did not add that she had deliberately fled London in the hope he would not follow her... at least, not until she was ready to deal with him.

To Elizabeth's surprise, Jacob did not press further on the matter. Nothing more was said, and at length, Elizabeth drifted on sleepy currents and eddies. At some point, she realized Jacob's hand no longer rested against her back, but she did not mind. She was warm and *almost* comfortable, and at last, she slept.

Truth be told, she slept more soundly than she had in years. Still, she woke once during the night, her mind foggy with confusion, until she remembered her *husband* shared her bed, and she quickly fell back to sleep, feeling strangely safe. And when she struggled to rise from bed several times during the night, Jacob was there, his great strength helping her from the bed with ease. Afterwards, he had helped her settle back in, snug and so warm on a cold December night, leaving Elizabeth with the unfamiliar feeling of contentment.

Despite the advanced state of Elizabeth's condition, Jacob knew from experience a thorough consummation of their marriage was possible, even desirable, although Elizabeth might never admit such desires... or even be aware that her body craved satiation. He slept close behind her and woke several times with his arm draped over her, his hand protectively splayed over her belly. Without any conscious thought on his part, his body instinctively remembered lying beside Maria, gone these long years, and her intense desire for him as she grew ever greater with child.

But Elizabeth was not Maria, and just sharing this bed felt like a major victory to Jacob toward winning her trust.

"How do you know so much about... 'expectant' ladies?" Elizabeth asked as he helped her from bed, cold sunlight struggling to brighten the chamber.

"I've known my fair share of expectant *women*—there were plenty enough among the camp followers—but I've never known an expectant *lady*."

"I imagine an expectant *lady* is much the same as an expectant *woman*."

Jacob nodded, all the while thinking *women* tended to be less fussy than *ladies*, especially women who followed the drum. Still, he could not stop thinking about what Elizabeth had said the night before. She had been compromised, a not unheard of event. But ladies who were delightfully compromised by ardent lovers only to be abandoned afterwards did not carry pistols on their person for protection at all times, especially within the sanctity of their own bedchamber. He knew, despite all her *bravado*—she was a fierce little thing—Elizabeth feared something. Probably some*one*.

The day progressed much as the previous day had—sans the wedding—with Jacob visiting tenants and learning the lay of the land. But to his surprise, before he departed, Elizabeth handed him a basket of baked goods for the Widows Thompson and Smythe, and then insisted he make sure the Claytons were sending over milk and eggs for the two old women daily, along with butter and cheese weekly. He soon discovered the women—one quite elderly, the other more silver than gold—inhabited a cottage rent-free, along with Mrs. Smythe's near-grown simple-minded grandson, who took instructions rather well and seemed more excited about Jacob's horse than the biscuits Mrs. Howard made for him.

The pair invited him in and, over tea, spoke kindly of their landlady and noted how much they missed her visits, once so frequent. He heard much the same from other tenants over the course of the afternoon, and as he made his way back to Worthing House, his mind considering the words and praise of common laborers toward their mistress, Jacob realized each lived in such well-maintained tenant houses, so unlike the drafty, dilapidated houses he remembered from the estates of his childhood.

Clearly, Elizabeth cared for these people, despite her temperament suggesting otherwise. All her coldness, her reserve, her distrust... all indicated an indifference with little regard for two old women and the tenants residing on her lands. But Jacob knew such thoughts false and unfair toward Elizabeth. Her marriage to him alone proved her willingness to sacrifice herself for another—in this case, her unborn child, a person she did not yet even know. A person who might grow to adulthood filled with animosity and distain for her. As Jacob had once felt for his own father.

There was plenty of work just around the house and the stables to occupy half a dozen men, and Jacob looked forward to hiring more servants in the New Year. But while he was now Lord Worthing, he was no dandy to sit about idly with nothing more important to worry about than the embroidery of his waistcoat and the intricacy of his neck cloth. So he busied himself until dinner.

That night, even though Mrs. Howard had aired and cleaned his room, Jacob, again uninvited, climbed into bed with Elizabeth, who was as grumpy as the previous night. Again, she attempted to ignore him with her book, but Jacob helped settle her in. Sleeping with a soon-to-be mother lacked the restfulness of his own bed, but Jacob found he did not mind. It portended hope for a new life he never thought possible.

And so, many nights went much the same. Until one night, Jacob stirred from sleep to find Elizabeth huddled close to him in the cold darkness, her body turned toward his. Neither spoke of it in the morning, the day progressing as usual, with Elizabeth seemingly indifferent to him, except to issue the occasional order on estate matters.

But the incident repeated itself the next night. Only this time, Elizabeth lay enveloped in his protective embrace, as if she belonged there, just as Maria had. *And why not?* Elizabeth was his wife, too. And he would be father to her child.

So strange, Elizabeth thought. By daylight, she and Jacob lived civil, almost indifferent lives with little beyond polite, mundane conversation—in many ways, a perfect ton marriage. At night, though, lying side by side in her bed, they felt like lovers. Or at least, how Elizabeth imagined lovers would feel—not in the physical sense; she possessed no experience in such matters—but spiritually, like two souls bound together. In truth, she never intended to reach out to him, to cling to him in the darkness, but warmth emanated from him, and she naturally gravitated toward him.

Over successive nights, she gradually realized she felt safe, for the first time in a long time. With Jacob, she knew she had nothing to fear, not from him, nor anyone else. Until he left for America, at least. And then, as before, she would have to take care of herself.

His attention to the estate impressed her, especially his visits to the tenants and his concern for their well-being. His plans to hire workers in the New Year gave her hope, but then she always reminded herself that as soon as Jacob had enough money to start anew, he would be gone. Despite that, she wanted to know him better, to talk with him and learn his thoughts, but she never felt brave enough. Consequently, without really meaning to be, she was often cold toward him.

In the end, though, she suspected his attentive nature toward her thawed her heart. Elizabeth awoke one morning with a bout of nausea—less common in these last weeks— and with barely a sound from her, Jacob had her head over a basin. While the anticipated sickness never materialized,

Jacob stroked her back and murmured soothing sounds to comfort her.

From the start, the attacks of sickness frightened Elizabeth. Even before she realized she carried a child, she suffered violent bouts. And now, as the day grew closer, it worried her still.

"What's wrong?" Jacob asked, his voice filled with tenderness as they sat on the side of her bed. When Elizabeth hesitated, he gently urged, "Tell me."

"They say such sickness indicates I don't want the child."

Jacob took a deep breath, set the basin back on the stand, and nodded. "*They* say a lot of things, but in my experience, *they* are wrong more often than not. Collective wisdom is rarely wise and little more than a stone's throw from mob rule." The words surprised Elizabeth, who never expected to hear such a thing from a now-former army sergeant. He continued, "By such reasoning, no woman ever wants a child. And if I know anything, I know that's not true." He looked her square in the face and asked, "Do you want this child?"

"Yes. Very much so." Elizabeth could not help but smile as he tucked her back under the covers and propped pillows behind her back so she could comfortably sit upright. "I suspect your familiarity with expectant ladies is more than knowing a few camp followers in this condition."

Sitting beside her, Jacob bluntly replied, "My wife— Maria—had a child. A boy."

"Oh." With a sad pain in her heart and a fair amount of embarrassment, Elizabeth felt like an intruder into the private sanctuary of his grief. But Jacob did not appear to mind her presence there and, with a small, wistful smile, he continued unabated.

"She spoke no English and I spoke no Spanish," and then he grinned, "but I knew when she was angry and I knew when she was happy. From the moment she related to me her condition, she chattered away to our son growing inside her—always with such joy." He almost laughed. "I'm pretty sure she preferred him to me."

"What happened?" Elizabeth asked, letting her curiosity get the better of her before instantly regretting it. "I'm sorry. I have no right to ask...."

"*You* are my wife now." Jacob spoke firmly but kindly. "You have every right to know what happened to the first Mrs. Burrows." He looked away from her, toward the window and the ever-growing day. "There was an outbreak of fever in camp. She died. Along with our son. I buried them in a vineyard. She would have liked that." He looked at Elizabeth again, and with a deep breath and a hint of a smile, he said, "Now, I've told you my sad story. Tell me yours."

Jacob didn't mind talking about Maria or their son. It felt good to speak of them both again. But he felt guilty for not telling Elizabeth the whole truth, that Maria, in the grip of fevered delusions, had given birth to a stillborn child... and died two days later. Elizabeth did not need to hear that, not in her condition, when anything could still go wrong.

But when he asked her to tell him her sad story, he never expected her to comply, not really. He thought she might ring the bell for Mrs. Howard or perhaps even feign another wave of nausea, all in an effort to avoid the discussion. Instead, she looked meekly down at her hands resting on her belly.

"No one ever came a-courting when I was plain Miss FitzWalter."

Jacob took one of her hands in his and said, "Never *plain* anything."

Elizabeth gave him a bittersweet smile before continuing. "We lived in London, but I had neither time nor the inclination to gallivant about Town like some debutante. Even then, I had people to care for—my uncle, for one—and estate matters to manage. He was unwell and Matthew was in Spain. And then everything happened so quickly. First Uncle Frederick. Then Matthew."

She looked up at him and with complete sincerity said, "But the moment I put off my mourning... throngs were at my door." Jacob heard the shock and dismay in her voice—she had no idea how lovely she was. But then she continued, "They weren't there for me. They were drawn by the chance to be Lord Worthing."

"Ah." That never occurred to Jacob. He certainly did not marry her for the title, but he could see any number of unscrupulous sorts vying for the right.

"There was one gentleman, more persistent than the others. An officer from Matthew's regiment. He was the one who brought word of Matthew's death. Said he was with him when he died."

Jacob recalled her contained fury when he had said as much on the night they met in the stables. He now understood her reaction to his claim that he had been with her brother when he died. But he couldn't figure out whom she spoke of. Jacob was well-acquainted with all the officers in the regiment, and several of them had been present when Matthew died.

"Everyone thought him so charming," Elizabeth continued, "and how fortunate I was to be courted by so handsome a suitor. I certainly didn't see it. His only redeeming quality was he was *almost* ginger-haired, and even there, he didn't quite measure up."

With that brief description, the face of the man immediately came to Jacob's mind. *Lieutenant Harris.* Jacob remembered him all too well. After Toulouse, the blackguard sold out, abandoning his brothers-in-arms to fight the Americans without him. Not that it really mattered. The man was a coward and malingerer at the best of times. And now Jacob wondered if Harris left in the wake of Matthew's death simply to pursue Elizabeth.

"He proposed," Elizabeth said, "much to my horror. I couldn't abide the man. So I refused him. Politely, of course. And I thought that was the end of it. But then...." She looked away, and Jacob took both her hands in his, suddenly realizing what was to come. "There was a garden party. In Richmond. He sought me out, said our hostess needed help. And I foolishly dismissed that voice warning me of danger— how could *he* possibly be dangerous? I even berated myself for being so ridiculous to think such a thing." She turned and looked Jacob in the face. "You understand... he just wanted the title. He wanted to get caught with me." She shook her head, the full extent of what had happened playing out in Jacob's mind. "I don't think he intended to take it so far. I simply refused to cooperate with his scheme. I just knew... if I made a sound, if someone came in, I would have to marry him. And that was so much worse than...." With a horrified look on her face, Elizabeth abruptly withdrew her hands from his. "You must think me utterly depraved. That I would allow…"

"Good God, no!"

But she did not seem to hear him. "I should have fought. Screamed. Done something. But not nothing."

"No." Jacob caught her hands again and made her listen. "Everyone thinks in a moment of danger, there are two choices—fight or flee. But sometimes, the most prudent course of action is inaction—to remain perfectly still. Even in war, this happens—hold your breath and wait for the danger to pass."

That calmed Elizabeth's agitation. She nodded and sat quiet before saying, "It was the only way I could think to escape him."

Jacob leaned forward and kissed her forehead. Then he pressed a handkerchief into her hand.

"I'm not going to turn into a watering can," she said with the faintest hint of a smile.

"Of course not." Jacob sat quietly with her for a moment and then gently asked, "Do you know where he is now?"

Elizabeth shook her head. "I fully expected him to follow me here—professing love and nonsense—he made it clear he would marry me. But I've heard nothing."

And so the pistol, Jacob realized. She lived in fear… *but no*, it wasn't fear he sensed from her. It was anger. That same fierce defiance he had known from her since their first meeting. He could not help but wonder what she had been like before.

Jacob stood up. But Elizabeth was not finished.

"You understand, this is my child, not his. The grandchild of my parents and my brother's heir." She lovingly caressed the great mound of her belly. "It wasn't the poor little fellow's fault. Yet everyone seems to think a child is nothing more than property, a man's property at that. As if I have nothing to do with it."

"I understand, Elizabeth. You never need to explain yourself to me."

"And what if it's the only one?"

"It won't be."

Elizabeth eyes went wide with the realization of the meaning behind his words. But before she could say anything, Jacob asked, "Now then, how does a cup of tea sound?"

As Elizabeth watched Jacob, wrapped in his new Banyan, leave the room, she thought perhaps she had misheard him. *It won't be.* To suggest that she might bear more children after this one…. The idea of having some semblance of a normal family was a dream long vanquished, and she imagined her emotions might have gotten the best of her.

Now, she regretted telling Jacob so much. She should have kept quiet. This was the reason she knew she could never marry—no man wanted to learn another man had had his wife. No man wanted to raise a bastard. Of course, it did not matter to Jacob. He would be bound for America soon enough. Only, she now found she did not want him to leave.

He returned shortly with a cup of tea for her. He spoke of inconsequential, everyday matters, Elizabeth listening but barely noting his words… until he said *Christmas*.

"Christmas?" she asked.

He grinned and replied, "Tonight is Christmas Eve. Or had you forgotten?"

Elizabeth smiled, a strange warmth filling her. "Yes, I

had." Memories of the aromas and delights of Christmas from her childhood with Matthew passed through her mind. How she longed to live such days again.

"Mrs. Howard is finishing with the Christmas baskets, which I will deliver," Jacob continued, "then there are presents to be wrapped...."

"Presents?"

"Well, there's just one for you." He gave her a quick smirk, his eyes flashing mischief.

The sense of joy faded from Elizabeth, guilt replacing it. "But I don't have anything for you."

"You have given me plenty already," he assured her before continuing with a few estate matters. He did not bring up their previous discussion, much to Elizabeth's relief. She had no desire to speak further on the matter but felt something comforting in confiding in him.

"And after that," Jacob was saying, "I will return with greenery for the drawing room. Owing to your condition, we can't open the house for revelries, but next year...."

Next year? That baffled Elizabeth as much as Jacob's earlier comment. She began to wonder if he intended to hold up his side of their agreement. Whether she felt hope or fear over the prospect, she could not say.

When Jacob returned to the house late that afternoon, snow dusting his broad shoulders, Elizabeth waited for him in the drawing room. A good fire burned on the hearth, and she had spent much of the day there, resting and reading, as she did not know when Jacob would return home. Mrs. Howard busied herself in the kitchen with plans for Christmas Eve dinner and a veritable feast for tomorrow, albeit for only two. None of them would attend Midnight service, but Mrs. Howard planned to visit with her sister in the village tomorrow after morning services.

As Jacob carried in bundles of pine boughs, Elizabeth—with some difficulty—rose and asked, "What did you mean?"

"About what?" Jacob asked without stopping his task.

"When you suggested this would not be my only child? And for that matter, Christmas *next year*? What did you mean?"

Jacob glanced over at her, the corner of his mouth turning upward, and then returned his attention to cutting the cord around a bundle. "Exactly what you think I meant."

That gave Elizabeth a start, accompanied by a fleeting mental image of her husband making love to her. "But you're going to America?"

"No," he said without the slightest pause as he spread out the pine boughs, "I have no intention of going to America."

"But we agreed...."

"No." This time, he stopped, stood up straight, and looked directly at her, his blue eyes piercing her. "*You* agreed. I needed employment, not your money. I have some money in a London bank, which is where I was heading after I delivered the letter to you. I've enough to get to America. I just needed to *earn* more to buy enough land. But all my plans changed when *you* asked me to marry you."

A frisson of doubt passed through Elizabeth, and she began to fear what his real intentions might be. "I thought you married me in exchange for money to go to America?"

"Hardly. I may be many things, but I am not a mercenary."

"Then why did you marry me?"

Jacob took a deep breath and calmly motioned to the overstuffed chair beside the fire. Elizabeth resumed her previous seat and watched in some amazement as Jacob knelt before her, slipped his hands about her ankles, and propped her feet up on a cushioned stool.

"Because God put me here at this moment for a reason," he said softly, gazing at her. "You needed me." He spread one hand over her stomach. "This child needs me. No one else needs me. Matthew was always there for me—and I will always be there for you."

With such reassurance, Elizabeth opened her mouth to respond, but Jacob stopped her.

"There's something more," he said. For a long moment, he knelt there, silent. "You told me your sad tale, but I only told you part of mine." An unsettling look descended upon his face, shame or embarrassment, Elizabeth could not determine.

"What is it?" she encouraged, placing her hand over his in an effort to reassure him.

"I do not know," he began, his voice low and quiet, as if he feared eavesdroppers, "if my father was... my father."

"Oh." For Elizabeth, nothing further needed to be said. Such things simply did not matter to her, especially given her own situation. But then a faint dawning beamed into her thoughts.

"You see, my mother was his second wife," Jacob continued, "And he already had four sons. He was a farmer, and she was a vicar's daughter. A strange alliance, but from my vantage, they seemed to like each other." Then he shrugged. "My childhood seemed perfectly normal, as far as I can tell, except I was taught by my grandfather—my mother's father—instead of going to the village school. He was an educated man, and plans were made for me. Maybe that built up resentment among my brothers, I don't know."

Jacob looked down, and as if needing strength and comfort before he could continue, took both of Elizabeth's hands in his and held them tight.

"Then one day, when I was about eleven, one of my brothers, in a fit of anger, turned to me and said, 'You're not even our brother.' Called me a bastard." Jacob whispered the word. "And I, like a fool, believed him. I accepted, without question…. Only, it explained why I looked nothing like my father or my brothers or even my maternal relatives."

He shook his head and looked up at Elizabeth. "I never said anything. Didn't ask my father. Or my mother—how could I ask her *that*? I just believed it."

Elizabeth's heart ached for the boy and mourned for his lost childhood. She imagined Jacob, much the same as now, only blonder with innocent blue eyes, so trusting, adoring his elder brothers as children do, only to be cruelly rejected.

"After that," Jacob continued, "I wanted nothing to do with my parents. I got into fights and all manner of trouble. And then I was caught poaching. They would've hanged me if not for a kind judge." He looked down at their still clasped hands. "My mother's husband—my father—was a good man. I just didn't know it at the time. I made the false assumption that he never loved me, that he loved my brothers more. But he did love me. He was a good father to me. And the truth is, I have no idea if my brother lied to me or not. But by the time I realized all that, years had passed, and it was too late. He was gone."

And then, without warning, Jacob lowered his head, his

ear resting against Elizabeth's stomach, and wrapped his arms protectively about her hips. And instinctively, Elizabeth gently threaded her fingers through his hair, brushed it back away from his face, and kissed his cheek.

"You understand." It was a statement, not a question.

"Yes, I do," she replied.

"It feels like justice, like a chance to redeem myself," he said without moving, "I need you, I need this child, as much as you and he need me."

"Oh!" Elizabeth cried out, just as Jacob jumped back in shock, a crooked grin on his face as he stared down at her stomach.

"The little fellow kicked." Jacob placed his hand on the spot, and they both waited to see if the child would kick again. But at length, when nothing further happened, they decided he had gone back to sleep.

Jacob remained kneeling before Elizabeth, both smiling at the wonder of life growing inside her, the creation of a new being. But then his smile faded, hers with it, and he looked at her with an unbearable intensity. Elizabeth could not turn away from that gaze. It drew her in, and she willingly succumbed as Jacob leaned in and kissed her. Softly. With only the faintest pressure against her lips. Until his hand cupped her cheek, and the kiss deepened, taking her breath away.

Jacob pulled away—much too soon, in Elizabeth's mind—and a hint of regret replaced the desire in his eyes. "I just wish we had met earlier," he whispered, his hand still pressed against her cheek, "that this child were fully mine, that I had some part in its creation."

"But you do. Perhaps not the child, but the person he..."

"Or she."

"...will become. He will learn what a man is... what a man is supposed to be... from you. You will be the father of the man he becomes."

Jacob's hand took hers. He sat back on his heels and turned somber. "As for my intentions, I will not have a sham for a marriage. I fully expect, in time, to fill this house with our children. I am your husband. You are my wife. This child is mine. And while this land and this house may not be mine, I am lord of this manor. I made a vow before you and God, and while you may not take that seriously, I do. I will never leave you. I will be there. For you, and your child. Come what may." He gave her a brief, reassuring smile. "You are stuck with me."

"For better or worse."

"Exactly." Jacob abruptly stood. "But there's one more thing."

Overwhelmed, Elizabeth tried not to sigh out loud, but she did not think she could take much more. All his words still echoed in her thoughts. He would never leave her. *How extraordinary.* With another man, such words would frighten her, but not with Jacob. They filled her with a comfort and peace so long absent from her life.

But rather than stating his thoughts on a further matter, Jacob left the room. He returned moments later, this time carrying a document folded and tied with red tapes, which Elizabeth instantly recognized as a legal document.

"Gifts are not unheard of at Christmastide," he said presenting it to her. "I obtained this when I first went to Gloucester."

Baffled, Elizabeth accepted it, untied the tapes, and

opened the single page. She quickly glanced down at the bottom to see Jacob's signature there alongside those of two witnesses.

"I consulted a solicitor there," Jacob explained as Elizabeth carefully perused the words on the page. "You'll see it's dated from before our marriage."

Elizabeth found the document concise and straightforward. Despite becoming the titular Viscount Worthing *jure uxoris*, Jacob renounced all claims to Elizabeth's lands, properties, income, monies, and even her person. Furthermore, the document stated Jacob would run the estate of Worthing House and receive recompense appropriate to an estate manager—that was, *between £50 and £100, as her ladyship sees fit.*

"Only a hundred pounds?" Elizabeth thought the sum horrifying. Jacob was worth so much more than that.

Jacob gave a brief laugh. "Well, I'm glad you prefer the greater amount."

"But you deserve so much more."

"But I do not *need* more." Again, he knelt before her. "I am no spendthrift. I do not gamble or drink or carouse about. My needs are modest, as are, I've noted, yours."

"But what about your desire for land of your own?" She felt a pain in her heart for him, for his lost dream.

"I have all I want here, now. So the house is already built and the fields are already cleared. It is still my duty to make sure the roof doesn't come down upon us and to make sure the crops are planted so we have food on the table. And in that, I am no different from any other man."

Elizabeth indulged in a small smile. "I suppose not."

And before another word was spoken, Jacob rose and

said, "I'm famished. How about some supper?"

Elizabeth nodded, so very grateful Jacob's plans for their lives did not match her own. She thanked God for sending him to her. And she thought of her brother Matthew, and knew how very pleased he would be.

Jacob helped her up and suggested, "After dinner, I can hang the holly and pine boughs, and you can tell me how to do it properly. I'm sorry but I didn't find any mistletoe."

"That's all right," Elizabeth said as they headed for the drawing room door, "You may kiss me whenever you wish."

Jacob gave her a mischievous grin and held the door for her. But before leaving the room, she glanced over to the side table, where her pistol lay alongside an empty teacup. But she did not rush over to retrieve it. She did not feel the need for it. After all, Jacob was here.

Jacob rose early. Beside him, Elizabeth finally slept after a restless night offering little comfort. Even his efforts to fortify her body with various pillows failed. He suspected she simply succumbed to exhaustion in the end. But as dawn crept into the room, Jacob found himself wide awake, thoughts of the day ahead and their future together filling his head. It was Christmas, after all, when hope abounded and anything was possible.

They had been up quite late the night before, making merry in the drawing room. Even Mrs. Howard joined them for a while. As he hung holly and pine, Elizabeth played carols on the pianoforte and even sang a bit. And all the while he thought, *Next year, next year, we'll fill the house with friends and neighbors. And there will be dancing and laughter and punch and pudding. A proper Christmas indeed. And children. Christmas belongs to children.*

He wished to go hunting. It occurred to him at some point in the night that he had yet to fulfill that selfish desire to hunt without fearing a gamekeeper or the magistrate. He knew Mrs. Howard already had a rib of beef for their Christmas dinner, and they did not need more meat. So he decided, should he bag a pheasant or hare, he would present it to the Widows Thompson and Smythe.

Mrs. Howard was up as well, and Jacob promised her he would return before her nephew came to take her to Christmas service in the village. He assured her he could manage breakfast well-enough for Elizabeth; a fireside hearth contrasted little to a campfire, in his experience.

A virgin snow covered the landscape, over the hills and forests, like soft down stretching to the horizon. More fell gently from the gray heavens, a stillness in the air amplifying every minute sound—the crunch beneath Jacob's feet, the heavy exhale of breath, the impact of each snowflake. Perfect weather for Christmas.

As the Clayton boys had yet to arrive—*yes*, even on Christmas Day, their duties would not wait, but mainly, Jacob and Elizabeth intended to give each a half-a-crown in honor of the day—Jacob saddled his own horse, all the while wondering if it were, indeed, *his* horse. Given Elizabeth's reaction to his gift the night before, Jacob imagined she would say it was, indeed, his horse. *And why not?* The responsibility of its care ultimately rested with him, whether he did it himself or paid another to do it. The lords of the land, really, were nothing more than caretakers. Of lands. Of houses. Of families. Despite all their greatness and wealth. And when Jacob married Elizabeth, when he said his marriage vows, when he signed that document in Gloucester, he took on that duty of care, to her and all he surveyed. He should have felt daunted by it all, the responsibilities he now carried, but instead, he reveled in the possibilities of a lifetime with Elizabeth, and he thanked God for bringing him here, at this time.

Over the course of a few hours, Jacob bagged two pheasants. He promptly delivered them to the Widows Thompson and Smythe—much to their delight—before declining their invitation to come in for a cup of tea; Lady Worthing was expecting him at breakfast, after all. He bid them Happy Christmas and rode toward home.

But as Jacob approached the stable yard behind Worthing House, he sensed something amiss. At first, he could not put his finger on it, but then he recognized the tracks to and from the house were all off. For one thing, they were much too busy. A pair of footprints, small—one of the Clayton boys, Jacob surmised. Then a set of wheel tracks—going away from the house as indicated by the hoof tracks. Someone had taken the gig out, but he could not understand who might have done so or why. Yet none of those tracks confused him as much as the lone set of horse tracks leading to the house, many atop the wheel marks in the snow. Someone had come to the house on horseback after the gig had departed.

And while it occurred to Jacob these were most likely the normal comings and goings at a great house on any morning, especially Christmas morning, the soldier in him realized—regretfully—that he had failed to reload his gun after the last shot.

He saw the horse in the yard before he spotted the

dismounted rider standing nearby. A black silhouette against the bright snow, the man stared up at the house and appeared unaware of Jacob's approach. The man's stance—great coat flung open, hands resting on his hips, head cocked to the side—reminded Jacob of one contemplating a purchase, the way a farmer considers a prize bull or an aristocrat ponders a great jewel before settling on the price.

Reaching the stables, Jacob swung his leg over the horse's head, his back never turning on the stranger, and slid down. As Jacob's booted-feet touched the snowy ground, the man turned around. At the sight of the face before him, Jacob felt a revulsion he had never known before, not even in the wake of bloody battle.

It was Lieutenant Harris.

Recognition quickly replaced the man's contemplation of the house.

"Sergeant Burrows," he called out with a previously alien tone of friendship, "Happy Christmas."

How peculiar, Jacob thought, slowly approaching his former brother-in-arms. Despite a long-held deep distain for the man, Jacob had always considered Harris a handsome fellow, tall and slender, the very cut of fashion, with flashing blue eyes and an engaging smile. But Elizabeth was right; the brown hair futilely endeavoring to grow in ginger proved his only redeeming quality.

"Sergeant no more," Jacob replied, his hand clinching into a fist and ready to strike.

"Finished your twenty, did you?" Harris smiled, white teeth gleaming. "Congratulations on surviving His Majesty's army."

"It's Lord Worthing now."

Jacob watched with pleasure as the smile faded from Harris's face, and Jacob wondered what carefully laid plans had brought him here. No doubt, the fool still thought he could win over Elizabeth, despite what he had done to her.

"She married *you*?" Despite Harris's forced laugh, Jacob saw the fury seething just below the surface and threatening to boil over. Then Harris shrugged. "Well then, I fear I must inform you, I was the first man she ever knew."

A splatter of blood accompanied his scream as Jacob's fist impacted with Harris's nose and sent him crashing to the frozen ground.

"No, you're not." Jacob stood over the prostrate man. Pain coursed through his hand... but with an unexpected satisfaction. "A villain, a blackguard, a coward, maybe, but no *man* ever knew her."

"Bloody hell!" Harris pressed his hand to his broken nose, blood gushing between his fingers and dripping onto the snow. "I'll have you flogged!"

"You are no longer my superior." Desiring nothing more than to give the scoundrel a thorough thrashing, Jacob reached down and grabbed Harris by the lapels.

"Think what you want," Harris spat, clutching at Jacob's wrists, "but I had her first, and she deserved to be taken down a peg. Nothing but a managing fe...."

A distinct click interrupted them.

Both men, painfully acquainted with the sound, instantly froze, their eyes darting toward the house.

There stood Elizabeth, a dozen paces from them, her pistol leveled at Lieutenant Harris. She still wore her night rail and silvery-blue dressing gown, her unbound brown hair flowing down about her. To Jacob, she looked much the same as she had that first night in the stable—her pale, chiseled features devoid of all emotion, cold as the icy world over which she presided.

That first night in the stables.

A flood of memories rushed over Jacob in the space of a heartbeat.

Elizabeth's words that night—*Oh, I'll just drag you into the house*—revealing a carefully calculated plan to deal with any potential corpse.

But not just any corpse.

One she expected.

Jacob stared down at Harris, immaculately dressed as a London gentleman, despite the blood staining his mathematically tied neck cloth and his waistcoat, the brocade silk crushed within Jacob's clenched fists.

Now he understood the purpose for the rank and tattered rags shoved up the chimney, from some well-paid passing beggar, no doubt.

Jacob released Harris and slowly stood upright. Harris scrambled to stand as Jacob stepped back, giving him a wide berth.

A corner of Jacob's mouth attempted to turn upward, and he resisted the urge to grin outright. He failed.

"Oh," he said, almost laughing, then quoted with pride, "'though she be but little, she is fierce,' this wife of mine." Elizabeth kept an unflinching gaze on Harris, the pistol steady. She reminded Jacob of an avenging Fury from myth— only he never considered one might be so cold and calm.

Harris brushed the snow off him and attempted a charming grin.

"I don't think you'll shoot me," he said to Elizabeth.

"Trust me," Jacob said, "She will. I suspect she's been preparing for this for..." He almost said *for nine months* but stopped himself as he realized Harris didn't know Elizabeth carried a child, since her garments hid her condition. "...a while. Didn't you listen to Major FitzWalter's stories? His sister taught him to shoot." It was a lie, but Matthew had been an excellent shot, and Jacob immensely enjoyed adding to Harris's discomfort.

Harris smirked with a cocky confidence. "They'll hang her if she does."

"No, they won't." Jacob found he admired Elizabeth's calculated plan, especially with it now laid out bare before him. "See, she'll shoot you in the face—you've seen what a gunshot to the face does. Bloody mess. Then I'll carry your body into the house. We'll strip you, burn your clothes, and dress you in some rags Lady Worthing has been saving just for this moment. And then she'll give a performance worthy of..." Jacob glanced over at his wife. "Who did you say?"

"Mrs. Siddons."

She spoke even words, without the slightest hint of distress in her voice, only a diabolical calmness that filled Jacob with a satisfying sense of pride.

"That's the one." Jacob nodded and returned his full attention to Harris. "A performance worthy of Mrs. Siddons... about how she killed an intruder—a lone female in house and all."

"But she's not alone. You're here." For the first time, fear and doubt crept into Harris's voice.

"Ah, no, I'm not." Jacob pointed to his horse, his gun secure on the saddle. "I'm out hunting. I even have witnesses. Respectable widows happy to testify before the magistrate."

"No one will believe it."

"Everyone will believe it. A lone female defends herself from one wishing her harm. Besides, if they have any doubts, well, she is a much beloved neighbor from an old, respected family. And if they don't," Jacob shrugged, "I'll confess to the deed."

"You wouldn't?" Shock covered Harris's face, and Jacob suspected Harris finally grasped the full extent of the danger he found himself in.

"In a heartbeat. Her brother saved me countless times. I'll gladly die for his sister. I'll gladly sacrifice myself for my wife. She is worth a hanging."

For the first time, Elizabeth glanced over at Jacob, a barely discernible shift of the eyes before returning her gaze to her intended victim. But in that same moment, her cold face subtly softened, her brown eyes brightened, just enough for Jacob to notice.

He returned his attention to the well-dressed gentleman staring down the barrel of the lady's pistol. "So I recommend," Jacob said, untying Harris horse, "that you run. After all, it's what you do best. She might still shoot you in the back but I wouldn't bet on it... Although, I could be wrong."

He dropped the reins and moved closer to Harris. Jacob glared down at him and spoke in a low voice. "If you ever return, if I ever see you again, my wife's pistol will be the least of your concerns." And then without warning, Jacob slapped the horse's flank, thereby sending it racing out of the yard... and Harris scrambling in the snow after it.

When the man and his horse disappeared from sight, Jacob turned to his wife, her pistol now lowered. Reaching her, he took the pistol from her. She let out a gasp and slumped against him.

"It's all right," he said, enveloping her in his arms and pressing his cheek against her head, "I've got you. You never have to worry again. That's my privilege now."

"Thank you," she replied, clinging to him, "but that's not it."

Jacob then noticed the strength with which her hands clutched at him, as if she were in pain, and he understood. Her time had come.

"When did this start?" he asked.

"Sometime during the night." She looked up at him. "I think." He wanted to scold her for not telling him sooner—he never would have left the house had he known—but she was probably ignorant of the earliest signs.

"Let's get you into the house, and then I'll go for the midwife."

"Mrs. Howard and Charlie Clayton already went to fetch the midwife." Inwardly, Jacob breathed a small sigh of relief—*so that explained the tracks of the gig in the snow.*

Now feeling the cold more than before—and with Elizabeth in her dressing gown—Jacob scooped her up into his arms.

"It's all right," she assured him, "I can manage...."

"I know you can. But you don't have to. Not anymore. We have each other now."

Without another word, he carried his wife into the house.

And so, 1815 retired and gave way to 1816. Jacob hoped the New Year would bring more temperate weather and gentle rains, all followed in due course by an abundant harvest.

But no, Old Joe proclaimed bringing the post that first day of the year. The pain in his knee warned him otherwise, that cold, miserable days would worsen and the harvest would fail, no doubt. *'Tis God's judgment on the wickedness of mankind—for 'llowing folks like Napoleon to thrive while there be cannibal savages in this world and respectable ladies still take sugar in their tea.*

Jacob tried not to laugh, but when he reported the conversation to Elizabeth, he saw she made a note to buy more corn.

There had been much coming and going at Worthing House since Christmas, first with the midwife's arrival, followed thereafter—at a most inconvenient hour—by the Honorable Mary Burrows-FitzWalter. Elizabeth surprised Jacob with the choice of Christian name—after his mother. Jacob, in turn, surprised Elizabeth with the choice of surname and declared if he had anything to do with it, the FitzWalter name would not die out. After all, he owed so much to Matthew.

Elizabeth admitted she was relieved to have a daughter, for sons would likely follow, and Jacob's son would succeed to the title one day.

Jacob, for one, found he did not care in the least, for he instantly fell in love with the tiny bundle presented to him, with her large brown eyes like those of her mother, all topped with snowy blonde hair. His daughter could scarcely be pried from the cradle of his arms, and he showed her off to anyone entering the house, from the new scullery maid to the solicitor and to, especially, the Widows Thompson and Smythe when they came to call on the little family. With them came the Smythe grandson, who refused to enter the house and insisted on visiting the stables instead. Jacob hired the boy on the spot, for while he wasn't the brightest candle, he had a good spark and enjoyed working with the horses.

Warmth now replaced much of the previous chill in the house, with fires lit and rooms aired, and well-paid servants to call for tea. Mrs. Howard happily fell back into delegating duties rather than doing everything herself. However, the new parents did not hire, as was customary, a nurse. In fact, the nursery had not yet even been aired, and Mary was never found less than arms' length from Elizabeth or Jacob. That would all change soon enough, but not for the present.

So as Jacob warmed himself before the sitting room fire and told Elizabeth of Old Joe's prediction, his wife held out a piece of paper to him. Folded and tied with red tapes, it reminded Jacob of the legal document he had given her on Christmas Eve.

"In olden times," Elizabeth explained as he took the paper from her, "it was customary to give gifts on the New Year. Of course, that was when the year began on April First. But I thought now is as good as any time." Then she raised her eyebrows and smiled. "And it's not unheard of to give a gift at Christmastide."

"What is it?" Jacob asked unfolding the single page.

"It needs but your signature." Elizabeth motioned to quill and inkwell on the escritoire.

After a cursory glance—and with a growing excitement in his stomach—Jacob said, "A lease for eighty acres?"

"In lieu of the land you wished to buy in America. I, of course, cannot sell or give you the land outright. It belongs to the estate. But it is yours to plant as you wish." Her eyes seemed red, and Jacob thought for a moment, she might be about to cry. But then she raised her eyebrows and turned mischievous. "I fear my new estate manager will be quite put out when he learns what I've done."

Jacob was too excited to read the document properly, and only snippets of words reached his brain.

"How is the income to be divided?" he asked.

"It won't be. You keep what you earn. For your lifetime." She raised her forefinger. "Of course, there is the rent."

Jacob quickly skimmed through the words in search of the amount. He barely contained himself when he saw it. "One pound!"

"A man can make something of himself with land like that."

Jacob nodded, hearing his own words quoted back to him.

"Happy Christmas," Elizabeth said.

Jacob leaned down and kissed her. "Happy Christmas," he said, and thanked God for all his Christmas gifts—his wife, his daughter, and the promise of their lives together.

About Anna

Anna D. Allen is essentially half-Finnish and half-Southern, which means she has no sense of humor and will shoot you for wearing white shoes after Labor Day... unless you are attending a wedding and happen to be the bride. She holds a Bachelor of Science and a Master of Arts in Language and Literature. She is a recipient of the Writers of the Future award and a member of Science Fiction and Fantasy Writers of America, but she also has a great passion for Regency Romances. It is generally acknowledged that she spends way too much time with the dead and her mind got lost somewhere in the 19th Century. Case in point, her website: http://beket1.wix.com/annadallen

Along with her contributions to the four *Christmas Revels* Regency anthologies, her available works include the Regency Romance novel *Miss Pritchard's Happy, Wanton Christmas (and the Consequences Thereof)*; the Regency Romance novelette "A Christmas Wager;" the novel *Charles Waverly and the Deadly African Safari*; and three short story collections: *Mrs. Hewitt's Barbeque*, *Lake People*, and *Lady de Kiernan's Headache*; as well as some boring scholarly stuff about dead people. Rumor has it she has run off with the

Doctor—picking up Matthew Brady along the way—and was last seen in 1858 in a hoop skirt and running shoes, but she doesn't believe it.

In the virtual world, she can be found on Facebook: https://www.facebook.com/pages/Anna-D-Allen/366546213501993

Home for Christmas

by

Hannah Meredith

Chapter One

Early November 1814
Somerset, England

Charity Fletcher fervently believed two truths—that she'd been born optimistic and that she'd been incorrectly named.

She had one older sister, Faith, and by logical progression, the next daughter should have been called Hope. Hope, the very essence of optimism. But for reasons forever unknowable, her mother had deviated from the standard pattern and leaped over Hope to land on Charity.

Despite this error in the naming process, Charity remained ever hopeful.

Nothing in her formative years had nourished this attitude. Not that her life had in any way been terrible. No, indeed. She was more fortunate than most. Everyone had disappointments along the way, and Charity had simply had her share. She still believed that everything would work out for the best.

She'd grown up at the family estate, Fletcher's Field. Her mother had died before Charity had a firm memory of her, and her father was ever absent, preferring the fast set in London to sheep in Gloucestershire. Nonetheless, Charity had an idyllic, if isolated, childhood and enjoyed a close relationship with her sister. Or at least she had, until Faith, being true to her name, married the local curate and followed him to China as a missionary. This left Charity, at the age of eighteen, in charge of the estate.

Fletcher's Field and its immediate environs was all Charity had ever known. She loved the inconvenient old house, the rolling green acres, the heavy curled horns of the rams, and the comical antics of the lambs. The larger world whispered to her through books and newspapers and rare letters from her sister, but the opportunity to travel never presented itself and she was content to be where she was.

If she were lonely on occasion—well, was not everyone? She did not care for the times her father appeared with his cronies, filling the house with cigar smoke, leaving circles from discarded glasses on the tabletops, and generally disrupting everyone's schedule. Charity would have been happy for her father to stay in London forever.

What she'd never anticipated was his death.

She had no sooner buried him in the family crypt, with more dignity than he himself had displayed in life, than her cousin Horace, the new Baron Fletcher, had arrived with his horde... changing her life forever.

Horace had only one strong point—he was a prolific breeder. Seven unsupervised children racketed around the house, and Horace's wife Portia looked to be increasing again. Fletcher's Field was an ancient but not particularly commodious house. The destruction to floors, walls, and furniture was inescapable—and heartbreaking, since Charity was no longer in charge and could do nothing about it.

Circumstances battered her native optimism.

She had become that most pathetic of all humans—the dependent, maiden aunt. Or, more accurately, the dependent, maiden second cousin. To give Horace his due, he did say Charity could stay on at her family home until she married. As if there were a plethora of suitors in rural Gloucestershire who were waiting to snatch up a dowerless, average looking, twenty-six-year-old. Horace evidently had better breeding organs than brains.

It quickly became obvious that while she awaited the arrival of her non-existent, potential spouse, she was supposed to assume the role of nurse-governess, a position she did not relish. But the fact was, she had no place else to go unless she could find a job as a companion—and those who needed a companion were even scarcer than suitors.

And then... her optimism was restored. She was saved!

A letter arrived from Nicholas and Sons, Solicitors, with the magic word *bequest* twice mentioned. The idea of a mystery inheritance wrapped a world of wistful possibilities around Charity, although she could think of no one who would leave her anything. Her own father hadn't been concerned enough with her future to avoid frittering away all of his wealth that wasn't entailed.

The morning after receiving the letter, she traveled the four, cold, muddy miles into Bristol. There the cherubic Mr. Nicholas, one of the sons indicated by the firm's name, had happily informed her a Sir Edward Pym had left her the amazing sum of five thousand pounds—and a summer cottage on the sea in Somerset.

She had nearly swooned with the shock of it all, and

Charity Fletcher never swooned.

Wealth! Wealth beyond all her imagining! Why, if she placed the money in a four percent consolidated annuity, she would have two hundred pounds a year—for life. A princely sum, especially considering she now also had a home of her own called Fairview Cottage. She saw herself becoming established in the nearby village of Blakely-on-Sea. She would be Miss Charity Fletcher of Fairview Cottage. A new start to a new life.

Had she danced around the solicitor's office? She hoped she'd not made such a spectacle of herself, but she had wanted to. Heavens, how she'd wanted to laugh and twirl.

To her amazement, all this bounty came from a man she had never heard of, and who had evidently never known her. Sir Edward's designated heir wasn't named but simply described as the daughter born to Lady Fletcher, née Olivia Taylor, on the eighteenth of September, seventeen eighty-eight. That could be no one other than Charity... and she chose not to examine the oddness of the bequest too closely lest it should disappear.

And so, it was with undeterred hopefulness that Charity and Lucy Dibble, the former under-cook at Fletcher's Field now promoted to Charity's housekeeper, had loaded their trunks onto a mail coach and trekked to the coast of Somerset.

If Fairview Cottage was more a dilapidated manor house than a cozy cottage—well, with repairs, it would be spacious and lovely. If Atlantic gales constantly buffeted the house—well, winter storms were to be expected. If the two women found the needed tasks overwhelming—well, Charity would make lists. She could think of no other way to stitch together

her fraying optimism.

Their third night of residence found both women huddled in chairs by a meager fire in the room they'd christened the small drawing room. Their after-dinner tea had immediately cooled to tepid, but they ignored this as they leaned toward the fireplace when a smoldering log suddenly flickered into flame. It was a ridiculous to think the additional illumination would instantly provide more heat. Unfortunately, the flame quickly subsided like an insubstantial dream, and they both settled back into the established warmth of their mounded quilts.

"I think a donkey and cart might be more practical," Lucy continued the discussion interrupted by the hope of heat. "Donkeys cost less to keep."

Charity wondered why she hadn't thought of this solution and thanked heaven, not for the first time, for Lucy Dibble's practicality.

Lucy's face took on a wistful expression. "Although a horse and chaise would give you more consequence, and if chosen carefully, you could use the horse for riding as well." Charity suspected Lucy liked the idea of being the housekeeper for someone of importance. Alas, Lucy was bound for disappointment.

"I hardly need consequence." Charity was already crossing *horse and chaise* off the disgustingly long list and writing *donkey and cart* next to it. Such substitutions already filled the page. Charity wished she could permanently cross off some of the items, but everything on the page was a necessity.

The need for some form of transportation had become apparent with one trip into the closest village, Blakely-on-

Sea. Walking that distance wasn't feasible, at least at this time of year, not if she and Lucy wanted any sort of social interaction. "The most important thing right now is to make the house habitable," Charity said, moving the donkey and cart further down the list.

By habitable, Charity meant warm. Oh, not summer warm. That would probably be impossible. All she wanted was enough heat to allow her to feel her extremities. And perhaps discard the many layers of clothing and quilts that made movement difficult. Poor Lucy, who was plump to begin with, was wrapped in so many covers she looked like bread dough that had risen too long. More correctly, bread dough with a current on the top. Lucy's nose was decidedly red.

"We'll definitely need more firewood," Lucy said, obviously also thinking of heat.

"It's number two on the list, right behind *fix the windows*." And in front of—Charity made a quick mental calculation—fourteen other items. Appalling.

Charity glanced toward the one window in this, the smallest room in the house. They'd pulled the heavy drapes and placed books along the floor to hold them in place—resulting in the window coverings billowing like a sail in a stout breeze. Frigid air continued to swirl about the room, however, unaffected by their stratagems.

Lucy followed Charity's gaze, "Do you have any idea how to make such repairs?" she asked.

"No." Charity recognized a certain amount of defeat in that single word.

How did one fix leaking windows? Glazing? Caulking? She hated she was at a loss but had faith a competent carpenter would know the solution. Assuming there was such a carpenter available in Blakely-on-Sea.

"I should have listened to Mr. Nicholas's caution more carefully," Charity said. "He kept stressing this was a *summer* cottage."

"Well, he may have gotten the summer part right," Lucy said through a yawn, "but he was confused about this being a cottage. I thought the house would be something small and snug."

"As did I." Charity had envisioned a whitewashed, thatched cottage nestled among the trees with a view of the water. What she found was a substantial stone house on a long, high promontory jutting out into the Bristol Channel—without a tree in sight. Well, unless you considered the four, wind-warped, ornamental somethings in the overgrown garden. Charity had no idea what type of trees they were. She knew the best type of grain to plant in a given field, but had managed to escape tutelage in the more refined art of ornamental gardening.

She mentally added *gardeners* to the pernicious list, but didn't want to commit that need to writing. She feared her yearly two hundred pounds had already been allocated. What had initially looked like unlimited wealth was quickly shrinking.

As if to underscore her need to economize, the last log in the fireplace crumpled into glowing coals with the sound of a sigh. "We should probably be abed," she said, thinking of the puny fires they had lit an hour before in their respective bedrooms. The fires would provide a pleasant glow to see the two women into their slumbers even if they did little to raise the temperature of the rooms.

She wondered if Lucy found the creaking and groaning of the dark house as unsettling as she did. Last night, Charity had taken a large candlestick into the bed with her to give her more security, although this was something she'd never admit.

When they'd first arrived, she'd offered to share Lucy's smaller room that abutted the kitchen, both for warmth and companionship. But Lucy had been so appalled that "Miss Charity" would consider sleeping with a servant, Charity had dropped the topic and climbed the stairs to her own spacious room.

Hers was the principal bedroom with impressive views out three large windows—windows that, if the shape of the stunted garden trees were to be believed, faced directly into prevailing winds. This seemed to be confirmed when the books anchoring the drapes constantly became displaced and the window coverings were left to flap like washing on a line.

Charity was not looking forward to adjourning to her bedchamber, but if she meant to be Miss Charity Fletcher of Fairview Cottage, the principal bedroom was where that personage should sleep.

And she *would* make this place her home.

All would come out right in time.

Over the past few hours, the pain that permanently lodged in his knee had expanded into both his calf and thigh. When the persistent throbbing migrated to his back, Colonel Lord Gilbert Narron simply *had* to stop and stretch his left leg.

He reluctantly brought his horse to a halt, kicked his foot out of the stirrup, and straightened his knee. He sucked in a deep breath of the frigid air and then slowly released it as the change of position brought some relief. But his leg still hurt like hell.

As it probably would for the rest of his damned life.

"Colonel, is there a problem?" Sergeant Holly yelled to make himself heard over the gusting wind.

"No, I'm just a little stiff from this bloody long ride." Stiff? Now there was an understatement. More worn out. Used up. Ready for the knackers. But still here, by God, still here.

Holly motioned with his hand toward the dark dot at the end of a narrow headland and he shouted, "I think that's it."

"I hope you're right," Gil yelled back as he put a hand under his knee to lift it and force his foot back into the stirrup. That he had to use his hand was a testament to his exhaustion. He'd spent months strengthening the leg and thought he was done with having to manually move the thing.

They both turned their mounts in the direction of the distant habitation, too tired and too cold to say more. This entire trip had been one disaster after another. Why else would its end find him on a horse, his left leg on fire, and the rest of him a block of ice?

At least the journey had been educational. Gil now knew all of the disparate parts of a carriage that could break. He'd had no idea there were so damned many of them. Given the condition of the roads, he anticipated broken wheels, or at least broken spokes. But a bloody pole followed by a shaft followed by an axel? Each blasted, broken part meant a delay in some obscure village while they waited for the damaged piece to be repaired.

Holly blamed the coachman for lack of maintenance, but Gil recognized there was no way to anticipate what would break on equipage as decrepit as what they were using. He'd thought his brother Charles had abandoned the old coach in the mews behind the townhouse because it was so ill-sprung. Gil now knew otherwise.

He still had no idea what a damned forecarriage was, but its demise had been the *coup de grâce*. They would have had to wait a week for some sort of gears to arrive. Against Holly's commonsense advice, Gil opted to rent horses and simply ride. It was only fourteen miles, after all.

Fourteen miles of sheer, bloody hell.

His arse had initially hurt as badly as his abused leg, but his backside had eventually lost all feeling. Most likely frozen solid. Like his fingers and his ears and his nose. The lumbering gait of his hired horse vividly reminded Gil of why he had chosen the infantry over the cavalry. If this beast had the oft-mentioned, rocking chair canter, then one of the rockers was askew.

Journey's end was finally in sight, however, for which Gil was eternally grateful. He wasn't sure he could stay in the saddle much longer.

They relied on the weak light of the moon's reflection off the scudding clouds to pick their way along the track that led down the promontory. Gil couldn't tell much about the house except that its dark mass indicated a property larger than he'd expected. At this point, however, he would have been satisfied with any dwelling that allowed him some place to get warm.

"As bolt-holes go, you've managed to find one of the most isolated in the country." Holly's voice overrode the sound of the wind. Their ongoing argument about their destination would evidently continue to journey's end.

"This isn't a bolt-hole. It's a place to regroup." Gil knew his distinction was a lie, but a man had to preserve at least a vestige of his pride.

"You could have *regrouped* at your family's home." Fooling one's sergeant was impossible, but Holly had been singing the same song for the whole bloody journey, and Gil was hardily sick of hearing how one should be surrounded by family as Christmastide approached. Holly had been an only child, and although his parents were dead, he had very strong feelings about responsibilities to kin.

"We've been over this before. As it is, we're only two days ride from Tilbury Park. I can easily go there when I'm ready." The problem was—Gil really didn't know when he would be ready.

Gil loved his mother and his brother. He even loved the odd woman Charles had married, and he was sure he'd love Charles's three children when he met them. But he simply couldn't make himself go to Tilbury Park for this Christmas season.

He'd held images of his childhood home tightly in his mind through all the war years and had called up those memories when he wanted to ignore the mud and the flies and the groans of injured men. Mentally, he'd run through the fields, he'd swum in the river, he'd taken his punishment for misdeeds, and he'd been victorious in wrestling at the local fair.

But he knew nothing would now be the same—and he *needed* it to be.

While he was gone, his father had died, and his oldest

brother Charles had assumed the title of Marquess of Teign. His middle brother Terrance had been killed at Talavera. Charles's children had been born. Their mother would have aged.

Gil wasn't ready to have all his memories proved false. There were still nights he needed them intact.

He wasn't even ready to face those things that were unchangeable, like the two graves behind the chapel that contained the remains of his youthful folly—his wife Alison and her infant daughter. How could he admit to their shades that he mourned more for all those young men under his command whom he'd buried in foreign soil?

Perhaps most cowardly of all, he didn't want his family to see how much *he* had changed. The physical difference was obvious. He walked with a limp, and sometimes, when he overdid, such as now, the pain was debilitating. But he remained eternally thankful that Sergeant Holly had fought the surgeons and the leg was still there, painful or not. He feared being cosseted, however, and didn't want to be seen as less than he had been.

The physical changes had been explained in letters home and wouldn't come as a shock. What he'd been unable to explain were the changes that years of brutality had made to his inner self. Even he couldn't fully understand them. He simply knew that there was a hole inside he'd been unable to fill. That, frighteningly, he suspected never *would* be filled.

And so, yes, he would hide out for a few months and hope the howling Atlantic winds would blow away some of his hurt and confusion. He would go back to Tilbury Park in the spring, when new life was returning to the earth, and he would be whole or nearly so. He had to believe this or go mad.

When they finally arrived at the front door, Gil painfully pulled himself off the horse. He had to hold onto the saddle for a moment to make sure his legs were working. Like an eighty-year-old, he thought with disgust. At least Holly had the good sense to resist offering to help.

He limped to the door muttering the filthiest curses he knew. He should feel bad about doing so since he'd vowed to work on eliminating this offensive part of his vocabulary. Years surrounded by soldiers in desperate circumstances had unleashed his tongue, and the act of removing his uniform had not replaced the restraint. Unfortunately, in his case, words-thought tended to become words-uttered, regardless of their inappropriateness.

He assuaged his conscience with the conviction that there were times when such words were necessary—and this was one of them. God, the pain in his leg was as bad as it had been when he first tried to use it after the crushed bones had knitted.

Under the porch's overhang, it was too dark to see the lock's location. He added more curses as he ineffectually poked the key around until he finally found the damned hole. When the key slid home and he heard the lock click, he leaned against the door as tired as he'd ever been after a long, forced march.

Holly's voice rumbled from the dark behind him. "There's a stable in the back and the agent said there would be enough hay for a while, so I'll take the horses around, get them bedded down, and bring back our saddlebags."

"Thanks, Holly," Gil said, pulling himself into an upright position, his back and leg equally protesting. "I'll find some candles and light a fire. It's bound to be colder than a witch's tit in a vacant house."

Holly grunted an agreement, then added, "I'll see if I can locate the wood pile. We're bound to need it." He gathered up the reins and led the horses toward the rear of the building.

Gil pushed open the door and entered what was probably a low-ceilinged entry hall. All that registered was Stygian darkness. He hadn't realized the difference even the reflected moonlight outside had made. Across the hall, he made out a doorframe, the opening lighted by the moon's illumination. He moved in that direction, stumbling over a low obstruction.

A form suddenly loomed over him. His mind registered what seemed to be a descending cudgel. He jerked back, putting all his weight on this left leg. Agony knifed through him. The pain made the sharp strike on his right shoulder seem no more than a strong pat. But he knew it for what it was. Someone had swung a club at his head—and missed.

Reflexes took over—reflexes that allowed him to ignore the torture of pushing off his left leg to transfer his balance to his right and drive his right fist forward with all his weight and power behind it. The shock of the strike shuttered down his arm. His fist burned.

His assailant crumpled with a loud thud.

Gil readied himself to attack again, but there was no movement from his opponent, no sound in the hall at all other than his own heavy breathing. The trespasser must be unconscious. He fumbled in his pocket for his flint and steel. He needed light to assess the situation.

He hobbled into the adjoining room where the pale glow coming through the window showed a candle on a side table.

He soon had the candle lit. He hurried into the hall and raised his light high.

"Bloody, bloody hell!" Gil's words echoed loudly in the silent house and were what greeted Holly as he pushed through the door, their travel bags filling his hands.

"Colonel?" Holly questioned.

Gil motioned to the figure on the stairs. On the damned stairs. He'd imagined his assailant was a tall man. Instead, a young woman lay amid the puffiness of a heavy comforter that had evidently been wrapped around her. She wore a plain, flannel night robe, now rucked up to show shapely legs and bare feet. Irrationally, he worried that her feet were cold. A long braid of brown hair snaked away from her head. If it weren't for the red and already swelling nose, she would have looked like someone's little sister, awakened in the night by a bad dream. Hell, she probably was someone's sister—and he was the bad dream.

The bags hit the floor with a thud. "Good heavens, what happened?" Holly asked. "Is she dead?"

"God, I hope not." Gil leaned forward, placing the candlestick on a step and carefully touching his hand to her neck. "Good strong pulse," he said. "She's breathing, so my guess is she's just knocked silly.

"And as for what happened—she attacked me in the dark. Clobbered me with a club of some sort. I struck back blindly. I thought my assailant was a man. A vagrant of some sort skulking in a vacant house. Seemed tall, standing on the stairs…" Gil let his voice trail off. Whatever he said sounded like a weak excuse for felling this young woman.

"Well, she's obviously where she shouldn't be." Holly stopped abruptly and looked to Gil's left. Another woman had entered the hall, and this one started to shriek as if murder had been done.

Chapter Two

Initially, only pain registered as Charity's mind fought for consciousness. Her entire face throbbed in agony. Panic quickly followed, however, when she realized she was restrained and being carried by a large man.

"Help! Help!" she yelled, bucking against the man's increasingly firm hold. Even as the sound reverberated around the stairwell, she realized her screams were nonsensical. Who did she expect to rescue her? If Lucy were wise, she would be hiding.

"Hush, now, Miss Fletcher." Lucy's voice, solid and unafraid, came from in front of her. "We're taking you up to your room so we can tend to your hurts."

We? Who was this we? Charity stopped struggling and pried open reluctant eyelids to get a look at the carrying part of Lucy's *we*. What she saw was not encouraging. Looking up from where she was clenched tightly to his chest, she viewed the long, narrow face of a man in his late twenties. He was in need of a razor and looked like a disreputable highwayman.

She turned her head and saw Lucy stop at the top of the steps, her candle held high to light the way for the highwayman. When he reached the top riser, she hurried down the hall. There was the sound of stumbling behind

Charity and a distinctive, "Hell! Would it be too much to ask that you didn't leave me in the damned dark?"

Charity stiffened and twisted her neck to see who followed, but her view was blocked by the man who carried her. She knew the voice, however. It was the cursing man—the one who had broken into the house. She'd heard him outside the front door.

And Lucy was acting like these men were allies... What was she thinking? Or perhaps she was being clever and pretending to agree with them until she and Charity could devise a plan to get away. Charity had to believe this was the case. Nothing else made sense. She forced herself to relax and wait until she and Lucy were alone.

Lucy remained on the landing until the trailing man caught up. Then the tiny cavalcade marched down the hall together and entered Charity's room. The open door increased the draft, and the drapes waved their greeting.

The slender man carried her to the bed and laid her down with surprising gentleness. The bedcovers were in disarray from her earlier hasty rising. She realized what she had taken for restraints was simply the tightly wrapped quilt she'd thrown around her shoulders when she left to investigate the suspicious sounds at the door.

The cursing man had stopped at the fireplace and glared at the meager flames flickering there as if they offered some offense. In the uncertain light, he looked demonic. His gaunt face was a study in light and shadows—high cheekbones and rather prominent nose were highlighted while his eyes and mouth were shrouded in darkness. He appeared massive, an impression no doubt fostered by the greatcoat he wore.

"Holly, I hope you located the woodpile, since we need to

increase this fire if Miss Fletcher isn't going to freeze tonight." He turned to face into the room and his entire visage was lost to the shadow. Charity felt alarm that the intruder knew her name.

"Yes, sir. I'll get more wood up here and then bring in some for whatever room you choose." The younger man jerked his attention away from watching Lucy light some tapers and started toward the door.

"Here," said Lucy, hurrying toward him. "You'll need the carrying candle to see your way."

"As will I," said the man by the fireplace. "I'll go with Sergeant Holly and see you ladies in the morning." He gave them a perfunctory bow, made an impatient shooing motion with his hand toward his compatriot, and followed the retreating sergeant from the room. He walked with a wavering gait, and his oddly staccato footsteps echoed down the hall. Was the man drunk? Her father's friends had taught her to distrust that condition.

Charity knew she should take some sort of action, but she felt detached from what was taking place, as if she were watching a play unfold instead of being a participant. Her head pounded and she hadn't the energy to rescind the order to get additional firewood, although she saw more of her limited income now disappearing up chimneys.

Lucy filled a washbowl with water left to warm by the hearth, picked up the flannel next to the basin, and carried them to the bed. She made a *tsk* sound when she began carefully washing Charity's face. "The colonel examined your nose downstairs, and he didn't think your nose was broken, but it certainly is swelling. And I'm guessing both of your eyes will blacken. The poor man was quite cut up about hitting you."

The poor man? Charity managed to jerk a hand out of the cocooning quilt and grasp Lucy's wrist. "Lucy, what in sweet heavens is going on? Those men broke into the house and attacked me—and you sound like you're making excuses for what they did. They're dangerous. We need to get away before they return."

With a gasp of pain, Charity struggled into a sitting position to make good their escape, but Lucy stopped her attempted flight with the simple expedient of putting a hand on her shoulder. "Miss Charity, it's not what you think. They didn't break in. They had a key because the colonel has leased the house. Mr. Nicholas gave him the key. He was most insistent about it and upset to find us here. They thought *we* were the intruders, and I had to do a bit of talking to convince them otherwise."

"Ridiculous! They can't lease the house because I *own* it, and we now live here." Of course, how were two single women supposed to evict two large men? Good Heavens. Those two men were now happily ensconced in the house— and there was no chaperone on the premises. Before she'd actually met most of them, the residents of Blakeley-on-Sea would know her as the *scandalous* Miss Charity Fletcher of Fairview Cottage. Even if nothing untoward happened, gossip would still make the rounds.

Of course, that assumed nothing did happen. Chilling thought.

"Are there locks on the inside of the bedroom doors?"

Lucy stopped her ministrations. Her brow wrinkled in thought. "No, I don't believe there are."

Urgency beat through Charity. "Then we have to leave

tonight. We really don't know anything about these men. We could be compromised or murdered in our beds." She again tried to sit up, but the movement caused an invisible hand to drive a spike between her eyes. She moaned and subsided against the pillows without even a prompt from Lucy. As much as her mind told her to flee, there would be no dashing out into the night for her.

"Don't take on so," Lucy said. "Both the colonel and the sergeant have been complete gentlemen. And the colonel really is a gentleman. Lord something. I'm sorry I missed the title in all the excitement, but he does have one."

Charity could have rebutted this argument by pointing out that anyone could claim a title, even if he didn't have one. Also, judging from some of her father's cronies who had appeared with him on his infrequent trips to Fletcher's Field, being a member of the peerage wasn't necessarily a guarantee of good character. Instead, she cut to the obvious falsehood in the intruders' story.

"How could these men have leased Fairview Cottage? Mr. Nicholas knows I have taken possession of the property. He would never have given someone else a key."

"It wasn't your Mr. Nicholas, the man you talked to in Bristol. A Mr. Nicholas in London gave them the key. And that man was under the impression the house was just sitting here empty." Lucy emphasized her statement by dabbing at Charity's nose with a bit too much vigor and Charity swatted at her hand.

"Well, even if what they say is true, they will have to depart tomorrow. They can hie themselves back to London and take the problem up with whichever Mr. Nicholas is there. This is my home and they cannot stay."

Lucy looked dubious. "That nice Mr. Holly would probably leave, but I'm not too sure about that Colonel Lord Whoever. He seemed pretty sure this was his house until March."

"March? Ridiculous! I'll have to talk with him tomorrow." Charity hated to admit that if the man were to enter her room right now, her head hurt too much to put forth a sensible argument. So tomorrow it would have to be. After their discussion, everything would come out right.

Both women jumped when there was a loud thump on the door. "I've more wood for your fire," a man said.

Lucy hurried to open the door. "Oh, thank you, Mr. Holly," she said, all smiles.

The highwayman entered with a large load of firewood and proceeded to add some to Charity's meager blaze. This, then, was the "nice Mr. Holly," which meant Colonel Lord Whoever was the demonic looking one. Charity definitely wasn't ready to take him on.

As much as she hated to see so much money being wasted, the large fire improved the atmosphere of her room, if not the actual temperature. Charity felt her body relax for the first time since arriving at Fairview Cottage, and sleep found her.

Gil chose a room that faced away from the direction of the wind. Not that the location seemed to make all that much difference. The windows still whistled and moaned. At least the free circulation of air made a good draft for the fireplace, and Holly soon had a large, cheerful fire burning in the grate. Gil was torn between the desire to sit in a lumpy looking chair and stretch his legs out toward the flames or to simply collapse onto the bed.

Holly moved the chair closer to the fire and said, "Mrs. Dibble said she'd bring by bed linen. I expect her shortly."

Gil subsided into the chair. He hated it when Sergeant Holly seemed to read his mind. "Hell! I was hoping to get horizontal. There's been many a night we didn't even have a bed, much less any damned linens."

Holly grunted as he pulled out the trundle and positioned it at the foot of the bed. "But now we're in England and can expect sheets and coverings. And you told me to remind you when your language was slipping. Well, it has slipped—and this won't do around the ladies."

"Ah, yes. The ladies." Gil dropped his head against the chair back, vowing again to get control of his cursing. "We'll have to figure out a way to nicely evict them tomorrow. Or at least as soon as Miss Fletcher is well enough to travel."

He still couldn't believe he'd hit the woman. Gil had lost most of his manners during the Peninsula Campaign, but toward the fairer sex, he'd remained chivalrous. Of course, it had been pitch dark. He'd been attacked. He had every reason to think his assailant was a vagrant.

He sighed. He could write out an entire page of excuses, but none of them could eliminate the clawing feeling of guilt or erase the image of narrow ankles and bare feet—probably *innocent* ankles and feet. The choicest of his unacceptable words flitted through his mind, but he managed to stay silent.

Holly pulled the desk chair to the opposite side of the fireplace and folded his lanky frame into it with a sigh. "I don't see how we can expect them to leave. Mrs. Dibble is positive Miss Fletcher is the new owner, and to my mind, owning trumps leasing every time."

"I'm pleased to know you're now a qualified solicitor." Sarcasm never worked with Holly, but Gil persisted. "To my way to thinking, I paid a great deal to live here and have a legal lease on the property. This money now belongs to Miss Fletcher—and in return, I'm owed possession of the house."

"But Mrs. Dibble says they have nowhere else to go. You, however, would be welcome at Tilbury Park—"

"That option isn't open for discussion." Gil glared at his supposed servant and Holly had the good sense to drop the topic. Damn it. Holly pressed too hard, even if he did so with the best of intentions. Sometimes Gil wondered what in the hell he was doing hauling his former sergeant around the country with him. But he knew he would never dismiss the man.

Holly had saved Gil's life on two occasions, the last time pulling him out from under the fallen carthorse that had crushed his leg. This was a debt Gil could never repay. When they'd returned to England, he'd offered to set Holly up in some business or to rent him a farm, but Holly had his heart set on becoming Gil's valet or butler. Gil had no idea where the man had gotten the idea that being an upper servant was superior to being a shopkeeper or small farmer. Perhaps a butler had come to his father's cooperage and acted like a lord. Whatever the reason, the idea had been firmly planted in the sergeant's mind and had grown into a massive, immovable tree.

During the war, Gil had gotten out of the habit of needing someone to help him dress, and Holly was ham-handed in any case, so the position of valet seemed a poor choice. Gil had no establishment that needed a butler, so he'd given Holly the title of Majordomo, explaining that he would be in charge of everything about Gil's household.

It was a natural choice. Holly was very good at getting things done, especially if one didn't look too closely at how this was accomplished. He also had an abundance of common sense, a useful trait Gil appreciated.

But sometimes the man was just so bloody managing. Gil had long been grown and didn't need a nursemaid, even if Holly didn't seem to recognize this.

"Then maybe we can *all* stay here," Holly said. "There's certainly plenty of room and anyone can see the place is in need of work only a man could do."

Gil suspected this was the point his new majordomo intended to make all along. He shook his head slightly in negation.

"Propriety is something we haven't had to worry about for some time," Gil said. "Countries at war don't have time to be concerned with absurd social niceties. But females cling tenaciously to propriety here at home. We can't stay here because there is no chaperone. Miss Fletcher and I could hardly pretend either you or the housekeeper was filling that position, and so, our staying here would be scandalous in the extreme."

Holy gave him a skeptical look. "We're in the middle of nowhere. So who's to know?"

"Well, let's see... the people we hire to fix the bloody windows for a start, and then there's the maid of all work who is needed to help your Mrs. Dibble, and the store keepers in Blakely-on-Sea where we need to buy supplies, and... Oh, hell, why don't we just figure the entire county will know there's an unmarried lady and an unmarried gentleman living here together within twelve hours of the first local person finding out."

"I could fix the windows. If there's one thing you learn in a cooperage, it's how to stop leaks."

"I'm sure you could," Gil said with a sigh, "but that doesn't address the problem. Word would still get out. Mrs. Dibble was very clear that Miss Fletcher was the daughter of the late Baron Fletcher and the cousin of the present one, so she is not someone to be trifled with. I do not relish a male relative showing up at the front door demanding I do the right thing."

Holly had the gall to grin. "Now that would be a predicament worth witnessing."

Gil's retort was interrupted by a soft knock on the door. With the alacrity of a hungry hound discovering a dropped meat pie, Holly leaped from his chair and hurried to let in the plump partridge of a housekeeper.

If he hadn't been so sore and tired, Gil would have been amused by the sergeant's evident interest in Mrs. Dibble. The man had never seemed to be much affected by the female of the species, so his behavior was atypical. As it was, Gil could only be thankful that Holly's insistence he help dress the beds meant the work went faster.

"Is there anything else you need?" Mrs. Dibble asked, giving the room a quick look to make sure all was in order. "I've checked in the kitchen to see if there were any spirits and couldn't find any, so that is not available. I know gentlemen sometimes like a nightly tipple."

"No, thank you, Mrs. Dibble. We appreciate all you've done for us and will see you in the morning." Gil couched his dismissal in courtesy. All he wanted was to be abed.

"Then I wish you a good night." She gave Holly a

significant look and departed.

As soon as the door had snicked shut, Gil commented, "If you plan on visiting the woman tonight, you might want to consider where *Mr.* Dibble is. Or did I misinterpret that last look she gave you?"

To Gil's surprise, Holly's long face reddened. "I wouldn't consider doing anything like that. Mrs. Dibble didn't give me any sort of look. She's just trying to be an efficient housekeeper, since she's new to the post. And there is no Mr. Dibble. Missus is a courtesy title because of her position on the staff."

Gil chuckled. "If you haven't noticed, Holly, there is no staff."

"Well, there should be, but Miss Fletcher and Mrs. Dibble arrived only two days ago, so there's been no time to arrange the household."

Two days? Hell, if they hadn't had so much trouble with the coach, he and Holly would have been in residence before the women arrived. It would have been easier to get them to move on if he'd already been in possession of the house. That, however, was a fight for another day.

Holly helped him off with his boots and then they both readied themselves for bed. The mattress was a little lumpy, but it didn't take Gil long to find an indentation that fit him well. He felt his tense muscles relax and anticipated sleep.

Which, to his irritation, did not come.

Instead, the events of the last few hours kept circling his brain. They had not been his finest hours. He'd knocked out a lady and now intended to throw her out of her house. Lord help him. When had he become so brutish? This was not how he behaved.

There was nothing to be done about the physical assault except apologize. But if Miss Fletcher truly had nowhere else to go, he could not make her leave—or stay himself. Unless she was aged, and then gossip would be unlikely. He could pretend to be her nephew.

Unfortunately, there was no way Miss Fletcher could be considered an old lady. Embarrassment had made him avoid direct eye contact, so he remembered her as pieces rather than a whole, but what he recalled were attributes of a young woman. Her feet had been small and her legs shapely. Her braided hair was a glossy brown. Her face, well, it remained indistinct. All he could mentally see with clarity was her abused nose, which he'd examined with some care. He'd thought she'd looked like someone's younger sister. Holly had it from the housekeeper that she'd recently inherited this house. Gil now saw her as young and cast adrift by a beloved father's death.

Dear Lord, this situation was getting worse and worse.

He rolled over and found a lump poked him in the chest, so returned to his original position. His imagination showed him a child wandering from house to house in the snow, the faithful Mrs. Dibble following behind.

Bloody hell. That scenario was ridiculous. Miss Fletcher wasn't a child... and it wasn't snowing. He was sure of the last fact since, had it been, the flakes would be circling around his room. The damned loose-fitting windows would not have kept them out.

Could he, in good conscience, leave the two women here in this uninhabitable house? Holly was right in realizing maintenance was needed, and it was possible Miss Fletcher didn't have the funds to make repairs. Holly believed he could do something to secure the windows and Gil could at least help. He was hardly a useless fribble. Hell, he'd successfully led men in battle for years. He simply had to plan the takeover of Fairview Cottage as if it were a campaign.

And so, as the fire in the grate diminished to a weak glow and the wind moaned, Colonel Lord Gilbert Narron made plans.

Chapter Three

It was three days before Charity was able to confront the interloping colonel. Three days of Lucy dosing her with willow bark tea while she lay prone in bed. The slightest movement sent painful shards of glass rattling around in her head and made her stomach rebel. She slept a good deal and felt hazy when awake.

Then, finally, she opened her eyes and the room was in focus. She could think clearly and could remember what had happened and tally the passage of time. She turned her head to the side and felt only the slightest twinge. A woman sat in a chair near a robust fire—a stranger.

Charity must have made some sound, since the woman looked up quickly, laid down what seemed to be knitting, and came to her feet. She was portly with graying hair that escaped the confines of one of the most fanciful caps Charity had ever seen.

"Are you awake, then, Miss?" the woman asked. Her face pulled into a grin as if she were viewing an accomplishment of her own making.

"Water, please." Charity didn't recognize the raspy sound of her own voice.

"Oh, of course. Yes." The woman bustled to the bed and

poured a glass from a pitcher on the side table. Then she gazed at Charity with round eyes and seemed at a loss of what to do.

Charity pushed herself into a sitting position and extended her hand. The unknown woman happily gave her the glass. The water tasted like fine wine. Charity drained the glass.

"Thank you," she said, stretching to place the empty glass on the bedside table. The woman took it instead.

"I'm so glad to see you're recovering. Your cousin was so worried about you after your terrible fall. But, what can you expect in such an old house. Uneven stairs are so dangerous. I can tell you, I'm very careful going up and down. But at least all the improvements you're doing will make the place nicer in the cold months. I was always telling Agnes that she needed to do repairs. It wasn't as if the woman didn't have the money. But instead, she hibernated in the kitchen and the study over the winter. Heavens, you would have thought she was a field mouse, huddled in her nest while the winds blew. There was no telling Agnes anything, of course. Why, she even ignored my nephew's counsel. He—"

Charity held up a hand to stop the torrent of words. Whatever was this woman talking about? Had Charity lost her mind? She didn't know who her own cousin was, or the woman's nephew, or Agnes, or even the identity of this talkative woman before her. She felt as if she was reading a novel from which the first few chapters were missing.

"And you are...?" Charity asked, deciding that was the logical place to start.

"Oh, goodness. I'm so sorry. I'm Mrs. Struthers, of course. The chaperone. Your cousin, Lord Gilbert, explained how his sister had taken ill and hadn't been able to make the trip with him, so when he arrived, there was no one in residence to act as chaperone in a house with two unmarried people living there. Although you and he are kin, I understand the relationship is off a couple of degrees, and so when Lord Gilbert brought the problem to my nephew, the vicar, dear George naturally thought of me to take the place of your cousin. I'm s—"

Charity was relieved the verbose Mrs. Struthers responded to hand signals since there seemed to be no other way to stop her. "Could you please call Lucy, er, Mrs. Dibble?" Hopefully, Lucy would be able to explain this convoluted mess.

"Oh, you need to attend to things of a personal nature. Of course, you do. I should have thought of that. I'll get Mrs. Dibble immediately." Mrs. Struthers bounced out of the room in haste. Evidently, she had no desire to help with things of a "personal nature."

Charity audibly sighed when Lucy's familiar face appeared at the door.

"Mrs. Struthers said you were awake and alert and in need of the facilities. I can't tell you how happy I am to see you looking so much better." Lucy's broad smiled reinforced her words.

"Mrs. Struthers decided I needed the facilities when I asked for you, but it's been mentioned so much you've convinced me."

Lucy chuckled as she extended her hand to help Charity from bed. Charity was thankful for the support. Her legs felt weak and unstable. She shuffled more than walked but made it to the commode chair and back.

As she was sliding into bed, however, she saw her reflection in a mirror and gasped. The face that looked back it her was decidedly her own, but her nose was enlarged and the area under her eyes bruised. "Lucy, you said I was looking better?"

"You are. Your face and nose are much improved. And what's more important is that you look at me with understanding. I was afraid your wits had gone wandering. It's good to see the essential Charity Fletcher is back."

Charity reached up and gingerly touched her face. It was tender without being sore. Good heavens. If this was an improvement, what had she looked like right after she's been struck? "I need you to explain to me what Mrs. Struthers is doing here and what all her mumbling about cousins was about. I'd particularly like to know about the supposed fall where I was injured. It seems to me a great deal of fabrication has occurred while I've been... resting."

Lucy, whom Charity would have sworn was one of the most honest people she knew, looked down and licked her lips, all signs that her friend and housekeeper had been complicit in whatever had occurred. "Well..." Charity prompted.

Lucy began fluffing the pillow and smoothing the bed linens. "The colonel, Lord Gilbert Narron, thought we needed a chaperone for propriety's sake, so he rode into Blakely and asked the vicar if there was anyone locally who could fill this role. The vicar, Mr. Thomas, recommended his widowed aunt. That would be Mrs. Struthers, who came here straightaway."

"And how much am I paying this unnecessary chaperone?" Charity asked. The list she'd already assembled would stretch her resources. She hated to think of anything else being added.

"Mrs. Struthers isn't charging anything—well, at least in money. She's obviously staying here and eating here. She said she was glad to help, especially since Lord Gilbert hired three maids and a number of workmen from the village. This is a slow time of year for both farming and fishing, and many in the area are in need of work."

Charity barely kept a groan from escaping. Heaven help her. Three maids and a number of workmen? She was now evidently the employer of choice for the parish. All of these new neighbors would hardly become friends when they discovered she couldn't pay them. So much for being Miss Fetcher of Fairview Cottage. They would throw stones at her if she dared to appear in town.

"Did the enterprising Lord Gilbert, who I'm assuming is supposed to be some sort of cousin, happen to say what I'm paying all these willing workers?" she asked.

"I think the colonel is paying them." Lucy wrinkled her nose. "Well, that's how he made it sound. He's a lord, after all, even if he said he was no longer a colonel, only a lord, so he can easily take care of the cost. Right?"

Oh, very possibly wrong, wrong, wrong. From his title, Lord Gilbert had to be the younger son of either a duke or a marquess. Impressive at first glance, but judging from some of the younger sons who had traveled to Fletcher's Field with her father, many such men had no fixed address and simply took advantage of the lodging, food, and entertainment at one house party after another. They were leaches sucking the blood of anyone foolish enough to invite them to visit.

And somehow, one had arrived on her doorstep and

insinuated himself into her household.

She couldn't fault Lucy. Even with her elevated position of housekeeper, she was not equipped to gainsay Lord Anyone.

"Perhaps you could explain to me how this happy hirer of half of Blakely-on-Sea suddenly became related to me." Chasity tried to keep a glare from her face.

"It all makes sense," Lucy assured her. "Lord Gilbert didn't want to embarrass you, so he made up a tale—"

"A lie."

"A tale," Lucy reiterated. "It was to keep you from being embarrassed at having to rent out the house to him."

"It seems the man is very conscious of my possible embarrassment," Charity inserted.

Lucy chose to ignore her and forged on. "Lord Gilbert told the vicar he was your second cousin, but that the family had always been close, and he and his sister were going to help you get settled in your new home, but his sister became ill and couldn't come at the last minute—"

"—Does he even have a sister? No, it's not important. Continue."

"And since his sister wasn't here, Lord Gilbert felt it would be better if a mature lady stayed here so all propriety was observed." Lucy frowned her irritation. "I thought it was kind of him to consider the possible ramifications of his presence."

"Possibly very kind. But I need to talk with Lord Gilbert so we can get our stories straight, since I need to be part of this lie. But first, I want you to help me dress. And then we can meet in the small drawing room. Since we are *cousins*, I'm sure there will be no breach of etiquette if we meet there without Mrs. Struthers."

"I supposed that's true," Lucy said.

"Good. And while I'm dressing, perhaps you can tell me who Agnes is."

Lucy gave her a blank stare. "I have no idea whom you're talking about."

Gil forced the sash into place with a loud bang. He'd been so intent on muscling the recalcitrant wood into position he'd failed to notice his little finger was wrapped around the edge. When the bottom of the window met the sill, he remembered.

"Damn it!" He shook his pinched figure vigorously and looked up to see the workman on the other side of the panes grinning at him. He was chagrined that he'd again lost control of his language and that he was doubtlessly providing fodder for laughter when the men met later at the Plough and Anchor.

He was doubly embarrassed that he had hurt himself while standing inside, out of the wind, with his feet on the floor rather than a ladder. Those working outside had a much more difficult task. Yet he was the fool with a blood blister rising on his finger.

"My lord?" A timid voice came from behind him.

Wonderful. He'd also performed for one of the newly hired maids. He nonetheless pulled his dignity around him and turned. "Yes?" he asked calmly, as if his previous outburst hadn't occurred.

She gave him a pert curtsy. "Miss Fletcher requests you join her for tea in the small drawing room."

"Now?"

The girl looked confused, as if having delivered her scripted message, she had no more words to say. "Eh, I guess now. The tea tray has been ordered and Miss Fletcher is there."

"Thank you." Gil gave the maid a curt nod of dismissal.

He was wearing an old shooting jacket, shapeless and comfortable. It had been ideal for manual labor, but wasn't meant to grace a drawing room. Now, however, meant now. And he was, after all, making repairs to her house. So he assumed Miss Fletcher wouldn't be offended at his casual attire. At least he hoped that would be the case.

He made his way to the designated room and knocked on the door. At her "Yes" he walked into—glorious warmth. A smile of triumph crossed his face. Shortly, he hoped, all of the rooms in use would feel the same. After standing by an open window for the last hour and walking down the chilly corridor, the heat felt like heaven.

Miss Fletcher ought to be pleased. He turned his smile in her direction and was met with a frown. A frown? Perhaps she was still in pain. Guilt washed through him, pulling the corner of his lips down as he looked at her more carefully. Oh, her poor face.

The skin under her eyes and around her nose was discolored. Black with brown swirls. The pattern on her face reminded him of a hedgehog he'd tried to make a pet of when he was a boy. The little animal had the same darkened areas. On a hedgehog, it was to be expected. On a lady, it was not.

Gil suspected he wouldn't have any better luck in making a friend of Miss Fletcher than he had with the hedgehog. He'd tried to take care of it, but the hedgehog had rolled into a tight, spiny ball whenever he touched it. Miss

Fletcher didn't have any visible spines, but he would swear they were there. Unfortunately, the lady had a better reason for doing so.

He gave her a bow and said, "It's good to see you up and about."

She nodded, motioned to a chair, and said, "Please be seated. I've not had breakfast, so have asked for a tea tray and some muffins. I hope you'll join me."

"I'd be delighted." He took the offered seat and then didn't know how to begin the conversation. He feared his party manners had become as rough as his clothing.

"I understand that while I've been recuperating, you've been rearranging my life and we are now somehow related. Since I plan to make this my permanent home, I'd like to hear the story you've been disseminating." Miss Fletcher evidently had the conversation already planned.

From her prickly tone, Gil was sure he'd been correct. The spines, while invisible, were nonetheless fully extended. At seven, he thought he was rescuing the hedgehog from some inquisitive dogs, but the little animal had never come to trust him. He hoped Miss Fletcher, as a reasoning human, would understand his current prevarications were an attempt to rescue her reputation.

He marshalled his argument as if he were persuading a superior officer to see the advantages of one strategy over another. "Since we're both in residence here, a chaperone seemed necessary. The logical person to ask was the local vicar and he kindly recommended Mrs. Struthers. She—"

"—isn't being paid, from what I understand."

"That wasn't what I was going to say." Gil hated when others tried to put words in his mouth. He felt as if he might start growing spines himself.

"I'm sorry. But I am most concerned about your employing so many people. I feel like the scale of your hiring could be construed as a bribe to get Mrs. Struthers to come here. How much is it costing to have all these superfluous people scurrying about?"

Gil seriously doubted Miss Fletcher was sorry about anything. "The cost is hardly your concern, since *I'm* the one paying. And no one here is superfluous. As it stood, your property was nearly unusable for winter habitation. Since I have no desire to live in a barn, I'm seeing the necessary repairs are being made. *Your* property. *My* expense. I hardly see what you're complaining about. Or have you failed to notice that you can sit here without being swathed in so many layers you can't move?"

"What I've noticed is that this huge fire is gobbling up a prodigious amount of wood."

"Wood that I've paid for. You might consider saying 'Thank you, Lord Gilbert.'"

"I might do so, but I couldn't use your name since we've never been introduced."

Blessedly, the tea tray arrived and they both quieted. Gil realized they had gotten rather loud. Hell and damnation, he'd not meant to shout at Miss Fletcher. He was here to make amends.

He watched as she went about the familiar pattern of serving tea. Her movements were graceful; her fingers long and narrow on the cup. She asked him his preferences in soft, modulated tones. She might have been pretty, although the discoloration on her face made it difficult to tell. It was all very civilized—and soothing. The calm after the storm, especially when there should never have been a tempest in the first place.

He now suspected a lack of funds prompted her concern with the cost of everything. She most likely didn't have the money to take care of the problems Fairview Cottage presented. He recalled she had just inherited the property and may have hoped to live here in genteel poverty. Many mature, maiden ladies were often reduced to this, and while she was younger than he, she was by no means in the first flush of youth. At least, the child in the snow image was now banished.

"Please let me apologize and begin again," he said when he had his cup in hand. "I have the advantage of knowing who you are, so let me introduce myself. I'm Lord Gilbert Narron. My brother is the Marquess of Teign of Tilbury Park in Devon."

She nodded, but whether she was acknowledging she knew his brother or was giving permission for him to continue was unclear. Gil chose the latter explanation.

"I've recently been a colonel in the infantry but sold my commission when the war with France concluded. The habit of command is still strong, however, and I fear I may have overstepped in my zeal to get things done and provide decent housing for both of us. If I have errored, it was with the best of intentions."

Gil gave her his most polite, social smile and hoped it would have the needed effect.

"And I too apologize for my easy irritation. I'm not the type of person who enjoys having things done for her. I realize I should be appreciative. And I am. It's nice to be able to feel my extremities." She returned his practiced smile.

"However," her face grew more serious, "I'm unsettled by your having to spend your money for what you've pointed out is my house. It doesn't seem fair... but I doubt I will be able to repay you, at least for the foreseeable future."

"There's no need to concern yourself," he said. "I'll be able to enjoy the improvements until March."

"March?" Horror filled in her voice.

"Well, yes, March. That is when my lease expires."

"But I assumed that you would not stay—not when you realized the house was occupied." She sat forward in her chair and Gil saw her quills again rising.

"I see no difficulty with both of us remaining. The property is certainly large enough to accommodate two people living independently, along with any number of servants. And of course, Mrs. Struthers, who is here to guarantee propriety."

"You're not leaving?" She seemed to wilt.

"No."

Miss Fetcher looked like she was ready to launch a rebuttal, so Gil hurried on. "And that was why I claimed kinship with you. I thought it would be the easiest explanation for the local citizenry to understand. I didn't want them to think you were reduced to taking in boarders, as it were."

"Boarders?"

There was so much disdain in that one word that Gil knew his further comments had been a mistake.

"You imagine I'm reduced to taking in boarders?" she continued. "I'm not destitute. I simply don't have money to throw about in a profligate manner like 'the brother of a marquess.' I'm the one on whose hospitality you've imposed.

And as your unintended hostess, I want you gone." She pointed her finger at the door with the same authority God must have used when he expelled Adam and Eve from the garden. "So you can get on your horse and ride to wherever in Devon your home is and stay there. If you leave an accounting of what you've spent so far, I will send you quarterly payments until the bill is satisfied."

Gil was watching her carefully and noticed she had paled under her bruising. There was no way in hell he was going to give her a bill she'd have to scrimp to pay—just as there was no way in hell he was going to Tilbury Park.

They would have to make an accommodation, and that didn't start with his yelling, *Bloody hell, woman*, as he wanted to do. He took a deep breath and imagined her as a raw recruit, afraid before his first battle.

"Miss Fletcher, you have just risen from your sickbed and are becoming overwrought. I meant no disrespect. On the contrary, everything I have done, and yes, all the prevarications I've made, have been in an effort for you to gain and retain the respect of the community.

"As to our relationship, I have remained purposely vague so you can fill in the blanks anyway you like. I do not want you to repay me, since I consider the money spent to be reparations for my striking you. I can only assure you that it would not have happened had you not struck first in the dark."

He could see a rebuttal again forming, and held up his hand. "*Pax*. Let us find a way to coexist. This situation can be resolved to both our advantages, but I suspect we will have to work at it. Sergeant Holly has pointed out that I am too gruff for genteel company, but I at least *try* to always be a gentleman."

He stood and made her a curt bow. "We will need to make this work, since my going home is an impossibility."

What he did then, he refused to call flight. It was, however, a strategic retreat. He moved so fast the door was closing behind him by the time she managed to say "Lord Gilb—". But if there were more, he was gone.

Chapter Four

"Oh, Miss Fletcher. Don't you look grand?" Tilda Harris, a maid-of-all-work pressed into service as a lady's maid, stood back to admire her handiwork.

Charity thought "grand" was a bit of an exaggeration, but she was nonetheless pleased with what she saw in the pier glass between her bedroom windows—a pier glass that was useable now that the windows no longer admitted a gale. The past two weeks had seen improvements on many fronts, and Charity's native optimism had returned with the increase in warmth. She'd never realized that creature comforts could make so much difference and wondered if her need for them indicated a character flaw.

She'd come to view Lord Gilbert's presence as fortuitous. His arrival was surely a sign that everything would eventually come out right. If she'd been solely responsible for all the repairs needed, it would have taken years for the house to reach the condition it had arrived at in weeks.

Her initial guilt at the amount of money the man was spending was assuaged by Lucy. Her housekeeper had passed on information she'd gleaned from Mr. Holly, who was of the opinion that Lord Gilbert needed a project. According to Holly, his employer had demons of his own that were best put to rest with activity and that his income was such that he didn't even notice the expense.

With what was probably a worse character flaw than her enjoyment of little luxuries, Charity chose to believe this reasoning. Just as she didn't question why a stranger would leave her an amazing bequest, she didn't question Lord Gilbert's desire to make repairs to Fairview Cottage. She'd always believed proverbs held accepted truths, and so she was not going to look the proverbial gift horse in the mouth. She was well on her way to becoming the Miss Fletcher of Fairview Cottage of her imagination—and it felt very good.

She smiled at her reflection. She did look better. The bruising on her face had faded, and a careful use of some face powder made the remaining discoloration hardly noticeable. The dress was old but still her favorite. She'd worn this teal blue gown to every important event she'd attended in the last three years.

And tonight *was* important. She was hosting her first dinner party at Fairview Cottage. The guests were just the vicar and his wife, but Charity felt like she was embarking on her life as a member of this community.

"I think my appearance owes much to your ability with hair," Charity said in complete honesty. Tilda had been promoted to temporary lady's maid on the strength of her assurance that she'd always arranged her three sisters' hair. Lucy, who'd assigned Tilda to her new tasks, had not been convinced, but Charity now was.

Her thick, heavy hair had been formed into what Tilda called a nautilus bun. A braid banded her hair in front and another braid wrapped the bun itself. Curling feathers of hair had been teased out around her face. The effect was very different from her normal style, which she did herself and consisted of pulling every strand of hair severely back and making a figure eight at the nape of her neck.

Charity thought the softer style made her look younger. Or did she simply look more frivolous? Heavens, she was getting a bit long in the tooth to pretend to be an empty-headed ingénue. She shouldn't even care—but she did. How long had it been since she wanted to be admired? The last time had to be the unfortunate house party her father had hosted when she was in her late teens. Nearly ten years ago. But tonight, she wanted to look her best—and it wasn't the Thomases she thought to impress.

She wanted that irritating, interloping Lord Gilbert Narron to see a poised and confident lady. Not a pathetic spinster who dwelt in a somewhat derelict house on the edge of the sea and worried about money. She was sure this was his impression of her since he behaved as if she were incompetent and he the take-charge male.

Not that she'd given him much reason to think otherwise. Good heavens, she hadn't even been able to remove him from her house. In a short time, her grumpy, cursing "cousin" had managed to insinuate himself into every aspect of her life—because he was the bringer of all those lovely creature comforts that were her weakness.

She didn't have to arrive at church this last Sunday on foot or in the yet-to-be-purchased donkey cart. No, she'd ridden to Blakely-on-Sea in the comfort of a massive traveling coach with a driver in the box. She didn't have to huddle under quilts before a meager fire. Instead, she could move around a warm house in regular clothing. And the rooms she entered gleamed and smelled of beeswax due to the diligent workers Lord Gilbert had hired.

She lived in luxury all while her four percent income remained unspent and kept mounting up.

In this way, Lord Gilbert had bribed his way into her life. Or at least, onto her property. He seemed perfectly happy to ignore her. They saw each other only at meals, and then there was no need for conversation since Mrs. Struthers could keep a monologue going that required no reply.

It was during these times, however, that Charity noticed Lord Gilbert was an interesting looking man. She suspected he was not handsome, as most people perceived it. The angles of his face were too sharp, as if all the softness had been burned away. With his normal, serious mien, he appeared harsh, but on the occasion of his infrequent smiles—oh, my, he took her breath away.

How had she ever thought him demonic? His eyes sparkled with intelligence and the lines around his mouth suggested someone who smiled often. His nose was of regal proportions, but it harmonized well with the shape of his head. The overall impression was of a genial if aristocratic man—one used to giving orders but willing to listen to suggestions.

Tonight, she wanted that man to notice *her*. And this realization was more lowering than her desire for comfort.

She took one more reassuring look in the mirror, turned to leave, and was surprised to see Tilda standing by the door with a lovely shawl over her arm. "I thought you might want this for the hallways," the maid said. "It would go well with your dress."

Charity smiled at Tilda's obvious effort to prove her worth. It would be a real coup for her to be permanently named Charity's lady's maid. Tilda let the shawl fall to its full length and swung it around Charity's shoulders. The fabric swirled with a kaleidoscope of colors and was as light as a butterfly's wing.

The same teal blue as Charity's dress featured prominently in the design. "Wherever did you get this?" she asked.

"I remembered seeing it at the back of a wardrobe while we were dusting one of the unused bedrooms. I thought it would complement the dress you'd chosen, so I retrieved it."

Charity turned to view herself in the mirror again. The effect was stunning, and the wool was the softest she had ever felt. "Thank you. It's perfect."

The young woman seemed to grow in stature. Charity had never had a designated lady's maid. She and her sister Faith had helped each other and after Faith married, Charity mostly looked after herself. She had to admit, however, that having someone taking care of her personal needs was nice. She nearly groaned when she recognized another temptation to enjoy creature comforts. But she was not going to relinquish the shawl.

Nodding to Tilda, Charity squared her shoulders and went to make sure that everything was in order before the Thomases arrived. She found Lucy in her element, marshalling her troops like a general—and making the new cook's life difficult with her suggestions. Mrs. Dibble, as Charity should now think of her, wouldn't give up her new position of housekeeper, but she still had definite opinions on how food should be prepared.

Lucy had been as seduced by Lord Gilbert's generosity as Charity had. She'd wanted to be the housekeeper in a place with social consequence, and now she had the staff, albeit small, that made her feel this was the case. On a personal level, Lucy seemed quite fond of Sergeant Holly and had been spending an inordinate amount of time helping him learn how to function as the majordomo.

Charity smiled at the thought. She doubted Holly needed quite so much instruction. Standing alertly in the entry hall, he seemed quite capable of collecting wraps when the vicar and his wife arrived.

After checking the dining room, she made her way to the larger drawing room to discover she was the last of the house's residents to arrive. Mrs. Struthers was waxing eloquent on some topic, but stopped speaking when Lord Gilbert leaped to his feet at Charity's entrance.

"Good evening, Miss Fletcher. You look most charming." He flashed her an odd smile. Charity felt somehow vindicated, as if she'd finally captured his attention. It was a strange reaction, but she didn't intend to examine why this was important to her.

Mrs. Struthers was also looking at her intently. "You have on Agnes's special shawl."

The older woman's tone was accusatory. Charity unconsciously gathered it more closely around her.

"One of the maids found it in a wardrobe. I had no idea it was hers."

"Who's Agnes?" Lord Gilbert asked.

"Agnes Turner," Charity supplied. "She used to live here." That sounded like a succinct answer, but in reality, it was all Charity had gleaned about the woman. All of the local people seemed to assume Charity should know about Miss Turner, and she'd not wanted to advertise her stupidity by asking pointed questions.

"Goodness, Lord Gilbert. I would have thought Agnes Turner was well known in your family," Mrs. Struthers said. "She was quite famous in this area for her eccentricities. For twenty years, she lived in this big house all alone except for occasional day help. Everyone initially assumed she hadn't any money, but she always gave generously to anyone in need. My nephew can tell you of the specific donations she made to the church. Why, after a big storm destroyed the steeple in 1802, she funded most of the restorations. Surely you've heard of her."

"She was from the other side of Miss Fletcher's family. We're related through her father's side." Lord Gilbert's reply was purposely vague since their pretend kinship wouldn't stand scrutiny. But he had inadvertently made it seem that Charity was related to Agnes Turner, and here her lack of knowledge would be telling.

"I don't see how giving generously to good causes could be considered eccentric," Charity said in an effort to deflect the conversation away from family relationships. "How did she earn that reputation?"

"Oh, Miss Turner wasn't considered eccentric because of her charity." Mrs. Struthers tittered at her unintended use of Charity's name. "She and I were on a number of committees together, so I'm familiar with her philanthropy. No, everyone hereabouts thought her odd because she spent so much of her time walking alone along the headlands, sketching weeds and such into her journals. And then, she was always getting mail from exotic places. She *said* the letters were from her brother, but as you can imagine, people wondered if the sender really was related in *that* way."

Mrs. Struthers suddenly appeared sly. "Did she have a brother, Miss Fletcher? He was the one who sent the wrap you're wearing—from India if I remember correctly."

Charity felt she had been caught in a trap. If she claimed knowledge of this unknown woman, she would likely get verifiable information wrong. She was already having to work her way through the imagined cousinship with Lord Gilbert. Another pretend connection would be one too many. She opted for honesty.

"I really have no idea whether Miss Turner had a brother or not. I never knew her. I inherited the property from Sir Edward Pym."

"Why that's the man she claimed was her brother," Mrs. Struthers said, her eyes alight with the possibility of juicy gossip. "If you were related to this Sir Edward, then you should know if Agnes Turner was his sister."

Charity wished she were comfortable with uttering some of Lord Gilbert's obscene words, since this would be a good time to use them. "I'm not related to Sir Edward. In fact, I was unaware of his existence until he bequeathed me this house."

"Then why would he have willed you anything?" Mrs. Struthers shifted from her usual soliloquies to interrogator mode.

"He was a friend of my mother." Since her mother was the only name mentioned in the will, this must have been the case.

Fortunately, Holly appeared at the door announcing the arrival of Mr. and Mrs. Thomas, and Charity was able to use greeting them as a diversion. She could only hope the Thomases proved a blessing rather than a curse. She didn't want to establish herself as a liar in the area she hoped would be her permanent home.

Gil wished he had on his dress uniform. There was something about the bright colors and shiny buttons that gave a man confidence—and since he'd been figuratively knocked on his arse when Miss Fletcher had entered the room, confidence was something he needed.

Miss Fletcher had breezed in looking nothing like herself, or at least nothing like he *thought* she looked. For the first time, his vision didn't surround her with the aura of his guilt. He didn't feel the familiar surge of protectiveness. Instead he felt interested.

Interested? Bloody hell. He couldn't be interested—at least not in the way his body was telling him he was. First of all, she was a lady, the type of woman one married. He'd foolishly married once and certainly wasn't going to do it again. And secondly, even if she'd been someone ripe for an affair, he had never liked difficult women, and Miss Fletcher remained a hedgehog of a woman.

So there was no reason for a tightening in his groin, for his imagining her in nothing but the colorful shawl that draped her shoulders. Especially while she was in the process of greeting the vicar and his wife. Dear, Lord. It was ridiculous. He had no idea what was causing this absurd reaction.

Yes, she was dressed more formally that was her wont. She'd done something different to her hair. Her face looked less bruised.

The minute this last explanation popped into his mind, it seemed right. She no longer looked like a victim. Specifically, *his* victim. This had much to do with the decrease in his guilt. And when that disappeared, he saw her simply as a woman.

A desirable woman. Once he was no longer focused on her injured face, he noticed she was curved where a woman ought to be curved. She wasn't unforgettably gorgeous, but was comfortably appealing, like a pair of well-worn boots.

Gil smiled as they progressed into the dining room when this thought crossed his mind. He would certainly never say such a thing to Miss Fletcher. Commenting that she reminded him of comfortable boots was guaranteed to bring up her spines. He admitted that he enjoyed baiting her, however. Her attitude was refreshing. She stood up for herself when so many ladies lacked opinions and simply echoed what some man said.

Gil had few female friends—what unmarried man did?—but he could see Miss Fletcher becoming a friend. He was thankful the busyness of seating the ladies and the arrival of the food saved him from further stupid observations.

Once the meal began, Gil realized his mother's insistence on having even numbers at the dining table was not just a silly social convention. Their group of five took up only half the table and so were all seated at one end. Had they been spread around the entire table, the distance between diners would have made conversation impossible. As it was, speaking to those in the adjacent chair was merely difficult.

Miss Fletcher sat at the head of the table, with the vicar, Mr. Thomas, to her right and Gil on her left. Mrs. Struthers sat beside the vicar and Mrs. Thomas sat next to Gil. This meant that if either of the gentlemen turned to talk to Miss Fletcher, the lady on his other side had no one with whom to converse. And if the men spoke with the end ladies, Miss Fletcher would be left in solitary splendor.

Gil searched his mind for some way around this awkward social situation—but Miss Fletcher solved it simply by speaking across the table to Mrs. Thomas. While the service was formal, evidently conversation would follow the pattern of a family breakfast. By the removal of the first course, performed by the two maids under the gimlet eye of Mrs. Dibble, the entire table was involved in a lively discussion of possible economic improvements in Blakely-on-Sea.

Perhaps because his audience contained those he thought could help alleviate some of the local problems, the vicar proved to be nearly as loquacious as his aunt. "Prosperity eludes us," Mr. Thomas said, "because we have no large landholder whose estate requires goods and services from the village. My parish is made up of tenant farmers, small holders, and fishermen. This means we hold the enviable position of always being able to feed our populace, but we must be able to sell our grain and seafood if we want ready coin to purchase anything else. Our isolation and the condition of the roads make this very difficult."

Gil barely restrained himself from pointing out that the isolation of Blakely-in-Sea and the poor conditions of the roads in the area were also an advantage. Enclosures and the decrease of production in the midlands due to Napoleon's exile to Elba had caused a great number of indigent people to move about the country in search of work. Many of these ended up on the parish poor rolls in whatever location they gave up their search. "I appreciate your problem," he said to the vicar. "But while the population here may be underemployed, they are employed."

The vicar nodded, but it was Mrs. Struthers who spoke up. "My lord, you must see that without better access to the larger towns inland, this area can do nothing but stagnate."

"I have not noticed any one living in obvious poverty," Miss Fletcher said. "But then, I have been here only a short time and have not seen that much of the area."

Mr. Thomas leaned toward his hostess. "Our young people, in particular, have a difficult time supporting themselves. For instance, the village blacksmith's son, Carl, is himself a fine smith and would like to marry the oldest Davis girl, but the smithy in Blakely-on-Sea doesn't make enough money to financially support two households. Therefore, I fear we will soon lose a fine young couple to another locale."

"The village of Fletcher's Run, which was adjacent to where I grew up, suffered from many of these same problems," Miss Fletcher said. "I fear it is the lot of all rural villages."

"But your home village had a manor to support it, did it not?" The hopeful look on the vicar's face made Gil wonder if he imagined Fairview Cottage would magically become a large estate.

"Yes, to a certain extent, Fletcher's Field supported the village and the surrounding countryside. We needed a consistent number of workers and goods, so the opportunity for work remained stable. However, it didn't increase, and so younger people had to look elsewhere for a place to make their lives. Even the most prosperous tenant farm is seldom able to support multiple generations."

"Did you grow up in this area?" Gil asked the silent Mrs. Thomas, both to draw her into the general conversation and to change the topic. He suspected the vicar was working up to suggesting some sort of philanthropic need. Gil didn't mind contributing to some worthy cause, but he didn't want Charity to feel she needed to commit funds she might not have.

Mrs. Thomas shook her head. "No, both my husband and I are from Cambridgeshire. Mr. Thomas was fortunate enough to get the living here fifteen years ago. It's a lovely place with congenial people." She gave him a shy smile. "You probably think I'm exaggerating about this being a lovely place, since you have only seen it in the midst of winter, but for the rest of the year, it truly is delightful."

"I'll have to use my imagination." He gave her a smile that brought a blush to her cheeks. Between her husband and Mrs. Struthers, he suspected Mrs. Thomas didn't get an opportunity to say much.

"Yes," Mr. Thomas said, "Blakely-on-Sea is quite popular in the summer. I believe this property has been leased every summer since the passing of your great-aunt? Cousin?" He looked at Miss Fletcher expectantly. "I'm sorry. I don't know your exact relationship to Agnes Turner."

The look Miss Fletcher gave the vicar suggested she was not enthusiastic about again visiting this topic.

"I don't know my exact relationship to Miss Turner either," she said. "I inherited Fairview Cottage from Sir Edward Pym, whom I understand was Miss Turner's brother. Sir Edward was evidently related to my mother, but she died when I was a baby and I never knew any of her family, so I'm unsure of the degree of kinship."

"Mrs. Struthers evidently knew Miss Turner well—" Gil began.

"—No, not really well," Mrs. Struthers said quickly. "You

must have misunderstood."

Gil doubted he'd misunderstood. Mrs. Struthers had acted as if Agnes Turner were her bosom beau.

"Agnes Turner was *my* special friend," Mrs. Thomas's soft voice said next to him. All eyes swiveled toward her. "Sir Edward was her brother, despite what some salacious-minded gossips would suggest because Agnes's maiden name wasn't Pym. These spiteful people didn't bother to ask Agnes if her mother had been married twice, which was the case. So Miss Fletcher, it's possible you had no blood relationship to Agnes, but were related to Sir Edward through a familial relationship between his father and your mother." Mrs. Thomas gave a self-deprecating shrug. "Family relationships can easily become convoluted."

Miss Fletcher's eyes sparkled, making Gil reassess his opinion of her beauty. He'd never had old boots that could be brought up to such a shine.

She turned her bright smile on Mrs. Thomas. "Is there a possibility we could meet sometime tomorrow and you could tell me all you know about Agnes Turner and whatever she said about her brother? I couldn't believe Sir Edward left me this house in his will, but if he's part of my family, however distant, I'd love to learn more about him. Both of my parents are dead and my only sister is now in China, so discovering any additional branches on the family tree would be wonderful."

"Oh, Miss Fletcher, I wish I had more to tell you, but you've now heard most of what I know about Agnes Turner's family. She was very private about anything personal. We often talked at length, but it was usually about things we could do to improve the life of others, some here in this area, some more distant. I'm sorry I can't tell you everything you'd like to know."

The glow that had momentarily surrounded Miss Fletcher dimmed. Gil wished there were some way to get it back.

"Don't you think much of this information might be in the journals Agnes kept?" Mrs. Struthers broke her unusual silence. Gil had never heard her sound so tentative. Perhaps she was embarrassed that her previous comments about Agnes Turner had identified her as one of those who were prone to gossip. Since his actions had introduced Mrs. Struthers into this household, Gil hoped her comments were prompted more by an attempt to find something to talk about than by malicious intent.

Mrs. Thomas shook her head. "Agnes didn't keep personal information in her journals. She kept her observations on the local flora and fauna in them."

"While that's true, I believe she kept diary entries scattered among her notes and drawings." Mrs. Struthers spoke with such vehemence that Gil was sure she had read some of the journals. Or at least pieces of them. He decided he needed to warn Miss Fletcher to keep her personal information under lock and key. Mrs. Struthers was evidently not above prying into areas that were not her business.

"Do you happen to know where any of Mrs. Turner's journals might be?" he asked, his tone unconsciously becoming the one he used to question recruits whose truthfulness he questioned. The older woman blanched.

"I, eh, have not seen them in years. Not since Agnes passed away. I was helping straighten the house before Sir Edward came to inspect the property and found what must have been twenty of them in the bookcase in the study. Since they're not there now, I assume her brother took them when he left."

Gil believed her, but it was obvious that she'd checked to see if they were still there while she was here in the house. Mrs. Struthers liked to poke around a bit too much.

"Then, alas, Cousin Charity, I'm afraid the journals are probably gone." He purposely used Miss Fletcher's first name, which had the desired effect of making her pause to look at him. "However, tomorrow you and I might make a check of some of the unused rooms to see if we can find any of them. Even if they contain nothing of a personal nature, they would be useful in guiding you on explorations of the area when the weather is conducive to roaming the countryside."

Before she could answer, Gil transferred his eyes to look at the vicar. "Since this is hardly the season for hiking about, perhaps Mr. Thomas could you give us an idea of what we can expect in the way of local entertainment during the Christmas season. Special church services or perhaps a local assembly?"

The vicar puffed up like a partridge at again becoming the center of attention. "The choir has been dutifully practicing a cantata, which will be performed on Christmas Eve. This program is usually very well received. And then on Twelfth Night, there will be a social gathering in the large room above the Plough and Anchor. It is always an enjoyable evening, although I'm not sure it will be grand enough to be called an assembly."

"I'd call it such," Mrs. Thomas said. "There are fiddlers and dancing."

"Oh, both activities sound so celebratory." Miss Fletcher seamlessly followed his effort to change the topic, again. "As a new member of the community, what can I do to help?"

"If you sing, would you consider adding your voice to our choir," the vicar said. "I'm afraid calling our efforts a cantata might be a bit grand, but it is always a moving service."

And so the rest of the meal passed with discussions of the upcoming Christmas season. Even Mrs. Struthers seemed to forget she'd shown herself to be a gossip and entered in with enthusiasm. By the time the dessert course was finished, Gil knew where to gather Christmas greens and the best recipe for Christmas pudding. His one accomplishment was avoiding becoming a member of the choir. Holly had heard him sing and would have added his veto to the idea if asked. Miss Fletcher also managed to sidestep the invitation.

Thankfully, the Thomases felt the need to return home before the hour grew too late, and he was saved from further small talk over tea. Both Mrs. Struthers and Miss Fletcher also declared they were tired and needed to find their beds.

So he soon found himself alone before a fire with a glass of excellent French brandy in hand. Even when he was actively involved in fighting the French, he'd still admired their ability to make a superior liquor. He raised his glass to the Cornish smugglers who had brought the brandy into the country and to Holly, who with his usual proficiency had discovered where to purchase it.

As he settled back in his chair and felt himself relax, two realizations hit him simultaneously. The first was that for the entire evening, not a single curse word had fallen from his lips—which meant, miraculously, none had crossed his mind.

He'd been trying to be careful with his speech so he could avoid offending Miss Fletcher. His diligence seemed to have finally paid off.

The second realization was even more important. After an entire day of being on his feet, his leg wasn't bothering him. Oh, it still ached, and he would forever limp, but the throbbing pain was absent.

He raised his glass to these two hopefully permanent milestones and took another sip. As the lovely libation spread warmth down his throat, a third and less salubrious observation struck.

He could not get the image of Miss Fletcher dressed in nothing but the Indian shawl out of his mind.

Chapter Five

Charity slowly came awake with the feeling that someone was prowling around her room. She lay quiescent, listening, but shot to a sitting position when the "someone" pulled back her curtains and pale winter light flooded in to illuminate a smiling Tilda Harris. Heavens, for the sun to be up, it had to be after eight in the morning. Charity never slept this late. She couldn't shake the habits ingrained by the needs of a working estate.

"Good morning," Tilda said. "I brought you some hot chocolate."

Charity nearly groaned as the wonderful scent reached her. It was very possible the smell of chocolate had roused her instead of motion in her room. She pushed herself further up in bed to lean against the pillows and Tilda handed her a steaming cup. What decadence. Chocolate in bed.

She had to take a sip first, and then she could greet Tilda. "Good morning to you. And thank you for this wonderful treat."

"Lord Gilbert suggested it when you were so late in coming to breakfast. He said his mother often slept in after entertaining and liked to start her day with chocolate."

"Wise woman," Charity muttered. Then more loudly,

"What time is it?"

"Almost half nine." Tilda took one of Charity's three everyday dresses out of the wardrobe and shook it. "Lord Gilbert said to remind you of your appointment with him to begin your search." Tilda raised her eyebrows in question. She was obviously curious about a mysterious search.

Charity saw no reason for secrecy when Mrs. Struthers would undoubtedly trumpet about everything that was said last night. "We're going to look for some journals the previous owner may have left here. And I am indeed late."

At least she assumed she was. She really didn't have a solid memory of setting a specific time to look for Agnes Turner's journals, but last night she'd been so carefully tiptoeing around the subject of kinship, she was unsure of exactly what she had said. She did remember anticipating the search. How exciting it would be to discover something about her benefactor, Sir Edward, and to learn more about Mrs. Turner. What if they were connected to her family from her mother's side? It would be amazing to discover more branches on the family tree.

She felt her pulse ratchet up and slipped out of bed to make a quick toilette. "I think the green dress," she said as she crossed the room to the privacy screen. Tilda was holding the yellow and Charity had always thought that dress made her look a bit sallow. It was ridiculous she wanted to look her best to crawl around in the dusty reaches of the house searching for something that might not even be there, but she couldn't help herself. Although she knew Lord Gilbert had already seen her any number of times in all of her day dresses, she nonetheless wanted to look good today.

She was becoming absurd. She could only hope that no

one else noticed.

Even with Tilda's help, Charity felt it took twice as long to get ready as it normally did. She grabbed a quick breakfast and then hunted down Lord Gilbert. She found him in the small drawing room where he was studying some sort of diagram.

"There aren't any journals or letters in this room," Lord Gilbert said without preamble, "but I did find this." He motioned to the paper he'd spread out on the table.

She leaned over to look but couldn't tell what the lines and boxes illustrated. She glanced up at Lord Gilbert with a questioning frown. "And this is...?"

"The floorplan for this house. At least I think it is. It's hand drawn and some of the dimensions are wrong, but if you imagine this is the front door," he turned the page so that side faced her, "all of the rooms seem to be properly placed."

Once she had the orientation, the drawing made sense. However, as Lord Gilbert had pointed out, many of the rooms were slightly off in size when compared to the others. It was interesting, but she couldn't see how the floorplan would help them find the journals, assuming they were even here.

"I think you're correct. It's this house, even if the drawing is a bit skewed." She turned toward him and realized how close their heads were as they both examined the drawing. If she were to lean just slightly she could place her lips... She jerked back. "Why do you think this is significant to our search?" she asked in a breathy voice.

"Look here." His finger ticked against the lower corner. "A.T. I suspect it stands for Agnes Turner. And so I asked myself, why would Mrs. Turner take the time to draw a vague floorplan of a house where she was living? Had it been to scale, it might have been usable, but this isn't good for anything. It looks like something she absently drew while she was thinking of something else. Doing so is not all that unusual. But then she initialed it and carefully put it away in a folio, one which contained some lovely flower illustrations, by the way, so the woman could draw well. Again, the question is 'why?'"

He looked at her expectantly, like a tutor anticipating the correct answer from a talented student. Leaving Charity feeling like the dunce in the corner. She had no idea if the initials were significant or why the drawing had been made. All she could see were his hands. Masculine hands. Long fingered with blunt, well-kept nails. Hands that looked both graceful and strong. She didn't think she'd ever noticed hands before.

"Why did she?" she asked.

"Because she's added an extra small room to this drawing. One that's not there. To make sure, I looked. And in the process of my examination, I think I found a space where the wall of one room doesn't correspond to the wall in the next. There seems to be a space between the wall here"—he pointed—"and the wall in the study. Come on. Let me show you."

Lord Gilbert impulsively grabbed her hand and pulled her toward the door. Charity should have been shocked by his forward behavior, but all she actually noticed was that his hand was slightly callused and dwarfed hers.

He stopped as they came to the doorway. "Now get a good visual image of the distance between the corner of the room and edge of the door frame. When we get on the other side of the door, we're going to mentally mark where the wall would be if it extended through into the hallway. Do you have it firmly in your mind?"

"Yes." She felt a quiver of anticipation. She wanted to push him out of the way and dash into the hall. What if there were a narrow, hidden room? What could it mean?

He seemed to catch her excitement and pulled her into the hall. She frowned at the blank wall before her. Then she walked forward and placed her hand on the smooth surface. "Here's where the perpendicular wall should be."

"I agree. Keep your hand there for a moment."

He ducked back into the small drawing room and reappeared carrying a needlepoint footstool. He placed it on the floor under the place she marked. "Now we know exactly where the drawing room wall is, and we can see if the one in the next room lines up."

She nodded and sped ahead, no longer needing him to urge her forward. She entered the study and turned sharply toward the wall between the two rooms. She didn't have to check the position of the footstool. The wall was significantly displaced from where she would have guessed it should be.

Lord Gilbert hurried up behind her. "How far off do you think the wall is?" he asked. "Three or four feet?"

"More. At least five. The bookcase causes visual clutter and makes it hard to tell." She turned toward him. "I think there *is* a hidden space between the walls."

He grinned. Gone was the normally sober and stern Lord Gilbert Narron. His expression belonged on a young, impish boy in the midst of an adventure. "I do too."

"How do we check?"

He laughed. "Well, we could go through the process of measuring—or we could take the books off the case and see if we can find a way in. The wall on the other side is plaster, so if there's a hidden door, it should be in the wooden section behind the bookcase."

"I'm not waiting to measure." Charity was already gathering up books. Lord Gilbert followed suit.

"Should we check to make sure none of these are journals?" she asked, carrying her first load across the room.

"There's no need. I looked through all the titles earlier."

"Earlier?" She continued to pull books out of the case and tote them to the other side of the room, where she stacked them in piles. She noted his book piles were much taller than hers. Probably because he was carrying twice as many books in every trip he made.

"I've been up for hours," he said. "Unlike some people who were content to sleep the morning away, I was anxious to look for the journals. And then, when I noticed the discrepancy in the location of the walls, I was absorbed by the mystery. I've always been interested in puzzles of all kinds—and this is definitely a puzzle."

"Is there a problem here?" They both jumped at the sound of a different voice. Lucy stood in the doorway. "I can get some people to move the books for you."

"No problem, Mrs. Dibble," Charity said. "And we don't need help. We're just..." Just what? Anything she said would make it sound like both of them had taken leave of their senses.

"We're checking the structural integrity of the wall," Lord Gilbert interjected. "One of the workmen upstairs thought there was some give to the floor above, and we wanted to make sure there wasn't any wood rot."

"So Lucy, if you hear banging on the ceiling and the

walls, you'll know we're making sure all the repairs we've done so far are on a solid footing." Charity smiled in complete sincerity. She'd never thought she had a talent for prevarication, but she didn't want to tell anyone else about the discovery she was sure was coming. Well, at least until there actually *was* a discovery.

'If you need help, please let me know." Lucy hovered at the door and seemed reluctant to leave.

"Thank you, Mrs. Dibble," Charity said. "I'll ring if this gets too much for us. I'm loathe to take any of the maids away from their regular work, however, so I'm hoping we can take care of this problem without bothering anyone else."

Lucy looked dubious, but went about her own chores.

It took them nearly half an hour to clear the bookcases that stretched along the entire wall. When they'd finished, Charity's arms were aching and Lord Gilbert's limp had become more pronounced. Then they both stood back and observed the empty shelves.

"I don't see any obvious indications of a door," Charity said.

"Neither do I. Maybe if we changed the angle of the light... Yes, that might work. You close the curtains and I'll light some candles. We can move them to different places and see if any suspicious shadows show up."

Charity pulled the heavy curtains and turned to see Lord Gilbert holding a two-branched candelabra. Another rested on a side table and she picked it up.

"I'll start at one end of the case, and you start at the other, and we'll work toward the middle," Lord Gilbert said. "Look for a shadow that shouldn't be there, even if it's slight." He pushed the library stairs into position as he spoke. "If you see any suspicious line, tap to either side of it. A door should sound hollow."

She put her candelabra on the bottom shelf and squatted down. "You realize if someone walks by, we will both look quite demented."

"I could close the door." He stopped with his foot on the lowest step.

Charity chuckled. "And then with the two of us shut up in a darkened room, we would look scandalous."

"Well, I'm sure as hell not inviting Mrs. Struthers in to chaperone... Eh, pardon for the language."

It occurred to Charity that this was the first time she'd heard Lord Gilbert curse in some time—and he'd even apologized for it. Oddly, she hadn't notice this change in behavior until now.

"Then I think we're better off looking insane," she said with a laugh.

They both set to work, moving their candles from shelf to shelf, squinting at potential cracks, and occasionally knocking on the wall. As they slowly both moved to the center of the bookcase, nothing unusual presented itself. It was possible they were delusional and there was no hidden room.

She'd just straightened, leaning to the side to get a kink out of her back, when Lord Gilbert said, "Bring your candles here and check directly below my position. I think I see something and the sound on either side is different."

Responding more to the urgency in his voice than to his actual instructions, Charity hurried to his position in such haste that the flames on her candles wavered wildly. She set the candelabra down on the third shelf and wedged her body between the library stairs and the bookcase. Perhaps because the light still flickered, a faint vertical line immediately became apparent.

"Yes, I see it." The excitement of discovery shivered through her. She tapped on either side of the line. "And it sounds different. But if it is a door, how can it be accessed?"

She heard a brief grunt followed by a scraping sound and then a laugh. "Found it!" he said triumphantly.

She backed away and straightened to look up at a grinning Lord Gilbert. He held a shelf from this section of the bookcase in his hands. He leaned down toward her. "Here, take this. It was covering the crack that must be the top of the door. I'm willing to bet all the shelves in this part are removable. And when they're gone, the door will be revealed."

He held out the shelf, but didn't pass it to her. "You should also close and lock the door. The only person who will believe we're involved in anything compromising will be Mrs. Struthers, and I think she'd be the last person you'd want to alert to the existence of a hidden room."

Charity took the shelf, surprised by its weight, crossed the room, and leaned it against the wall. She then closed and locked the door. When she returned, he had pried the next one loose and was waiting with it in his hands. One shelf later, he was able to move the library stairs and work from the floor, where he speeded up the process by the simple expedient of placing the shelving to one side. Soon the entire faint door shape was visible.

"I should have guessed the door was in this section," he said. "Wasn't this the area with fewer books and more objects d'art."

"Well, there were more objects, although I'm not sure the 'd'art' part is accurate," she said with a laugh. "But it would make sense to have fewer things to move to get to the door." Looking at the cleared expanse, the outline was now obvious, but there seemed to be no handle or latch. "Now that we've found it, how does it open?"

"That's a good question." He followed the outline with his hands, pushing at various places along the seam. She did the same on the lower portion. When she came to the bottom corner there was a faint click and the door protruded out slightly.

Lord Gilbert wrapped his fingers around the exposed edge and pulled outward. A narrow door swung open on silent hinges. Charity felt unable to take a breath. Lord Gilbert reached over to retrieve one of the branches of candles and pushed through the opening with Charity crowding behind him. He placed the candles on a shelf that seemed to be provided for that purpose and they both looked around in amazement.

The small room was lined with shelves, all of them crammed with what were definitely objects d'art, and this time the emphasis was most definitely on "d'art". Statues of strange looking beings were wrought in glittering gold. A small chest seemed to be covered with gems. Stacks of brightly colored porcelain lay in a clutter on the lower shelves.

"Oh, my," she whispered. "It's a treasure."

"And the journals," he said, pointing to a higher shelf.

She felt a strong flush of discovery. This tingling must be what an explorer experienced when he stepped onto a just discovered island. Excitement and joy washed over her.

Almost without conscious thought, Charity reached up and pulled Lord Gilbert's head toward hers. Then she went up on her toes and kissed him, full on the mouth, as she'd only done once before in her life.

She kissed him. A celebratory kiss. He was sure that was what it was. After all, there was much to celebrate. He should take a step back and give her a quick peck on the forehead in parting and that would be that.

His brain sent him that message. The rest of him ignored it. Instead, he gathered her to him until he could feel her breasts brushing his chest. The two soft points of contact sent waves of desire washing south of his waist.

She fit well into his embrace. Sturdy without being overly plump. Alison had taught him to avoid dainty, doll-like creatures. From the distance of years and experience, he couldn't understand why he'd ever felt an attraction to such a fragile woman. He'd learned to appreciate real women, like the one he was holding.

Only Charity didn't seem like one in a long line of similar women. She seemed fresh, different. Her lips were plump and moist and quivered uncertainly against his. It was obvious she was fairly untutored when it came to kissing. What she lacked in finesse, she made up for in enthusiasm. When his tongue tickled her lower lip, she trembled and let her mouth relax. He lightly stroked the interior, eliciting a soft moan.

It was hardly a lascivious kiss, yet it felt more complete than any of his memory. The woman felt more right in his arms than any had before. His desire to bring his hands into play, to push her back against a wall and press firmly against her was overridden by a need to cherish her.

A shaft of alarm shot through him. He'd put tender emotions away and hadn't expected them to reassert themselves after he'd thought them long dead. Sexual attraction was normal, but affection—affection could lead to disaster.

He eased his lips away from hers and then he did peck her on the forehead, since the act seemed to be lodged in his mind. He did not release her, however, instead he settled her with her head against his chest. She didn't pull away. And so they stood heart to heart in the dark, hidden room while candlelight caused gold and jewels to flicker like fireflies around them.

"Why did you never marry?" he asked over the top of her head. He knew the inappropriateness of the question, but it now seemed so improbable that no one had seen her worth and swept her into matrimony.

She stiffened and didn't speak. He thought she probably wouldn't. The question was too personal. He should not have asked.

"I suppose you could say the opportunity never presented itself." Her voice rose up from his chest, hesitant but clear. "Since our mother was dead and our father generally away, my sister Faith and I grew up in isolation at Fletcher's Field. I guess we got used to a solitary existence, and pushing our father to take us to London, or even to Bath, never occurred to either of us.

"Then Faith, who was five years my senior, became enamored with the new curate at the village church. Our father, who'd never done anything to help find us husbands, was against the match, but Faith was of age, so married whom she wanted. She and her husband left shortly to become missionaries in China."

"And then you were completely alone?" If she and her sister had felt isolated, now her isolation was complete. Something long dormant rose up within him and he wanted to make sure she was never so alone again.

She chuckled, the vibration moving up through his chest. "Hardly alone. At eighteen, I was left to run a large estate. There was the land steward as well as staff in the house, tenant farmers, shepherds, and to a certain extent all the people who lived in the village of Fletcher's Run. No, I was not alone."

All of the people she'd named would have offered a working rather than a personal relationship. Gil noticed that she had not mentioned a single friend. Was it possible she'd had none? As far as he could tell, she'd been abandoned by her father—or if not abandoned, at least ignored. "Were there no potential spouses in the area near Fletcher's Field? None that your father knew and could introduce you to?"

"I did meet a man when I was nineteen and imagined myself in love." She made a sound that was a cross between a laugh and a sigh. "What girl that age isn't swayed by a nice smile and a little attention? That year, my father had one of his occasional shooting parties at Fletcher's Field. He invited his usual friends from London and one of them brought his son. He was young and bored and we spent a lot of time together. I foolishly thought it meant something and ended up embarrassing myself." The sound she made this time was definitely a self-deprecating laugh. "So now you know my darkest secret."

"He must have been very young to be so foolish." To his surprise, Gil realized he meant every word. How could a man

Charity valued not value her in return? But he could easily imagine some callow boy, caught in a company he found boring, gravitating toward an attractive young woman. But he must have done more than simply admire her if Charity had been led to "embarrass" herself.

"No, I was the one who was young and foolish. I now see his rejection as one of life's lessons. Painful at the time, but necessary for growth. Since then, I've matured and learned to be content with the life I have. The legacy from Sir Edward has offered me more opportunities than I thought possible."

He looked at the amazing collection of artifacts before him. "I believe you're the recipient to an even larger legacy than you anticipated."

She pulled back, and he reluctantly loosened his arms. She simply turned around to view the objects on the shelf, however, and didn't move away. "It is a treasure, isn't it?"

"Yes, I think you're about to become a very wealthy woman. And to that end, you need to decide how you're going to handle this discovery. I suspect you'll need some legal help. And I'm not sure you should tell all and sundry what we've found until you've made an inventory and given some thought to what you want to keep and what you want to sell. Some of the Hindu gods are probably museum quality and would appeal to collectors."

"Is that what the golden figures are—Hindu gods?"

"Yes. Sir Edward probably sent them to Mrs. Turner, just as he sent her the Indian shawl. Whether they were gifts or just items she was holding for him, we'll never know. But Mrs. Turner knew their value or she would not have put them in this secret room. Do you want to close the hidden door and put everything back on the shelves until a later date?"

"I want to remove the journals and then shut everything else up... for a while." Her tone was decisive.

He nodded agreement and then realized she was looking away from him. He started to edge forward, ready to gather the journals. She stopped him by grasping his arm.

"Stay for a moment, please. It's only fair. I gave you my truth and now I'd like to hear yours. Why have you never married?"

He was blindsided by the question—and shouldn't have been. He was the one who had introduced this personal topic. Naturally, she'd assume that he would be willing to answer the same query.

"I did marry," he said. "Years ago. My wife died in childbirth while I was in Spain." It was a succinct recounting that masked all the hurt and confusion he'd felt at the time.

She turned to look at him, still standing very close. "What a sadness. I'm so sorry. Did your child survive?"

"No. She's buried with her mother."

Gil was horrified to see her swipe at her eyes. He had long distanced himself from any pain that chapter in his life had caused. One of the reasons he didn't want to go to Tilbury Park was to avoid facing the situation again.

"Losing your child must be the most difficult thing in the world," she said tightly.

He hated that what he'd said had made Charity cry. The situation wasn't worthy of her tears. "I would have done everything for her, had she lived," he said. He'd always told himself that he would have cared for the child. He hoped it was indeed the truth. He hated to think he could be the kind of man who would blame a child for the frailties of its parent.

"I think there has been enough truth in the dark," he said into the silence, knowing he would never tell Charity more than the bare bones he'd already presented. "Let's move the journals into the study and get this place closed up."

Without speaking, they went about their tasks, and soon all was as it had been except that the insignificant objects d'art had been crowded together and the journals were now placed on the shelves obscuring the hidden door. Neither mentioned the confidences that had been given on the other side of the secret door.

Chapter Six

Reading Agnes Turner's journals soon became an obsession—and it was one Charity couldn't seem to control.

She'd initially planned to scan each page quickly, looking only for any personal references. These appeared infrequently among commentaries of Agnes's walks and some rather exquisite drawings of the local flora and fauna. Armed with carefully cut strips of paper with which to mark the locations of potentially useful information, Charity thought she would dash through each book, leaving it bristling with bookmarks for later examination.

Her mistake was beginning with the oldest journal in the stack—the one written when Agnes first arrived at Fairview Cottage and Blakely-on-Sea. From the very first page, Charity was struck at how similar her own reactions were to those of Agnes. Charity and Agnes shared a similar surprise at the size of the house and an identical delight at the awe-inspiring expanse of sky and sea that could be viewed from every window. Charity felt as if the two of them were walking hand in hand. The need to discover information that would be helpful in determining kinship disappeared. It seemed unimportant when Charity felt an affinity to each word and impression. She could hear the surf pounding against the promontory cliffs from Agnes's vivid description. An illustration of a lapwing with its rakish narrow crest leaped from the page so true to life, Charity could almost see it turn its head.

"You've been at it for hours. Have you found anything of interest?" Lord Gilbert's voice jerked her from Agnes's description of the butcher in Blakely-on-Sea.

Charity rolled her neck to work out a kink. "Heavens. Has it really been hours?"

"Five hours. It's approaching tea time."

Five? Impossible! She was only half way through the first volume.

"I lost track of my purpose," she admitted with chagrin. "I became mired down in the bits and pieces of Agnes's story, you know, all those details that make her a real person. I know I should be searching for clues to how I ended up here and instead, I stupidly got caught up in the narrative."

"I think your reaction is normal. We're all attracted to stories. If you want, I could go over some volumes too. I doubt I'll form an emotional attachment to the writer and can cover more ground." He gave her an easy grin. "I suspect you'll be doing me a favor. Since I sometimes have trouble sleeping, reviewing the journals for pertinent information will give some purpose to my wakeful hours."

"Please by my guest." She motioned to the shelf that held a daunting number of gray-backed books.

He chose a couple of books at random. "I'll see how long it takes me to get through these. Then I'll know how many I'll need for any potential late-night reading. I think you should lock this room when neither of us is in it. At least if you don't want Mrs. Struthers' help with the project."

"No. Mrs. Struthers would just want to…"

"Pry?" he supplied at her hesitation.

"Exactly."

"Then we are of the same mind. Let me get to work on these," he said and quickly left the room.

The suggestion the study be kept locked was a good one. Mrs. Struthers was entirely too anxious to insert herself in others' lives. Lord Gilbert, however, was good at keeping his own counsel. This was the second time she'd seen him today, and neither time had he made any reference to what Charity thought of as "the kiss." The irritating man acted like it had never happened.

This attitude wasn't particularly welcome. Whenever she was not engrossed in the journals, Charity's mind went back to the hidden room. She should be thinking about the potential wealth to be found in the stored objects; instead, she relived the feeling of Lord Gilbert's arms about her and his lips on hers. They had awakened longings she thought she'd long ago put aside. Had *wanted* put aside. It was silly to yearn for what would never be.

She wondered, not for the first time, if she had learned nothing from her encounter with Harold Muir all those years ago. Then she had imagined a romance where there was none, and when he'd kissed her, she had blurted out her love and elaborated on the happy life they could have together. She only stopped when she realized he was laughing.

At least she hadn't said anything *that* stupid after kissing Lord Gilbert. Instead, she had admitted to her earlier romantic encounter, which, when viewed in retrospect, might have been equally ridiculous. His reaction again seemed to be to make himself scarce except for meals. But his recent appearance showed he was still interested in helping her solve the mystery of her bequest.

For this reason—and of course, for this reason only—she was disappointed when he did not appear the next morning with the journals he'd taken the previous evening. Instead, he'd eaten an early breakfast and left before she'd arrived in the dining room. He'd not sought her out in the study since. She was loath to admit she was anxious to see him and tried to become lost in the world as seen through Agnes Turner's eyes.

"Good, you're here." Lord Gilbert's voice made her jump—a reaction perhaps caused by her body trying to keep up with the flip made by that most foolish of all organs, her heart.

She smiled at him as he leaned casually on the doorframe. "Here, and at the same time, out on the promontory walking with Agnes in what was much better weather than what we're enjoying today." As if to reinforce her comment, the wind changed enough for sleet to tick on the windows. Blessedly, while the cold still penetrated the glass, no breeze circled the room.

"Yes, it is a good day to stay indoors and read by the fire." He held up his journal. "And we will need to do a lot of reading, since I think I've discovered the key to finding the information you want."

"What?" She came to her feet, the journal she'd been reading sliding off her lap and landing on the floor with a soft thump. "You found the familial connection?"

"Not exactly. I said I'd found the key. Sit back down and let me show you."

She resumed her seat on the settee and he sat next to

her. "Have you noticed that occasionally there's a tiny E in the upper, outside corner of a page?"

He pointed to a small mark she had seen before but had ignored. "I thought that was a check mark, but can see where it could be an E." She felt her heartbeat increase from a mixture of excitement and Lord Gilbert's proximity. "Do you think it has something to do with Sir Edward?"

"Yes. I believe Mrs. Turner put a small E at the top of a page when it contained something she wanted to include in a letter to Sir Edward. This is supposition, of course, so let me show you what I mean."

He opened the book he'd had overnight to the first page and began rapidly leafing through it until he came to a page with the mark at the top. "Here. See the short paragraph set off by itself."

Charity leaned over and read, *The crocuses are a riot of color. My garden has been worth the work.* She looked up and raised her eyebrows in skepticism.

"Give me a few more chances," he said, "and I think you'll see what I'm talking about." He flipped through more pages and stopped when he saw the symbol. This time he read what he thought were the appropriate sentences. *Mr. Stone delivered three large crates this morning. Excellent quality and selection. It could take a year to sell without notice.*

It was his turn to raise his eyebrows. "Doesn't this sound like a reference to the kind of things we found in the hidden room?"

"Yes, but it doesn't make sense."

"I have an idea what it's about, but right now I'd rather concentrate on how to locate the information you're seeking." He turned more pages until another E appeared. He handed the book to Charity.

To her surprise, the sentences she was looking for seemed to jump out at her. *Relieved E. is coming home. Here or Y?* she read. She unconsciously reached over and covered his hand with hers. "I think you're right. This makes sense. Mr. Nicholas, the solicitor who contacted me about the bequest, said Sir Edward lived in Yorkshire. That was one of the reasons they had trouble finding me."

He gave her one of those smiles that made her toes curl. "By just reading the pages with an E in the corner, we can rapidly find the references we need. Then if we start at the beginning and read the sentences chronologically, we should be able to put together Agnes Turner's side of an ongoing conversation. Or at least the topics she covered. Mrs. Struthers commented on the large number of letters Mrs. Turner received from abroad, so it's only logical she would answer them."

"Why would you think these are necessarily prompts for a letter? We could be imagining the significance of the E." But if it were true, Charity could see where it would greatly simplify their search. As Lord Gilbert had said, the E was a key, and in Charity's experience, such keys were seldom easy to find.

"When I was a young boy away at school, my father made it clear that if I did not write to my mother weekly, my allowance would not arrive monthly." He chuckled. "At that age, the lack of an allowance was horrifying. But the first few times I sat down to pen my dutiful letter, I couldn't think of a thing to say. It seemed I had done nothing worth noting for an entire week, or at least nothing I wanted to tell my mother about.

"And so I started making little notations in my copy books of innocuous bits I could tell my mother. The score of a cricket match I saw. A prank some boy had pulled. An unreasonable assignment one of my teachers had given. Minutia, but put together they made a letter—and evidently an interesting one, since my mother has admitted she's kept every one."

She saw him return to the present from whatever past he'd been mentally viewing. "When I saw these unrelated groups of sentences, they looked much like what I used, and discovering the E at the top of the page seems to confirm it."

His reasoning seemed solid and she felt her excitement mount. "I think you're right. The E is the key. Will you help me mark the pages?"

"Of course. I'm as anxious to find the answers as you are. I told you I enjoyed puzzles, and you've certainly presented me with one. Today is the perfect day to sit inside by the fire and collect evidence. There's only one thing we need before we start."

"What?"

"More slips of paper to mark the appropriate pages."

She laughed and got up to get more paper and scissors. When her hand slipped from Lord Gilbert's, she noticed he had turned his hand over and had been holding hers the entire time.

Although they were both anxious to begin their more organized search, they spent the next quarter hour making paper strips. She used the scissors and snipped away. Lord Gilbert located a ruler and used it as a guide to tear his pieces. To her irritation, his pile of bookmarks grew more rapidly than hers.

"I think that should be enough," she finally said. "You only found three marked pages in the volume you read last night, so I think we can assume there will be a similar number in most of the other journals."

"Of which there are forty-five," he observed. "Mrs. Turner was quite prolific and filled nearly three books a year."

"And I'm sure we must have a couple hundred markers. That will surely be enough. I think we need to get started." She picked up the book she'd been reading and returned to her place on the settee.

"Wait, before we begin, I have one other organizational suggestion."

Charity sighed theatrically. "You are the most irritatingly organized person I know."

Instead of looking offended, he grinned. "I've commanded troops in wartime. If I weren't organized, people could be killed. I'm afraid the habit has become ingrained. My suggestion is one that will save us time in the end.

"So far, the pertinent sentences on the marked pages have fallen into three categories: general information, like the state of her garden; discussion of goods received—and I do think we will find more of those; and personal information, such as that about Sir Edward's returning to England. If we put a letter on the top of every strip we inserted—a G for general, an A for anything about artifacts, and a P for personal—we could then go back and read them by category, obviously starting with the personal. This would help us make sense of what is there."

As much as she hated to support his obsessive organization, he was right. "Yes, I think that would be helpful."

"Good, then I'll start with the last volume and you can start with the first and we'll both work toward the middle."

"Stop organizing," she said with mock severity.

"Yes ma'am." His humility was equally false and she would have thrown something at him if she'd had anything at hand other than one of the precious journals. He settled into a wingback chair by the fire and stretched his stiff leg out to settle on a footstool.

Then all that could be heard was the shuffling of pages.

Gil laid his journal on the stack next to his chair with a sense of real satisfaction. "That's it for me," he said. The space the journals had occupied on the bookcase was empty. The book Charity held was already decorated with a collection of bookmarks. She too was nearing the end.

The day had been unexpectedly agreeable. He and Charity had sat in companionable silence most of the time, each absorbed with his or her own tasks. Even the interruptions had been kept to a minimum: Mrs. Struthers poking her head in to ask if she could help, an offer that was rejected in the nicest possible way; Holly coming in occasionally with more wood for the fire, all the while grumbling that in a proper household this would not be the job of the majordomo; Mrs. Dibble insisting they have afternoon tea and then bringing it in.

At first, there had been the temptation to read particularly significant passages to each other, but Charity had put a stop to that. "No," she said. "I want us to have the full story before making suppositions."

Of course, she made this difficult with an occasional

indrawn breath or softly muttered "Oh, my." He so wanted to ask her what she had found. Reading chronologically, he could understand how the brief comments might form a story. Since he was reading backwards, it was some time before the sections he marked began to coalesce into a logical narrative. But when it did, he echoed her desire to see it as a whole.

"Finished," Charity said triumphantly, placing her final book on the stack by the settee. "And before dinner. Amazing. Your discovery of the key certainly made our search easier. I'm dying of curiosity to see what you've discovered, but..."

"But?" he encouraged when she did nothing but stare into space.

"I'd like us to concentrate on the personal information for right now. I've uncovered some amazing facts I'd like to pass on to you with the hope you have found similar references in the sections you've read. Would that be agreeable?"

She looked at him expectantly. She seemed to quiver with excitement and trepidation, like a spirited horse at the starting line of a race. "All of these decisions are yours," he said. "We can go over what we've found in any way you want."

Her shoulders relaxed, as if she had been expecting opposition. She leaned over and retrieved one stack of books and then the second, turning them upside down to reverse the order as she set them on the settee next to her. She shuffled through the first group and pulled out one journal. "Personal information was scattered throughout all the volumes, but only a few seemed to apply to my situation. I've put a circle around the P on those.

"This is from 1799," she said. She opened the book and read, *To my joy and surprise, my daughter has at long last married. A wool merchant from Bristol, Lemuel Newberry. Thank God, Julia has finally put the mistake of '88 behind her.* She looked up expectantly.

Gil wasn't sure what he was supposed to see in the passage, so recited the bare facts he'd gleaned. "Well, this lets us know Mrs. Turner had a daughter, Julia, who overcame some mistake she'd made eleven years before she married a wool merchant. Is there anything else significant about this passage?"

"Of course, there is no way for you to know, but we sold our wool to the firm of Newberry and Pride. I'm assuming Mr. Newberry may have been one of the buyers who came to Fletcher's Field, although I can't be sure since the land steward always handled the sales. What struck me most was the phrase 'mistake of '88' since that was the year I was born."

He nodded encouragement, unclear where this was going. She must have seen his hesitancy and said, "This will make more sense when you have more context."

She looked through some more books and finally pulled out one. "It is now 1802. Mrs. Turner writes, *Against my advice, Julia traveled with Lemuel and has seen the girl. They did not speak, so Julia has abided by the agreement she made when Mrs. Epps found the kind woman who took the girl to raise in place of her babe who'd died.*

Realization struck. "You think you're the girl who is mentioned."

"Yes. There are too many pieces that fit. Mrs. Epps was the name of the midwife in our local village. The earlier reference to the mistake of 1788. And a kind woman taking a child to replace another. This latter could explain why I'm named Charity rather than Hope. There was a second daughter, Hope, but she died. It also explains why Sir Edward made his bequest to the daughter of Lady Olivia Fletcher born on September eighteenth in seventeen eighty-eight. He knew when I was born, or at least supposedly born, but he didn't know what I'd been called."

The flush of accomplishment from solving a puzzle was quickly overshadowed by something that looked very much like despair. Gil had to restrain himself from crossing the room and gathering her into his arms.

"If this is true, the family I thought was mine, was not. It might explain why my father ignored me and made no provisions for my welfare after his death."

He wanted to hold her with a desire that was almost pain. But he knew that could likely lead to kisses which could lead to... a situation he didn't want to contemplate. "I can see how you came to your conclusions from what was written," he said, "but I think you are wrong about not being part of the family in which you were raised. If it is true you were not Olivia Fletcher's natural child, she chose you and would have loved you had she lived. Many children don't have the luxury of being chosen, they just appear at inconvenient times and are raised by indifferent parents. I suspect an indifferent parent describes your father, who probably had no idea you were not his daughter by blood. Didn't he treat your sister Faith with the same casual disregard?"

She nodded.

"And weren't you close to your sister?"

"Yes, I love Faith dearly. I hate that she is half a world

away, but we both write so letters arrive about every six months, even if they are terribly out of date."

"Would your feelings change if you knew for sure you didn't share parents?"

She was quiet for a moment. "No, I'd feel the same."

"Proving that family is made up of those you love, regardless of the type of actual kinship. And I think you also need to remember that while what you've found supports your theory, the notations are not conclusive."

Charity opened another book. "This 1805 entry makes it conclusive. Agnes wrote, *Lemuel reports the girl is alone since her sister married*. Faith married in 1805, so all the evidence points to my being the girl who is mentioned. This would make Agnes Turner my grandmother and Sir Edward Pym my uncle. Is there anything in what you read that would refute this?"

"There was nothing about 'the girl' in the sections I read, but there were some personal notations. I didn't know who they were when I marked the place, but Mrs. Turner noted her sadness that Julia and Lemuel had died of cholera in eh…" he shuffled though the books until he found the right one, "1805."

He chose two of the last books. "Then toward the end of her commentary, in December of 1811, Agnes Turner is thrilled to know that her brother has received a knighthood and that he will be returning to England after years in India. But this is the last entry, made in February of 1812."

He handed her the journal.

The sharp pain from this morning has returned, she read. *It takes my breath away. I fear I will not be here to greet Edward when the wild cherry trees bloom as we had planned.*

"How sad. She never saw her brother." She shook her head and looked to the side, as if he wouldn't still see her tears. "All of these people, the members of my family, were gone before I ever heard of them, much less got to know them."

He was silent a moment, pretending to look though one of the volumes. He wanted to give her time to collect herself. She surreptitiously wiped the back of her hand across her eyes and fiddled with the book lying on the settee, then she took a deep breath and straightened. "I wonder if I would have liked them," she said.

Gil recognized the strength of her character in that observation. "You're wise to consider that. Blood ties do not always lead to affection, even in close families. Did you love the man you thought of as your father, Viscount Fletcher?"

"Yes. Or at least I wanted to, since I wanted him to love me back. But I suspect he never did. He was too self-absorbed to love anyone but himself." She gave a muffled snort that may have been a laugh. "I'm fairly sure, however, that I didn't *like* him most of the time."

"And it would likely have been the same had you known Agnes Turner or Sir Edward Pym or even Julia Newberry. No one is always perfect or perfectly lovable. My guess is that Julia was not married to whoever fathered you. Had she kept you, your life would have been stunted by this fact. Instead, whether it was by accident or design, you were left to become the daughter of a peer in a household where you would never know want. Julia Newberry did the best she could to ensure you a future. And your uncle left you a legacy that has allowed you an independent living."

"Do you think Sir Edward left me the bequest so I'd find

out about his family and my connection to it?"

"It would be nice to think that, but I doubt it." Gil hoped he wasn't disillusioning her, but he had to be honest. "I think he wanted you to be comfortable and he wanted you to have the house that evidently meant a lot to his sister, but I'd be surprised if he knew about the hidden room. If he had, he would have taken what was in it."

"You mean the treasure?"

"Yes. I'm sure he would have taken the artifacts and probably the journals as well. At the end, Mrs. Turner might have had a premonition she was dying, so it is possible she left the poorly drawn floor plan to lead Sir Edward to the hidden room. If he saw it, he evidently didn't notice the discrepancies in the location of the rooms, so he never looked for the hidden one.

"In the section of the books I scanned, there were a number of entries that dealt with deliveries and sales. I think Sir Edward was sending goods from India to his sister, and she was selling them in such a way that wouldn't draw attention to her or her brother."

Gil didn't want to tarnish Miss Fletcher's perception of her newly discovered relatives, but she needed to realize that the very expensive items in the hidden room were probably plunder taken by Sir Edward in India. It was a typical practice, and not illegal, but to Gil, looting items from another country was uncomfortably close to theft.

There was nothing slow about Charity Fletcher, however. She immediately asked, "Are the jewels and the statues contraband? Is that why they were hidden?"

"Calling the items contraband might be a little harsh," he said with a smile. "Sir Edward probably sent back what he considered to be spoils of war. I served with a number of officers on the Peninsula who had been involved in the Maratha Wars in India and they told tales of huge caches of gold and jewels taken from maharaja's palaces. I suspect an example of that plunder is in the secret room."

"It really is treasure, then?"

"Yes, enough to make you a very wealthy woman."

An odd looked crossed her face. "I only gave the artifacts a quick glance. I really have no idea what's there." She got up, walked toward the bookcase, and then turned back. "I supposed ignoring the gold and jeweled statues was unnatural."

Gil too had gotten to his feet when she rose. "Not unnatural. You were specifically looking for the journals. They were what was important to you. So, when you saw them, all else paled."

She gave him a rueful smile. "That's my excuse for ignoring incredible wealth. What's yours?"

"What was important to you was important to me." The minute the words were out of his mouth, Gil recognized their truth. He had been single minded in his desire to make Charity Fletcher happy. Hell, when had that happened? When had the woman become so important to him? The realization caused a titanic shift in his perception.

She turned toward the wall of shelving and then reversed to look back at him. She was so caught up in her thoughts, Gil's admission of interest didn't register. "Tonight, after everyone in the house is asleep, could we meet here and really examine what else is in the room?"

"I don't see why not." Of course, his mind was screaming all sorts of "why nots," starting with the inadvisability of meeting an unmarried lady alone in the dead of night. Especially when he now realized he cared about that unmarried lady. "I'll meet you here about half an hour after the house settles."

"I'll come as soon as Mrs. Struthers begins to snore." She giggled like a naughty schoolgirl, and he grinned back.

Yes, this assignation was foolish, but he would not miss it for the world.

Chapter Seven

Dinner was subdued, since both Charity and Lord Gilbert were careful not to disclose what they'd learned from the journals or what they had planned for that night. Mrs. Struthers' monologues were punctuated by more questions than usual—questions that were either deflected or ignored.

Curiosity about what lay behind the locked study door seemed to consume the older woman. Charity took a mischievous delight in suggesting they had found salacious information about Mrs. Turner, since she knew that was what Mrs. Struthers most wanted to hear. However, after they had taken tea in the drawing room and no details were forthcoming, Mrs. Struthers gave up and retired to her bedroom to write some letters.

"She evidently no longer feels the need to closely chaperone you," Lord Gilbert said. "I wonder if I should take it as a slur on my manhood and be offended."

Charity laughed. "No, I suspect Mrs. Struthers has convinced herself that you and I are spending our day looking at obscene drawings in the study and so feels my virtue has already been compromised."

They exchanged a conspiratorial smile and then each went to their own rooms to linger until the house slept.

Tilda was waiting for Charity, and there was no way to dismiss her until Charity had changed into her flannel nightgown with her hair brushed and braided. After the maid departed, Charity went to her wardrobe to redress. She stood in the wardrobe's open door for the longest time, however, her eyes not really focusing on the clothing. She didn't *want* to redress. She enjoyed the comfort of her nightclothes. Besides, she would look less suspicious if she were found wandering outside of her room. No one would dress to get a glass of milk from the kitchen or a book from the study.

Instead of a dress, her hand closed on a heavy night robe. She slipped into the warm, shapeless garment, confident in her excuses for not dressing, for excuses were what all her rationalizing assuredly was. What she wore could hardly be considered seductive, but she liked the idea of meeting Lord Gilbert in dishabille. If any of the novels she had read were true, this was guaranteed to inflame his passions.

Oh, she was ridiculous. She didn't want inflamed passions. She wanted another kiss. A real one, not one of those friendly pecks on the forehead. The first kiss had been so nice, but Lord Gilbert had not seemed prone to repeating it.

She paced the room as the hands on the mantel clock moved with exquisite slowness. Finally, the house was silent except for the rhythmic and loud exhalations coming from Mrs. Struthers' room. She opened her door with care and scuttled down the stairs, the key to the study door in one hand and the other trailing along the wall to keep her oriented in the dark.

She'd just pushed open the study door to find the

welcome flickering light of the dying fire when a form materialized behind her. She dashed into the room and turned to face the door.

"If you try to brain me with a cudgel again, I can't be responsible for my actions," Lord Gilbert said, entering.

"It was a candlestick." She barely controlled a childish impulse to stick her tongue out. Heavens, Lord Gilbert was teasing her. He seldom did that. Perhaps he had a stash of liquor in his room and had been imbibing.

"Same effect. And the reason we need more light. I'm not taking any chances." He crossed to the fireplace and added a few logs. Then he lit a spill and used that to light a couple of candles.

"Well, let's get the hidden door cleared," he said as he pushed the library stairs into place. "I'll take the top again."

He looked at her expectantly. Like an idiot, she had been standing in one spot since he'd entered. Her mind had been focused on the unfairness of the world. He didn't seem in the least bit overcome with passion at seeing her in nightclothes—although she now realized her comfortable robe was not particularly alluring since it had been washed out to the sickly-green color of something that might grow on a poorly preserved ham. It was not a garment that would make the heart beat fast.

Whereas Lord Gilbert looked... very appealing. He was in his shirtsleeves. Coat, waistcoat, and cravat had been discarded. The fine linen of his shirt lovingly hugged his broad shoulders and powerful arms. His pantaloons neatly outlined his thighs and, when he leaned over to push the library stairs, his very nice derriere was highlighted. She felt her face heat as she dragged her gaze from his hindquarters.

With effort, she kept her eyes focused on the books and art objects Lord Gilbert handed her as they rapidly cleared the shelves.

"It's certainly much faster now we know what has to be removed." he said, pushing on the release and opening the secret door. He picked up a branch of candles. "Shall we see just how wealthy you are?" He entered with her treading on his heels.

As she remembered, a huge selection of objects d'art spread across the shelves. They glittered in the candlelight. The beauty of the display took her breath away. Only her obsession with the journals' contents could have pulled her attention away from such incredible works of art. That hunger for knowledge about her relationship having been assuaged, the amazing collection now captivated her.

A massive gold statue of a many-armed woman held pride of place. She reverently touched some of the waving hands. "Do you have any idea what this is?" Charity realized she was whispering. It seemed the proper reaction to such opulence.

Lord Gilbert leaned over and took a closer look. "It's one of the Hindu gods; sorry I can't tell you which one. They have a quite extensive pantheon." He motioned to a darker statue sitting next on the shelf. "Look at this jolly fellow with an elephant's head. I suspect he's made from silver that just needs to be polished to give the full impact."

They worked their way down the shelf, commenting on each of the exquisite statues. Most seemed to be made of either gold or silver. A few had jewels implanted in their foreheads, but all were beautifully rendered.

They finally came to the jeweled box. "Do you think the

gems are real?" Charity asked. Some of the attached stones seemed impossibly big.

"I'm no expert," Lord Gilbert said. "You'll need to hire people who are to do the evaluation. But my guess is that they are completely real—" He stopped speaking as he opened the box. "Good Lord!"

She leaned in for her own look and responded with an indrawn breath. The jewels attached to the outside of the small chest look insignificant compared to what lay within. A jumble of magnificent stones of every size and color filled the box to nearly the brim. "It's every child's dream of pirate treasure," she said.

"And I cannot imagine these are not real." He suddenly hugged her to his side. "Charity, you are not just a wealthy woman, you're incredibly wealthy, and we haven't even gotten to the Chinese porcelains."

"Chinese porcelains?"

"All of the plates, vases, and jars that are on the lower shelves. I recognize a couple of the blue and white patterns as ones my mother has—ones she keeps where they cannot be inadvertently broken. So I know this type of thing is also costly."

He gave her another one-armed hug. She was tempted to turn in the arm that rested on her shoulder and face him. She wanted more of an embrace, specifically an embrace that would lead to a kiss. Oh, how scrambled her wits were. To entertain such thoughts when surrounded by a fortune. But he'd called her by her Christian name... which he seldom did.

What was it about this man that made her feel so needy? She needed to get control of herself. She straightened, pulling from his arm. "How wealthy am I?"

"Very. But I have no way of attaching an amount. You will have to have professionals give you appraisals. For now, do you want to take the box of jewels into the other room and spread the contents out on a table?"

The suggestion made her want to laugh. Who would not want to play with pirate's booty? "Yes," she said, surprised when Lord Gilbert pressed the cask into her arms rather than carry it himself. But then, it was hers. For some reason, she kept thinking of the treasure as theirs, perhaps because he had been so instrumental in finding it.

He did lead the way, however, and found a clean cloth to place on the tabletop to keep the gems safely contained. When the jewels were spread across the surface, they were awe-inspiring.

"Sir Edward left me five thousand pounds and this house. Do you think all this is worth that much?" She absently pushed a large ruby around the table like a child's toy.

Sir Gilbert laughed, a lovely deep, rumbling sound. "I'd guess much more. At least ten to twenty times that amount."

Her hand stilled. She pressed her fingers against the tabletop to keep them from trembling. "Surely not that much?"

"It's a conservative guess."

Charity imagined her careful list with all the less expensive substitutions. Forget a donkey and cart. Two horses and a carriage became a possibility. No, a certainty. The small staff she'd worried about paying once Lord Gilbert left could now grow. Why, there was no need to even stay here. She could buy a large manor, some place with a home farm and sheep.

"I could buy an estate—with sheep," she said, the wonder of her situation washing over her.

Lord Gilbert looked confused. "I thought you wanted to make this your home, to become Miss Fletcher of Fairview Cottage."

How could she explain that was what she *had* wanted? But now her horizons could change. A possibility she'd never considered. "When Fetcher's Field, the only home I'd ever known, was no longer my home, I was thrilled to be offered another. We all need a place that is ours, that we can become a part of. And I could be very happy here, but... I miss tending fields, I miss the sheep."

How stupid and silly that sounded, but he nodded as if she were making perfect sense.

"We all need some place where we belong," he said. "A place where we're accepted, flaws and all. We think of that place as home. Its memory gives us strength even when we are far away from it. You're trying to replace your old home, so it's understandable that sheep would play an important part of your vision." He suddenly chuckled. "But I have to ask, why sheep?"

She smiled back at him. "I know they have the reputation for stupidity, but they are also placid and friendly and in the case of Horned Dorsets, which is my preferred breed, they are easy to keep. Besides, with their curling horns, they always make me smile."

"So your ideal home has Horned Dorsets wandering around?"

"If I could afford the acreage to keep them—and it now seems I can." The realization hit her anew. She was going to be wealthy. She could be Miss Fletcher of anywhere she wanted to be. "Yes, now I can."

At some point during her recitation about what made a home for her, Charity's hand had stopped fiddling with the jewels and slipped into his. Lord Gilbert's hand was significantly warmer than a gemstone and decidedly nicer to hold. She had a fleeting thought that something in his firm grasp seemed like home as well.

"I have to start over finding a home," she said. "You're fortunate that you have a home awaiting you—when you're ready, of course."

He stroked his thumb across the top of her fingers. "I'm a coward. I hate to admit that time has made changes to the home I remember—and in how those who live there remember me. I'm afraid if I go to Tilbury Park, the people I love will expect me to be someone I no longer am. They will see things they think are broken and try to fix me, when I've been working hard to fix myself. There is a tyranny to being loved by those we love in return. And I don't know if I can stand it."

He suddenly grasped her hand more firmly and pulled her toward him, bending across the table to meet her half way. And she allowed it. No, she actively participated, turning her face up to his, finding his lips with her own. The kiss started softly, his tongue tracing the seam in her lips until they relaxed and he entered to stroke the sensitive roof of her mouth. She found herself straining toward him, her hands clutching his shoulders while one of his steadied her head and the other fondled her unsupported breast.

The feeling was exquisite. Heat pooled between her legs and her breathing became ragged. She wanted to be closer. To press her body along the length of his. But the table with a king's ransom is gems stood between them. She shifted and heard some of the stones patter to the rug on the floor—and she did not care.

But the sound broke the spell. "Gil," she moaned as he broke the kiss, straightening his arms and pushing her away.

"I'm sorry," he said, shaking his head in negation. "I shouldn't have... I can't offer you what you deserve. I..." He shook his head again and dropped to his hands and knees to retrieve the fallen stones.

She sat frozen as he gathered up her treasure and returned it to the jeweled box. She wondered if she had become part of the tyranny he'd spoken of, for she suspected she loved him, and could only hope she was loved in return.

He stood. "We need to put these back for safe keeping and close everything up." He moved to do so, only a more pronounced limp indicating he was in any way affected by what had happened.

"Tell me," she said. "Did you love your first wife so much you can't imagine any other woman in her place?"

He stopped abruptly and turned toward her, his face an oddly blank mask. "Why do you ask that?"

Most probably to make a fool of herself. No woman should ask a man why he shied away from kissing her, but Charity was sure if she didn't ask, she'd never know the answer. "Whenever we kiss"—even if it had only been twice, it counted as everything to her—"you stop and seem to run away. I assumed it was because you felt you were being disloyal to her memory."

"Disloyal?" He put the jewel box on the table and ran a hand over his face. "There is no way I could be disloyal to a memory I have diligently tried to erase from my mind. The fact is the child born to my wife was not mine."

As if he could see the question forming on her lips, he hastily continued. "Yes, I'm absolutely sure I was not the babe's father. I only lay with my wife once, on our wedding night. The rest of my marriage was a mummers' play."

She unconsciously moved toward him, but he shook his head.

"No man wants to admit he's been played for a fool. But Alison Beckwith, or at least her family, certainly played me. I met her on one of my breaks from the university. I took one look and was smitten. She was tiny with a head of golden curls. She seemed otherworldly, like a fairy creature. And she looked at me as if I were a god." He chuckled derisively. "What man at twenty doesn't want to be a god?

"In my self-absorbed stupidity, I thought the wedding night was the stuff of dreams, but when I tried to reprise the delight the next morning, I was met with cringing and tears and the announcement that she had long loved another. She found me big and clumsy, but swore she'd try to do her duty if I would just give her time."

"Oh, Gil." Charity reached out and touched him. His arm was as unyielding as one of the golden statues.

"I'm not worthy of your sympathy. No one equally delusional would be. I did my best and gave her time, trying to recapture the wonders of our courtship without any physical demands. We'd been married eight months when she told me she was expecting a child. She would not disclose the identity of the father, but investigation showed the only man she saw with any regularity was her half-brother."

Dear Lord. Her half-brother. The horror of the situation shot through Charity, leaving her lightheaded. She may have gasped, since Gil's eyes fixed on hers.

"I felt flayed to the bone," he said. "I now saw her parents' enthusiasm for my courtship in a different light and couldn't believe how easily I'd been gulled. I had no idea what to do. I was too cowardly to confess the truth of my situation, so I deserted Alison at Tilbury Park, where my mother was ecstatic about the arrival of her first grandchild—and I ran away to war."

He looked down, as if embarrassed by his admission. "I'm still running, unwilling to go home and face my failures and my ghosts. I'm still a coward. When I kiss you, I feel such a cascade of emotions I'm frightened and all I can think of is to run." His eyes came up to meet hers. "I thought I loved before, and I think I love now. A very different kind of love, but powerful, nonetheless. I'm trying to be strong, to not inflict such a broken man on you."

"Gil, I think I lo—" He placed his hand over her mouth, cutting off all that wanted to come bubbling out.

"No. You must realize you've been given a wonderful future—a future with gamboling sheep and laughing children and a whole man to stand beside you. All I have is a past."

He picked up the box of jewels and hurried with it to the hidden room. He didn't look at her while he replaced the shelves and items. She didn't help. Her limbs refused to respond. She could only stand like Lot's wife while tears washed her face.

Since it was approaching breakfast time, Gil found Holly overseeing the placement of the buffet items on the dining room sideboard. "Would you get your coat and come walk with me?" he asked.

Holly nodded, as if unsurprised by the request. He knew some topics were best discussed outdoors where one couldn't be overheard. Gil already wore his greatcoat and had a wool scarf wrapped around his ears. He probably looked like a doddering old man, but the breeze was brisk and the temperature cold.

Similarly swathed in layers of clothing, the former sergeant arrived quickly in the hall. Together they exited the house and took the path toward the cliff edge. The distant water was hidden by a swirl of fog. They walked in silence, the only sounds the sighing wind, the thrum of the incoming waves, and the crunch of the shell pathway under their boots.

What do two grown men say when they discover each other sneaking about in the dead of night? When it happened, they had simply nodded and continued on their way. But Gil had brought them to Fairview Cottage, and he felt the subject needed to be addressed. He'd done Charity enough disservice and didn't need to add any problems for her housekeeper, who was also her friend.

Holly abruptly stopped and turned toward Gil. "I love her," he said, each word showing up as a distinct puff of mist in the air. "Lucy, eh, Mrs. Dibble, and I have an understanding. I was waiting to say something to you until after she talked with Miss Fletcher. We want to make plans for the future but are torn by conflicting duties. Lucy feels it is her responsibility to stay here with Miss Fletcher, while I feel it is my responsibility to leave with you in the spring."

Gil was momentarily nonplussed. He'd anticipated a dalliance and was prepared with admonitions about not toying with the plump little housekeeper's affections. Holly had cut a wide swath through the available women on the

Peninsula, but Lucy Dibble was a different type of woman. Now it seemed Holly's emotions were involved, and these feelings were evidently mutual.

It was lowering to realize that both Holly and Mrs. Dibble felt they had to look after their employers. Charity had been competent to run a large estate. And Gil believed he'd been an able commanding officer. He'd bought his captaincy, but the additional two ranks had been earned. So why would Holly and Mrs. Dibble think their employers couldn't muddle on without them?

In his case, perhaps it related to the question that had haunted Gil all night. "Holly, do you think me a coward?"

"What? Colonel, have you run mad? That damned horse wouldn't have fallen on you if you'd not dashed into the heat of battle to help those poor fool artillerymen and their mired guns. Oh, I've heard you called a stubborn ass, but that's no bad thing in a commander. There wasn't a man in the whole of the army that didn't want to be in your regiment. Your men knew you'd look after them and not allow them to be blown to pieces so you could cover yourself in glory. No, sir, coward is one word no one would ever use."

Gil didn't want to point out there was physical bravery and emotional bravery, and he failed in the latter. If he were not such a coward, he would have declared himself to Charity last night. He would have admitted she filled his senses and made him feel whole. He would have asked her to marry him. Hell, he would have taken her on a gem-strewn tabletop as he'd wanted to.

His life was filled with *would haves*—and he wished he could change it. But in the end he was afraid. Damn that honest word. He wouldn't put himself in the position to be so hurt again. He had long ago determined that being alone was less painful. But if he were to marry, she would be his choice.

The realization was astonishing. What had seemed like an irritating case of adolescent lust was more. He liked the woman in all her prickly quirkiness. She made him feel relaxed and at ease. When he was around her, his leg hurt less, he was a nicer person, he slept better, hell, he had even stopped cursing—well, mostly.

He was not sure when it had happened. Miss Fletcher... Charity... had become integral to his enjoyment of life. It was an uncomfortable discovery when nothing could come of it. He didn't want anything to come of it. She was his friend, only that.

Because he was afraid.

Holly, however, was made of sterner stuff. "So, you and Mrs. Dibble plan to marry," Gil said. "My congratulations." He held out his hand, which Holly vigorously shook. "My offer to set you up either on a farm or in a business still stands. You needn't worry about me, and I doubt Miss Fletcher would hold your Lucy to any agreement that would get in the way of your happiness."

Holly seemed less than pleased. "Mrs. Dibble and I would prefer to stay in your service. It is not unheard of for a butler and a housekeeper to be married, and these are our chosen professions. Particularly after last night, I thought you might be considering making Fairview Cottage your permanent home."

"After last night?" Gil had lost the thread of the conversation.

"Well, I assumed we were both returning from visiting our ladies—and I assumed that you were not trifling with

Miss Fletcher's affections. I would hope that is not the case. Ladies like Miss Fletcher are due serious respect. You should not think she is available for a liaison."

"There is nothing untoward occurring between Miss Fletcher and me," Gil said.

"Then you are not pursuing her for either sport or marriage?" Where had Holly learned to mimic the expression of a disapproving vicar?

Of course, Gil had no good answer to the question. "Miss Fletcher is my friend," he said with honesty. "I've been helping her find out more about her heritage and a potentially large inheritance. We have had to meet at odd times to thwart Mrs. Struthers' interest."

Holly didn't look convinced, but he nodded at the last statement. "Now there is one of the nosiest women I have ever met. Lucy says if she appears in the servants' hall without invitation one more time, someone is bound to accidently drop a tureen of soup on her."

Gil smiled at the image. If it happened, he hoped the soup was something creamy and viscus. Before he could put the thought into words, however, his attention was drawn to the approach of a coach as it wended its way down the bumpy track leading down the promontory to the house.

"It has to be coming here," Gil said. "There is no other reason to take this road, unless it's someone who wants to see the view, and with the fog, today there isn't one."

Holly also squinted at the oncoming conveyance. "I think there's a crest, but I can't make it out."

And then, Gil knew. Just as he knew pain would follow the stab of a bayonet, he knew who was in the coach. "You wrote him, didn't you, Holly? You wrote to my brother

Charles. You could not leave it alone. You had to try to pull me back to the bosom of my family for the Christmas Season." Gil's voice had risen with his growing anger.

"No, Colonel. I'd never...I wouldn't—"

But Gil walked away from him and toward the coach. He thought to do—what? Stop the coach before it reached the house? Order the driver to turn around and disappear? He logically knew none of this would happen, but he marched straight on with the same cadence he'd used to approach the deadly French muskets.

The coach did indeed stop before it ran him down. The door swung open and a man leaped out. For a brief moment, Gil was a boy again, a boy who wanted to cry out "Father" and run to his embrace—but the man was his brother Charles. Charles, grown into the position of Marquess of Teign and looking much as their father had when Gil was young.

It was Charles, not his father, who hurried toward Gil and embraced him and held him and brought all of the now undeniable changes flooding in. Tears gathered in his throat and all Gil could do was hug his brother back. He had not wanted this yet, but the present was here to make a lie of all his false, comforting memories.

"Why are you here?" Gil asked when he was sure he had control of his voice.

Charles pushed himself back, but kept his hands on Gil's shoulders. "To take you home for Christmas, of course. I could understand your wanting to get used to England again by staying in London for a while. But when you disappeared, with only a brief note that you would come to Tilbury Park in the spring, the family became concerned. Then, after the vicar brought word that you were here at the end of the earth, holed up with your ladybird for the holidays... well, mother was bereft. And you know what mother is like when she's upset. There was nothing for me to do but come and bring you home."

As a statement of purpose, Charles's little speech was effective, but Gil had lost the thread of the argument at *holed up with your ladybird*. Was Charles referring to Charity? How absurd. Gil would admit to having lustful thoughts and feelings about Miss Fletcher, but his *ladybird*?

"What in the bloody hell are you talking about?" he demanded in what must have been his parade ground voice, since both coach horses jerked back in their traces.

"Can we get into the coach to discuss this?" Charles evidently didn't want to entertain either Holly, whom he didn't know, or the coachman, whom he did.

"Why? Are you afraid someone will overhear? You've already impugned a lady's good name to all and sundry."

"No, you ass. I'm simply freezing my balls off." As Charles turned and walked back to the coach, Gil realized his brother wore no hat, no scarf, and no gloves. So the man would be cold. Telling the coachman to continue on to the house, Gil followed Charles into the coach, which began to move as soon as he'd pulled himself through the door.

Gil settled back in the seat, appreciative of the more comfortable temperature. The brass foot warmer on the floor obviously still contained coals. "I leased this house from a solicitor in London," he said. "I arrived to find the new owner, who had recently inherited the property, in residence, a Miss Fletcher, the daughter of the late Baron Fletcher and cousin of the present one. So Miss Fletcher is a lady in fact as well as demeanor. She is most definitely *not* a ladybird."

Charles didn't look relieved. "So, you have been cohabitating with a lady for what? A month now? I'm assuming the banns are being read."

"Good Lord, no! It's more like I'm her house guest, or perhaps she's mine. It makes no difference. Mrs. Struthers, the local vicar's aunt, is in residence to act as a chaperone, although the woman is prone to gossip and involving her may have been a mistake."

Charles looked out the window, then shook his head. "If what you say is true, then Mrs. Struthers *was* a mistake. It was she who wrote to our vicar's mother with the news of your life of debauchery."

Gil uttered a word so vile even he used it sparingly, but he knew Mrs. Struthers would be departing immediately—and that he would soon follow. Charles would cajole and demand and conjure images of their mother prostrate with grief until Gil accompanied him to Tilbury Park. Many times, Gil had told recruits that bravery was overcoming fear, not lacking it. He might as well rely on his own advice and accept the inevitable graciously.

Also, once Mrs. Struthers' veneer of respectability was removed, Charity would be placed in a compromising position if he stayed, especially if Mrs. Struthers had distributed her slander far and wide. He had no choice but depart—and it was the last thing he wanted to do.

Chapter Eight

"Are you sure you want to give everyone a holiday for Christmas Day?" Lucy asked for what seemed the hundredth time.

"Yes. I think it's better to make tomorrow very busy, so the next, Christmas Day, is one that everyone can spend with their families. The small staff that is left—you, Holly, and the coachman—can enjoy the day anyway you'd like. I do not require constant attention."

Charity had the irritating suspicion that her name was finally correct. When it came to those who worked at Fairview Cottage, she had become a charity case. Everyone seemed to think she needed help and attention since Lord Gilbert had been whisked away by his brother.

But this wasn't the case. Charity was complete unto herself. She was very busy. She wasn't in the least lonely. She needed to make this plain to others so they would stop constantly watching for her to fall apart.

Why, anyone could see how complete her life was just by looking at her list of activities—a list that had happily replaced the original that had dealt with things to buy and repairs to be made. Fairview Cottage was now in good condition and she was the proud possessor of an antique carriage as well as a sturdy team. She couldn't call herself the owner since Lord Teign had only loaned the conveyance, horses, and coachman to her until his brother's return.

During wakeful nights, however, she wondered if she had become the de facto owner. What if Lord Gilbert never returned? What if Lord Teign had left the coach with her to assuage his guilt at basically kidnapping Gil? Oh, he'd used logic to convince his brother to go to Tilbury Park, but Charity felt Gil's departure was an abduction nonetheless.

She hoped she was wrong about Lord Teign. She'd liked the man, who seemed to be an older, softer version of Lord Gilbert. She and Lord Teign had enjoyed a lively discussion of the relative merits of various sheep breeds, even though Lord Teign was a proponent of the continental Merinos. She guessed she couldn't blame the man for following what his wrong-headed estate manager had recommended.

The click of objects being rearranged on the mantel drew her attention. Lucy had lit candles against the encroaching dusk, but was still poking around the room. "Lucy, please leave. You're hovering like a bird whose chick has fallen from the nest. I'm sure you have a lot to do to prepare for the feast we're planning for tomorrow."

Lucy gave Charity a Mrs. Dibble stare that had been designed to keep maids at their work, then nodded and left. Charity returned to the list of upcoming activities to make sure everything was covered. The greens had already been gathered and waited in a wagon in the barn. She placed a check by that notation. Tomorrow she and the staff would decorate the house. Last week she'd purchased an obscene amount of red ribbon. Perhaps she should have continued to economize, but she believed Gil's assessment that she was soon to be a very wealthy woman. So she'd made sure the house would be festive.

Then in the late afternoon, she would join the staff for an early Christmas feast. Holly was even putting together a wassail bowl. She'd only had the heady, mulled punch once before and was looking forward to it. The evening would be given over to the Christmas Eve service at the church in Blakely-on-Sea, during which the choir would present this year's cantata. Afterwards, everyone would go to their family homes.

In the space next to Christmas Day, Charity had written *Reflection and Contemplation*. She pointed to these words every time Lucy suggested Charity join her and Holly for some activity. Charity didn't want to intrude. The couple planned to have the banns called after the first of the year. They needed their private time.

And Charity certainly had a lot to contemplate. Mr. Nicholas had recommended an appraiser in Bristol who was willing to make the trip after Christmastide, providing the roads stayed passable. This man would undoubtedly know reputable dealers who could sell the bulk of the hidden treasure, at which point she would be wealthy and she could… she could…

There was the sticking point. She wasn't sure what she wanted to do. Hence the need for a day of refection.

The idea of purchasing an estate had stayed with her. Fletcher's Field had long been her home and it wasn't surprising that she wanted to recreate it for herself. Perhaps she should have felt more at home in Fairview Cottage, since this was where the woman who had been her grandmother had lived. Although reading Agnes Turner's journals had made the woman live and breathe, Charity felt no innate connection to this house or this area. She was the product of the life she'd led. Faith would forever be her beloved sister. She would even remember her lackadaisical father with a modicum of affection. She could appreciate what Mrs. Turner and Sir Edward had done for her, but she could not love them.

She recognized the desire to duplicate her past, but at the same time she wanted to put her own imprint on her future. And that was the conundrum—what did she want to make of the rest of her life? She had thought she wanted to be Miss Fletcher of Fairview Cottage, perhaps because that was the only alternative she could imagine.

Her horizons had now been expanded. This should have supported her optimistic assertion that all would come right in the end, since financially that was the case. There was a very important part of her change of fortunes that was not coming out right, however, and this change had very little to do with the potential for great wealth. In the most honest part of her heart, she wanted to be Mrs. Narron of Anywhere. More exactly, she wanted to be Lady Gilbert Narron of Anywhere. Her difficulty was that Gil had not asked her to fill that position and she could well understand his not wanting to marry again.

Now he was gone—and she missed him more than she had thought possible.

She'd hoped she had more time. Until March, at least. He was such a part of the upheavals the recent discoveries had brought that she couldn't imagine going on without him. The treasure seemed to be *their* treasure. The estate with frolicking sheep seemed to be *their* estate. The only future she could see was *their* future.

She missed his conversation. She missed his steadying presence. And above all, she missed his drugging kisses.

He'd kissed her right before he left. Soft, sweet, warm, a meeting of souls as well as lips. Charity had wanted to cling to him, and Gil had seemed reluctant to leave. But he was the one to break the embrace. He dropped that irritating peck on her forehead and said he had to be home for Christmas and left. Dear Lord, she could not—would not—think of that as their last kiss. There had to be more to come. She optimistically clung to that hope.

And while she waited, she would fill her days with activities and plan for a future she could enjoy, alone if need be. Tonight there was only dinner to get through. She would take it here in the study with her lists and thoughts... and dreams.

Gil had pressed to get to Blakely-on-Sea before sunset and had nearly made it. Darkness was complete by the time the coach turned east onto the road leading down the promontory, however, and the coachman was probably wise to walk the horses. But the lack of speed was galling. He could see the lights in the windows of the house, and like a moth, he wanted to fly to that light.

It occurred to him that he had made certain assumptions and that he might be making a colossal mistake. But he was now committed to this path, and it had seemed the right one when he'd fled Tilbury Park.

It had only taken a few days for him to become a person he didn't much like. He'd been wrapped in the love of his family, which had left him feeling stifled rather than protected. He'd had to get away. To again become the Gilbert Narron he had found at Fairview Cottage.

His mother, his sister-in-law, hell, even the children, had tried to do everything for him, as if he were either an invalid or an imbecile... possibly a bit of both. As if responding to the atmosphere, his leg began to hurt more than it had in weeks, which accentuated his limp. His sleep, always erratic at best, was now punctuated by nightmares. He felt the hard, outer shell he'd believed was sloughing away, begin to reform. His tendency to curse reasserted itself, even around his nieces and nephews, much to the horror of all in residence.

He'd had to return to Fairview Cottage or lose his mind.

He knew the actual location had little to do with his wellbeing. Miss Charity Fletcher was the essential ingredient. And since this is where she currently resided, it was where he wanted to be. He harbored the hope that he was as necessary to her happiness as she was to his. He was as nervous as a recruit in his first battle. What if she didn't want him?

By the time the coach horses had plodded to a stop, Holly was at the door. Holly with a broad grin on his face. This had to be a positive sign.

"Lord Gilbert, you're back before we expected you," Holly said, taking his coat. "And glad we are. My Lucy says if she sees one more list she will scream."

Gil could think of no response. When had Holly become cryptic? "Is Miss Fletcher at home?"

"She's in the study, finishing dinner. I'll bring you a tray there if you'd like."

"I won't be disturbing her?" Gil suspected that was his insecurity speaking.

"I guess you've been spoiled being at the home of a marquess," Holly said. "I certainly wasn't used to announcing you before you left, and you managed to come and go from rooms just fine on your own."

"Right." Gil nodded and strode down the hall to the study, where the door was closed. Should he knock? He'd previously walked right in, but he had been gone for nearly two weeks... He compromised and knocked as he opened the door.

Charity was sitting at a library table, her dinner before her and odd papers scattered around the tabletop. He remembered her sitting there with rubies and emeralds and sapphires spread between the two of them. At the time, he'd wanted to push a king's ransom to the floor and spread Charity on the surface instead. Hell, the impulse was still there.

Charity stood. Her mobile face first reflected surprise, quickly followed by what he hoped was delight. "Lord Gilbert, you're back. I thought you meant to be home for Christmas."

"Now I am." He moved across the room and gathered her into his arms. She felt completely right. Perfect. The tension that had griped him for the last week melted away. "Now I am home. I've discovered that anywhere *you* are—is home."

He kissed her as he'd dreamed of doing since he'd left. No, he'd wanted to kiss her this way even longer. He put into the kiss all he was and all he hoped he could be. He didn't hide his desire, not only for her lush body, but for her very self.

Before his emotions could overtake all caution, he broke the kiss, drew her hands into his, and backed away two steps.

It was hard to do in the face of Charity's confused expression, but he was on a mission—and he was going to accomplish it.

He dropped to one knee. If he was going to do this, he was going to do it right. "Miss Charity Fetcher, would you do me the honor of becoming my wife? I promise to spend my life ensuring your happiness." He had planned to say more, but was distracted when she gripped his hands as if he were a lifeline thrown to a drowning sailor.

"Yes." She said the word softly, but it echoed in his head like a cannon volley.

He came to his feet. "When? Tomorrow?"

"Tomorrow what?" Her face was a study in confusion.

"Marry me tomorrow." He reached into his coat pocket and pulled out two papers. "In a fit of optimism, I purchased a Bishops license that allows us to skip the banns. We've been in residence here for over four weeks, so there is no impediment. All we need are the vicar's agreement and two witnesses."

She opened her mouth hopefully to agree, but Gil placed a finger over her lips. "Before you let me hurry you into marriage, I wanted to make our respective financial situations clear. You are about to become an obscenely wealthy woman. I don't want you to ever think that this was in any way part of your attraction. I'm wealthy in my own right. Both my father and my maternal grandmother left me large sums in their wills. I had Charles's solicitor make up this settlement, which only lacks your signature. It's very brief, stating that all monies and goods you bring to the marriage will remain yours to do with as you see fit. The only expense that is specifically yours is for the purchase and maintenance of livestock for a mutually agreed upon estate."

He felt the edges of his lips tip up. "I didn't want you to think I'd choose the wrong kind of sheep."

To his horror, Charity's eyes sparkled with unshed tears. Dear Lord, he'd done it wrong. He'd moved too fast.

"Oh, you fool," she said. "I don't need a settlement. Whatever is mine is ours together."

Relief left him standing on trembling knees. "But I do. In the wedding ceremony, I say 'with all my Worldly goods I thee endow.' That is my promise, not yours. I don't want succeeding generations ever questioning your right to do as you please with your inheritance."

"Then yes, I'll sign your silly paper—and tomorrow sounds like the perfect day for a wedding." She laughed. "A feast is already being prepared."

He kissed her laughing mouth, ran his hands over the soft curves of her body, and very simply wanted more. They were soon both breathing like thoroughbreds at the end of a race. Clothing had become loosened. And the damned library table was again looking enticing.

"Come upstairs with me," he said. "There's another part of the wedding service we need to explore."

"Another part?"

"'With my body I thee worship.' I think some worshiping is in order."

Gil knew it was an improper suggestion and was immensely gratified when Charity took his hand and led the way.

Did all brides view their wedding day as if they were standing at a distance, watching rather than participating? Charity was sure she'd seen the brief ceremony at the church in Blakely-on-Sea from somewhere in the rafters. Gil, looking so tall and straight and military, until he smiled and became himself. Lucy had assured her she was a beautiful bride—and the look on Gil's face seemed to indicate this was the case. Even Mr. Thomas looked resplendent in rose-colored vestments.

The small church was cold but smelled of fresh greens. Gil's hands were warm and he smelled of bergamot soap. The ring he slid on her finger was a plain gold band. He assumed she would replace it with one containing one of the stones in the hidden treasure box. In this, he was wrong. The gold band that had been his grandmother's was all she would ever want.

Did every bride struggle with laughter when her new husband promised to worship her with his body? Probably most weren't sure what this worshiping entailed. However, Charity now knew and struggled to maintain her decorum through the final prayers. She was convinced that this type of worshiping was one the greatest gifts to humankind.

From high above, Charity watched her hand sign the registry as Charity Rose Fletcher for the last time. She would henceforth be Lady Gilbert Narron or just Lady Gilbert. Oddly, she felt unchanged.

The wedding party then returned to Fairview Cottage. The feast that had been designed to be a day early so the staff could spend Christmas Day with their families was quickly changed to a wedding breakfast by the simple expediency of moving it forward a few hours. If the vicar and is wife thought it odd to celebrate with staff, they made no demur. Everyone had a rollicking time, perhaps fueled by Holly's wassail, to which a large quantity of apple brandy had been added at the last minute.

Charity had begun to think the breakfast would never end—and then it did. As if in answer to some secret signal, the vicar and his wife departed and all the servants dashed to complete chores so they could go into town together. Gil had provided both the coach and a wagon for transport and all wanted to take advantage of that opportunity.

Then it was just the two of them and Charity seemed to drop from a distance back into herself. "Well, Lady Gilbert," Gil said, "do you want to go over your list of what you want in the way of an estate or would you like to watch the light fade from our bedroom window?"

"Goodness, it isn't quite four, is it? What will everyone do in Blakely-on-Sea for the hours until the Christmas Eve service?"

Gil came up behind her and nuzzled her neck, sending a swirling warmth to the lower part of her body. "Some will enjoy extra time with family and some will spend the money I gave each of them at one of the shops or the pub. I can promise that all will be entertained."

Charity feigned a wide-eyed innocence. "Well, I am rather too fatigued to discuss acreage, so perhaps I should go up and have a rest."

"Yes, I think *we* should." He then swung her into his arms as if she were a sleepy child and took the stairs at a fast pace. Their laughter filled the stairwell where not so long ago, a woman had confronted an intruder, and had shown him the way home.

Epilogue

December 24, 1817

Lord Gilbert Narron paced from one end of the old medieval hall to the other. When he and Charity had bought the property, the hall had seemed vast and was one of the features that had convinced them this was the home for them. Tonight, the dimensions seemed to have magically decreased. He was on his fourth circuit when his brother Charles's voice stopped him.

"For God's sake, Gil. This is your third child. At this point, you should be relaxed about the entire process. Come sit down and have a brandy."

"Is that what you do? Meet every new offspring in a state of inebriation?" Gil had to admit, however, that the idea had some merit, and he joined Charles by one of the two large fireplaces in the hall and poured himself a brandy.

"You are going to have to stop doing this," Charles said. "Mother was complaining on our way up that we haven't had Christmas at Tilbury Park for the past three years due to Charity's lying in. When we talk about Christmas, the children assume we will celebrate it here."

"If you think I'm going to stop what I think you're suggesting, I can promise that isn't going to happen for, hopefully, at least fifty years."

Charles chuckled. "Fifty years? You certainly are optimistic. I was going to suggest you do something like employ French letters for the month of March."

Gil took a sip of his drink, his attention directed more to any sounds from upstairs rather than what his brother was blathering about. "March?"

"Well, let's examine the evidence. Your first born, Ned, arrived on December twelfth of eighteen fifteen. Then Agnes arrived on December tenth of eighteen sixteen. And we are now awaiting the arrival of another child on—December twenty-fourth. Unless your brain has been too fixed on the gestation periods of your ewes, I think you can see that the keels to all these boats were laid in March."

Gil grinned. "You may have a point. I never considered the timing."

"So, you won't be surprised when a case of French letters is delivered in February?"

"Charles, don't even think about doing it. Not unless you want something similar to arrive at Tilbury Park in July. My nieces and nephews all seem to be born at the same time as spring lambing, which, I might point out, is damned inconvenient."

"Touché." Charles lifted his glass. "But at least I don't make it a yearly event."

"Early marriage enthusiasm?" Gil countered. "As I understand it, as one ages, one becomes less enthusiastic."

"Be very careful where you're stepping, baby brother."

What could have been a spirited sparing match was

interrupted by a call from their mother that brought them both to their feet. "Gilbert. Congratulations. You are the father of a healthy baby girl. Give us fifteen minutes and you can come admire mother and child."

Charles shook Gil's hand and slapped him on the back. "Congratulations, indeed."

Gil blinked, finding his eyes misty. A girl. This made complete the list of the unknown people he and Charity always wanted to be remembered. Ned for Sir Edward Pym, Agnes for Agnes Turner and now Hope for the child whose death gave Charity the life she'd had.

He raised his glass. "Welcome Hope Elizabeth Narron," he said in a voice that could be heard throughout the expansive house. "We're glad you made it home for Christmas."

About Hannah

Hannah Meredith's father wanted her to be a doctor, so she dutifully trekked off to Southern Methodist University with this in mind—but somehow ended up with a Master's Degree in English and minors in history and religion. Along the way, she'd discovered she was not really fascinated by the actual "insides" of people, but rather by the people themselves and the stories they made of their lives.

The story of her life has been a happy one. She married her high school sweetheart and they have recently celebrated their 50th wedding anniversary. They have one wonderful son and four clever grandchildren. They moved around the mid-South as her husband's career advanced but are now permanently located in a charming North Carolina town. She's taught at the high school and college level and sold real estate, always staying very busy.

Then life slowed down... and she had the opportunity to write some of the stories she'd been imagining for years. Under another name, she sold over a dozen speculative fiction short stories to major Science Fiction and Fantasy magazines. She now concentrates on historical romance. She currently has five romances available: *Kestrel*, *Indentured Hearts*, *Kaleidoscope*, *A Dangerous Indiscretion,* and the newest, *Song of the Nightpiper*, which is a fantasy romance with a medieval setting. Hannah's novellas have also appeared in the three previous *Christmas Revels* anthologies.

If you'd like to keep up with Hannah as she examines the human heart (without a scalpel), you can find her at:
http://www.hannahmeredith.com and
http://www.facebook.com/HannahMeredithAuthor

A Memorable Christmas Season

by

Kate Parker

Chapter One

Susanna Dunley, Dowager Countess of Roekirk, directed the footmen to replace a few more sprays of greenery on the banister and then nodded her approval. As the footmen cleared away the last of the fading branches, her son's wife, Rose, hurried toward her, her face a mask of misery.

"Rose, what's wrong?"

"I—I just cast up my accounts. I don't think I can go through with it now. Not tonight of all nights."

The girl burst into tears and Susanna gathered her in her arms. "Hush, now. The ball will be the best of the year. Your first party will be a crush and will make your reputation as a hostess. Everything is ready. Except us."

Susanna felt the girl's arm. "You're freezing. Is it that cold in your room?"

She nodded and sniffed as she straightened.

"Let's go upstairs. Sit by the fire to warm yourself before you dress for the ball. You'll feel so much better once the guests begin to arrive." Susanna led the girl upstairs while mentally checking off all the tasks that needed to be done to put on a successful ball in the week between Christmas and Hogmanay.

All the members of the ton who were in town for the

Christmas season had been invited to the ball. Many of them were Scottish like Roekirk, his wife, and his mother, and unable to go home, as the roads to the north were impassable.

Once Christmas Day and Boxing Day were past, there had been nothing planned until the Duke of Derwin's New Year's Eve gala. Rose had carefully chosen the perfect date. December 28th.

Susanna hoped it would take both their minds off the date.

"Your first time hosting a Christmas ball. Your first Christmas as a married woman. I know you're nervous," Susanna said as they reached the first floor landing. "It will be fine. Wonderful. Don't worry. Just warm up and get ready."

Rose had nearly opened the door to her room, but before entering, she dashed down the hall after her mother-in-law. "Are you sure the house looks all right? Will the musicians be here on time? Oh, I should check the food—"

The girl would make herself sick again if she didn't calm down. "Rose, all will be well. Relax. Take a deep breath. Now, go make yourself even more lovely. And wear Roekirk's Christmas gift to you."

"Those emeralds are so beautiful. Yes. Yes, I will." Rose hurried down the hall and went into her room to dress.

This ball would go a long way toward helping Rose find her feet. Rose only lacked seasoning, and seasoning was something Susanna could supply. And once Rose was confident in her role as countess, then Susanna could—dear heavens, be what? Dowager. An ugly word for someone without purpose.

Now was not the time to study the future.

After long years of practice, Susanna and her lady's maid quickly readied her for the ball. She'd had time to read a chapter of a gothic novel before there was a scratching on her door. Her maid opened it and Rose walked in.

Susanna gave her an encouraging smile. "Oh, is it time to go down, Rose?"

"I think so. I heard Richard on the stairs a little while ago."

"I suspect to get into the brandy ahead of time. He hates balls. So like his father." The thought of the late Earl of Roekirk ruined Susanna's tranquility. She snapped her book shut.

Rose looked at the ornate mantle clock and said, "It's only twenty minutes until the guests will arrive." Susanna glanced over to see she was bouncing on her toes again.

They went down the broad staircase together and lingered in the front hallway for a minute, until Birdwell, stationed near the door, cleared his throat.

"Perhaps we should check each of the main floor rooms to make sure all is in readiness. One never knows where guests might wander during a ball. Especially young guests." Susanna smiled and started on her tour.

Rose followed, a blush on her cheeks. Does she think we don't remember our courting days when we get older, Susanna wondered? Thoughts of summer days in the glen when she was younger than Rose warmed her face.

The front drawing room, red fabric on walls and cushions blending nicely with the holly on the mantle and over paintings, was pristine. The music room, ebony furniture and ivory walls and draperies, was cheered with the fire in the grate and improved with mistletoe over the doorway and the mantle. The mauve and rose dining room had the chairs removed. The long table was set for the buffet with punch bowls at either end. Under the chandelier, the silver sparkled from many polishings.

Without saying a word, the two women walked past the closed door to the study. Richard was in there.

They went on to walk around the ballroom once. The floor had been waxed until it reflected the candles in the chandeliers. Most of the chairs in the house were against the pale blue walls. A great deal of greenery balanced over the draperies closed against the chill of the winter night.

Susanna entered the morning room first. The yellow walls and upholstery made this a charming room in the morning. Tonight it was dreary, without Christmas decoration or fire.

"I don't think anyone will come in here," Rose said and walked off.

Next was the library, all leather and paneling touched with mistletoe on the mantle and a fire in the grate. The card room, in shades of green, was set up for two tables of card play. Susanna had decided the blue drawing room hadn't been redecorated for a hundred years, but tonight she found it slightly less hideous with liberal helpings of greenery and red ribbon.

"The servants have done a wonderful job, haven't they, Rose?" the dowager asked.

"Yes," Rose answered as she turned toward the front hall to await the first guests.

"Just the green drawing room left," Susanna said and started in that direction.

With a sigh, Rose followed. "Do you think anyone will bother wandering that far from the party? There won't be a fire in there tonight and the draperies are closed against the cold, hiding the lovely view of the garden you so prize in the summer."

"We must make certain that everything is as it should be," Susanna said. She opened the door and felt cold air tumble out the door and strike her where she stood in the warmer hall. The cold breeze from the room made her suspect the French doors to the garden were ajar. "Perhaps we should have a fire laid in here?"

Susanna reached for a candelabra from a table in the hallway and stepped forward while Rose lingered outside the room. In the flickering light, she could see a hand on the arm of a high-backed chair. The chair faced away from the hall, toward the drapery-covered French doors.

Had one of the guests arrived early? But why would they come back here? Had one of the servants thought this was an appropriate place to bring her guests?

"Good evening," Susanna said as she reached the chair. Then her hand holding the candelabra shook so violently that light rolled up and down the walls.

She took a step back with a gasp. "Rose, could you please fetch Birdwell?"

Instead of obeying, Rose moved to stand next to her mother-in-law and looked down on the man. An arrow stuck out of the breast of his deep red and blue waistcoat.

The deep red was blood.

Rose wailed, "This will ruin everything," before she collapsed in a heap.

Susanna looked down at the unconscious body of her

daughter-in-law and murmured, "What a wretched time for that silly girl to faint." Leaving the door open, she hurried to the front hall, hoping none of the guests would choose this moment to arrive.

They had five or ten minutes, at the most, to rectify this disaster.

Fortunately, no guests were in sight and Birdwell was still there. "Find a footman to take your place and come with me," she told him.

At that moment, the bell rang and a footman, unaware of the tension flooding Susanna, opened the door. A man walked in, shaking the cold and snow from his broad shoulders, and Susanna thought for a moment she might faint.

Will? In her house? After all these years? Tonight of all nights?

Pull yourself together, girl.

"Lord Keyminster, what brings you here?" Susanna said with a curtsy on shaking legs.

He swept her a low bow. "The new countess invited me to the ball tonight. I came early, to allow you the opportunity to deny me entrance without bringing either of us embarrassment."

"I would never turn you away." Susanna realized with a shock that she had spoken aloud.

"My thanks, milady. Shall I leave now and come back at a better time?" His face had aged thirty years, there was gray in his dark hair, but his smile, wicked and wry, hadn't changed a jot.

A plan half-formed in Susanna's mind. "No. As long as you are here, you can perform a great service for me, as a leading diplomat and as a friend."

With another bow, he said, "I am at your service."

"Please, follow me. Birdwell, bring more light. We'll have need of you."

Susanna turned and hurried toward the green drawing room, certain the men would follow. Birdwell was paid to follow orders. She had never been certain why Will Marsden, now the Earl of Keyminster, did anything.

As she entered the green drawing room, the door open as she had left it, the countess groaned and sat up. "Good. Rose, pull yourself together. Your guests will start arriving at any moment. Do you want me to call your maid?"

"No, I'm all right." Then she looked horrified. "But what do I tell the guests?"

"If they ask, tell them I will join them shortly. A minor household emergency is keeping me from them at present. And tell Richard nothing."

Unfortunately, the silly girl looked at the chair, the hand still draped over the arm, and gasped as she slid on her bottom away from the dead man.

"Come, come. You'll ruin your dress that way. Be brave, Rose. Rise and put a smile on your face." Susanna stood by her, bent over with a smile, offering her hand.

Lord Keyminster gave Rose, Countess of Roekirk, his hand which she took. Susanna stood by while he helped Rose to her feet. Rose rewarded him with the coquettish smile that had won her husband, Richard, the new Earl of Roekirk.

Enough of this. Susanna ignored her jealous annoyance, took Rose's hands and said, "This is the ball you've been planning for weeks. Go and enjoy it. Lord Keyminster and I will take care of this. Now, not a word about what you've seen. Smile. Have fun. Enjoy your ball."

"I'll go up the back stairs and repair the damage before I come back down the front staircase," Rose said with a weak smile.

"Very wise," Susanna said to encourage her as she walked her to the door. Once the girl was on her way up the stairs, Susanna shut the door and turned to the two men. "What do you make of this?"

"I have no idea how he gained admittance, milady," Birdwell said.

Lord Keyminster lifted the man's chin with one hand and held a candle close with the other. "Do you know him?"

The dead man was perhaps forty, with light brown hair and a thin face. Blood—where had that come from?—had trickled onto his collar, and death had robbed him of any individuality. She shook her head. "I didn't make up the guest list. Good heavens, I didn't know you had been invited."

"He's Sir Benjamin Atwell."

"The traitor?" Susanna felt her eyes widen as she looked at Lord Keyminster. It was hard to think of him by his relatively new title while depending on him to help her rid herself of an unexpected corpse. "Why, the scoundrel. I know him only by reputation, but he wouldn't be admitted to my house."

Sometimes she found it easier to ignore that she was the dowager countess. It was no longer her house. And ignored that she unfortunately did know Sir Benjamin. She took a breath and continued. "Didn't he sell British battle plans to the French, causing the deaths of scores of British soldiers?"

"Something like that." Keyminster glanced down and shook his head, a motion she remembered all too well. "The question is why murder him here?"

"Everyone in the ton who's in town will be here tonight. Perhaps they wanted to be in the crush when the body is found."

"How did he get here? Birdwell, is it? How would he find this room here in the corner of the house?"

"Perhaps from outside, milord." Birdwell walked over and pulled aside the draperies covering the window facing the dead man. Behind it was a French door leading to the garden.

Will, as he'd always been in her mind, walked over and examined the door handle. "Easily forced." He opened the door, sending in a wave of bitter air. "The snow on the ground outside has been churned up here. Was the staff outside this room for any reason?"

"No, milord. The rear staff entrance is on the other side. There's not any greenery here that they would have cut to decorate inside."

Will stepped outside, peering at the snow glittering from the light coming from the room. Susanna followed him, trying to ignore the cold.

"There are three sets of footprints coming to this door and one going past it and back again. What is back there?" Will asked.

"A shed." Susanna shut her eyes when she realized what that meant.

"What about this shed? And come inside before you freeze." He swept out his hand for her to proceed him. Then he pulled the door shut and locked it before Birdwell closed the draperies again.

Fortunately, the rug by the door was large enough for

them both to wipe the snow off their shoes.

Shivering, Susanna hugged herself for a moment before standing gracefully. "We keep gardening supplies in the shed. We also keep the bows and arrows and targets in there for summer archery practice." Susanna put her hand on Will's arm. "Someone knew all this and brought this man into my home to kill him. Why?"

Chapter Two

This was as close as Will had been to Susanna, to the dowager Countess of Roekirk, he corrected himself, in thirty years. It had been a long thirty years full of war and diplomacy, of missions for which the crown had rewarded him, and of missions the crown didn't want to see the light of day.

Thirty years had changed the gangly boy Will Marsden, son of a solicitor, into the stately Earl of Keyminster, elevated by a grateful sovereign. Now that he was worthy of Susanna, fate had thrust them together over the body of a traitor. Fate had a wicked sense of humor.

"I don't know who brought him here, milady, or why." He kissed her gloved hand. "With your permission, I'll endeavor to find out."

"We'll find out. Please, find out everything you can from the body, and then we'll put it in the shed until after the ball is over."

Susanna had always been practical. No vapors. No hysterics. He'd often wondered if the Earl of Roekirk had known what a jewel he had won. "If you and Birdwell will hold the candles up, please, I'll see what we can learn."

First he tipped the body forward, finding the arrow had

gone through and the tip had pierced the back of the chair. "Begging your pardon, milady," he said as he worked the tip out of the chair, one hand on the shaft in front of the body and the other behind.

Both the lady and the butler were looking away with sickened expressions. Neither noticed the heavy blow low to the back of the skull. If the blow was inflicted first, the arrow was not necessarily the cause of the man's death.

"Not too much damage done," he told her.

"You were always very neat. Very practical," she told him, and the boy inside the man puffed up with pride.

The corpse had bled little from the front and back wounds, soaking the clothing around the hole but not spilling all over the chair. Will searched the corpse's pockets next. He'd done it so many times over the years he felt not a twinge of horror or pity.

Especially for Atwell. He knew the real story, and it was far more traitorous than what Susanna had heard.

There were some nice coins in his purse, "He wasn't short of money, despite his villainy," and then he found what he expected to find. And something extra.

He slipped the something extra into his pocket until he had time to study it. "Here's a note, giving directions to enter this room from outside. It set the meeting for seven o'clock."

He looked up to see Susanna's eyes had widened again. She looked down and closed her eyes. "That's when we ordinarily would have been sitting down to dine before the ball. On the far side of the house."

"But that's not when you dined this night?"

She raised her head and stared at him. "No. Rose was so nervous we moved dinner up to six. We'd left the table by seven. Instead of everyone being in the dining room, family and servants both, we were all over the house. Someone may have seen the archer."

He frowned. "Is that likely, with the dining room and the ballroom both on the far side of the house? The servants, at least, would be carrying out last minute assignments."

"Do you suspect my family? Me?" This was the Susanna he remembered. Fiery. Proud. Beautiful.

"I suspect everyone who is familiar with this room and the shed with the archery equipment, everyone who's been here in the summertime."

"We're talking hundreds of people."

"Who are also in town tonight and no doubt at your ball."

She shook her head. "Rose's ball. We are still probably talking about a hundred people. Well, perhaps fifty."

"How many of them would want Atwell dead and want to embarrass you, your son, or his wife?" He held her in his gaze, wishing he could touch her still creamy skin and kiss her still red lips.

"There was a time when *you* would have loved to embarrass me." She pressed her lips together, looking as if she might burst into tears.

"That time has long passed. I learned many years ago that you had no choice but to marry Hubert, the Earl of Roekirk. I had nothing to offer you then. I lost my chance."

"Fate was cruel to both of us," she whispered. She glanced at Birdwell staring at the far wall and then back at Will.

"Birdwell, we've kept you too long from your duties with this ball. Her ladyship and I will dispose of the body and conduct a more thorough examination."

"We'd appreciate it if you directed people away from this room without calling anyone's attention to it," Susanna said. "Your discretion, as always, is appreciated."

"Thank you, milady, milord." Birdwell fled the room, shutting the door behind him.

Susanna let loose one giggle before she regained her composure. "I can only imagine the picture in Birdwell's mind of me lugging a body around the house."

"It will be much easier to explain a dead man shot with an arrow outside your house rather than inside. I'll just need to finish my examination before I slide the chair across the room and tip the body outside. Once there, it will only take a moment to manage the scene. The snow should obliterate any footprints."

"Will, you sound like you have experience with this sort of thing."

He was glad to see she said that with a smile. She had no idea. "Diplomacy requires a man to think quickly. Since there's no need to hide the body forever, and no one will see back here in the dark, a discovery in the morning of a body in the snow will suffice."

"You make it sound so easy."

"No, not easy. But it needs to be done. I'm going to need you to lift him slightly so I can finish searching him."

He had Susanna lift from behind the chair so he could work from the front, her gown protected by the chair. Also, she wouldn't have to look on that dead face or touch his dead skin. She'd only touch the corpse's well-tailored clothes.

He quickly spotted the thin rope tied around the man's cuffs and the chair arms that he expected to find, but no corresponding marks on the wrists. The knot would have been easy to release if Atwell had been alert when he was tied up.

More than one person was involved in this killing over a period of time. Keeping his voice neutral as he removed the thin rope, Will told her, "There's nothing else of interest here."

She let the corpse drop back into the chair with a thud, then shook out her arms.

"I think we'll leave his purse and watch on him. If some scavenger in the night robs him, may it be to their benefit as a Christmas gift."

She looked at the inconvenient corpse sadly. "He won't need it anymore. I'll have to see that he gets a Christian burial." She must have seen the look of shock Will knew was in his eyes, because she added, "Anonymously, of course."

"Of course."

She swallowed with a shiver and then faced him. "Tell me what you want me to do, Will."

This was going to be most distasteful. On the other hand, Susanna trusted Will to make this as easy for her as possible. Will had been a gentleman, even as a boy.

"If you don't want to do this, I'll find a way to handle it, Susanna."

She saw the gentleness, the sympathy in his eyes. Almost as if he knew... "I doubt either of us want to do this, but while I must get this body out of my house so as to keep the revelers at this ball from gossiping about us forever, you act only from kindness. Tell me what to do."

"Can you lift the back of the chair?"

She grabbed the back by the sides and gave him a nod. He bent over and lifted the front, standing between the corpse's knees. She tried to lift, but the chair was too heavy. Everything, chair and body, nearly tipped over onto her.

Will quickly set down his end. "That won't work. We'll have to slide this across the floor."

"It will gouge the floor. The servants will notice. Wait. I have an idea." She walked to the doorway and picked up the rug meant for wiping feet. "We'll set the chair on this, and drag the chair over to the door."

"I'll just carry him across."

"You'll get blood on you, Will. And blood is so hard to wash out. Someone will remark on it."

He nodded. "I'm afraid I didn't come dressed for moving bodies. The rug it is."

It worked quite well, Susanna tugging on the rug while Will lifted chair legs and slid the rug under the weight. Then they found, with effort, they could slide the man across the room in a matter of seconds.

Will opened the curtains wide and then both French doors. At his nod, Susanna lifted the back of the chair and he guided the body out onto the snowy ground, landing on its side. "Don't want to damage the arrow. Someone might become suspicious."

Susanna could see his breath in the moonlight. "Come in before you freeze."

Will adjusted the corpse's limbs, looked down, nodded to himself, and came back inside. As he shut and locked the doors and pulled the draperies, Susanna pushed the chair back. Then it was only a moment to lift the empty chair from the rug and put the rug back by the door. Sliding the rug over the floor wiped up any trace of snow on the wooden boards.

"You have the note?" Susanna asked as she brushed off her gown and shook out her skirts.

"I have the note. And the rope from around his wrists. Did you recognize the handwriting?"

"No."

"Oh. I thought you might."

The calm way he spoke frightened her. "What do you mean?"

"You correspond with a great number of people. Ladies. And that is a lady's hand, I believe." He pulled out the note and showed it to her again.

She looked up at him and knew her defiance showed in her eyes and in her voice. "Does it matter now?"

"Yes. This isn't your hand. I'd know your writing anywhere. But this is clever enough for you to have planned the entire affair. Which brave British soldier, sold out by Benjamin Atwell, has been avenged by wife or mother or lover?"

He stood too close, dangerously close, and Susanna found her heart melting for him again as it had when she was only a girl. "Why do I think you know all my secrets?"

"Because I knew them once, that summer, when I asked you to—"

The door behind her opened and a young man spoke as a girl giggled nervously. "Beg pardon, sir. I didn't realize this room was occupied."

"Is it?" Will looked down at her.

She took a breath as she composed her features. "Not any longer." She gave Will her arm and he escorted her out.

The young couple's eyes widened as they saw the gray in

Will's hair and the age in Susanna's face. Bursts of laughter could be heard before the door completely shut.

"I suppose we will need to speak later. For now, let us enjoy the ball, milord."

His wry, wicked smile made a quick appearance. "Go in to the ball. I will endeavor to arrive a minute or two later. We don't want to start tongues wagging prematurely."

"Yes. They won't be able to stop tomorrow, will they?" She gave him what she thought might be a conspiratorial smile and walked off alone to the ballroom by a back hallway.

Susanna slipped into the ballroom in the middle of a dance and worked her way along the side of the room without seeming to do so. She began to greet guests warmly, responding once or twice with, "I wondered where *you* were. In this crush, no wonder we missed each other."

The dance ended and Rose hurried over to her. "What are we—?"

"There's nothing to concern you, Rose. We've taken care of our domestic problem. The ball seems to be going beautifully. Any complaints about the ladies' retiring room?" They were using the blue drawing room.

"Only from Lady Willowfield."

"Let's hope that's the only thing she complains about," Susanna murmured.

"What was that?"

"Nothing, dear. Oh, there's Richard. Go tell him to dance with you. That will rescue him from Lord Morton. Go on."

Rose looked shocked at being so forward as to ask her husband to dance. Fortunately, she'd fallen into the habit of carrying out the dowager's suggestions, and off she went.

As Susanna watched, her son looked grateful to excuse

himself from the tiresome old man, even if it meant dancing. With practice, and some careful management, the newlyweds would make a success of their marriage.

Unlike the last Earl and Countess of Roekirk.

"Lady Roekirk."

Susanna, drawn from her reverie, turned with a practiced smile to find herself facing Will Marsden. "Lord Keyminster." She dropped him a graceful curtsy as she tried to hide the jolt of excitement that seeing him gave her. A jolt she'd forgotten in the past thirty years. A jolt she'd now experienced twice that evening. "I didn't realize you were back in the country."

"I am, and very glad to be in London so I could attend your lovely party." He bowed over her hand.

"Not mine, my son and daughter-in-law's. They married not long ago and this is their first ball."

And then came his wicked smile. "I can't believe you're old enough to have a married son."

Her tone was dry. "I *can* believe you are the sovereign's favorite diplomat."

He kept his wicked smile as he said, "We'll speak again later."

"I look forward to it."

As he walked off, Susanna was certain he'd be watching her. How would she be able to tell the archer that while the plan had been changed several different ways, all was well. The blackmailer had been disposed of.

Chapter Three

Either Susanna had planned Atwell's demise or she knew who had and approved wholeheartedly. All Will would have to do was watch her closely and he would know the identity of the killer. Before he was the Earl of Keyminster, he'd had too much practice over too many years with the best spies and assassins in the business for her to keep anything secret.

She wouldn't be able to hide the truth from him.

But then he'd have to decide what to do about it. He wasn't looking forward to that challenge.

With part of his mind, he carried on pleasantries with acquaintances, commenting on the weather, hunting, and politics with the men, and complimenting women on their gowns. The rest of his brain was at work watching Susanna. Watching who she talked to, every movement of her hands, and where she looked.

Quite frequently, she looked at him.

He was finding that gratifying. Not because it told him she was worried about when he'd catch her and what he would do then, but in a wholly separate way. In the way he enjoyed knowing Susanna watched him when they were both young. Then it had given him hope that he stood a chance with her.

Poor fool, but he'd hoped. Until the day he learned she would be married to Roekirk and asked her to run away with him. He was discovering tonight that he still hoped. Was he still a fool?

He catalogued the people she spoke to. Her daughter-in-law Rose, Lady Winterbury, the Duchess of Innavarna, Lady Beatty and her lump of a daughter Charlotte. He kept his eyebrows from raising when he saw her deliberately cross paths with the politically well-connected Lord Stabler. Why would she be talking to him?

Lord Stabler blamed Sir Benjamin Atwell for his son and heir's death. And he was right.

Somehow, in the midst of the Christmas season, it didn't seem right to repay evil with evil. To avenge Stabler's son's death on the man who had led him to that death was something Will understood. But to do so at Christmas and involve Susanna? As hardened as he was by what he'd had to do all these years, Will found that a step too far.

He couldn't see Susanna taking part in a revenge murder. And certainly not at Christmas. Not the Susanna he knew. Somehow, he couldn't believe she had changed so much.

Susanna walked away, and Will was certain nothing passed between them but words. Perhaps Stabler wasn't the archer.

She shared a smile with Lady MacEwen and then brought Lady Robertson forward to introduce Lord Grant to her. Will nodded his head slightly in approval. Grant was a wealthy widower with grown children, Lady Robertson was a well-to-do widow, and they were both shy and reported to be lonely. As Will watched, he was certain she was mentioning a few acquaintances they had in common and perhaps an interest or two that they shared.

Then with a smile, she left them and walked in his direction. Finally. The thrill that washed through him told him he'd been eagerly waiting to talk to her again.

"Are you enjoying the party, Lord Keyminster?"

"I don't know when I've enjoyed anything more. I do wonder why I was invited."

"You are part of the ton and you are in London for the Christmas season. Rose invited everyone who met those criteria."

"Truly?" He couldn't help smiling at his good fortune, although the explanation did seem lucky in the extreme considering how quickly he was put to use.

"She didn't know we'd known each other as children. She wasn't certain if she should apologize, but I told her our childhoods were a long time in the past."

Susanna's smile was beautiful, even more so for not being forced. Could this be true?

"And she's recovered from her earlier shock?"

"Quite." The smile drooped off her lips.

"Did you know I would arrive early to make certain of my welcome?" He realized he wasn't smiling either and tried to put on a less stern expression.

"No." She began to turn away and he snatched her arm, being careful not to grab too hard or let anyone see the urgency of his movement.

"It was just fortuitous that a person who would know how to remove an unwanted corpse happened to arrive just as you needed him."

Her eyes snapped with anger. "No. I would say you were a year late."

He let go of her arm. As she walked away, her surprising words rang in his head. *You were a year late.*

Whatever happened then must have led to tonight's murder.

He stationed himself on one side of the room and watched his hostess more closely. Part of his brain was telling him something was very wrong here while the other part proclaimed what a fine looking woman she still was.

"I'm sorry. If you or the dowager countess are suffering from any embarrassment, it's my fault."

Will turned to the young woman who was speaking to him. Rose had recovered her color since he'd seen her on the floor near the body and now looked like every other pretty, young, society hostess.

Susanna hadn't looked like every other pretty, young, society hostess. She was uniquely, beautifully Susanna, and he found he had to leave the country for a series of diplomatic, and not-so-diplomatic, missions once she married.

He kept his thoughts out of his voice and off his face. "No. There's no embarrassment on either side. Just a vague regret that so many years have passed since we've seen each other." He gave her his diplomatic smile.

"Susanna is an amazing woman."

"Why do you say that?" he asked, surprised to hear his thoughts spoken by someone else.

"Nothing upsets her. On the other hand, I don't believe I've ever heard her laugh."

Will glanced over to see that Rose was looking at the

dancers and not him. "That's a shame. She used to have a beautiful laugh. Was it the loss of Roekirk?"

"Oh, the old earl never made her laugh. No, she hasn't laughed about anything or with anyone since long before the evening he died. That was before Richard and I were married, but we've known each other since childhood."

"What happened to the old earl?"

"There was a dinner party a year ago tonight at their castle and the guests were all staying over. It was snowy and cold. I could tell Susanna was in a foul mood when dinner started. The old earl was terrible to anyone who disagreed with him, however mildly. He was looking for a fight. I don't know what happened, but she hasn't returned to Castle Roekirk since they put his body in the crypt."

The sense that had kept him alive in some harrowing situations told him he needed to learn more about that night. "Could it have been one of the guests who upset them?"

Her voice became soft. "I think it was."

"Who was it?"

"I don't remember his name. I'd not seen him again until tonight. He was the man we found with an arrow through his heart." She took on a ghostly pallor. "And I once loved that back drawing room."

"But now you'll have bad memories of it?" He made his voice soothing.

"Terrible, frightening memories. That room was once my hideaway. I'll never be able to use that room again."

Susanna was trembling when she walked away from Will. She wasn't sure if she were angry or terrified, but she'd have to control this trembling. She needed to keep it from him and everyone else.

For lack of a better escape from the party, she checked on the dining room. Refreshments would be served in fifteen minutes. The candelabras were ready to be lit; the chandeliers were already ablaze. Plates, glasses, silverware, serviettes, cold foods, and punch were in readiness.

She gave Birdwell a nod and left to return to the ballroom, only to find Lady MacEwen waiting for her in the hall.

"Are you all right, Susanna?" she asked in her heavy brogue.

Susanna gave her a smile. Rebecca MacEwen was a fighter. Her beautiful red hair had frightened off many a man, but Lord MacEwen had been certain there was more to Rebecca than a shrew when he proposed. Perhaps not even Hamish MacEwen knew how loyal a friend Rebecca could be. "You worry too much."

Rebecca leaned in closer. "Not me. But you do. Tell me your conscience is at peace."

"I made my decision a long time ago. There's nothing further to be said." If she wasn't happy, that was her own fault.

"A long time ago?" Rebecca persisted, staring her down.

"The decisions that led to tonight. I can trace every event through the years to that summer day. I couldn't change that first decision, turning him down, and I haven't been able to change anything that has come of it."

"You poor lamb. You're shaking." Rebecca put her hands over Susanna's in an attempt to warm them. To let her know she was with her.

Susanna forced a smile. "I'm fine."

"And Rose?"

"Poor child. She's been badly frightened. Life does that to some people."

"Will she keep her silence? She was involved. She saw him. And she's not stupid." Rebecca watched her closely.

"She'll keep her silence." Susanna shook off her mood. "Now, let's rejoin the ball. There's still plenty of dancing to be done."

They walked back to the ballroom. Susanna was more worried about Will's interest in tonight's events than Rose's. She couldn't begin to guess what Rebecca was thinking. Bless Rebecca for her support when she didn't even know why it was needed.

Susanna went up to Rose and very quietly said, "Everything is ready in the dining room for the ball supper. I think at the end of this dance?"

Rose looked relieved. "Wonderful. I'll see that it's announced then."

"The party is going beautifully. Your first ball will be a success. See, you had nothing to worry about."

"Except..."

"Except nothing. It's a success."

Rose squeezed her hands. "Thank you."

Susanna lingered in the ballroom, speaking to guests as they left in groups or knots to get food and drink. The musicians slipped out to the kitchen where they could get a break as well as something to eat. She breathed a sigh of relief when the last of the guests left the room, leaving her alone.

"Rose tells me you haven't laughed in years," said a quiet voice. His words caressed her bare skin at the nape of her neck. "Long before the night a year ago when Earl Roekirk died and before Richard and Rose married."

She turned and looked up into his chocolate eyes. They didn't look threatening, but *beware* echoed in her ear. "She—she must be mistaken."

"I'd know your laugh anywhere, Susanna, and I've not heard it tonight."

"I'm afraid tonight I don't feel like laughing. I found earlier to be—upsetting."

"With good reason. Particularly since you told me earlier you had never met Sir Benjamin, and now I've learned you had him as a guest for dinner."

"His lordship invited him. Not me." Only one in a long list of sins committed by the old earl.

"Nevertheless..." He fell silent as Susanna heard the door open. She turned with a welcoming smile on her face.

It was two couples more Rose's age than hers, apparently eager to resume dancing, as one of the men asked, "When will the musicians begin play again?"

"In a few minutes. You have time to have another Christmas cake or walk around the room before they return."

They all bowed and curtsied before Will said, "Perhaps you'd do me the honor of joining me for a plate in the dining room?" When Susanna looked at him, startled, he added, "Or perhaps a cup of tea?"

"I'd love to." There would be people there. People who would prevent Will from questioning her too closely.

If she were smart, she'd be able to keep people around her the rest of the evening.

She realized, as everyone was bundling up in cloaks and

hats and gloves, that she'd barely exchanged a dozen words with Will since the dinner break. She'd be able to relax soon.

The crush was soon a crowd and then only a gathering as coaches arrived out front and people climbed into them. Some of the horses' tack had bells attached to ring during this season, adding to the general merriment. The snow had reduced its strength to flurries. Susanna turned to find Will, bent slightly forward, talking to her petite daughter-in-law and holding one of her hands. Rose looked pleased at his words.

She wasn't surprised. He was a kind man. And soon he'd be gone and she wouldn't have to see him anymore or worry about Sir Benjamin. All in all, a good night.

The hall was practically empty as Will stepped in front of her dressed to go out into the winter chill. He bent over to kiss the back of her hand. As he straightened up, he said, "I'll see you in the morning."

The room lurched for an instant as her heart crashed against her chest. The nightmare wasn't over.

Chapter Four

Muffled in a warm scarf, heavy greatcoat, hat, gloves, and boots, looking more like someone camping on the battlefield than he had in a long time, Will took a walk the next morning. He tapped his cane in the heavy snow, kicked up great powdery clouds of flakes that had fallen during the night, kept to a stroll, and looked around him like a man without pressing business.

He slowed when he reached the hedge that separated the Roekirk house from the one next door. Glancing down the stretch of snow covered grass and flower beds toward the back of the house, he saw the lump he expected to see. And someone bent over it.

"Hallo," he shouted as he marched across the ground at a swifter pace.

The live figure stood straight up, showing himself to be a boy in rags. In his hand, Will could see the purse and the watch. The boy turned to run toward the back of the property and ran smack into a tall bush. One foot slid on the ice and he crashed to the ground.

Before the boy could get to his feet again, Will was over him. "The coroner will set up a hue and cry after the pocket watch. Take the purse and this for your trouble."

The boy looked at the sovereign Will slipped into his hand in amazement.

"Now, get out of here before somebody sees you."

The boy scarpered, kicking fresh powder from last night's snow and obliterating any tracks toward the shed behind the house. Will checked over the body quickly, finding it was in full rigor or frozen, slipped the watch back into its easily reached pocket, and hurried around to the front of the house.

The butler answered his knock and tried not to look surprised to find an earl on the doorstep this early in the morning.

"Birdwell, I need you to send a footman to the coroner immediately. There's a body in your grounds."

"A body, milord?"

Good. Birdwell recognized him. All the better. "Yes. A man's body."

"Very good, milord. Would you care to wait in the—"

"I need to stand guard over the body until the coroner arrives. Please send a footman with all possible speed." Then he decided to add the unnecessary, "It's cold out."

"Very good, milord." Will heard him call for a footman before he shut the door.

Fortunately, the coroner, the stocky, gloomy Lord Exham, arrived before Will's feet turned to blocks of ice. "Morning, Keyminster. How is it that you found the body?"

He sounded vaguely accusatory, but Will knew that was his normal tone. A handy trait in a coroner.

"I felt the need for a morning stroll. I've been indoors too much lately. I glanced over and an odd-looking lump caught my eye. I went to investigate and then I sent for you."

"Do you recognize the man?"

"I believe it to be Sir Benjamin Atwell."

"Yes." Exham stared at the body as if disappointed. "Too bad he couldn't have died in a less populous area. Still, there will be people happy to hear of his passing."

"I would think his family will grieve." While that was true of most men, Will doubted it in this case.

"His mother might. She was always a silly woman." At Will's surprise, Exham said, "A friend of my aunt's. The rest of the family couldn't stand the traitor."

It was too cold, even with the bits of sunshine breaking through the clouds. Will rubbed his gloved hands together. "What do you need me to do for your investigation?"

"Oh, you mean the arrow. I suppose there must be an investigation. Pity. I sent for the surgeon and the constable—ah, here's Mister Oliver now."

The surgeon, Oliver, turned out to be a young, thin man with cheeks burned rosy with the cold. After a brusque bow, he knelt down by his patient and did a quick examination. Rising again, he said, "He's been dead since yesterday evening and outdoors at least that long. The arrow might be the fatal blow, or it might have been this wound on the back of his skull. I won't know until I take him back to my surgery and thaw him out."

"Thank you, Oliver. We'll arrange to have him sent over after the constable gets here." Exham stomped his feet.

"All right if I get on with the living?" Oliver asked the coroner.

"Yes, yes." The two men bowed to each other. Both had ignored Will the entire time.

"Just one moment, Mister Oliver. Do you recognize him?"

Will asked.

The surgeon faced him for the first time. "Yes, I know the traitorous Sir Benjamin. But if I'd have killed him, I'd have used poison. Much more accurate than a bow and arrow or a cosh, at least in my hands." He bowed to Will and was gone.

The constable arrived a few minutes later, but to Will, stuck in the cold for too long, it seemed like eternity. At the coroner's direction, he searched the body. When he found the pocket watch, the coroner declared that he'd not been robbed.

At least that poor boy would be safe.

Leaving the constable to arrange to move the body to the surgeon's residence two blocks away, Will and the coroner asked to speak to the Earl of Roekirk and were escorted into the dining room.

Unlike the night before, the chairs had all been put back at the table and serving was done from the server, not the table as they'd set it up for the ball. The servants had rearranged and put everything back in a few hours. They must have worked hard in that time, and Will, who believed in efficiency, was impressed.

Will was even more impressed to find Susanna at the table, drinking a cup of tea. When they entered the room, she paled for a moment before her expression changed to mild puzzlement.

Richard, Earl of Roekirk, set down his cup with a click. "Why are you here so early?"

Will let the coroner tell him, "We've found a body on your grounds. There needs to be an investigation, and I want to start my questions here."

"If some vagabond chooses to wander onto my land and

freeze to death, it has nothing to do with me." The new earl sounded a great deal like his father. Poor Susanna, married all those years to a man Will remembered as sounding as aggrieved as his son.

"He wasn't a vagabond, and he was shot with an arrow."

"Nonsense," Richard said and took another sip of tea.

Foolish Richard. This was no way to treat a coroner. Susanna put on a welcoming smile and said, "Gentlemen, please have a seat and some tea to warm you before you ask your questions."

Both men bowed to her and sat down, the coroner saying "Thank you, countess."

Servants set out teacups before them and poured out steaming tea, then brought the milk and sugar. Will, she noted took neither, but he seemed grateful for the warmth between his large, bare hands.

He had chosen to sit next to her, just as he had many years before. He'd set his gloves on his thigh. The gloves were a richly tanned brown leather with a bit of sheepskin lining peeking out, no doubt warm in this freezing weather.

"What brings you out this morning, Lord Keyminster?"

"I'm used to an outdoor life, and I've found this weather has kept me inside too long. I went for a walk, probably the first to come this way, and I spotted the unfortunate in your grounds."

Well done, Will. "Shot with an arrow? How dreadful." She looked down to give an appearance of ladylike horror. The coroner hadn't said who the victim was yet, so there hadn't been any comments of "served him right" coming from her son.

"It was rather—surprising," Will said, glancing at her with that devilish smile in his eyes.

"I imagine it must have been." Susanna thought of his arrival and their work in the small parlor the night before. She wondered what he thought of.

The coroner, who had gulped down his tea and seemed the better for it, now said, "Did anyone in the household mention hearing a disturbance outside last night?"

"Don't know how they could have. What with a ball going on until the small hours of the morning. Didn't see you there, Exham." Richard sounded as accusatory as the coroner.

"Had a body to examine. They turn up at inconvenient times," the coroner replied.

Susanna shot a glance at Will, who looked at her with eyes gleaming with humor. So, he saw the irony in the coroner's words, too.

"Two bodies in under a day? It makes me feel less than safe in my own home."

"Then you must stay inside, Mother," Richard said. The silly boy could sound so much like his father on occasion.

"Was the other person anyone we know?" Will asked, earning Susanna's gratitude. She'd almost slipped up and asked that herself.

"An officer in the same regiment as the body found outside this house."

"He was an officer?" Richard sounded surprised. Of course, he would be. No one who knew anything in this house made the mistake of telling the earl. And no one would dare make that mistake twice.

She never had to warn the servants not to tell the earl.

Father or son.

"The body found at supper time yesterday was Captain Josiah Ferringdon, a well-decorated soldier. The body found in your garden this morning was Sir Benjamin Atwell—"

Richard interrupted the coroner to bellow, "The traitor?"

Susanna thought he might order the corpse to move himself elsewhere.

It would have been worse if the corpse had been found inside the house. Thank goodness Will had been present to help her get rid of that problem.

"Was he expected at the ball last night?" Exham asked.

"Certainly not." Down went his cup again with a clink. Richard sounded as if he might break the poor thing.

"You have no idea why he might be here?"

"None. And if you have no further questions, good day, Exham."

"I do need to question your servants."

"Birdwell, organize it for Lord Exham."

"Very good, milord." Birdwell went off, while Lord Exham and Will remained seated at the table.

Susanna wondered how long Will would stay. She'd like to talk to him and find out what he knew about the investigation. Find out how close it might come to her.

And find out who killed Captain Ferringdon. He didn't deserve to die.

"Excuse my curiosity, Lord Exham," Susanna asked, "but were both men killed the same way? Were they close friends?"

"Mother. It's not seemly."

"It's all right, Roekirk. She has a right to her curiosity. We're interrupting her household," Lord Exham said.

"Ferringdon was stabbed in the back. Atwell was shot in the front with an arrow as well as smashed over the head. And they were implacable enemies due to Atwell's sinister behavior in France."

"Then it sounds like poor Captain Ferringdon will be mourned." Rebecca certainly would. Had she known about Josiah's death before the arrow entered Atwell's breast?

Rose entered the room, and seeing company at the table, gave them a lovely curtsy. "My lords, welcome."

They had both already risen from their seats to bow to her. Richard, after a glare from his mother, rose as well. "You gave a magnificent ball last night, Lady Roekirk," Will said.

"I'm so glad you enjoyed it. Is that why you're here this morning?"

Oh, please don't tell her about finding the body. Susanna found she was holding her breath to see what her daughter-in-law would say in response.

Exham glanced at Richard and it was Richard who said, "No. They've come on another matter. Nothing to worry your pretty head about."

Blast that son of mine. Hadn't he learned by now that just made Rose more curious.

She smiled sweetly but doubt shone in her eyes. "It must be of some import if two lords have come out on a winter's morning to sit at our table. And why are there men walking through our front garden carrying something heavy?"

Lord Exham apparently decided to answer. His somber tones filled the room as he said, "I regret to inform you that I'm here in my capacity as coroner. A body was found in your garden this morning."

"Good heavens. Who was it?"

"Sir Benjamin Atwell. He was found shot through with an arrow and battered about the head."

Before any of the men could reach her, Rose slid gracefully to the floor in a faint.

Chapter Five

The next several minutes were spent in sending for Rose's lady's maid and her smelling salts, then in helping her up and having her taken to her room.

In the midst of seeing to Rose, Birdwell came and took Lord Exham away to question the servants. Besides a footman, Richard was now the only one at the table with Susanna and Will, and Richard never showed any inclination to budge from the breakfast table on a winter morning.

The unfortunate habit meant her son was developing a small paunch.

"This is rather awkward, but Lord Exham hasn't released me yet from my duty as the finder of the body," Will said.

"Oh, we'd never dream of throwing you out into the snow, Lord Keyminster. Perhaps we could adjourn to the drawing room?" Susanna tried to use her eyes to tell him to agree.

It must have worked, because he immediately said, "That is kind of you, my lady."

They both rose, nodded to Richard, and left the room. Not until they were shut in the blue drawing room with a fire burning in the grate and no servants present did Susanna feel safe to widen her eyes and say, "What have you learned so far? Don't worry, no one will hear us unless the door is opened."

"Sit down, Susanna."

She'd been so anxious she'd forgotten her manners. "Yes. Please sit, Will." She was flattered that he joined her on the sofa. Of course, he might only be taking this added precaution so they could keep their voices lowered.

"I know the name Captain Josiah Ferringdon meant something to you."

"How?" slipped out as she felt the color drain from her face.

"Your paleness. The change in your breathing. Even the change in your pulse."

She had to smile at his words. "How could you tell that, Will?"

"I studied you as a young man. I study you now, and I find you haven't changed. Not in the things that are important. Not in the things that matter. And you are not a natural liar, Susanna."

"And I suppose you are?"

"I had to learn. It saved my life more than once."

She felt her heart ache for the boy she had loved and all he must have gone through. "Oh, Will."

He gave her a grim smile. "It's all in the past."

"Thank heavens for that. But it's so sad to think of you far from home, staying alive by your wits—"

"Please, don't romanticize it. Now, it is all formality in gilded palaces, but in the beginning it was cold, dirty, ugly work. Made more so because I knew if I failed, no one would care. No one would ask what happened to me."

"I wouldn't have dared ask, Will, but I would have cared. Sometimes, thinking of you was all that kept me going."

"Hush." He put his bare finger to her lips. His touch was rough and calloused, emphasizing his words about his work. "You would have pictured me in the glen in summertime, with sunshine and flowers. While my reality was quite different."

"So was mine. Picturing you in the glen in sunlight was the only beauty in my life." No. She wouldn't think of Elizabeth.

"You had Richard."

"Not after his father decided he was old enough to join him. Join the world of men."

"How old was he?"

"Eight."

Will shook his head as he gazed at her. "He's been luckier than me. He never had to kill."

Susanna took his hands, trying to give him comfort. "You did what you had to do. We all do."

Then she pulled her thoughts away from the dark place they were going. "You must have some idea of what's going on. Two members of the same regiment, killed on the same day in London. And one of them believed to be a traitor."

"Do you want me to find out?"

Some of it. The parts she didn't know. Not all of it. "Yes. I keep thinking of poor Captain Ferringdon stabbed in the back. He never had a chance."

"Unlike Sir Benjamin, who was tied to the chair when he was shot with an arrow."

"What?" How did he know that? And why was it done?

"You sound surprised."

"I am. He was tied to the chair we found him in?"

"I removed the thin rope used to tie his wrists to the chair. Not that there was any need. It was all for show." His entire expression was grim. Sad. Disappointed.

"Was that what you were doing? I wondered where you found that rope." Would they hang for what they did? "I suppose the coroner will find out about the binds on the body."

"Only if you or I say something. Lord Exham is perfectly happy to not investigate this. How did Sir Benjamin come to be tied up?"

"I don't know." Her confusion leaked out in her voice.

"Susanna. This is me, Will, you're talking to. I know nothing goes on in this house that you don't know about."

"I thought that once. And then I learned differently." What a disappointment that had been. And now it had led to another death.

"You're not talking about last night. Are you referring to a year ago when Sir Benjamin came to eat at your table?"

"That wasn't here. That was at Roekirk Castle. Do you remember the castle?"

"I remember the light never seemed to make it inside through those narrow windows. I remember it was always chilly. I remember that leaving the castle, even the public rooms, always felt like escaping a dungeon."

Susanna watched him as he talked. His memories of the castle had marked him, just as they had marked her. "I haven't been back once the snows melted after Hubert died. I hope never to go back."

"It was never a fun place," he said, his voice edged with irony.

"It was never a nice place. It was never a home, for all the time I lived there."

"You only had the one child?" he asked, and her heart snapped in two.

"There was a second child. A little girl."

"She died?"

She nodded, not trusting her voice.

"What was her name?"

"Elizabeth." Elizabeth, her darling daughter, was number one on the long list of grievances she held against her husband.

When the light of life left her husband's eyes, she had thought of Elizabeth.

❖ ❖ ❖

Will was glad Susanna still held his hands. He could feel her pulse and gage her emotions. The other side of his mind said, forget the craft of his trade, these were Susanna's hands he held. How he'd longed for her touch over these long, sad years.

Nevertheless, he had to ask. "What happened when Sir Benjamin was a guest at Castle Roekirk?"

"The food had spoiled. Everyone took sick. Hubert died." Her voice was flat. Lifeless.

"Do you think Sir Benjamin poisoned your dinner?"

"Of course not. He was never near the kitchens."

"Who else was at dinner?"

"What does it matter? Sir Benjamin was murdered in London, along with this Captain Ferringdon. That is what is important."

"I know Richard and Rose were present at that dinner. Did they sicken, too?"

"Yes. As did I. As did Sir Benjamin's niece. And the Copleys and Lord and Lady MacEwen."

"Who are the Copleys?"

He felt her pulse calm as she said, "The minister of the local kirk."

"And Sir Benjamin's niece?"

Her pulse raced. "A young woman in her early twenties."

He needed to learn more about Sir Benjamin's family.

There was a scratch at the door and they dropped hands before Birdwell came in and said, "Lord Exham is ready to leave now, Lord Keyminster, and wishes you to attend on him."

No. He wants me to solve this mystery in a way that doesn't ruffle any feathers, Will thought. "Of course. Thank you so much for your hospitality, Lady Roekirk. It would have been a cold wait outside if you had not taken pity on me."

"On the contrary, I should thank you for your diverting stories."

As they were both standing now, Will bent over to kiss the back of her hand and then left the room in search of Lord Exham.

Will found him near the front door, pulling on his coat, hat, scarf, and gloves. Will took his coat and hat from a waiting footman and bundled up before they braved the elements.

Susanna didn't come to see them off. Will realized he was annoyed and hurt at her absence beyond all reason.

"It's a short walk to Oliver's. Shall we?" Exham said, and they set out. The snow now crunched beneath their boots and their breath froze in their throats. Will was glad when they reached Mister Oliver's home and surgery.

The surgeon's assistant led them downstairs to a large, low ceilinged room where the body lay on a large table surrounded by candles. Oliver, who looked even thinner in a large apron than he had in a heavy coat, had already removed some of Sir Benjamin's clothing.

"Well, Oliver, what can you tell us?" Lord Exham asked.

"Not nearly as much as the corpse can. I've removed the arrow, and it's not a good strong hunting arrow. It's just a target practice arrow with a thin shaft and a neat little metal tip. If it was fired from a target practice bow, it would have needed to have been fired from very close range to penetrate the clothing and the body."

"Who would be playing at archery in this weather?" Lord Exham asked in exasperation.

Will could have made a guess, but remained silent.

"Not only penetrated," the surgeon went on, "but traveled through the body and broken out the other side."

"Did it hit his heart?" Will asked.

"Yes. There seems to be a great deal of blood loose inside the body, as if the heart was punctured and sent blood spilling out around the other organs."

"And the cut on his head?"

"Cracked the skull. See, you can feel it here."

Lord Exham shuddered and looked away.

The surgeon continued. "If he didn't die from his head wound, then the arrow through the heart would have been instantly fatal. It is my opinion that death occurred because of the two events. You could almost say he was killed twice."

"A nasty way to go," Will said.

"Indeed," the surgeon agreed.

"And well deserved. He was a man who earned such a death," Lord Exham added. "Have you notified his family?"

"Yes. I've had a message sent to his mother. I've not heard back yet."

Turning away, Exham said, "That will be our next port of call. Coming, Keyminster?"

Will turned just as the surgeon said, "There's more. I found rope fibers on his cuffs. This man was restrained."

Exham turned back. "You mean this wasn't just a lucky shot?"

"Not lucky for the corpse," Will murmured.

"No. And it couldn't have happened where the body was found because there was nothing there to tie him to," the surgeon continued. "The blow to the head was severe enough that he should have been unconscious, if not already dead, when he was tied up and shot. And there was nothing near the body that could have been the cosh."

"So he was killed elsewhere and dumped there in a nice, convenient, dark spot," Will said. Hopefully, Exham would buy that story. He, on the other hand, needed to consider if the person who struck the blow was the person who wielded the bow and arrow. Indeed, how many people were involved?

"Definitely elsewhere. No one goes out in this weather without heavy outer clothing. But Sir Benjamin was dressed in evening clothes. Not so much as a scarf or hat," the surgeon pointed out.

"Blast. He could have been killed anywhere in London or the countryside and dumped on my section of London. But why drag him into the yard of a house where everyone in London is headed?" Exham asked.

"Who's going to notice a couple of extra men in the area of a house where there's a great deal of activity?" Will suggested, making his tone sound as if this were the only answer. "At any other house, with no one expected, a servant might notice activity and raise the alarm."

Exham nodded. "It'll be impossible to find the culprit. And here I'd hoped to enjoy my Christmas holiday." He grumbled and added, "I'm calling on the family with nothing to tell them. Come on, Keyminster. I'll need your diplomatic skills for this."

They went back outside, where bright sunshine now loosened the icy grip of winter just enough to fool people into thinking it might be warm out. Sir Benjamin's house was not far down the street and across a park, but Will was half frozen by the time they arrived.

A footman answered the door and, after handing off their outerwear to a maid, led Will and Exham into the front drawing room.

It was easy to spot the grieving mother of Sir Benjamin. She sat, dressed in black, sobbing loudly and inconsolably. Will decided since Exham was coroner, it was his duty to handle this vocal woman. He was welcome to this chore. Will walked over to a man of about forty, Sir Benjamin's age, seated across the room and bowed. "Lord Keyminster, sir. The deceased was your...?"

"Cousin. I'm Thomas Atwell. Our fathers were brothers. His was the elder, hence Benjamin inherited the baronetcy."

"And you, sir?"

"Inherited a thriving shipping business. Even more thriving now that the French war is over." He looked quite pleased with himself.

"Then you are to be congratulated. Is that your mother with Sir Benjamin's?"

"Yes. Poor Mama. I can claim business and escape the din, but Mama has to stick to the task, no matter how much her ears must hurt. Sir Benjamin had no sisters to deal with the lady."

"Is the entire family here?" Will looked around, but there were no young ladies of any age in sight.

"Yes. Benjamin was an only child. I have one sister, that's her over there with her husband and son." They looked ready to bolt like frightened horses. "This is my wife," Will gave her a small bow, "and my two sons."

"No daughters?"

"No."

The boys were perhaps six and nine years old. Both his sister and his wife were well into their thirties. "Is there no family on his mother's side?"

"None. She was orphaned young and brought up as the ward of the old Lord Margrave, a friend of her father's. The Margraves, like anyone who could, have avoided Benjamin for years. The avoidance included his mother." His expression said he wouldn't be here if he could have not come.

So who was Sir Benjamin's niece that he took to Castle Roekirk for that terrible dinner?

Chapter Six

Across the room, Will heard Lord Exham trying to learn something useful from Lady Atwell. The older woman was still bursting into noisy tears every minute. How could that woman carry on for so long at such a pitch?

"When did you last see your son?"

"At luncheon yesterday, but I didn't think it would be the last..." Anything beyond that was lost in her sobs.

When her shrieks settled down to moans, Exham said, "Do you know of anyone he planned to meet yesterday?"

"He never confided—Noooooo."

Exham gave Will a look that said "save me."

It might be a mistake, but it was worth a try. Will walked over and bowed to the grieving mother. "Lady Atwell, I'm Lord Keyminster. I recently learned your son had visited Scotland last year. In particular, the area of Scotland I come from."

That startled Lady Atwell so much she stopped crying. "You don't sound Scottish."

"I had to lose my accent to serve in the diplomatic corps."

"Was it difficult to learn to speak like a proper Englishman?"

Will cringed inwardly at her snub, but he spoke blandly. "Not at all. Tell me about Sir Benjamin's trip to Scotland. To Castle Roekirk."

"Such a silly name. Roekirk. Benjy went to his castle two or three times. The last time, everyone at the dinner came down with food poisoning, and Lord Roekirk died. Benjy said he didn't get sick at all, but he hadn't touched the haggis. Terrible things, haggis. The whole castle deserved to get sick, eating such filth."

"Have you ever had haggis, madam?"

"Never."

She was an opinionated old harpy, but at least she was calm. Behind him, Will heard her nephew's sigh of relief.

"What did Sir Benjamin tell you about Scotland?"

"They're an ill-mannered lot, much given to Presbyterian ideals. Except in their private lives. And that was how Benjy bought me a carriage and two fine horses."

"I don't understand," Lord Exham said.

Will was afraid that he might. The late Lord Roekirk had a reputation people only muttered behind their hands.

But rather than answer Exham, Lady Atwell cried out, "How will I be able to afford my coach and horses now?" This was punctuated with more sobbing and wailing.

Exham signaled to Will and they both walked out into the front hall followed by Thomas Atwell. "Thank you, my lords," Atwell said. "You managed to stop her outbursts for a few minutes. I shall try talking of food and see if any will suit her. Chewing might quiet her for a bit."

"That was well done, Keyminster," Exham said. "Although why talk about Scotland? He was murdered here, well," he looked around, "somewhere near here."

"I was trying to distract her. We do that in the diplomatic service on occasion when a king begins wailing too loudly," Will told them.

Both men smiled as if he'd spoken in jest. If only the world knew.

"It would be helpful, Mr. Atwell, if you'd identify the body and let the surgeon know what disposition you have planned," Lord Exham said.

"As soon as I can talk some sense into my aunt." Thomas went back into the drawing room, looking as if his shoulders were weighted down with care.

Will took his outer garments from a maid and readied himself for the outdoor chill. "If he waits until that woman sees sense…"

"He'll be waiting for the Second Coming," Lord Exham said, wrapping his scarf around his neck and walking outside.

"How will you find the place where the murder took place?" Will asked, genuinely interested. If there was any chance Exham would bring the hunt to Susanna's door, he needed to know so he could deflect it. He suspected she was involved in this murder up to her wide blue eyes, but whatever the reason, he was certain she had already paid for this crime.

"I'll leave that to the constables. When one of them finds a likely spot, I'll investigate. Until then, I'm off to enjoy the rest of this Christmas season with my family." Exham started to walk off. He turned and said, "Thanks for your help, Keyminster."

"My pleasure to assist. Christmas greetings to Lady Exham."

With a wave, Exham headed across the street and

around the corner toward his home. Will headed down the street. After all these years, he finally had a house. It was an impressive house, with servants to give his life ease, but it was not a home. He had no one to share it with. He never had.

He resolutely put one foot in front of the other and headed toward his house.

A few hours later, after what felt like an eternity broken by being shaved, dressed, and fed, Will entered the home of Lord and Lady MacEwen. Already the musicians were playing a waltz somewhere in the depths of the building. Shimmering fabric and glittering jewels could be seen on beautiful women moving gracefully toward the music.

Where was Susanna?

After Will had shed his outer garments, Lord MacEwen joined him. Unlike Will, who'd never had the opportunity to wear a tartan at a formal occasion, MacEwen wore his proudly as a formal waistcoat. "You look like a man who would like a wee dram, Keyminster."

"I admit to not being much of a dancer—"

"Dancing's got nothing to do with it. When my wife and Lady Roekirk spend the afternoon with their heads together, there's nothing better than a drink."

"That might affect you, but I should be safe from the wiles of those two lovely ladies."

"Not when you were the subject under discussion." Lord MacEwen raised his bushy gray eyebrows and smiled like some evil Scottish gnome.

Susanna Dunley, the dowager Countess Roekirk, and Lady Rebecca MacEwen. Those two could have easily hit Sir Benjamin over his head, tied him up, and shot an arrow through his heart. But how to prove it? And did he want to?

What good would it do?

"Thank you, MacEwen. I think I'll take that drink."

Will followed the short, older man to a side room that proved to be his study. MacEwen poured a large swallow into each of two glasses from the cut crystal decanter, and then he handed one to Will.

"Why were they talking about me?" Will asked, moving closer to the fire burning merrily in the grate. The greenery over the mantelpiece was tied up with plaid ribbon, reminding him of his long ago childhood in the highlands.

"My wife believes Susanna should cart you off to one of our spare bedrooms and have her way with you. Susanna, ever the lady, thinks you should have some say about it."

Will downed his whisky in one gulp. Long practice kept him from choking over MacEwen's words. "And you, my lord. What do you say?"

"Susanna's had so much unhappiness in her life. You know what that beast Roekirk was like. She deserves to have you if she wants you."

"So you're on your wife's side."

The gnomish smile returned. "Will, lad, I have no choice but to be on my wife's side. She gets her way sooner or later."

"I was out of the country when Roekirk earned his reputation. Why was he notorious?"

"He was a brute to young and old. To his servants, his tenants, and his family. In his mind, everyone was stupid, lazy, useless. No one ever did anything well enough to suit him. That included Susanna and his children. That's why their daughter's death was so terrible. If he had been a better man, she never would have run away into the snow."

Will felt the blood leave his head. Susanna said her

daughter died. Not...

He found his glass had been refilled. "Best get that down you," MacEwen said. "You look like you've had a shock."

Down in one burning gulp. "Susanna's daughter froze to death?"

"Aye. Ten years ago, or was it eleven, the child had sewn her father's initials on handkerchiefs for a Christmas present. Her little fingers had bled for weeks as she worked on his present. Not that the bully would have appreciated it. When she gave them to him, he laughed. Said they were hideous things, poorly made, and threw them on the fire."

"Good grief." Will found his hands were in fists, frustrated that there was no outlet for his anger.

"Elizabeth ran out of the room crying. When Susanna moved to go to her, Roekirk pushed her back onto her chair and ordered her to stay put. Said the child needed to learn to stop crying over everything. They didn't realize until too late she had run outside. Apparently, she grew disoriented in the snowstorm. They didn't find her until the next morning. At the bottom of a ravine."

"Oh. Good. Grief." Will dropped into a chair and put his face in his hands. If Roekirk were still alive, he would have killed him. "Is Susanna here?"

"Not yet. But she's expected."

Susanna kept what she hoped was a surreptitious eye on the door to the ballroom while she spoke to the other guests. All the time, Rebecca's advice kept playing in her head. Just take him upstairs to a guest bedroom and enjoy him.

Enjoy him. She'd always enjoyed Will, no matter where they'd been when they'd been young, and the few times she'd seen him in the years since then. His conversation, his laughter, his wisdom, the touch of his hand.

He'd always treated her as an intelligent lady, and she appreciated it. Roekirk should have taken lessons from him.

"I understand you wanted to see me."

Susanna jumped when she heard Will behind her. "Lord Keyminster," she said, curtsying.

"Lady Roekirk," he replied, bowing. And there was that smile that reminded her of sin and sunshine.

"I wondered about that incident this morning. Perhaps we should find a less public spot if we're going to discuss something so unfortunate," she said.

"I am at your disposal."

She wished his words were true. "Lady MacEwen said we could speak freely in her morning room."

He held out his arm. "Lead me to it."

They found a cheery fire burning in the small blue morning room. She sat on the couch and he joined her, but sat at the other end. Still, they were within touching distance.

"You have questions, my lady?"

"What have you learned about the corpse Rose and I unfortunately found in our back parlor?"

"The information you most want to hear is that since the surgeon showed Lord Exham the fibers from the bindings on his cuffs, and since there was no place outside to tie him up, and since the victim was dressed for being indoors, the constables are on the lookout for a place in London or vicinity where the attack could have taken place."

"So Lord Exham won't need to bother us anymore?"

"No."

She let her relief show. "Rose found the questioning

arduous."

"Not only Rose, I imagine."

"No one likes to be questioned."

"Susanna, I know where I first saw him."

She closed her eyes, then opened them to stare into his. "Will, I appreciate what you've done for me. For Richard and Rose. We'd never live down finding anyone, much less Sir Benjamin, dead in our back drawing room with an arrow through his heart."

"So which one of you did it?"

The cold in his words froze her blood. "N-none."

"Don't lie to me, Susanna."

"I'm not. I swear to you, none of the three of us did it. Nor did any of our servants, so don't even think that." She managed to maintain an enraged tone, partially by strength of will, partially because she truly was angry. How could he think she'd do such a thing?

She had only ever been that angry with someone once. Someone who deserved it.

"But you know who did. No one could sneak in and kill someone in your house without you knowing about it."

She wanted to tell him not to press her. He had once before, when she told him she was to marry Roekirk. He had been right then, that it was a mistake and she'd never be happy. And he was intelligent. It was only a matter of time before he figured out what had happened.

And then he would hate her. Even if she didn't hang, she'd lose his love and respect.

"Susanna?" His voice was very quiet.

"It's not my secret to reveal."

He turned her head to face him with the slightest

pressure of one hand. "You can't go around murdering people."

He was so wrong. Anger drove the words out of her mouth. "Why not? Roekirk did."

"What?"

"He chased our daughter, he chased Elizabeth, out into a blizzard with his cruelty and his impossible expectations. And he wouldn't let me go after her. We thought she'd gone up to her room. No one saw her leave. If I'd followed her, she wouldn't have died." Tears ran down her cheeks unchecked. She didn't care.

He gripped her arms with his hands. "I wish I had been there. I would have stopped him."

"You were in France." She didn't bother to hide her scorn. He hadn't been there to help. No one had.

"I'm sorry, Susanna."

"She worked so hard on those handkerchiefs and was so proud of them. I should have realized she wouldn't have just gone to her room to cry after he did something so devastating. I should have fought back when he threw me back in my chair and ordered me to stay with him, that it was my duty to stay with him in the drawing room. But I was so afraid of him. And so I let my daughter die."

He let go of her and leaned back, as if touching her burned his hands. Perhaps he saw her as a failure as a mother. She did.

Chapter Seven

It had been a long time since Will had heard something that truly sickened him to the pit of his stomach. "I am so sorry, Susanna. Elizabeth must have been a beautiful child."

"Oh, she was." She looked, and sounded, shattered, forced to recall the horror. There was no other word for it.

The investigator in him had to know. "Was this the reason Sir Benjamin had to die?"

"No. Elizabeth's death is on her father's head. Sir Benjamin had nothing to do with it. His sins were of a more impersonal, monetary sort." She brushed her tears away with her fingers.

"You know who killed him."

"I know who killed Josiah Ferringdon." Her eyes were too bright. She looked feverish from having to relive this horror.

All right. He'd ask. "Who?"

"Sir Benjamin Atwell. Ferringdon found out what Atwell was up to and confronted him about it. He died for his decency."

"What was Atwell up to?"

She made a face as if she tasted something rancid. "Blackmail."

Blast and double blast. Atwell was a traitor and a blackmailer? That explained the coach and horses his mother mentioned. "How do you know?"

"How does anyone know anything in the ton? Gossip." She wrapped her arms around her middle, looking broken.

Susanna was not a gossip. But what could Atwell have blackmailed her about? Her daughter's death was a terrible accident. The whole incident showed Roekirk in a bad light, but Susanna wouldn't have paid blackmail to protect the old rogue's name.

"Why was Atwell blackmailing you?"

"He wasn't."

He reached into his pocket and pulled out the second note that had been in Sir Benjamin's possession when he had first examined the body. Handing it to Susanna, he said, "Are you certain about that?"

She opened the note, glanced at it, and blanched. Written there were the words LADY ROEKIRK, I KNOW YOUR SECRET. ATWELL. "He tried. I refused to pay."

He was openly impressed. "That was very brave of you."

"Not really. Saying I killed my husband is an unprovable charge. No one would believe it."

"But the ton would be alight with gossip about you."

"It doesn't matter. As long as the scandal doesn't touch Richard and Rose, it makes no difference what they say about me."

"But you know better. The talk would spread to both of them."

She stared off to the side, her mind far from a London party. "He took both of my children away from me when they were eight. Upsetting Elizabeth with his cruelty until she ran away into a storm and perished."

Shaking her head, she continued. "A few years before, Richard was taken away to toughen him up. One day Hubert rode the boy so hard he burst into tears. He was only a child, but Hubert said I was turning him into a molly-boy, his words, and I'd have nothing more to do with his upbringing. He sent him away to a strict boys' school and Richard came home sullen and bitter."

A sob and then, "It was Rose, not me, who helped him become a better man. He blames me for his being sent away, and he blames me for his sister's death."

Will kept his voice low so he didn't frighten Susanna. She was visibly upset. "Why would Sir Benjamin try to blackmail you? You've done nothing wrong."

She smiled grimly. "I think Sir Benjamin knew if he claimed I killed my husband, it would make me hated by every man in the ton."

Sir Benjamin. Who didn't have a niece. "Sir Benjamin procured young women for the earl."

She nodded, her chin dropping to her chest.

He had to know the rest. "When did your husband die?"

"This time last year. Between Christmas and Hogmanay. December twenty-eighth."

"Of bad haggis."

"Something spoiled. We all became ill."

"Sir Benjamin didn't."

She stared into his eyes. "Where did you get that idea?"

"He told his mother that others were sick from the haggis, but he wouldn't eat it."

"And you never told your mother stories?"

He smiled, hoping she would tell him the truth if he

guessed right. And he was almost certain his guess was correct. "Susanna. You were mistress of the house. No one would think anything of you going down to the kitchens and adding herbs. Then, when the earl was weakened, you suffocated him with a pillow."

"We hadn't made haggis in weeks. How would I know which haggis we'd eat on which day and which day I wanted to make everyone sick?" She hadn't moved, but she watched him closely.

"Then it was some dish that would be served that night that Sir Benjamin didn't eat." He was right. He had to be.

"I poisoned some unnamed dish that Sir Benjamin refused to eat but my husband did, and so he died. Except Sir Benjamin ate from every dish put on the table. Or I suffocated Hubert while he didn't have the strength to fight me off. Except there was never a moment of our marriage that the earl didn't have a great deal more strength than me." She shook her head sadly.

She rose and stared at him. "I'm going back to the party. It's the Christmas season and I'd prefer to be around joyous people rather than an inquisitor."

Will rose with her. "I'm not trying to be an inquisitor. I'm trying to figure out what happened."

"Why? What's done is done, and the dead do not return to life." Susanna strode to the door, opened it, and left, leaving a puzzled Will behind.

Left alone, he went in search of Lord MacEwen. He found him in his study. "Come in, Keyminster. Want a dram? Did pretty Susanna have her way with you?"

"She walked all over me," Will muttered.

"That's not the Susanna I know. Did you two quarrel?"

He handed Will a glass.

"The night that Lord Roekirk died, did you get food poisoning from Susanna's dinner?"

"No. Neither Rebecca nor I."

"Then what did Roekirk die of?"

"Heart failure. Not easy to believe in a man without one, but there you are. He ate a big dinner, he fought with Susanna, and his heart stopped." MacEwen shrugged and took a sip from his glass.

Will decided to trust him. "Atwell tried to blackmail Susanna over her husband's death."

"Poor lass. She should have received a medal, not trouble from the likes of that man."

"Do you remember the Christian name of Atwell's niece? She was at dinner at the castle the night Roekirk died."

"Laddie. Don't you get it? She wasn't Atwell's niece. She was some light-skirt off the streets. Sir Benjamin paid her a pittance and then made Roekirk pay him handsomely for her."

Will took a stiff belt of the whisky and felt it burn his insides. "How old was she?"

"At least Richard's age. Hubert found out his son hadn't had a woman yet and decided to give him one for Christmas. Make sure he was practiced before he wed Rose. Once again he was calling Richard a molly-boy and angering the young man. And afterward Hubert was going to have the lass himself." MacEwen stared into the fire.

The old Lord Roekirk didn't deserve Susanna. How had she managed to survive thirty years of marriage to the brute? "What happened to Roekirk?"

"What does it matter? The sinner's dead."

Will knew he'd get nothing more from the canny Scot.

Susanna took a deep breath, put a smile on her face, and entered the ballroom. Roddy, Lord MacEwen's brother, came up and twirled her around. "Susanna, my love. How about a dance?"

"Why, thank you, kind sir."

Roddy burst out laughing. He took her hand and led her out onto the dance floor where they waltzed in sweeping style among the other dancers.

Following Roddy's lead, her feet moving fast and without time to think, Susanna felt sadness and worry lift from her shoulders. Between one rotation of the room and the next, her heartbreak resolved and her sorrow evaporated.

By the time they finished that dance and the next, Susanna was gasping for breath. Everything that bothered her before was gone in a flurry of dance steps and spins. "Thank you," she panted, "but I'm going to have to give up now, or I will surely collapse."

"Ah," Roddy said, equally out of breath, "I believe you wore me out, bonnie lass."

"Then it must be my turn," came from a pleasant voice behind her. "Shall we have a drink before we dance? Do you mind, Mr. MacEwen?"

"Not at all, laddie. She has spunk enough for both of us."

Susanna turned and faced Will. "That would be nice." She gave him her hand the way she had when she was still half grown, winked at Roddy, and walked with Will to the dining room.

She chose the watered wine and fruit punch. He poured

two cups, handed her one and kept one for himself. She drained her cup and then smiled at him. "Roddy is an enthusiastic dancer."

He handed her his cup. "You may want this."

She took a sip, already beginning to cool off. "I'm looking forward to New Year's."

"Hogmanay?"

She shook her head. "New Year's Day. A new beginning." She needed a new start, since she couldn't start over.

"What do you have planned for the New Year?"

"Nothing special. I just plan to face forward, face the future, and leave the sorrows of the past behind. And you? What do you have planned for the New Year?"

He looked down, and for a moment she thought he wouldn't answer. Finally, he said, "I'm done with traveling for the crown. I've retired from the Foreign Office with the thanks of a grateful nation and an adequate reward. The road before me lies empty. I get to choose, for the first time, where this road will go."

"What a beautiful thought." Will always put magic in his words.

"But a very empty life without someone to share it." He held her gaze, and Susanna hoped against hope that her future could be spent with him. When he reached for her hand, she gave it to him willingly.

"When we were young," she began, and then didn't know how to end the sentence.

"No," he said, putting a finger to her lips, "no looking back."

She stared into his eyes and wondered if that was possible. "And now?"

"Now is all we have. We should take our now and go forward. Together." He held her hand in both of his. Then he bent his head and kissed her.

"Ah, Keyminster, I've been looking all over for you."

They jumped apart like guilty children. Susanna felt her face heat.

"Lady Roekirk, my apologies," the man continued. "I didn't see you there."

"Lord Exham, were you looking for Lord Keyminster?" Well, of course he was. That silly remark was worthy of someone Rose's age. Placing a smile on her face, Susanna said, "I think I'll go watch Roddy dance. My lords." She curtsied to them both and left the room.

Behind her, she heard Lord Exham say, "I apologize if I interrupted anything."

She didn't hear Will's reply.

When she returned to the ballroom, Rebecca MacEwen came up to her and whispered, "Exham has a witness to something in your garden before or during your ball. The part of the garden where Sir Benjamin was found. I don't know if this witness could identify anyone or even if he saw anything compromising."

"Perhaps it was nothing." Even as she spoke, Susanna knew that wasn't true. Exham wouldn't go looking for Will in the middle of a ball for no reason. He'd have waited for him to come into the ballroom and greeted him there if it were nothing.

Rebecca gave her a dry look.

They were in trouble. The question was, how much, and could they be hanged?

Chapter Eight

Will stared at Exham, angry he had destroyed any chance at furthering his new relationship with Susanna. Exham ignored him as he poured himself a glass of punch.

When he turned to face Will, Exham wore his funeral face. "We have a witness to carrying on in Roekirk's side garden shortly before their ball. It was a man and a woman."

"Go on." Will's mind raced as he schooled his expression to one of polite curiosity. Years of spying followed by years of diplomacy allowed him to mask his fear. Someone had seen Susanna and him move the body outdoors.

How was he going to deflect this new danger?

"Apparently, they were foreign."

Will's eyebrows rose. Not what he expected. "French, perhaps? A crime of passion? Sir Benjamin cut a wide swath through French society at one time."

"That was my thought. I'm going to question this witness tomorrow morning. I'd like you along in case anything points to a diplomatic connection."

"I'd be pleased to, Exham."

They set a time, and after Exham finished his drink, the two men walked back to the ballroom as if there was nothing on their minds beyond a pleasant night's entertainment.

Will knew he was acting. The tension in Exham's lower face said he was, also.

By adroit conversational maneuvers, Will made his way across the crowded ballroom to Susanna's side before the last dance. "Madam," he said bowing, "I hope you've saved the last dance for me."

"Of course, my lord," she replied, curtsying.

Will took her hand and led her onto the dance floor for the final waltz. Once she was in his arms, all pretense of formality ceased. "There's a witness to what happened in your side garden," he whispered.

She stiffened. "We were seen?"

"No. They were supposedly foreigners. Exham suspects a French connection, and so do I."

He felt her relax into his arms.

She felt so good there, fitting perfectly into the crook of his arm, that he hated to ask, "Do you know any French people who might have been at your ball?"

"No. They're not very popular right now."

"Perhaps someone from the *Ancien Regime* who fled France years ago?"

"No. No one who fits that description."

"Any that might have been at your house? A lady's maid, perhaps?"

"No. This wasn't like a fortnight at the castle. The ball was only for one evening, and no one came early or stayed over."

He had to ask. "Any French men or women who were familiar with the archery equipment in your shed?"

She looked up at him, her eyes wide, and shook her head. Then she stared at his shoulder. He could feel her pull away from him ever so slightly.

"You're angry with me for questioning you."

"No."

"Yes, you are."

Her eyes flashed fury when she glanced up at him this time. "This is supposed to be a Christmas season dance, but you have me telling you my deepest sorrow and then accusing me..."

"No."

"Accusing me of inviting French murderers into my home."

"You are a sociable and a kind woman, Susanna. I imagine you have invited thousands of people to dine or to dance under your roof. You can't be held responsible for what someone does later with the knowledge they've gained of your household."

He hoped he was diplomatic enough to soothe her. He had never worked as hard to pacify a foreign ruler.

She danced, her face expressionless for a moment before she nodded. "When will you know more about these people's identity?"

"Exham and I are questioning the witness tomorrow."

He felt a shudder run through her body and knew she hadn't told him the truth. He was surprised to find he wasn't angry. He was disappointed.

Will was ready on time the next morning when Exham called. Once outside in the still cold air, he noticed the snow was tired, sinking into itself and becoming icy. He suspected the sunshine was responsible. The temperature was too low to cause any amount of thawing.

"I'm tired of this. Give me a wet garden and plenty of footprints any day," Exham grumbled, "with windows open and neighbors listening to every word."

"Have you made any progress on Captain Ferringdon's murder?"

"No, and I won't be until a witness comes forward."

"How did we get a witness to what happened in Roekirk's side garden in the dark and cold?" It seemed unlikely.

"A bit of luck there. One of the footmen had been filching food from the larder in the house next door to Roekirk's. When they called in the constables, they convinced the other servants to turn in the guilty party. The footman, it turns out, had been stealing from his employers for a while and selling the goods on. Problem was, he got greedy and took too much..."

"They so often do," Will said, shaking his head. If criminals didn't get greedy, half of them would never get caught. A philosophy that had kept him safe in some harrowing times.

"The thievery was discovered by the mistress who had called the constables. When confronted with evidence and testimony, this footman admitted the crime but said he had evidence of his own to give against the murderer next door. His employers are keeping him on at the moment at our request, but I wouldn't give much chance to him staying in that household afterward."

Will glanced at Susanna's house as they walked to the front door of the next house. He followed Exham to the servants' hall below stairs where a young man sat at the table, closely watched by a larger man who was clearly employed to do physical labor.

"That's all, Gregson," the butler said, and the big man lumbered off.

While the butler stood at a distance, Exham and Will sat across the table from the prisoner. He looked miserable. He'd apparently been forced to sit up all night and his clothes looked wrinkled and dirty. A bruise was growing around one eye and dried blood marred one ear.

"What's your name?" Exham asked in his usual grumbling tone.

"Croft, my lord."

"I'm Lord Exham, the coroner. I'd like to hear what you saw and heard the night of the ball next door."

"It was before Milord and Milady went to the ball. Except for those dressing them, we were at leisure for an hour. I had something I wanted to—pass on to a friend, and I'd arranged to meet him by the side of the house. It's dark back there and no one comes that way."

"You were alone when you heard or saw something?" Will asked.

"Excuse me, who's he?" Croft asked, obviously panicked.

"I'm Lord Keyminster, assisting Lord Exham," Will said. "I'm just making sure we get all the details correct."

"Yes, I was alone. I was waiting for my friend. I didn't see anything, but I heard two voices. A man and a woman's. They came from the front and they spoke for a moment. Then one of them walked off."

"How do you know that?" Exham asked. "Could you see them?"

"No. Not with no light and those thick bushes there."

"Then how do you know?" Exham sounded annoyed.

"I heard the footsteps. The snow crackled under their feet. That's why I had to stand really still or they'd have heard me. Just about froze out there waiting for them to leave."

"How long until the other one left?"

"First one came back from behind the house after a minute or two. Then they opened the door into the side of the house. That's when I heard them clearly. The woman said, 'He's dead.' Like she was surprised."

"He's dead. You're sure?"

"Yes I'm sure. Then the man said, 'Come on, lass. Let's make it look good.'"

Aloud, Will said, "Make it look good? What did they mean by that?" even as he was thinking, *I know who it was.*

"I don't know, do I? Then the woman said, 'She wouldn't have.' Then they shut the door. My friend came and we— spoke quickly, it was terrible cold out, and then I went inside."

"So that's all you have to tell us?" Exham said.

"Yes, my lord."

"Then why did you say they were foreign?"

"Cuz of the way they talked. They had an accent. Like English wasn't their real language."

"Do you know what kind of accent?"

"No. It just sounded funny."

"Can I hand him over to the constables to put in jail?" the butler asked.

"Yes. I'm done with him," Exham said, sounding disgusted as he rose.

"Tell the constables I may want to talk to him again," Will said. Both Exham and Croft looked at him in surprise.

Will shrugged. "It's a possibility. Tell the constables to keep him available for me."

He rose and followed Exham out. Once they reached the outdoors, Exham said, "You know something."

"No. If nothing else works, we may want to have a native French speaker talk in front of Croft to see if it's the right accent. It could narrow down the suspects."

Exham made a grumbling noise. "Sorry to bring you out in this cold. I'd hoped he'd be able to tell us more than that."

"Would have been nice if he could. Good luck, Exham. And a happy new year to Lady Exham."

They split up at the corner. Instead of going home, Will headed to MacEwen House.

Lord MacEwen and his brother Roddy were in his study sitting by the fire. Will was glad to see neither had started drinking yet.

"Ah, Will. An excuse to pour a dram in the glass," Lord MacEwen greeted him.

"Hamish. Roddy. Which one of you did it?"

The two men looked at each other, and Will felt the sinking sensation that he had guessed right.

"Roddy didn't find out until much later. Leave him out of it."

Will nodded. Roddy rose, patted his brother's shoulder, and left the room. The door clicked quietly behind him.

"How did you find out?"

Will sat in the vacant chair. "There was a witness on the other side of those thick bushes. He heard you and Rebecca. So far, I've convinced Exham he's looking for someone with a French accent, not a Scottish one."

MacEwen gave one loud guffaw. "How long until

Exham's knocking on my door?"

"He won't if I can help it. But tell me, did you really find Atwell dead?"

"Aye. We opened the door to find him sprawled on the floor, face up. He wasn't breathing. When we checked him out, we found a horrible gash in the back of his head. There's a fender in front of the fireplace. It looked like he'd hit his head on that. We tied him to the chair and shot him with an arrow from the shed. Then we left the way we came."

"Why shoot him with an arrow? The man's skull was cracked open." That seemed to Will to be overkill.

"To confuse the issue. I didn't realize you'd come along and move the body. Next time, we need to coordinate our efforts."

"I hope there isn't a next time, Hamish. But why didn't you remove the bindings?" That had been foolish in Will's opinion.

"We wanted everyone to think he died from the arrow through the heart." He smiled ruefully. "You look like you could do with that dram now."

Will nodded, staring at the fire until MacEwen put the glass in his hand. "So who hit him over the head? Was he hit over the head or did he hit his head on the fireplace fender? And if he hit his head on the fender, how did he end up smashing his head against it?"

MacEwen shook his head and took a sip of his drink.

"And why were you breaking into the side of Susanna's house?"

"Ah, that one's easy. She sent a messenger, one of her staff, with a note. I've burned it, in case you wanted to read it for yourself."

Will felt the edges of his mouth curl up. Hamish MacEwen never missed a thing. "Why would Susanna bash Atwell over the head? He was trying to blackmail her, but all she had to do was deny it. No one would believe him."

"There's two things wrong with your thinking, Will."

"What?"

"He wasn't killed for trying to blackmail her. Susanna is much too sharp for that."

"Are you saying Susanna didn't hit Atwell over the head?"

All he received for that shocked question was a nod from MacEwen.

"Who? Why?" What was he missing in all this?

"She's trying to keep all this from you, lad."

"And she's doing a fine job of it, too." He thought Susanna trusted him. Had he been wrong about that? "What is the other thing I have wrong?"

"Ask Susanna. Tell her I told you to ask her."

"She won't tell me. I love her. I always will. But there's this big secret standing like a mountain between us."

"Assure her you'll always love her. And you'll keep her secret and her heart safe." MacEwen rose and stomped to the fireplace. "Good heavens, lad. She loves you. You love her. Why are you making heavy weather out of such a simple thing?"

Why, indeed? And if Susanna wasn't guilty, why keep these secrets from him?

Chapter Nine

It was Hogmanay. New Year's Eve. Susanna looked out the window into the dusk and hoped the next year would be better. Fewer lies. Fewer deaths. Fewer ghosts.

They were hosting a small dinner party for their Scottish neighbors in London before tonight's ball at the Duke of Derwin's palatial home. When Rose asked if she should invite Lord Keyminster, Susanna had raised no objections.

She hadn't yet decided if that was wise.

A scratch on the door made her look up as Birdwell entered. "The Earl of Keyminster, milady."

"He wants to see me?"

"Yes."

She hadn't seen him in nearly two days and she'd missed him. She'd been safer without him, but she missed him. "Please show him in."

She was still standing by the window, feeling the chilled wind slip into the room when Will entered. He bowed and she managed a curtsy on shaking legs.

Rebecca had sent a note saying Hamish had admitted practically all to Will. But in the important details, Hamish had told Will to ask her.

He stood close to her by the window. "I love you,

Susanna. I always will."

She hadn't expected to hear that. "You wouldn't if you knew the truth."

"I know you didn't kill Atwell. You cleaned up someone else's mess. That's what you've had to do for years. Clean up Roekirk's messes."

A sound between a sob and a chuckle slipped out. "Amazing, isn't it? He's been dead a year and he's still leaving messes for me to clean up."

"Tell me, Susanna. Tell me and then leave me to clean up whatever's left."

"I can't." How she wished she could. "You believe in the law and honesty. You and Exham, finding killers and hanging them."

"No." He took her fists in his and kissed her knuckles. "That's Exham's job. I can't remember how many I've killed. Law? Honesty? That has nothing to do with diplomacy or espionage."

He was as damaged as she was. She could hear it in his voice. Oh, how she wanted to lay down this burden. Confess all and leave it behind.

"Oh, Will. It's not a pretty tale."

"Let's get it out before midnight and leave it with the old year."

"Rebecca went to see Captain Ferringdon. He was her late brother's best friend. She passed Atwell as she rounded the corner and found Ferringdon stabbed in the back. There was no one else around."

"And she immediately came and told you."

How well Will knew them, for not having lived among them for years. "Yes. So later, when I found Atwell's body in the green drawing room, I asked them to mask the cause of death."

"And the only problem was I showed up too early."

"No." She managed to give him a weak smile. "Your plan was much better than mine. You kept the death from my door."

"Who killed him?"

"I won't tell you. He wasn't killed for being a blackmailer. I will tell you that much."

She could see his brain working furiously behind his eyes, but his expression remained placid.

"How did Atwell know you killed Roekirk?"

His words were spoken so softly and calmly that they forced a gasp out of her.

"That's why he tried to blackmail you. Because he knew you had killed Roekirk. What happened? It was this time last year. In a cold and gloomy castle. No escape from him."

She wanted to put her hands over her ears. His voice was like the steady drip, drip of snow melting.

"I'm not going to judge you, Susanna, nor turn you in. I have no room to judge after the things I've done for Britain."

"You acted for your country. I acted for my son and his future happiness."

He looked shocked. "What happened?"

"I found Hubert ordering Richard to lie with a lady-bird. I knew Hubert did such things. I didn't care. But Richard said he wouldn't demean his love for Rose that way. I backed him up, and Hubert went after me. He pinned me in a corner and put his hands around my neck. I couldn't breathe. I struck out, catching him in the throat."

She swallowed and then said, "A moment later, he

collapsed on the floor, taking me with him. He was still and dead, with a horrified look on his face." She put her arms over her sore stomach. "I just left him lying there. Richard had already left the room and hadn't seen any of this, but when I opened the door to escape seeing that dead accusing face, Sir Benjamin was standing there in the hall with the whore. He looked in and saw Roekirk. He immediately knew I'd killed him."

"Did he tell you that?"

"He didn't have to. I knew from the pleased look on his face."

"Pleased?"

"He'd as much as caught me in the act."

"No. Roekirk died because his heart stopped. The excitement was too much for him. He'd never taken care of himself." He put his arms around her, and Susanna sank into the comfort of his embrace.

"Are you sure?"

"Yes. That shocked look on his face is a sign of instant death. His heart just stopped. You were trying to help your son and Rose have a better life than you had. Roekirk's death is on his own head."

"Oh, that is a relief." She stood, brushing away the tears from her eyes, and stepped out of his embrace.

"So he couldn't have blackmailed you."

"He wasn't trying. Not when he died."

She felt the instant he realized what she had said. Stupid mouth. It had put her in trouble again.

Will nodded, his eyes watching her. "The Countess of Roekirk. Only Sir Benjamin wasn't trying to blackmail you. But Rose is such an innocent. How could he have anything to threaten her over?"

"He didn't. Rose went into the green drawing room, her favorite room, after dinner, and found Atwell in there. He said something about what a pretty little piece Richard had married and tried to force himself on her."

His face showed his anger and horror. "Oh, good grief, he was as depraved as Roekirk."

"Yes. They were quite a pair. They loved the darkness and whisky and fallen women. Never mind the damage they did. And Atwell procured whores for Roekirk for a handsome fee."

"And nothing would stop them short of death." He shook his head.

"Richard heard the commotion and went in and caught Atwell fondling his wife. He grabbed him and threw him. Off balance, Atwell fell and hit his head on the fireplace fender. It was an accident."

"So why shoot him with an arrow?"

"I came in a minute later and found Rose sobbing in Richard's embrace. He was being very kind to her, not like the way his father treated me." Memories crashed through her, but she shook them away. "I told them I'd take care of everything. I sent a message to Rebecca and unlocked the French doors for them."

"But the arrow didn't disguise any of this."

"I know. Your plan was much better than ours."

"Why not admit it was an accident?"

"You weren't to know, Will. No one was. To have this follow Hubert's death? The gossip would have never stopped." And she was very good at keeping secrets. So why was she telling Will everything?

"Richard shouldn't know I told you any of this. He is never to know." Her voice found the strength to demand he obey her wish.

"Understood." Will answered in the tone he used to his commanding officers when he would follow their orders to his death. Fortunately, it had never come to that. Otherwise, he wouldn't be able to try to mend Susanna's hurts. "Do I know the full story now?"

"And what a bloody story it is. Atwell killed Ferringdon. Richard accidently killed Atwell. Roekirk's actions killed our daughter. I killed Roekirk. And Rebecca fired the arrow."

Will pulled her close and kissed her forehead. "That scene was as much Hamish as Rebecca, I think. So who wrote the note?"

"I disguised my handwriting when I answered Sir Benjamin's note, in case he tried to use it as evidence against me."

"Only Rose came in to the room before you had a chance to meet him and throw him out." Bad luck had started this chain of events. Now Will was determined to stop the chain and make things right for Susanna again.

"Yes. This is all my fault." Susanna leaned against his chest and sobbed until he thought her heart would break.

All he could do was hold her. Whisper that everything would be all right. That he loved her. That she never needed to go back to Castle Roekirk in Scotland.

He had no idea how long he stood there, holding her as she wept out the years of misery and terror. Birdwell scratched at the door and then peeked in at one point, but Will gestured him away with a shake of his head.

And then they were alone again until Susanna finally

stopped crying. She sniffed into her handkerchief and then said, "I'm sorry. I've dampened the front of your jacket."

He kept his arms around her. "It's a dark color. It won't show."

"I must look a mess."

"You look like the woman I want for my wife."

She froze in his embrace for a moment before she raised her gaze to his eyes. "Me? I've just confessed to killing my husband, or at least forcing his heart to fail. Are you sure you want to take on that position?"

He smiled at the sight of her shocked face. "I haven't chased my daughter into a storm, terrified my tenants, or bullied my servants. I wouldn't. So I think I'm safe from your homicidal urges."

"I'm old. I'm sorrowful. I'm broken."

"You're beautiful." He kissed her forehead. "Deep inside you're the same goodhearted girl I fell in love with many years ago. And you're the only one who can heal me."

"Heal you? Will, you've been made an earl. You served the crown for many years and came home in one piece. You hardly need healing."

"I have an empty house and no family. I have no one to share my home and my life with. I've waited all these years to share it with you. Please say yes and make us both happy. Fix our mistake from all those years ago."

She shook her head, and his heart dropped. "It wasn't a mistake. We couldn't have run away together and had any kind of a life. You hadn't finished your solicitor training. I was still a silly girl. We both had a hard life, alone, but now we're free to make up for all those bad years. Together."

A "whoop" escaped from Will's throat as his heart

soared. "Is that a yes?"

She nodded.

"We need to tell everyone tonight at the ball at midnight. Make our announcement the first thing to happen in the new year."

She went up on her toes and kissed him, and he felt her claim him and put her mark on him. "I love you, Will. I'll be proud to be your wife."

"There is one thing I need to do to make certain everyone is safe." He saw the panic in her eyes. "No, this is all right. A footman next door heard Hamish and Rebecca when they came in the house with the bow and arrow. He's currently locked up for stealing from his mistress, and Exham thinks the accent he heard was French. I'm going to try to get him released in the morning and shipped off overseas before Exham thinks to find out what kind of accent the burglars had."

"How will you do that?"

"I'll get Hamish to loan me some of his lads to see the footman onto a ship bound for America down at the docks. I'll cross a couple of palms with silver and have him out of here before the wedding."

She looked at him with her brow furrowed. "Why?"

"Rebecca has been a good friend to you, and I want to protect her. Protect you. I love you and I want our new life to go smoothly."

"It's a good idea. I'd like that as my wedding present." She put her arms around his shoulders. "There is one thing while you are sending this young man far away. We can send him with Sir Benjamin's coat and scarf."

Sir Benjamin's missing outer clothes. Exham had

apparently forgotten about those. "That is a good idea. Get that evidence out of London."

"Now what would you like for your wedding present?" Susanna asked.

"Having you as my wife." He let go with one arm to reach into his coat pocket and pulled out the tiny box. When he handed it to her, he saw surprise followed by amazement as she opened the box and saw the tiny ring.

"Oh, it's beautiful."

"I bought it for you that summer. Before we were parted all those years ago."

She tried to put it on, but it wouldn't go past the knuckle of her third finger. "Yes. Many years ago."

"I'll get you another. One that fits."

She shook her head and slipped the ring on her smallest finger. It fit perfectly. And then she laughed, the joyous, free sound he remembered from that summer in the valley, many years before.

And he knew they both were healed.

About Kate

Kate Parker grew up reading her mother's mystery stories and her father's collection of history and biography books. Now she can't write a story without someone being murdered, and everyday objects are studied for their lethal potential. She's encouraged to write historical mysteries by living in a nineteenth century town, fortunately improved by twenty-first century conveniences.

Kate is inspired to write by her husband, who wants to know when the next book is coming out because he needs something to read, and by two of her children who are also writers. She considers it a triumph over their upbringing that neither writes about murder. So far. She takes no credit at all for her four perfect grandchildren.

During the past year, Kate closed out the five-book Victorian Bookshop Mysteries series by marrying her sleuth, Georgia Fenchurch, to the Duke of Blackford. Now she is hard at work on the third in the Deadly series, set in pre-WWII London with a society page reporter, Olivia Denis, as sleuth. *Deadly Fashion* finds Olivia worrying about her Army captain beau as Hitler moves into the Sudetenland and war comes nearer.

Next up will be *Deadly Deception* when our intrepid reporter finds herself caught between rival spies.

Follow Kate and her deadly examination of history at
www.KateParkerbooks.com and
www.facebook.com/Author.Kate.Parker/

A Perfectly
Unforgettable Christmas

by

Louisa Cornell

Chapter One

December 1816
London

"Winterbourne is a dead man."

Lucien Rollinsby, Viscount Debenwood, heaved himself into an upright position on the side of his bed, scratched his *arse*, and squinted a glare at the strand of sunlight that dared to slither past the dark blue drapes drawn on his bedchamber window.

Clang!

That made seventeen.

"First I'm going to kill the architect who designed my bedchamber to hang over every banging garden gate in Grosvenor Square."

Clang!

Eighteen. How many damned servants and trunks did it take to move one woman into a townhouse?

Lucien fumbled about in the bedclothes in search of his banyan. God forbid he sit naked on his own bed and frighten the upstairs maid. Again.

"And then I'm going to kill Winterbourne."

"Will you be dressing for the occasion, my lord?" Redford, the single-most condescending butler in the history of condescending butlers, inquired from somewhere across the room. The man had finally learned, for his own personal safety, not to light any of the lamps until after two in the afternoon. It was a sacrifice of biblical martyrdom that Redford lit any lamps at all. The task was completely beneath the butler, and well Lucien knew it. Redford's reasons for taking on the role of valet were his own. Lucien tried not to dwell on them overlong.

The last of his valets had left in an indignant huff over a year ago. Lucien could hardly blame him. A valet had no use for a master who never left the house, never dressed beyond breeches and shirtsleeves, bathed and shaved only a few times a week most of the year and not a single day in December.

Good God, would his head never cease pounding with his every heartbeat?

With his left hand, Lucien covered his eyes in an effort to keep them from jarring out of his pounding head. With his right, he opened the bedside table drawer—after three tries—and captured the tinderbox therein. Once he managed to light the candle on the table he shoved the candle holder in Redford's general direction. "Be a good man and put this next to the chamber pot."

Clang!

"Nineteen. Wellington didn't take this much baggage to the third siege at Badajoz." Lucien inched closer to the edge of the bed. His bare feet curled against the texture of the thick Persian rug. A sharp pain shot from the sole of his left foot to the back curve of his left hip.

Badajoz.

Weston and Bridges had died there. Fools. Why had they ever listened to him? Why had any of them? Had he not been such an arrogant young fool, he might have been there to save them or at least to die by their sides.

"Is there a reason I am required to illuminate the chamber pot and nothing else in his lordship's dungeon... ahem, bedchamber?" Redford placed the candle on the floor and made a hasty retreat into the shadows next to the mahogany wardrobe.

"Target practice." Lucien leaned forward onto his right leg and stood, right hand braced on the bedpost. "How many can boast of a master who can hit a chamber pot at twelve paces? You are a most fortunate butler, Redford."

"So I tell myself every day, my lord. I am the envy of every butler in London."

"Sarcasm does not become a man in your position." Lucien dropped back onto the edge of the mattress and continued his search for his banyan. Several times his hand landed on a lump under the covers. Each time the lump wiggled a moment, grumbled, and settled with an exasperated sigh.

Clang!

This time the skull-splitting noise came accompanied by several loud thumps. The screeches of a querulous banshee wafted into the room from the slightly ajar French windows on the other side of the bed. Such a voice heralded only one thing. The creature Winterbourne moved into the house next door had a Scotswoman in her employ. God help them all.

"What kind of mistress comes with enough luggage for an invading army and a Scotswoman with a voice like a West

India dockhand? Mistresses do not require clothes at all if they are any good. Redford, for God's sake, where is my damned robe?"

The butler lifted the candle to the bureau across the room and opened the banyan, which had in all likelihood been draped over his arm the entire time. When he moved close enough Lucien snatched it from him and struggled into it.

"My lord, I am quite certain Lord Winterbourne would not be so ill-mannered as to move his mistress into Grosvenor Square." Redford moved to the French windows and closed them with a militant click.

"Who do you think the last fair occupant of the house was?"

"If memory serves she was the Countess of—"

"She was the penniless widow of the Earl of Hiddleston. She lived next door for precisely six months and left considerably plumper in the pockets and bejeweled than she was when she arrived."

"As you say, my lord." The butler, silent as a cat, placed a pair of brocade slippers next to the bed. One of these days, the man was going to frighten the life out of him with all his skulking about in the dark. Good thing Lucien had no fear and very little life left in him.

"Winterbourne cares even less for Society's good opinion than I do."

"I find that difficult to believe." The opening of the wardrobe door indicated Redford, as he did every day, intended to lay out clothes he knew Lucien had no intention of wearing. "Of course, his father is a duke. I would think much might be forgiven the heir to a duke."

"His father is a nightmare. If he were my father I'd move an entire brothel of mistresses into Grosvenor Square."

"To be sure, my lord. However, this lady is not Lord Winterbourne's mistress. I have it on the best authority she is his sister." As if the cacophony in the mews and garden next door were not enough, Redford began to tidy up the bedchamber. He started with the noisy items first—brandy bottles, wine bottles, and glasses.

"Winterbourne doesn't have sisters of an age to set up their own establishment. Could you leave those for later in the day, Redford? It is too early in the morning for this."

"It is three in the afternoon, my lord. And Lord Winterbourne has five sisters, all grown and out in Society."

Lucien whipped his heard towards the latest banging of glass on glass so swiftly the room began to spin. He fell back across the mattress. "I've known the man for ten years. Why have I not met these grown sisters?"

"Pardon my impertinence, my lord, but if you had sisters of an age to be introduced, would you introduce them to you?" A muffled grunt indicated he'd tripped over something in his patrol of the bedchamber. Good.

"Stubble it, Redford." Lucien stared at the gold threads in the canopy over his bed. The meager candlelight made them wink in and out like stars. The wiggling lump edged closer to him and with another sigh went still.

"Stubbling it, my lord."

Clang!

"Six years in this house. Six years and he comes up with a sister of age and insists on moving her in here in the middle of the night with every bonnet, slipper, and bit of frippery she owns."

A lamp flared to life on the mantel. "In here, my lord?" The man stared at him expectantly.

"Very well, next door. It is still an imposition."

"To move his sister into his own house?"

"Yes."

Another lamp began to glow on the cluttered desk in the corner. Apparently, even Redford had his limit when it came to stumbling around in the dark.

Lucien had not yet reached his.

A chorus of bottles and glasses landed in the empty coal scuttle. With a snarled curse, he sat up and clasped his hands to his head. The bump under the covers barked once and nudged Lucien's good hip. "For the love of God, man, show a little mercy." He winced as the banshee in Winterbourne's garden began to screech again.

"Perhaps the noise would not be so bothersome had the amount of brandy you had with dinner not been so much. My lord." In spite of the weak glow of the few lit lamps in the monstrous bedchamber, Redford made no attempt to hide the "I-told-you-so." expression on his face.

"I had dinner?" He said it only half in jest. Days and weeks had begun to meld into each other these last five years. He'd only just begun to admit it.

"Eels, my lord, in wine sauce."

Lucien's stomach roiled. Those eels threatened an encore. Not the sort of target practice he fancied. He lurched to his feet and sat down the moment his left foot touched the floor. In two steps, the butler was at his side.

"I can do this myself, Redford. I'm not a complete invalid." In spite of his words, Lucien allowed the man to pull him up.

"Of course not, my lord. I am simply helping you conserve your strength."

Once they made it to the French windows, Redford opened one of them a space. The cool winter air cleared Lucien's head. If he didn't move too much the eels might stay put. "My strength? For what?"

"You announced your intention to kill an architect and Lord Winterbourne. I should think such an endeavor might well tax your strength. I suggest the black wool Weston jacket for murder, my lord. It is less likely to stain."

Clang!

The bed erupted into a fury of barking.

The Scottish banshee began to cast dispersions on the parentage of some ham-handed cart driver.

"One more word, Redford, and I am going to stab you with my father's ivory handled letter opener."

"Very good, my lord. And then?"

"Then I'm going to kill Winterbourne."

A quiet sojourn to London?

Muttering under her breath, Lady Caroline Chastleton McAlasdair closed her eyes and fell back against the plump squabs of the carriage. She'd have done better to put a Good Friday vespers in the charge of Prinny than to task her brother with her *discreet* return from exile. Lord Alexander Chastleton, Marquess of Winterbourne, had once disrupted a funeral with a bout of fisticuffs. In the midst of seducing a vicar's wife, he'd set a conservatory on fire during a Christmas house party. He was the outside of—

"Mama, what is *ostentatious*?" Blue eyes the color of a Highland loch on a summer's day regarded Caroline from a delicately grave face tilted to the side beneath a ridiculously expensive white ermine cap.

"Your Uncle Alexander is the first thing that comes to mind, Lily, dear." She pushed the velvet curtains away from the carriage windows. The view had not improved. They travelled the well-paved, elegant streets of Mayfair. Not simply Mayfair, but the heart of Mayfair. She'd asked her brother to find her a little house on a quiet street in a modest neighborhood where she and her daughter and a small staff of servants might spend the Christmas holidays in peace. Caroline knew these streets as well as she knew every golden hair on Lily Rose's head. Modest and quiet they were not.

Grosvenor Square. The carriage steered a course as unerring as the sun's passage across the sky. He'd landed her right under their father's nose. She'd half a mind to tell the coachman to turn around and take them straight back to Scotland. What the devil had she been thinking?

"Yes, Mama but what does ostentatious mean?" Lily sat on the seat across from Caroline, her little traveling secretaire before her and quill poised to add this new word to her collection.

Caroline tossed a speaking look at the prim governess seated beside Lily. Miss Grace Howard, who had briefly, very briefly, been Caroline's own governess, merely raised her eyebrows and chased a slight smile from her features.

"It means no knowledge of how to behave without causing a riot on a daily basis."

"Really, my lady." Grace gave Caroline the look she'd given her a dozen times a day when she was only a few years older than Lily. "Ostentatious means overdone or designed to draw attention. Your mother might say the lovely cap Lord

Winterbourne sent you for the trip from Scotland is ostentatious."

"And what do you say, Miss Howard?" A twenty-year-old coquette lurked in the gangly body of Caroline's only child. She tossed her head and petted the silly cap, all the while batting her eyelashes. At only nine years of age, she charmed everyone she met. God help them all once she made her come out.

"I find it very becoming and quite lovely," Grace assured her.

"You would." Caroline rolled her eyes. "And don't you 'my lady' me, Grace Howard."

"You are the daughter of a duke and the widow of the wealthiest baron in Scotland." Grace leaned over to check Lily's penmanship. "What would you have me call you?"

"An idiot for ever agreeing to this return to the bosom of *society*. What on earth made me think this was a good idea?"

Grace made no attempt to hide her grin this time, and Caroline had no choice but to join her.

"Lady Rose McAlasdair," They said together and then laughed. The mere thought of Lily's formidable grandmother ever elicited one of two reactions—laughter or abject terror.

"Grandmama is a force of nature," Lily observed as she labored over the leather-bound journal strapped to her secretaire.

"She is indeed," Grace concurred. "She intends you to become a great lady, Miss Lily. That is why we have made the return to London." This last said for Caroline's benefit, more than the governess's young charge.

The carriage slowed to turn, hit a slight bump, and continued. Caroline glanced out at the stately mansions and dignified townhouses facing the garden square made only a little austere by December's icy hand.

"A discreet return to London." Caroline flounced back into the seat and threw up her hands. "Is that not what I wrote?" She waved around the luxurious interior of her brother's travel carriage. "First he sends this boudoir on wheels to fetch us."

"It is a very comfortable conveyance." Grace said. The fleeting grin was back and then gone.

"I like Uncle Alexander's carriage. There is room for me to sleep without wrinkling up my legs." Lily brushed her quill across her lips and bent once more to her journal.

"There is much to be said for unwrinkled legs." Grace coughed behind her hand. The woman was about to burst to keep from laughing. Drat her.

"I asked for a small house on an out of the way street." Caroline snatched the curtains back from the carriage window. "Does this look out of the way?"

"I am certain Lord Winterbourne has ascertained the whereabouts of the duke for the holidays. Your neighbors will no doubt be respectful and discreet."

"Discreet?" Caroline noted the tinge of hysteria and tried to modify her tone. She leaned away from Lily and lifted her hand to the side of her mouth. "My brother has all of the discretion of a Covent Garden doxie."

"Caroline," Grace warned. She inclined her head towards the seemingly oblivious Lily.

"He would not know discretion if it walked up and bit him on the *arse*."

As if to prove Caroline's point, the carriage gently rocked to a halt before the largest townhouse in the most elegant row of townhouses facing the most precisely planned garden in all of London.

With the precision of an opera ballet, a footman made quick work of the carriage door and let down the steps whilst the door to the townhouse opened to reveal her brother's personal butler, Brooks. Caroline took one look at the ornate steps and carved front façade rising at least four floors above the street and closed her eyes.

"My lady?" The footman stood ready to hand her out of the carriage.

"Brooks!" Lily plucked her journal from her secretaire and leapt from the carriage past the astonished footman.

"Lily." Caroline stepped from the carriage and glanced back at Grace.

"Miss Lily, a lady does not jump about the streets of London." The governess tugged the hem of her skirts free and followed her charge into the house. "Nor does she gallop up the steps two at the time."

"She does if she has been allowed to run wild in the glens of Scotland for five years." Caroline looked at the houses on either side of the *small, quiet* dwelling her brother had chosen. At present, they had the virtue of no curious servants, lords, or worse, ladies, peering from the long sash windows marching three and four across the front of each house. It had been five years since she'd lived cheek by jowl with her neighbors. And then only briefly. Mere weeks, in fact. She'd spent the majority of her young womanhood in her late husband's home—a fierce castle turned manor house in the Highlands. Her prison.

"Will there be anything else, Lady McAlasdair?" The coachman's inquiry jolted Caroline out of her unwelcome reverie.

Footmen, laden with the personal baggage from the carriage, stepped around her to ascend the steps into the house.

"No, thank you, John. That will be all for today." She glared at the lions on either side of the steps and marched into the entrance hall.

"Welcome, Lady McAlasdair." Brooks inclined his head and signaled for one of the footmen to take her cloak, bonnet, and gloves.

"Thank you, Brooks." Caroline looked around the marble hall and up the graceful staircase curving along one side of it to the first floor. "It is good to see you, but—"

A frothy blur of blue muslin and lace came bounding down the stairs and launched herself at the butler.

"It is so beautiful here, Brooks." Lily gushed, her arms wrapped about the butler's legs. "I am ever so glad you are going to be with us for Christmas."

"As am I, Miss Lily." Brooks being Brooks, plucked her ermine cap from her head and handed it to the waiting footman, all without batting an eye or cracking even a hint of a smile. His eyes, however, glowed with fond affection.

"Lily Rose McAlasdair, you do not bowl into your uncle's butler like a runaway sheep." Good Lord, perhaps they'd arrived in London just in time. Although a childhood here had done little to make Caroline a proper lady. It had taken something else entirely to do so.

Having divested herself of her own cloak and bonnet, Grace stepped up to peel Lily away from the unflappable butler. "Still in Lord Winterbourne's service, Mr. Brooks."

"We all have our crosses to bear, Miss Howard."

"My deepest sympathies, sir."

"Indeed, miss."

"Brooks, did you know discretion doesn't have teeth?" The little girl looked up at the solemn servant with equal solemnity.

Solemnity in Lily Rose McAlasdair never boded well for her governess. Or her mother.

"Miss Lily," Grace warned.

"Indeed, Miss Lily. That is good to know." Brooks, the devil, knew what came next would, in all likelihood, be inappropriate in the extreme.

"Because if it did have teeth," she said and danced towards the double doors just before the staircase. "It would bite Uncle Alexander in the *arse.*"

"Lily!"

"Miss Lily!"

The golden-haired imp in the guise of Caroline's daughter winked at Brooks and flung open the double doors. "What's in here? Books! Oh, look, Miss Howard, books, and books, and books."

Caroline and Grace exchanged a look.

"Miss Lily, what have we said about the removal of impolite words from our vocabulary?" Grace followed her charge into the library.

The butler bowed and waved a hand at the staircase in invitation.

"Was I ever that incorrigible, Brooks?" Caroline picked up her skirts and followed him up the stairs.

"No, my lady. However, I suspect Miss Lily's vocabulary was expanded by the same person who expanded yours when you were a girl."

"My brother's language has ever been far more colorful than polite company allows." Caroline stopped, stunned, and gazed at the large portrait hanging at the top of the first-floor landing. "And he has help corrupting my daughter in the person of her grandmother." She had not seen this painting in over ten years. A woman of twenty or so, wearing a hunter green riding habit and holding the reins of a magnificent bay stared back at her from a face so like her own she might have been looking in a mirror.

"I hope you left the other Lady McAlasdair well."

"Well and complaining about the evils of Sassenachs and their molly-boy manners." She turned to find his regard pointed and serious to a fault. "Where did he find this, Brooks?"

"His lordship has had your mother's portrait since the day your father bade me burn it, my lady." He stepped forward to adjust a vase of red roses on an inlaid Chinoiserie table beneath the portrait.

"Oh, Alex," she murmured. A communion of sorts passed between her and the brash young woman in the portrait. She and her sisters had each lost something when their mother died, but Alex, he had lost his heart. Caroline never understood the depth of that loss until Lily Rose. Not a memory she cared to explore at the moment.

She started down the thickly carpeted corridor. "I am glad to see you, Brooks, but why are you here? I assumed my brother would hire staff from an agency when he rented the house rather than take you away from your duties."

The first door she opened revealed a lovely drawing room, with some very familiar furnishings. Next came a music room. The large Broadwood grand in the middle of the room, while polished to a brilliant shine, looked well-used by someone who knew how to play.

"Brooks?"

"Yes, my lady?"

"Answer the question."

"The question, my lady?"

Caroline crossed her arms over her chest and narrowed her eyes. The man, servant or not, had been around her brother entirely too long.

"His lordship is visiting friends in the country for Christmas, my lady. He has no need for my services at present, and I believe he thought a familiar face might be welcome, especially for Miss Lily." He pretended to wipe some dust from the rich oak wainscoting, which met an exquisite gold silk wall covering halfway up the walls.

"He didn't rent this house, did he, Brooks? This is his house, isn't it?"

The butler chose to nod, rather than give voice to his answer.

Caroline groaned. "Does the duke know?"

"He is aware his lordship owns the house, my lady, but we have it on the best authority His Grace has retired to Chastleton Hall and will remain there indefinitely."

"Indefinitely? Why?"

"I do not know, my lady." Brooks was her brother's creature, but he did not lie. Not for anyone. Which was the reason he'd left the duke's service once Alex removed their sisters and threatened their father should he try to intervene. Alex had been too late to save Caroline, and he'd done everything he could to make up for it since.

"Are you aware there is a portrait very like you at the

top of the stairs?" Grace asked as she traversed the corridor to join them. "What is the matter? Caroline?"

Her face must have looked grave indeed for her former governess to address her by her given name in front of Brooks. "This is my brother's house. He owns it. And the duke knows."

"I thought I recognized the library."

"Please tell me you did not leave my daughter in a room full of my brother's wicked books."

Brooks raised a hand to interrupt. "The wicked books are on the top shelves, my lady and the library ladders are all in storage in the attic."

"Your brother knows his niece all too well." Grace tucked her arm through Caroline's and opened the last door on the left of the corridor to reveal a cozy parlor with an inviting fire in the hearth. "Might we have some tea, Brooks?"

"Right away, Miss Howard." He went to the bell pull to summon a maid. "And Miss Lily?"

"Is in the library completing an essay on discretion and the reasons we do not use the term *arse* in polite conversation. She may have tea and some of Mrs. McGillicutty's gooseberry tarts when she has completed her essay."

"Mrs. McGillicutty?"

"My cook, Brooks. She should have arrived this morning."

"Ah, she cooks. I knew she must serve some useful purpose."

Caroline looked at Grace and they tried not to laugh.

"Has she been causing you trouble, Brooks?"

"Not at all, Miss Howard. She has been no trouble at all

unless one counts terrifying the maids, threatening to string the pot boy up by his toes, and announcing her presence to the entire square."

"Good Lord." Caroline collapsed into a chair by the fire. "She'll have the neighbors up in arms."

"No need to worry about the neighbors, my lady. The house on one side is closed up for the holidays, and the house on the other is occupied by an eccentric lord no one ever sees."

"How do you know he lives there if no one ever sees him?" Grace never settled for less than every bit of information to be known. It made her a tyrant as a governess, but an infallible ally when one was fighting a despot of a duke.

"Lord Debenwood does venture out of the house one night a year. Only the one night." Brooks went to the door to let in the maid with the tea tray. He instructed her to place it on the tea table next to Grace's chair. With a modicum of movements and a brief curtsy she was gone.

Caroline's stomach clinched. Grace began to pour the tea. She said something about the oddities of peers and how society tended to ignore them. Brooks and Grace, the room, the tea service—they swam just out of reach in a blur of sound and motion.

"What night?" Her mouth said the words. Somehow.

"My lady?"

"What night is it? The one night he comes out?" She didn't want to know. Not really.

"Christmas Eve, my lady. As regular as clockwork for the last five years."

Grace paused in the pouring of tea. Brooks looked at her

and then at Caroline expectantly. "I think we have everything we need, Mr. Brooks."

He hesitated but a moment, bowed to Caroline, and quitted the room.

"Debenwood," Grace said softly. "Is that..."

"Lord Lucien Rollinsby. Viscount Debenwood." Caroline had not said the name aloud for five years. "The man who helped me kill Dickie Forsythe."

Chapter Two

Lucien had finally done it. After years of trying, he'd actually managed to shock his servants. His male servants, that is. He had an unfortunate tendency to shock his female servants on a regular basis. None of them cared for his penchant for lying around half-dressed. Which might be quite lowering if he gave it much thought.

Today, however, he'd turned his small, disciplined brigade of footmen into gawking, fumbling, country bumpkins. Lucien had taken a bath. Whilst this was not a completely unusual occurrence, he bathed now and again, whether he felt the need to or not, his servants had behaved as if it were nothing short of Admiral Nelson's resurrection.

Before his life went to hell, he had bathed every day. Once his self-imposed exile began, he saw the point less and less. When one seldom left the house, why bother? And in the month of December he never bathed at all. Which was part of the reason the footmen stared at him as if he'd sprouted a second head until Redford dismissed them with one of his lethal, down his considerably pointed nose stares.

December crept up on him this year. Not bathing for the entire month was part of his penance. Any servant within sniffing range paid the penance as well, but Lucien always made certain his Boxing Day gifts were more than generous.

He sat on his bed in a clean robe, his hair still wet from washing. No explanation came to mind. He'd grown accustomed to wallowing in his guilt. The entire household had grown accustomed right along with him. Yet, this morning... He glanced at the ormolu clock on the mantel. Very well, this afternoon, he'd called for a bath. And it was December.

Perhaps it was in honor of the blessed silence, which had at last descended on his new neighbor's back garden. Winterbourne's sister had been in residence a mere twenty-four hours, and the noise of her arrival had finally ceased.

It was too much to hope the banshee in her employ had hied back to Scotland. Perhaps her ladyship had muzzled the woman once she terrorized every creature within the sound of her voice. Which included all of Mayfair and the greater part of London. One of those creatures wiggled from beneath the heavy comforter and nudged his furry head beneath Lucien's hand.

"You should have a bath as well, Bonaparte." He scratched behind the little fellow's ears absently. "Your odor is damned pungent when it doesn't have mine to compete with it." The white scrap of fur jumped down and trotted to the French windows.

Lucien levered himself off the bed and limped over to let him outside. He followed Bonaparte onto the balcony overlooking his own back garden. The neat flower beds and cleanly swept paths lay dormant now. In spring and summer someone, Redford, no doubt, borrowed a gardener or two from Debenwood to stir the small piece of the country into an artist's palette of colors and life. God alone knew why.

Lucien never ventured farther than the balcony, save for one night a year.

Bonaparte bounded down the stone steps onto the small terrace outside the downstairs drawing room. Lucien watched him sniff along a square of boxwoods and disappear behind a fountain of Neptune driving a pair of dolphins. The lord of the seas and his team looked a bit forlorn as the fountain had been turned off for the winter. A few minutes later, his mission apparently accomplished, Bonaparte trotted along the ivy-covered wall between Lucien's garden and Winterbourne's.

The wind flung tiny needles of cold at Lucien's face. At least he'd remembered to slide his feet into the slippers Redford left at his bedside. The slivers of ice would soon turn to rain or even snow in a day or two. The sky had the settled-in look of a chill determined to stay, like unwanted distant relations come for a visit.

An insistent bark drew his attention back to the garden wall. Bonaparte spun around in circles at the far end of the wall where it met the wrought-iron fence that portioned the garden off from the mews. Foolish creature. He barked, scratched at the ivy-covered wall, and spun in circles again. What was he up to?

Lucien tightened the belt of his robe and took two halting steps toward the stairs. He nearly tripped over the quilted black velvet wrapped around his body. What the devil. Two things halted him in his tracks. Besides almost falling *arse* over teakettle.

First, he never left the balcony.

Ever.

Damned dog.

Second, this was not his robe. He glanced down and ran his hand over the fabric. It was thick, warm, and perfectly suited for brisk weather. It was new. He had not ventured out to purchase such a garment. He had not summoned a tailor to the house to measure him for such a garment. He had neither wanted nor needed new garments of any sort in years.

Redford.

Damned butler.

"Bonaparte!" he bellowed. "Stop that barking and come."

The little mongrel ceased long enough to give Lucien an impudent look and returned to his rapier sharp canine serenade. Silly creature had hardly made a sound above a grumble in five years and now he set Lucien's teeth on edge with his barking. Yesterday a shrieking Scottish harridan. Today a yapping dog. Not to mention an interfering butler. How was a man to sink into comfortable misery with all of this with which to contend?

He'd hired estate managers, men of business, and secretaries to deal with his responsibilities to his mother— God save him—his title, his lands, and his people. Apparently, he needed to hire someone to manage his butler and his dog. Perhaps the same person. Redford had the tenacity and nagging bark of a hound, and Bonaparte had the haughtiness and persistence of a butler.

Lucien braced his hands on the balcony balustrade and leaned over in an attempt to discover what had Bonaparte in such a frenzy. The garden marched from the terrace and fanned out to the stone walls at the sides and the ornate fence at the back in the same ordered formation it always did. Not a creature stirred within its confines save the lunatic dog dancing in the back corner and nipping at the ivy.

"Bonaparte, bring your mangy carcass into the house and cease that racket!" For a moment, Lucien sounded like the cavalry officer he'd been years ago. With all the roads to guilt he had to travel, he didn't care to venture down this one. Especially as his best imitation of Captain Rollinsby had not fazed Bonaparte in the least. Almost as lowering as the maids complaining about his state of dress.

"Fine. Stay out here and freeze to death." Something Lucien would never do as his butler seemed determined to protect him from every conceivable means of ending himself. Redford was either in service to Lucifer or to the Viscountess Debenwood. Which of the two might be the worst master, did not bear contemplation.

He made his way slowly back into his bedchamber and dropped into one of the comfortable chairs before the fire. The volume of Marcus Aurelius he'd started months ago mocked him from the side table. Bonaparte continued to bark outside. Damn it. Lucien yanked the bell pull and picked up the book. He stared at the same page for an interminable time—at least he thought so—before he heard a scratch at the door.

"Come."

A young footman stepped inside bearing a tray of food, a pot of tea, and a bottle of brandy. Redford was a coward, but a clever one. The food smelled good, as the butler intended, but the brandy had the higher appeal. Once the footman placed the tray on the table, Lucien dismissed him with a murmured *thank you* and an absent wave, ignored the tea, and poured himself the first brandy of the day. Once it hit his stomach, he decided a piece of toast might be in order. It was hot and freshly buttered. All part of Redford's diabolical plan to make him eat something.

After the second piece of toast he settled into the chair, propped his feet on the hearth, and immersed himself in Aurelius's wisdom. Before long the warmth of the fire, combined with his full belly and the brandy, sent him into a doze. He had no idea how long he'd been reading and nodding off when it suddenly occurred to him Bonaparte had gone silent. Not exactly silent. Somewhere in the room a dog's steady pants and thumping tail indicated he'd made his way back into the house.

Lucien glanced up from his book towards the bed. The heavy tome slipped from his fingers and thudded on the carpet. He wiped his hand across his face. Twice. He checked the bottle of brandy. How much had he drunk? He gained his feet so quickly the pain he normally experienced did not have time to make the journey from his leg to his mind.

Seated on his bed, stroking the head of an ecstatic Bonaparte, was a girl. A blond-haired, blue-eyed girl of indeterminate age in a frilly blue dress and unbuttoned wool coat. She smiled up at him. There was a slight gap between her front teeth.

A little girl.

Ice crept into his veins. Around his head, a thick London fog lay siege to his brain. He'd finally run mad. And it wasn't at all what he imagined. No raving. No screaming. Simply a little girl petting a dog and swinging her legs off the side of the bed. She pulled a biscuit from her coat pocket.

"Would you like a sugar and spice? They're ever so good." She jumped from the bed and approached him, the slightly crumbled article in her outstretched hand.

Cinnamon. And nutmeg. And something more exotic.

Poppy seed, perhaps? Did hallucinations have a scent? She touched his arm. Her fingers were warm and sticky. Warm? Lucien stumbled back into the side table and sent the half-eaten tray of food and the tea pot flying.

"Get out," he rasped.

"But..."

"Get out!" He lurched towards her and raised his arm. "Go! Get out!"

Bonaparte barked and shot off the bed to stand between him and the child, who appeared ready to burst into tears.

"Go, damn you!"

The girl shrieked, dropped the biscuit, and fled out the open French windows. Bonaparte scurried after her.

"Bonaparte!" Lucien's left leg gave way and sent him crashing onto the remains of his breakfast. After two attempts to rise, he rolled onto his back. Sprawled on squashed eggs and kippers, it took him a few breaths to contemplate his situation. Lunacy turned out to be smellier, messier, and far less peaceful than he'd believed it to be. Damned inconvenient too. He'd taken a bath for this?

For a moment, perhaps two, all Caroline wanted to do was laugh. The entire house stood up in arms. Brooks, poor soul, had had to restrain Mrs. McGillicutty three times so far, and she looked to be arming herself for a fourth attempt to march out the kitchen door. The noise of chattering servants, a barking dog—where had he come from?—and the ever-sensible Grace Howard brought to mind an image of villagers who were armed with pitchforks and scythes, and were ready to go after some fairy tale monster.

Then she gazed at Lily's tear-stained face and her rage

fired anew. She'd vowed never to allow anyone or anything to ever hurt her daughter again, and God help any man who interfered with her fulfilling that vow. Whilst Lily's behavior—not only invading the man's garden, but his bedchamber as well—was the result of her somewhat unfettered upbringing in a remote area of Scotland where she was the doted upon daughter of the local laird; it still didn't excuse Lord Debenwood's behavior.

Ranting like a lunatic and chasing her out of the house. How dare he. Recluse or not, the man had no right to frighten the life out of a helpless little girl. He'd sworn at her. True, that particular detail had been Lily's favorite to relate, and she'd done so with great relish, but that was beside the point.

Right. To battle.

Caroline took the black mourning bonnet from the breathless maid who'd rummaged it from the half-unpacked trunks and raced into the kitchen to deliver it. She jammed it on her head and pulled the veil over her face.

"Lady McAlasdair, are you certain this is wise?" Grace spoke like any other household retainer, but a world of warning filled her tone.

"Look at her, Grace. She is terrified."

The governess turned her gaze to Lily, now seated on a bench by the fire, wrapped in a thick Scottish plaid with a mug of tea in one hand and two biscuits clenched in the other. A captive audience of footmen, maids, a groom, a coachman and the pot boy surrounded her as she regaled them with the tale of her narrow escape. For the fourth time.

"Very well, she *was* terrified." Caroline made for the kitchen door. "What sort of ogre swears at a little girl for offering him a biscuit?" She stepped outside and Grace followed her.

"The sort who has had his garden breached, his bedchamber trespassed, and his dog stolen," Grace pointed out. "A known recluse and a peer of the realm. We're fortunate he did not pitch her back over the garden wall. Where are you going?"

Caroline marched back into the kitchen and lifted the dog from his spot at Lily's feet.

"But, Mama!"

"He is not your dog, Lily Rose. You would do well to remember it the next time you climb over someone's garden wall. There are more than essays in store for you, young lady. Miss Howard and I both will be deciding your punishment for trespassing into a stranger's garden and breaking into his house, into his bedchamber, no less, like a common criminal. I am very disappointed in you."

"I didn't climb over. There is a door at the bottom of the garden. I went through the door. And I didn't break into the house. The doors into the house were open. I didn't know it was the gentleman's bedchamber until I was already inside. Bonaparte showed me."

"Bonaparte?" Caroline looked at the scrap of white fur and pointed ears in her arms. He tried to kiss her through the veil.

"His name is Bonaparte. I heard the man call him." Her wide blue eyes took in Caroline's black wool cape and the mourning bonnet. "Has someone died, Mama?"

"That remains to be seen, dear. Mrs. McGillicutty, do put down that meat cleaver. I am not certain I can explain the justice in gelding a lord of the realm to a Sassenach magistrate. Brooks, will you see that everyone remains here and resumes their normal duties?"

"Yes, my lady, but are you certain I should not go with you?" The butler glanced from the dog under Caroline's arm to the shiny cleaver still clenched in the cook's fist. "Or perhaps I might return his lordship's dog for you? Such a task is certainly beneath your dignity." How on earth had her brother landed such a devoted and high-minded butler?

"Perhaps. However, dealing with Lord Debenwood as he deserves is most certainly beneath yours."

"But, my lady—"

Mrs. McGillicutty growled as she drove the cleaver into the knife block. "Her ladyship ken wallop the likes of a Sassenach lunatic without the help of the likes of you,"

"There you have it, Brooks." Caroline tucked the little dog closer under her arm and strode into the back garden. Grace matched her stride for stride.

"Would it not be better to try the gentleman's front door one more time and have yourself announced?"

"We tried twice, Grace. If I have to hear that poor maid stammer through—*His lordship is not receiving today. Or any other day*—one more time, I will not be responsible for my actions."

"Bearding the gentleman in his den, so to speak, will possibly make him a little less disposed to an amicable discussion of Lily's wild highland sensibilities."

"If the man were a gentleman, yes. A man who swears at children does not own that distinction." Caroline threw the veil back over the bonnet and began to search for this supposed door.

"If he is the person you believe him to be, this constitutes a very bad idea, Caroline." Grace joined her in searching the ivy along the wall. "Do you truly believe this," she tugged on the veil, "Will hide your identity from him?"

"Yes, it is a very bad idea. But as I haven't had a bad idea in the past five or more years, I believe I am allowed this one. Aha!" She tugged several stands of ivy free to reveal a heavy wooden door imbedded in the wall between the two gardens. It stood ajar just enough for a nine-year-old girl to slip through. "Help me, Grace."

Together they managed to drag it open and Caroline stepped inside Lord Debenwood's garden.

"Caroline..."

"With luck, he won't know who I am beyond Winterbourne's sister. We've never even been formally introduced. That night was..." She glanced up at the balcony overlooking the quiet garden. "I doubt he remembers my name, let alone my face. I'm going to return his dog, offer an apology for Lily's behavior, demand an apology for his, and let him know exactly what I think of grown men who traumatize children. I'll be back here before you know it."

Grace touched her arm. "You didn't kill Lord Forsythe, Caro. It was an accident. An unfortunate accident no one in London even remembers."

"I remember." She did and for more reasons than anyone knew. "Let us hope Lord Debenwood does not."

"And if he does recognize you and you don't come back?" Grace smiled, but only a little and too nervously to be reassuring.

Caroline drew the veil down over her face and squeezed her friend's hand. "Send Mrs. McGillicutty with the meat cleaver."

Her courage and righteous indignation were all well and

good when it came to landing her in such situations. They tended to skulk off into the dark, however, when Caroline actually decided to take some action. Death was too good for her brother. She'd come up with a suitable fate for him later. Presently, she wanted to traverse Lord Debenwood's rather lovely garden without drawing attention to herself. No mean feat, when wearing a black bonnet the size of a coal scuttle and swathed in an entire bolt of black lace.

Fortunately, the more she contemplated the man's complete disregard for Lily's age and innocence, the angrier she grew. Anger had steeled her spine through the worst days of her marriage and lately through her dealings with her father. This hermit of a lord did not stand a chance. She reached the stone staircase that led to the monster's lair, squared her shoulders, and marched up the steps. The pair of French windows stood open in spite of the brisk wind that had been sweeping through the square all morning and into the afternoon.

"Lord Debenwood, might I speak with you?" Caroline called out. She waited a few moments and repeated her question, knocking lightly on one of the French windows's panes. Still nothing. Perhaps the element of surprise might serve her best. She knocked insistently, pushed the windows wide, and stepped into the room.

"Lord Debenwood."

"What the hell!"

A serving tray and a brown teapot flew past her head. Something very like a kipper landed on her foot. The dog jumped from her arms to snatch the kipper and run under the bed. And there, in a stained and rumpled velvet robe, stood what remained of Captain Lucien Rollinsby, Lord

Debenwood now. Tall, lean, and far thinner than she remembered, with sharp cheekbones, overlong black hair, and faded green eyes—but still him. Except at the moment, he looked as if he'd seen a ghost.

"Who the devil are you? And why are you dressed like a crow?" He limped to a bell pull and yanked it three times. Hard.

He didn't recognize her. So far, so good. "I am Lady McAlasdair, my lord. I am dressed like this because I am a widow. And I am here to demand—"

"Did you frighten him to death too?" He poured a glass of what looked like brandy and downed it in one swallow.

"Did I frighten whom to death?"

"Your poor benighted husband, madam. You do realize you are in my bedchamber." His eyes looked less faded now. Or at least she thought they did. Looking at him through a veil didn't help matters.

She took a step towards him.

He made a clumsy step back and braced his hands on the back of the armchair by the fire. Was he afraid of her? Good.

Caroline renewed her verbal assault. "My daughter was in your bedchamber earlier, my lord. If she was brave enough to enter, I see no reason for me to be afraid. Do you have any idea—"

"Do all of Winterbourne's female relations intend to invade my privacy or can I expect—"

"Will you please stow your wids, you great sheep's head." She hadn't meant to shout. Nor to resort to vulgarity. Then again, this man obviously ate vulgarity for breakfast. Even better, he'd finally stopped talking. She'd better say what she came to say before the shock wore off.

"My lord, you frightened my daughter and sent her home in such a state it took half an hour to calm her down enough to discover what was the matter. Are you accustomed to swearing at young girls for the crime of offering you a biscuit?"

Stow your wids? She was Winterbourne's sister and no mistake. Nice figure of a woman too, if a man ignored her shrieking at him like a fishwife. Which it appeared he was content to do. Tall for a woman and slender with the exact curves he preferred, if he were in the market. Hadn't been in the market for quite some time, but today he had a notion to look. Once he realized she wasn't a demon of death come to drag his soul into Hell. What sort of woman swept into a man's bedchamber dressed like that?

"I offer you my sincere apologies on behalf of my daughter. She will be properly punished. And you will apologize to my daughter, Lord Debenwood, for your boorish behavior. As you are intent on receiving no visitors, I suggest you keep your doors locked and perhaps post a guard before you subject another child to your monstrous behavior."

"What color is your hair?" Nothing like coming off as a bedlamite to stun a woman to silence. For a moment or two, at least.

"I beg your pardon. Have you been listening to me at all, my lord?"

"You would have better luck making me listen if you would remove that ridiculous hat." He leaned on his right leg, tested his left, and moved slowly across the room towards her. "I am not in the habit of being vilified by self-righteous shrubbery." He didn't know why he wanted to see her face, only that he did.

She took a breath, probably to reload for her next tirade. Lucien chose his moment and snatched the bonnet from her head. And was rewarded with an indignant shriek. Even that did not put paid to the loveliness of Lady McAlasdair. Her hair was a rich brown, not chocolate, darker and with more warmth to it. Her eyes were a gray-blue color, fired with flecks of gold as she was in a state of high dudgeon. How soft her skin must feel to the touch. A cheek such as hers would defy any artist's brush. Shrouded in relentless black she glowed as fair as any angel he'd ever dreamt in any fevered imagining.

"My God, you're beautiful."

"W-what?" In that instant, she seemed frightened. Terribly so. Then she actually stomped her foot at him and scowled. And she was still beautiful. "Are you mad, Lord Debenwood?"

"Definitely." He took a step back and flung her bonnet onto the bed. It must be a favorite of hers as she didn't take her eyes off it. "You were saying?"

"Oooh!" She flung up her hands.

"Yes, after that." He couldn't stop himself.

"My daughter—"

"Has a great future as a house breaker, my lady. She slithered in here before I knew it and absconded with my dog and what little bit of peace and quiet I have had since your brother chose to foist you off on the inhabitants of Grosvenor Square."

"She is not a house breaker. She is a child." She kept looking away, which made it dashed hard to admire her. Perhaps he had lost his mind. God knows he'd tried long enough. "She has had an unusual upbringing and is unused to living where she is not welcome in every household. I will use this incident to teach her better. She followed your dog. She was curious. Children are, you know."

"One of the many reasons I do not like children, my lady."

"Then it is fortunate you do not have any, isn't it?"

Now she'd touched a nerve. Damn it. And he'd been too slow-witted to hide it from her.

"Oh dear. You don't, do you?"

"Don't what?"

"Have children."

"None of which I am aware, madam." Time to get the lovely Lady McAlasdair out. His hold on civility had reached its limit. "If there is nothing else, I would appreciate it if you, and your curious child, and the bellowing banshee you have in your employ would cease to plague me and leave me to live my life in peace."

"Nothing else?" She stalked towards him and pushed her delicate finger into his chest. "Nothing else! You owe my daughter an apology, sir. I have endeavored to assure her you are a gentleman. I try always to be honest and truthful with her. Do not make me a liar." She continued to poke her finger into the folds of his robe until she reached flesh.

She gasped. Her head snapped up. Her eyes met his. Lucien looked down at her finger and slowly followed it to her hand, her wrist, her arm, her shoulder, the curve of her neck, and finally her face.

Well, hell and damnation. Nothing for it. He grabbed her shoulders and crushed her body to him just before he captured her lips with his own.

Chapter Three

In her twenty-four years, all Caroline wanted, in her heart of hearts, was to be cherished for her flawed, irreverent self. When God wanted to punish you, he gave you what you wanted. Or so her brother always said. And right now, Caroline wanted Lucien Rollinsby to go on kissing her as if she were the most cherished woman alive. Nothing else could account for a brutish hermit of a man who, with nothing more than two hands and his mouth, sent her to a place so cool and fiery and soft as where she now stood.

She framed his face with her hands and gave more of what he'd already taken. He groaned and cupped the back of her head as his tongue teased and tempted and caressed hers. It went on and on, the heavenly meeting of their lips, the sighs, the moans. When neither of them had breath in their lungs, they broke apart with a gasp. He touched his fingers to her sensitive mouth.

"What is your given name, Lady McAlasdair?" he whispered.

Oh Hell's front parlor, what had she done? Wait. He started it.

"Why on earth did you kiss me?" She stepped out of his arms and commanded her limbs to stop shaking.

He grinned. He actually grinned. "It seemed a damned good idea at the time."

Of all the...

She drew back her fist and cracked him in the jaw. And it felt good. His stunned expression as he cupped the imprint of her knuckles on his face felt even better. God had a perverted sense of humor. Now she knew He was a man. She dragged her bonnet off the ludicrously large bed and marched to the French windows.

"I thought ladies slapped men who took liberties. Who taught you to punch like that?"

She turned to find him rubbing his jaw, his unshaven jaw. Had the man no sense of self-preservation at all? For tuppence, she'd draw his cork and kick him whilst he was down.

"My Scottish cook. And if you ever speak to my child again I will turn Mrs. McGillicutty loose on your nether regions with her meat cleaver."

She was halfway across the garden when she heard him call from the balcony.

"Lady McAlasdair? If I cannot speak to your daughter, how shall I apologize?"

Caroline refused to look back at him. "Write her a bloody letter, you insufferable crack-pate."

Of all the foolish, unthinking, reckless things she'd ever done, this one took the cake. Years of dignified, ladylike, irreproachable behavior thrown out the window for a few moments in the arms of the most rude, boorish, arrogant— *Where was the door into her own garden where she belonged?* She fumbled along the ivy-covered wall, scratching her hands on the stones in her haste to escape her own folly.

"Caroline, over here." Grace stuck her head around the door and motioned to her frantically.

"Thank God." She scooted past the governess and slammed the door shut. "He is without a doubt the most debauched reprobate in London."

"Did you just tell a viscount to write your daughter a *bloody letter?*"

Caroline stared at her former governess. They both burst out laughing. They laughed so loudly Grace tugged her across the garden and towards the house lest Lord Debenwood still stood on his balcony, the lord of all he surveyed. Idiot.

"I take it he recognized you?"

Grace's question halted Caroline mid-laugh. He had not recognized her. Not in the least.

"No, in fact, he didn't. It was the oddest thing. He didn't remember me at all." The realization stole all the merriment out of the situation. Why?

"That is a good thing, isn't it?" Grace squeezed her hand and peered into her face. "Isn't it, Caro?"

"Of course it is." She slapped the bonnet against her skirts. "It is a very good thing." An insulting thing. An infuriating thing. A most—

"Peculiar, isn't it?" Grace asked as they went through the kitchen to the front of the house.

"It was dark," Caroline mused. So few words to throw her back to the very worst moments of her life.

Grace looked at her askance.

"That night. It was dark, too dark to see my face. And we were all half seas over." She handed her cloak and the bonnet to the footman and she and Grace started up the stairs. "It was so very dark."

Grace looped her arm through hers. "You never told me, Caro. Not all of it."

She patted her friend's hand. "I don't remember all of it, Grace. I don't want to and apparently, he either can't or won't. Best all around if it stays that way."

"If you ever need to talk about it, I am here. Not only as Lily's governess, but as your friend."

"You are keeping enough of my secrets, dear thing. No need for you to take them all on. You haven't called me *Caro* in years."

"We have called each other many things over the years, Lady McAlasdair. Whatever the occasion calls for."

They entered the upstairs parlor to find a fresh tea tray waiting for them in front of the fire. Brooks was such a treasure. She hoped her brother paid him well.

Her brother, the fiend.

"I still cannot believe you told that poor man to write Lily a *bloody letter*." Grace handed her the cup of tea she'd poured. "Wait until Lord Winterbourne hears of it."

Caroline slumped into the overstuffed yellow chintz chair and sipped her tea. "Oh, Winterbourne is going to do more than hear of it."

"This does not bode well for your brother."

"I had contemplated killing him for landing us in Grosvenor Square. I have decided to do far worse than kill him."

"Which would be?" Grace adopted a similar unladylike posture in the matching chintz chair across the tea table from her

"I am going to introduce him to every unmarried girl in

London."

"Oh dear."

"And their mothers."

"Ouch!"

"And I shall tell each and every one of them he is in search of a wife."

"I think your brother may prefer you kill him."

Redford blinked at him and cleared his throat. "You need what, my lord?"

"A toy, Redford. You must have had some sort of useless plaything when you were a child." Lucien eyed the butler. "You were a boy at some point, weren't you?"

"I believe so, my lord. And I do have a vague memory of what a toy is and its purpose."

"Thank God for that because I haven't a clue. All I remember being interested in when I was a little boy was little girls."

The man sniffed and looked about the room. Which was a shambles, to say the least. "I see you enjoyed your breakfast, my lord."

Lucien glanced up from his desk. "I enjoyed it. Bonaparte enjoyed it. The little girl enjoyed it. Lady McAlasdair didn't enjoy it, but I did somewhat toss it at her."

"You tossed your breakfast at Lord Winterbourne's sister?"

"Somewhat." He continued to rummage through drawers and stacks of papers. "Send someone to Bond Street to purchase a toy for a girl."

"What sort of girl, my lord?" He plucked a clean piece of foolscap from the bookcase behind the desk and handed it to

Lucien.

"One who trespasses in gardens, slips unnoticed into bedchambers, and steals dogs." He picked through a series of quills crammed into a short, fat flower urn. "Where is Bonaparte, by the way?"

Redford nodded towards the French windows. The canine in question lay facing the closed windows, his head on his paws. On hearing his name, he looked at the two of them for a moment, sighed, and went back to his vigil.

"Don't even think about it, my shaggy friend. Those two women are nothing but trouble. We'll send over my letter of apology, and a nice gift, and if luck is with us we'll never set eyes on them again. Quill knife, Redford?"

He placed it on the desk and stepped back. "It isn't as sharp as your father's letter opener, but I prefer to be safe rather than sorry, my lord."

"Very funny." Lucien went to work on the best of the bedraggled quills.

"Am I to understand Lady McAlasdair's daughter—"

"Yes, you neglected to tell me Winterbourne moved a child into the house as well as his very lovely sister."

"I did not know, my lord." He had the good grace to busy himself setting the breakfast tray to rights and ringing for a footman. Redford always was a terrible liar.

"Bollocks. You know everything, Redford." He set down the newly sharpened quill and waited for the man to face him.

"I assumed you would never see the child, my lord."

"And you thought it might upset me." Lucien waved away the butler's response. "We didn't count on her breaking into the house, did we?"

"Indeed not, my lord."

"Well I cocked it up in fine form. I looked up and she was just there. I thought she was... well, I didn't handle it well. I sent her screaming from the room and then her mother showed up and punched me." Lucien rubbed his jaw and winced.

Redford handed him a cold, wet cloth. "That's going to leave a bruise."

"She learned to punch from her cook."

"The Scotswoman?"

Lucien applied the cloth to his face and nodded.

"Ah."

"Yes, well, I did worse with the mother than I did with the daughter and got this for my trouble." He turned up the lamp on the desk. What in God's name were all these papers? Ah yes, the end of the year reports from his stewards and men of business. He left the daily running of his estates to them, but had not been able to rid himself of the need to make certain all was done as it should be. A sense of duty was more often than not a pain in the *arse*. As was writing... "A contrite letter and a gift for the child and we should see the back of them."

"I realize you frightened the child, my lord, but a punch to the face seems a bit extreme for a woman of Lady McAlasdair's breeding and upbringing."

"I kissed her." Lucien pushed some of the papers into a basket on the rug. He looked his butler in the eye. "I kissed Lady McAlasdair and she punched me. Then she told me never to speak to her daughter again and to write her a *bloody letter*."

"*She said*?"

"She did. Now could you please send someone for a damned gift for the little girl and leave me to compose my letter in peace?"

"Of course, my lord."

Damn it all to hell. The problem with women was they dragged a man's emotions out of the pit into which he'd thrown them when it was hard work to shove them into the pit the first time.

"Redford, wait."

The butler turned and raised an eyebrow at him.

"None of this is your fault. You may not approve of the way I live my life now, but you must admit being a recluse has calmed my temper. I shouldn't take it out on you."

"You may do with your temper as you wish, my lord." He raised the latch and pulled open the door. "I am glad to see you still have one."

"I'm not. It's damned inconvenient."

"You kissed her, my lord? Was that wise?"

"Not in the least. It may well be the worse decision I've ever made in my life." Lucien rubbed the back of his neck and tossed Redford a grin.

"On the contrary, my lord. I think it may well be the best idea you've had in a dog's age."

"Stow your wids, Redford."

"Stowing them, my lord."

Tick-tick-tick-tick-tick

Caroline paused on the first-floor landing. The case clock to the left just behind her tolled the hour. *Four o'clock.* She knew the time even before the clock began to strike. The insistent *tick* of canine toenails on the ruthlessly polished parquet floor of the foyer and the chiming of the clock bore witness to odd routine into which her life had fallen of late. She started down the stairs and peered over their curved descent to see exactly what she saw every evening at this hour.

Lord Debenwood's Bonaparte. On his way home.

The furry white whirlwind on tiny clicking feet made his rounds as punctually as any beadle on the watch. Each day for the past week, Bonaparte had arrived at the kitchen door promptly at six in the morning. One could hardly blame him as Mrs. McGillicutty, a firm believer in the notion an army marched on its stomach, cooked a hearty breakfast for the servants before a more refined one for the rest of the house. Bonaparte had only to follow his nose to land at the back of their townhouse. He followed the kitchen maid in from her daily journey to fetch fresh milk for the household. Mrs. McGillicutty had expressed her opinion of London milkmaids' slugabed hours in two languages, complimentary in neither. She had it on the best authority cows gave the freshest milk first thing in the morning, not at noon as these heathenish Londoners believed. The best authority, of course, being herself.

Once inside, Bonaparte scurried up the back staircase to the nursery, jumped up to lift the door latch with his nose, and was settled under the counterpane with Lily when Caro came in to wake her for the day a few hours later. The little fellow spent every moment after at Lily's side. Whether listening, head cocked, to Lily and Grace at lessons or wagging his tail through Lily's practice at the pianoforte, his loyalty never faltered. Banished from her dancing lessons by the disapproving dance master, Bonaparte lay forlornly at the doors to the small ballroom until said lessons were done. After which, he growled at the dancing master and marched away behind the object of his affection, tail in the air, highly offended.

However, each evening at precisely the same hour, he abandoned Lily and returned to his master's house. No manner of inducement swayed him from his daily departure. Or so Caroline had been told.

This particular evening, she reached the foyer in time to see the white flag of his tail disappear down the corridor beneath the staircase towards the kitchen. Curious as to the exact manner of his departure, she followed him. To her astonishment, once in the kitchen he received a sugar and spice and a *"Good lad"* from the irascible Mrs. McGillicutty. The young pot boy hurried to open the door into the garden and closed it behind their shaggy visitor. The poor lad's eyes widened when he turned and saw Caroline standing on the kitchen side of the green baize door from the corridor.

"Beg pardon, milady," he mumbled as he doffed his cap and crumpled it in his hands.

"Not at all. Tom, isn't it?" Caroline crossed the kitchen to push aside the worn brocade curtains and look out the window over the large sink. "I wanted to know how our friend makes his escape to Lord Debenwood's." She let the curtain fall back into place and smiled at the boy.

"Yes, milady." He tugged his forelock and nodded. "I lets him out or Millie does. He goes through the door at the back of the garden wall."

"Makes his escape?" Mrs. McGillicutty snorted and lifted the lid on a pot simmering on the stove. "More like he escapes every morning when he leaves that madhouse next door."

The heavenly aroma of her thick beef stew filled the kitchen. Caroline, Tom, and Millie, the kitchen maid, paused in eye-closed appreciation of its magnificence.

"It's a wonder he leaves at all with the smell of your cooking in the air," Caroline said with a wink for the two younger servants. "But he is Lord Debenwood's pet."

"Amen," they responded with conspiratorial grins.

"Pet to a madman, I says." The stalwart cook blustered around the kitchen in an attempt to make them all believe she was untouched by their compliments. "Abed all day, up all night crashing about the house in the dark. Doesn't eat. Drinks all hours. Never sees any callers, not even his own mother." She turned from the work table, a carrot in one hand and a butcher knife in the other. "And, from what I hear," she said in what passed for a Scottish whisper as she waved Caroline closer. "He sleeps in the nude and frightens the poor maids to death of a morning when they come to make up the fires."

Caroline ignored the suppressed giggles behind her. "Mrs. McGillicutty, a good Scotswoman like yourself has seen many a man wearing but a kilt or a plaid with nothing underneath but what God gave him."

"Aye, milady, but God usually gives a Scot more worth looking at than a skinny, Sassenach lord. And the Scot has the sense to keep it covered up so's it don't get up to any mischief."

"Quite right." Caroline swallowed the bark of laughter fighting to escape her lips. She hurried out of the kitchen and back into the foyer before the image of Lord Debenwood shivering in a kilt overtook her. Her merriment, however, stopped short when she remembered what else her plain-spoken cook had said.

"Abed all day, up all night crashing about the house in the dark. Doesn't eat. Drinks all hours. Never sees any callers, not even his own mother."

She'd done this to him. Perhaps. Their paths had crossed that night because both of them had led lives bent on self-destruction. All the young men in his circle of friends did. Caroline had formed an attachment with one of them. A barely there, tenuous attachment which had led to that young man's death and Lord Debenwood's present state. Her reasons for courting reckless excitement had been raw and new then. What had his been? Would he have ended up a drunken recluse without the events of that long-ago Christmas Eve?

"Caroline, are you all right?" Grace stood in the library doorway, her expression one of concerned curiosity.

"Perfectly." Caroline shrugged. "Or nearly so. I followed Lily's beau into the kitchen."

"Ah." Her friend led her into the library. A robust blaze crackled in the fireplace. The Turkish carpet just beyond the hearth rug sported an array of picture books open to illustrations of tropical flora and exotic birds. "We created our own jungle as it was too cold for our walk today," Grace explained as they each took a chair before the hearth.

"I doubt Lily thought it too cold."

"Indeed. Miss Lily has her grandmother, Lady McAlasdair's, fondness for highland winters."

"And did Bonaparte enjoy your trip through the tropics?" Caroline used her slippered foot to rotate the largest book the better to see the exquisitely rendered flower and tree illustrations.

"He was with Lily," Grace replied. "Of course, he did. Though he slept through much of the journey."

Caroline settled into the velveteen comfort of the oversized armchair. Bless her brother, his affinity for life's luxuries had its virtues. She stretched her legs towards the fire and wiggled her toes in her shoes. When she raised her eyes, it was to meet Grace's rapier patient scrutiny.

"Mrs. McGillicutty had a great deal to say about Lord Debenwood's habits."

"She has struck up a friendship with his cook." Grace mimicked the Mrs. McGillicutty's disapproving scowl. "Neither of them approves of his lordship."

"I fear Bonaparte is the only creature in London who does approve of him." Caroline stared into the flames. "I have never asked why Bonaparte comes here every day. He loves Lily. That much is obvious."

"You want to know why he returns to the viscount every evening," Grace observed.

"I fear it is more than that."

They sat in silence. A log shifted and sent a sizzle of sparks up the chimney. Something spattered in steady beats against the long windows overlooking the square. Rain, or perhaps sleet. Caroline tasted it in the air. The wind had whooshed through the streets all day. It whistled still in the darkness outside those windows.

"It isn't your fault, dear," Grace finally offered in the soft voice Caroline had come to rely on over the years. "Whatever demons chase that man are not your fault."

"I cannot share your certainty. You don't know—"

"I have no need to know. We all have choices in life. No

matter what happens to us or who acts against us, we have the choice to fight back or to give up."

A tiny pang settled beneath Caroline's ribs. It had very probably started at Lord Debenwood's first arrogant, go-to-the-devil utterance. Somehow, the sight of the sturdy little dog making his way across the garden in the snow to a master who only ever insulted him or offered him a brusque dismissal made her wonder.

"Has he given up, Grace? Is that why he behaves as he does?"

"The man drinks every waking moment, never leaves his house, refuses the attentions of his physician, ignores his mother, and limps about the place in the dark clutching a brace of pistols. Either he is mad as a March hare or he is miserable and determined to stay that way." Grace blushed at Caroline's censuring cocked eyebrow. A skill Caroline had learned from her brother.

"Mrs. McGillucutty isn't the only one who has befriended our neighbor's servants."

"Mr. Redford is a loquacious fellow," Grace admitted with a shrug. "He felt it incumbent upon him to explain the viscount when he called to deliver the man's gift and letter of apology."

"Mr. Redford?"

"Lord Debenwood's butler."

"What else did he tell you?" Caroline fought to keep the urgency from her question. She'd known Grace for nearly ten years. It was nigh on impossible to hide fear from your average governess. And though Grace had been but twenty when they met, she was no average governess, then or now.

"Only that the viscount injured his leg five years ago, in a carriage accident. He was unable to rejoin his cavalry regiment and seems intent on self-destruction because of it." Grace narrowed her eyes and leaned forward. "Why?"

Caroline trapped the sigh of relief forming in her chest and let it join the pang beneath her ribs. Grace knew almost everything about her past. Almost was good enough. "I simply wondered what the man said to explain Debenwood's behavior."

"He explained it. He does not excuse it. You were there that night, Caroline. Debenwood was injured and young Lord Forsythe was killed." Grace touched the back of Caroline's hand. "You were there as were a dozen other people. Drunk or high-spirited or both, none of you is responsible for what happened. It was an accident. Lord Debenwood's response is his own. As is yours."

Unable to sit a moment longer, Caroline pushed out of the comfortable chair and paced across the room to peer out the window into the snow-flurried blackness. "I should not have been there. My husband had been dead but three months. And my daughter, my little girl—"

"Your husband," Grace sneered. "A hateful man over twice your age whose own mother despised him. What sort of monster marries his daughter, a girl just turned fifteen, to such a man?"

"The monster who hoped I would produce a son and secure the McAlasdair lands for the family empire." Caroline walked from the window to the huge globe in the corner. She spun it carelessly with her fingertips. "He was so disappointed I only bore the baron a daughter. *'Just like your mother'* he said. Just like your mother." She shook the memory from her head.

"Little does he know Lady McAlasdair will make certain Lily gets it all once she is gone." Grace's smile of satisfaction was a frightening thing to behold. She hated His Grace almost as much as his children did. Except perhaps Alexander. No one hated their father as much as Caroline's only brother did.

"Let us hope we can keep that secret from His Grace for as long as possible. He'll have me declared incompetent and seize custody of Lily if he thinks there is a profit in it." Caroline finally wandered back to the hearth and subsided into her chair once more. "The point is, I was here that night with Lord Forsythe when I should have been in Scotland observing my year of mourning. If I had been, that handsome flirt of a man would be alive and Lord Debenwood—"

"Probably would have died at Waterloo if his present life is any indication." Grace collapsed against the back of the plush chair and stretched her feet towards the fire. "I daresay had his injuries been earned in battle his grief might be less. Men tend to see the survival of wounds of war to be somehow more honorable."

"I don't know, Grace. Perhaps I cheated him of rejoining his men against Napoleon, even if he joined them in death.

"Caroline, you are only held accountable for your own behavior, nothing more. You should not have to pay with a lifetime of penance for a few weeks of madness and a night of poor judgement on the part of others."

"Is that what you think I am doing?"

"You have become a tedious, modest, retiring old widow at the age of twenty-four."

"Tedious?"

"Very. Save for your recent assault on our reclusive neighbor."

"Assault? I would hardly call it an assault."

"You planted the man a facer, and you demanded he write your daughter a *bloody letter of apology*." Grace gave free to a gust of laughter. "I have never been so proud of you in my life."

"Well." Caroline grinned, in amusement at her former governess, and in no small measure in relief she had not pressed her for more information about that awful night. "He did write her a very elegant letter. And the doll is quite the most magnificent I have ever seen."

"Indeed. The little plaid sash was an inspired addition to *Miss Debenwood's* ensemble."

"I cannot believe she named the doll after him." Caroline rolled her eyes.

"I can. Your brother will have to come up with quite the Christmas gift to surpass Miss Debenwood."

"Heaven help us. I do not want to think what Winterbourne will contrive to give her this year. Ah, Brooks, your timing is beyond compare," Caroline said as the butler entered the library bearing the tea tray. "I have been longing for a cup of tea."

The butler made a quiet, stately progression across the thick carpets to deposit the abundantly appointed tray on the tea table next to Caroline's chair. "I thought as much, my lady. The weather has turned rather cold and miserable in the last hour. Will there be anything else?"

"Nothing here, Brooks, but could you send one of the maids up to fetch Lily? I doubt this plate of sugar and spices is for Miss Howard or myself."

"Right away, my lady." He quitted the room with the same dignified stealth with which he'd entered it.

Grace prattled on about Christmas preparations and Lily's abhorrence of her dancing lessons, whilst Caroline poured their tea and only half listened. She'd told her friend the truth, but not all of it. For her own sake, she counted it an act of cowardice. But her life wasn't the only one in the balance when it came to the secrets she kept. For a moment, she wished Lady McAlasdair were here. She alone knew all of Caroline's secrets. And the lies, so many lies. The ones before Caroline's ill-fated trip to London five years ago to keep her safe from her father. And the ones after that trip to keep Lily safe from the world.

The formidable Scots dowager had been the one to spin them when Caroline had returned from London out of her mind with guilt and denied grief. None of it mattered now. She had not let herself refine on it overmuch in the last five years. Trust her brother to land her next door to the one man who had the power to cut through the lies she and Lady McAlasdair had spun – if he remembered. Thank God, he did not.

A scratch at the library doors and Brooks's uncharacteristically rushed footsteps across the carpet snapped Caroline from her brown study.

"My lady. Miss Howard. It appears we have misplaced Miss Lily." The butler's tight lips and clenched hands gave weight to the earnestness of his announcement.

Caroline patted his shoulder. "Miss Lily has no doubt misplaced herself," she assured him. "Grace, where was she supposed to be last?"

They both left the library and started up the stairs, Brooks fast on their heels.

"She excused herself to the nursery to help Miss

Debenwood change for dinner once Bonaparte left. Colleen went up with her to do some mending and keep an eye on her."

Colleen was Mrs. McGillicutty's niece and had come down from Scotland with them as nursery maid and an extra pair of hands when needed. She was young, but steady, and not one to put up with Lily's nonsense.

"Apparently, the maid excused herself and when she returned from the water closet Miss Lily was gone," Brooks informed them as they reached the second-floor landing.

The wide, carpeted corridor was in ferment. Maids and footmen scurried in and out of the bedchambers. Colleen came down the narrow staircase behind the inset door at the end of the corridor. Young Tom, the potboy, stuck his head from behind another section of the silk damask papered wall designed to hide the narrow steps that led down to the kitchen.

"I was only gone a moment, milady," Colleen pleaded.

"Undoubtedly, Colleen. Lily is to blame for causing such an uproar, not you." Caroline, unlike her father and later her husband, never blamed a servant unjustly. Lily had managed to escape under the watch of every single servant of the McAlasdair household on more than one occasion. Not to mention the times she'd slipped away from both Caroline and Grace's watchful gazes.

"She's not below stairs, milady." Tom announced.

Grace came out of the nursery. "I've searched every possible hiding place in the nursery, the schoolroom, and her bedchamber. Wherever she is, she is not alone." She held up one of the dresses from the considerable wardrobe that had arrived with Miss Debenwood. "The doll's coat and hat are missing, as are Miss Lily's."

"She can't have gone out in this weather." Brooks, face aghast, looked from Grace to Caroline.

"Oh, yes she can." Caroline exchanged a glance with Grace. "Colleen, fetch my wool cloak from my bedchamber and bring it to the kitchen door, please."

The girl bobbed a curtsy and dashed down the corridor to do her bidding.

"Grace, if you will supervise a continued search, I will go next door and see if my daughter has gone where I think she has gone." Caroline headed towards the hidden door from which Tom had appeared moments ago.

"You don't want me to come with you?" Grace asked as they walked down the corridor together.

"No, you stay here and keep Brooks calm. He is not used to disappearing children, poor dear." They turned together to watch the normally serene butler barking orders and pacing up and down the intricately patterned blue and gold carpets.

"Unless one counts your brother," Grace offered.

"Grace," Caroline admonished half-heartedly. "If I am fortunate, by the time I don my cloak and reach the door in the garden wall, Lord Debenwood will have frightened Lily into running home."

"And if he hasn't?"

"As tedious as it sounds, I will endeavor to retrieve my child without assaulting a peer of the realm. Again."

Chapter Four

Lucien fought to steady his hands as he accepted the unsteady cup of tea his little guest offered him. She'd slopped half the tea into the saucer when she'd poured so perhaps she would not notice should he slop a bit more. He glanced at Redford, standing at the open bedchamber door with an expression of beatific amusement on his damned face.

"Would you like another sugar and spice, my lord?" a childish voice inquired.

He turned his attention back to the tea table. The golden-haired child proffered one of the rather tasty biscuits she'd dumped onto the tea tray from a paper packet in her coat pocket. Bonaparte, seated at the end of the tea table closest to the fire, stretched his muzzle none too discreetly towards the tempting treat. Lucien plucked it from the girl's hand.

"You've had enough, Bonaparte. You've eaten all of yours and most of poor Miss Debenwood's." Lucien looked pointedly at the empty plate before the dark-haired doll at the other end of the table.

"She doesn't mind," Lily Rose McAlasdair assured him. "Miss Debenwood is not fond of sweets."

"No doubt," Lucien muttered. Redford cleared his throat.

"I understand the difference between a Covent Garden doxie and any other sort of doxie, but why did Mama say Uncle Alexander has the discretion of a Covent Garden doxie?" Blue eyes, very like those of the uncle in question, if memory served, blinked up at Lucien.

Redford had a sudden fit of coughing.

When Lady McAlasdair's house-breaking daughter showed up in his bedchamber this evening, Lucien found himself a bit better prepared but no less disconcerted. How did she manage to do this not once, but twice, without a great hue and cry going up next door? Children usually trailed an entire retinue of servants behind them, or such had been his experience. At least children who lived in Grosvenor Square did. Those who sold flowers on a corner in Covent Garden in the heart of a winter storm had no one to look out for them. No one to mourn their passing save a scrap of fur that snored in bed and a broken-down cavalry officer held here by guilt and the efforts of a stubborn butler. The memory of that child lay in wait around every corner of his mind, ready to remind him of his duty.

"Lord Debenwood?"

Lucien sat up and took a sip of his tea. His stomach rebelled almost at once. He swallowed hard and gazed at the bottle of brandy atop the chest of drawers across the room.

"Knowing your uncle, Miss McAlasdair, I am certain your mother did not mean it as a compliment." He licked his lips and forced himself to concentrate on the imp seated on the footstool across the tea table from him.

"Miss Howard says Mama insults Uncle Alexander because he is her brother and that is what sisters and brothers do."

"Miss Howard has the right of it. I haven't any brothers or sisters to insult anymore. I have to make do with Redford."

"I don't have any either. Brothers or sisters, I mean. And my Papa is dead so I won't ever have any."

"My condolences." Lucien bit into the biscuit. For some reason his belly had no difficulty with the gingery concoction. Perhaps Bonaparte was onto something.

"I think I should like to be your doxie," the angelic little girl declared.

Lucien choked down an entire biscuit and reached for his tea.

"Oh, dear," Redford muttered.

Oh dear?

His butler nodded repeatedly in the direction of the French windows, rather like a seizing chicken. The mysteriously *opened* French windows. The windows in which a horrified Lady McAlasdair now stood giving Lucien a glare of reproach so powerful as to turn him to a pillar of salt should he remain under it for long. Lucien lurched to his feet. A lightning bolt of pain shot up his leg. He grasped the mantel to keep his feet.

"Lady McAlasdair." He executed a shallow bow. "Would you care for some tea?"

"I should like to know, Lord Debenwood, precisely what you have been telling my daughter." Never had he seen a lady lovelier. Or more deadly.

"I asked Lord Debenwood what a doxie is and he told me, Mama." She dragged her cloak-clad mother to the footstool and indicated she should sit. To his astonishment, she did. Then again, the child had managed to persuade him to take tea with her, a doll, and a dog.

"And what made you ask his lordship such a question?" She stroked her daughter's hair and all the while accused Lucien with her eyes.

"You and Miss Howard wouldn't tell me. I came over here to thank Lord Debenwood for my gift and to bring him some of Mrs. McGillicutty's biscuits. He said I could ask him anything." She sent Lucien a dazzling smile. He hated to think of the men of London once she reached her mother's age. They didn't stand a chance.

"Oh, he did, did he?" For a man who had given up on feeling anything years ago, Lucien found himself aroused and indignant at the same time. She raised an eyebrow. A dare if ever he saw one.

"I made the offer after she plied me with biscuits and had already asked me every question imaginable. I didn't see the harm in one more." He offered a Gaelic shrug, only because he suspected it might annoy her. It did.

"One more? Biscuit or question?" She spied the child's coat and hat on the blanket chest at the foot of the bed and fairly shot up from the footstool to fetch them.

"Both."

"Why on earth would you answer such a question?" She wrestled her daughter into the coat and settled the wool hat on her head.

His leg tortured him mercilessly. Only yesterday he'd have sat down throughout her visit and damned all gentleman's manners and intruding neighbors to perdition. He wasn't exactly certain what made him remain standing now. "I was endeavoring to be honest and truthful with the child." He grinned in spite of the scolding scowl on Redford's face.

She stopped fastening her daughter's coat and slowly crossed the room to stand close enough to shake the snow off her cloak onto his bare feet. "You are endeavoring to be a horse's *arse*. And succeeding. Admirably," she muttered huskily between clenched teeth.

The rough timbre of her voice scraped across his skin with a pleasurable sort of pain. The pain brought about when coming from someplace very cold into someplace warmer than he'd ever imagined.

"Quite," Redford affirmed quietly.

"Stow 'em, Redford."

"Yes, my lord."

"I don't understand, Mama. Don't you want me to be a doxie?" Seated on the blanket chest, Miss Lily stroked Bonaparte's head. "I think it would be very nice."

Redford began to clear the tea table. Lucien couldn't be certain, but he thought he heard the man mumble, "Stop talking." Good advice. Too bad he'd never been very adept at taking the advice of others.

"What exactly did you tell my daughter?" Lady McAlasdair demanded.

"He said doxies are women who are paid to be nice to men who are lonely," Lily offered before he could answer. "Some men aren't good at making friends so they have to pay them. I think Lord Debenwood is lonely. That's why he is so angry all the time. I should like to be his doxie, but he wouldn't have to pay me. He's already given me Miss Debenwood, and he lets me have Bonaparte during the day. I could be his doxie as a trade."

Every time the child said *doxie*, Lady McAlasdair's color deepened from pink, to pinker, to pinker still. Lucien wondered if the color was the same all over her body. He raised an eyebrow exactly as she had done. He'd put on a pair of buckskins under his dressing gown for the sake of his little female visitor. Lucien crossed his arms over his chest to draw the mother's gaze to the vee of naked flesh where the garment gapped open.

"I am going to kill you later," she promised.

"I look forward to it."

"Come along, Lily." She took her daughter by the hand. "You've interrupted his lordship's usual evening activities long enough."

The pain in his leg had reached excruciating. In spite of that, he bent down to retrieve the doll from her place at the table and handed it to Miss Lily. "Thank you for bringing Miss Debenwood to tea, Miss McAlasdair," he said, his voice far more gruff than he intended.

She let go of her mother's hand and came to take the doll from him. For the first time, he noticed a slight hesitation in her step. Lily McAlasdair had the tiniest of limps. Perhaps only a fellow sufferer would notice, but he did. He handed her the doll. She tugged his hand and he bent down. She kissed his cheek.

"Don't be lonely, Lord Debenwood." In that moment, a soul as old as time peered at him from those childish blue eyes. Just as quickly, it was gone. "Good night, Bonaparte. I will see you in the morning." She skipped out the French windows into the night.

Lady McAlasdair stared at him, a petite frown creasing her brow. "Pray, what else have you told my daughter, my lord?"

"I told her one does not discuss doxies and lonely

gentlemen in polite society." He added a solemnity he reserved for conversations with his mother. "I told her all gentlemen are lonely but don't wish to be reminded. And ladies are jealous because there are no male doxies, a fact of which they too prefer not to be reminded."

Redford, who had given up on coughing discreetly each time Lucien said the word doxie, sounded ready for the undertaker.

The lady looked ready to make Lucien follow close behind him. She pulled her cloak tight, nodded at Redford, and stalked towards his balcony. "Good night, Lord Debenwood."

"Good night. Caroline."

"How did you—"

"Discover your given name? Bonaparte told me. He hears everything."

With a soft gasp, she hurried out the French windows behind her daughter.

He stumbled into his chair and bit back an agonized groan. Eyes closed, he massaged his thigh in an effort to persuade his screaming muscles to release their viper-sharp grip on him.

"Brandy," he gasped. "Now."

"Are you certain, my lord?" Redford, his cough miraculously healed, moved the tea table out of the way and positioned the footstool to lift Lucien's bad leg onto it.

"That's the only thing I am certain of, Redford." He gritted his teeth and opened his eyes. Bonaparte subjected him to a quizzical study from his spot on the bed. Lucien retrieved a stray sugar and spice from the floor and tossed it to his canine turncoat.

"What have you dragged me into, you shaggy flea tenement?"

Caroline stood outside the small, first-floor ballroom and watched her daughter storm down the corridor to the door leading below to the kitchen. Neither Lily nor Bonaparte looked back. It was safe to say they were both in high dudgeon. Grace came up behind her and squeezed her shoulder.

"She will understand the importance of all this in time, Caro. We knew it would be difficult at first."

"I allowed her to run wild for too long. This is my fault." She linked her arm with Grace's and they made their way to the drawing room across the corridor.

"Nonsense. I have been her governess for these four years, and I can tell Lily McAlasdair is a bright, happy, and healthy child. You have every reason to be proud."

"She called her dance master a pompous, old molly-boy." Caroline leaned her forehead against the mantel.

"I can just imagine where she heard that particular term." Grace moved to draw the heavy drapes against the cold.

"Lord Debenwood," Caroline fairly growled his name. "What is it going to take to keep her away from him? I thought surely after the *doxie* incident he understood I did not want her to visit him."

When Grace didn't respond, Caroline raised her head and searched the room for her. The governess stood at the window one hand holding the curtain aside and the other one at her throat.

"What is it?" Caroline asked as she joined her friend at

the window. Those at this side of the house looked across the narrow divide between her brother's house and Lord Debenwood's. Where pandemonium appeared to have erupted. "What is Lily's dancing master doing in Lord Debenwood's parlor?" The thin, balding man ran past the windows. And then back again.

"I'm not quite certain, but he appears to be—"

"Running for his life, apparently," Caroline mused. Lord Debenwood, actually somewhat dressed in breeches and shirt, limped past the window brandishing a—

"Is that a pistol?" Grace pressed her face to the glass and promptly jumped back to clap her hands to her face.

"Come along," Caroline grabbed Grace's arm and pulled her towards the drawing room door. "We have to get over there."

They stumbled down the front staircase so precipitously Brooks dropped the post in astonishment. Caroline snatched two cloaks from the stand by the door and tossed one at Grace.

"My lady, may I help you?" Brooks danced around the foyer in an attempt to help her into her cloak.

"Only if you know how to disarm a cupshot viscount," Caroline replied. "Grace, hurry."

Grace finally took her cloak from the footman trying to help her and flung it around her shoulders.

They dashed past the shocked servants and out the front door. The icy steps nearly did them in, but they managed to make it to Lord Debenwood's. Their insistent knocks were answered by a white-faced, wide-eyed maid.

"Where is he?" Caroline demanded as she stormed into the entrance hall.

"His lordship isn't receiving—"

"Oh, for heaven's sake. Grace, up here." Caroline took the stairs two at the time.

She and Grace arrived on the first-floor landing in time to see the dancing master, screaming like a young girl and hands batting the air, scurry out of the drawing room into the middle of the corridor. A disheveled Redford blocked the door with his body.

"I suggest you run, sir," the butler gasped. "I cannot hold him back indefinitely."

"Get out of my bloody way," the viscount roared from the drawing room. "Do it, Redford, or I'll shoot you too."

"Mr. Ballantine, what are you doing here?" Caroline took a step towards the beleaguered dance master, but stopped when he shrank from her in fear. "I thought you were in the library waiting for Brooks to have the carriage brought round."

The sound of glass breaking in the drawing room made him jump. "I was. This ruffian,"—He indicated poor Redford who kept glancing over his shoulder at the noisily irate Lord Debenwood.—"Arrived and asked me to step over here to speak with his master."

"I never dreamt he meant to harm the man," Redford replied. "My lord, please put down the pistol. There are ladies present."

A shot whizzed past Redford's head, narrowly missed Mr. Ballantine, and shattered a tall Grecian urn against the far wall. It was all the encouragement the dance master needed. He dropped to his knees, crawled past Grace and Caroline, got to his feet at the top of the stairs, and fled.

"Why did his lordship send you after poor Mr.

Ballantine?" Grace asked Redford.

An inkling of a notion tapped at the back of Caroline's neck.

"Did I hit him, Redford?" the viscount shouted from the drawing room.

The butler, arms braced on either side of the door looked to Grace and Caroline, obviously at his wit's end.

"Where is she?" Caroline crossed the corridor to stand directly in front of Lord Debenwood's long-suffering butler.

"She, my lady?" His cravat askew, his face covered in sweat, and his hair on end, it wasn't fair of her to put him in the middle of it, but he had fetched Mr. Ballantine, nearly to his death.

"Where is my daughter?"

His shoulders sagged in defeat. "She and Bonaparte are down in the kitchen with Cook. His lordship sent her down there before, well before..."

"Before he tried to kill Mr. Ballantine. Grace, come along. Redford seems to have everything in hand here. We are about to take my daughter in hand."

"Good luck, Redford," Grace murmured as she joined Caroline on the stairs.

"And to you, Miss Howard. Lady McAlasdair."

After a few wrong turns, Caroline found Lord Debenwood's kitchen. Seated on a high stool before the hearth, Lily was about to take a bite of a scrumptious looking gooseberry tart. As expected, the appearance of her mother and her governess in Lord Debenwood's kitchen served as something of a surprise.

Amidst the curtsies and bows of the servants, Caroline took the tart from Lily's hand. She lifted her off the stool, into her arms, and walked to the door into Lord Debenwood's garden. The cook opened it without a word. Bonaparte jumped up from his spot on the hearth. Caroline stayed him with a look. She suspected her face had this expression frozen on it from the time she'd entered her lunatic neighbor's house.

"But, Mama," Lily started. "It isn't four o' clock."

"Close enough, young lady. And the time is the least of your worries."

She and Grace trudged across the snow-covered garden. Twilight had not fallen, but it waited in the wings. The crisp, cool air did its best to compete with the ashy smell that was London in the heart of winter. Caroline had a momentary longing for the bracing cold and simple life of Scotland. Raising Lily had been so much easier there.

Grace struggled to push the garden door open.

Caroline handed Lily to her. "Let me try." She raised the latch and put her shoulder to the old wood and iron portal.

"Lady McAlasdair."

Lord Debenwood stood at the top of the steps leading from his balcony into the gardens. He'd even donned Hessian boots and an open greatcoat for the occasion.

"Caro," Grace said softly.

"I'll deal with him. Take Lily inside, please."

"But, Mama." Lily raised her head from Grace's shoulder.

"Now, Lily McAlasdair, or you'll be writing essays until your wedding day." In spite of her frustration with her harridan-in-the-making, Caroline smiled and squeezed her little hand. "Go with Miss Howard, love. I won't hurt Lord Debenwood."

"Promise?" Lily called as Grace chuckled and made her

way to the door Mrs. McGillicutty already held open for them.

Chapter Five

Caroline crossed her arms beneath her cloak and stared at the man at the top of the stairs. She refused to go to him. Men who swore and fired a pistol in her presence and chased off the best dance master in London deserved no concessions on her part. Of course, when she saw the effort it took for him to limp down the stairs, her conscience did prick her a tiny bit. The vibrant trepidation with which he prowled across the garden, like a wild creature caged too long, suddenly set free, and none too happy to be so, made her inexplicably sad.

He stopped a few feet from her and stared, as if he might discern her thoughts through her eyes. She shivered, and not from the December chill.

"What is it, my lord? It is cold, about to be dark, and I have had quite enough excitement for one afternoon." Perhaps Grace was right. Her remarks of late had gone to the tedious and prim.

The viscount scowled at her. He actually scowled. And then he lowered himself onto a stone bench against the wall between their houses. He shoved his hands in the pockets of his great coat and hunched his shoulders. Eyes closed, he leaned his head back against the wall. The wind rattled the limbs of the oak tree at the back corner of her brother's garden. The tree grew in one garden, but the branches hung over into the other. Still the man said nothing.

"I don't have time for this." Caroline started to leave.

"He makes fun of her."

"Who?" She stepped closer to catch his expression in the waning light.

"That prissy horse's *arse* makes fun of Lily." He opened his eyes. Rage burned there. A righteous rage born of some deep hurt. "When he is teaching her, he tells her she will never dance like a real lady because of her limp. He told her he would never have agreed to teach a cripple, but she is a duke's granddaughter, so he has no choice."

"I'll kill him." Caroline fairly shook with fury. How dare he? How dare that little worm!

"I tried." Lord Debenwood shrugged and shifted over to offer her a spot on the bench. "You and Redford objected to the notion." He stared out into his barren garden.

The trees and shrubs rattled in protest of the sudden onslaught of a toothy wind. It gnashed at Caroline's bones, but the pain of what her daughter had suffered for weeks at her behest made the pain of a winter's chill as nothing. Lord Debenwood turned from his perusal of his small section of London and glanced at the empty place on the bench.

Caroline reluctantly took a seat beside him. She didn't want company. His least of all. She wanted time to lick her own wounds before she attempted to heal the damage she'd done to Lily. How could she not have known? No. How could she not have listened? Lily had all but shouted it to the rooftops. Late to her dance lessons. Insistent Bonaparte attend and furious when Mr. Ballantine banished her furry champion to the corridor outside the ballroom. Angry and truculent once the lessons were done. A child who had danced every reel at every fete they'd attended in the Highlands suddenly despised even the idea of dancing. And Caroline had been oblivious.

"Don't cry." The rough words came accompanied by an even less gentle brush of large, calloused, thumbs across her cheeks. "Your eyes will freeze over and your face will crack. Put these on." Lord Debenwood shoved a practically new pair of fur-lined leather gloves at her.

"I don't need these." Caroline dropped them in his lap and scrubbed at her face.

"The hell you don't. You've been rubbing your hands together and sniffling since you left the house." He slapped a handkerchief in one of her hands and began to wrestle a glove onto the other.

"Will you stop?" In spite of her objection to the gloves, Caroline did make use of the handkerchief. That is, until he snatched it from her bare hand in order to work the other entirely too large glove over it. When he'd finished, he handed her back the linen square, shoved his hands into his pockets, leaned back against the wall, and closed his eyes once more.

Caroline cast about for something to say. Anything to avoid a conversation as to her failure as a mother. "You didn't tell me these gloves were so warm, my lord." She clasped her hands together beneath her cloak. "Where did you purchase them? I should like to have a pair made for myself."

"I had no idea if they were warm or not. Redford shoved them in the pocket of my coat. He has a nasty habit of buying clothing for me I neither want nor need. He's worse than my mother."

"I daresay you would not have attempted to shoot Mr. Ballantine had your mother been in residence."

"Wouldn't have to. She'd have shot him herself. She once chased a tutor out of the house with a lace parasol because he made fun of my brother when he struggled to read." His eyes remained closed and his pose never changed, but she saw a hint of a smile crease his lips.

Caroline leaned back against the wall and watched a few flurries of snow tumble about in the fading light. The quiet between them grew heavy, but not cumbersome. The pistol brandishing madman remained, somewhere just under the surface, but this Lord Debenwood offered a peaceful stillness just short of complete serenity. It settled her enough to order the turmoil threatening to boil over into grief or rage, whichever won out first.

"She never said a word," she finally said. "Not to me. She chose to tell you."

"She didn't actually tell me."

"If you say Bonaparte told you, I shall have no choice but to send for the men from Bedlam, my lord."

"I have tried to send for them myself. Redford keeps sending them away. Of course Bonaparte didn't tell me."

"I am relieved to hear it."

"He told Cook."

"I see."

"Miss Lily came to console herself with some of Cook's gooseberry tarts, clever girl. She told Bonaparte over tarts and tea. Cook overheard and lumbered above-stairs to interrupt my nap and demand justice for the *poor little angel*."

"I hope you didn't frighten Cook the way you frighten

your maids."

"I do sleep in the nude, Lady McAlasdair, but the sight of me naked ceased to shock Cook years ago. It's rather humbling actually."

"I made her apologize to him."

He finally opened his eyes and looked at her, his head cocked slightly in inquiry.

"She called him a molly-boy. I made her apologize to Mr. Ballantine for insulting him."

"You spend a great deal of time on apologies, my lady."

"I suspect you spend no time on them at all."

"On the contrary. My entire life is an apology."

"For what?" She regretted the question the moment she asked it. She didn't want to hear the answer. She feared she knew the answer. He'd spent the last five years living an apology he did not owe. Caroline had to tell him the truth. "My lord, I—"

He staggered to his feet. "Good evening, Lady McAlasdair." The viscount limped slowly back towards the staircase which led to his bedchamber balcony.

"Lord Debenwood, wait. I must tell you something." Caroline hurried after him. She clutched the arm of his greatcoat. He turned, his green eyes appeared a hardened jade color in the deceptive glow of twilight. She was suddenly afraid. Not for herself. For him.

"I'm a terrible mother," she blurted. She released his coat and turned her gaze to her hands, clasped tightly at her waist. His fingers, long and strong and made red by the cold, slowly covered hers. The leather squeaked as he squeezed. "Lily swears. And she climbs trees and can shoot a pistol. She drives a gig as well as most men. And she breaks into gentlemen's bedchambers and steals their dogs." Caroline raised her head to see his slight smile amidst a face composed of patently false solemnity. "She was ill when she was small. I wanted to make her strong."

"I'd say you've accomplished that, my lady. And then some." He tucked her arm through his and led her back to the bench. They sat down and leaned back against the wall together. He didn't release her hand. "How does that make you a bad mother?"

"My mother would be horrified. I brought Lily here to make her a lady. I forced her to study dancing with that horrible man. She told me she hated it and I didn't listen." Caroline's voice caught on a hiccup of a sob. "I didn't listen."

"You wanted her to be the belle of the ball. Just as you were, no doubt. A worthy notion for a lady." His eyes were closed once more, but an amused chuckle rumbled in his chest.

"I never attended a ball. I was married and shipped off to Scotland before I was sixteen."

"Good God." He pressed her hand tightly in his own. It sent an odd falling sensation rolling over her.

"Yes, well, God was undoubtedly sleeping, my mother was dead, and my brother was away at school. There was no one there to save me. I have Lily for my troubles. It was a fair trade. And now I've gone and mucked it up." His handkerchief dropped into her lap once more. Livid, she wiped her face. It had been ages since she'd cried. Years.

"I know little of your lady mother, but your father is hardly a model of parental accomplishment. I say you've done well for someone who became a mother so young and had no example to follow."

"You are acquainted with my father?"

"Somewhat."

"Would you allow his granddaughter to enter society as anything less than ladylike perfection?"

"Before or after his death?"

Caroline snorted. "You do know him."

"Enough to hope Miss Lily never has cause to meet him."

"She is a wealthy heiress. My late husband left her a fortune. His mother will leave her nearly a quarter of the land in Scotland."

"That settles it. I'll marry her. She has already applied for the position of my doxie." He looked at her now, eyes daring her not to laugh. She lost the dare.

"Good Lord. Can you imagine my brother's response to such a match?"

"Hell, no. Before last week, Winterbourne had never thought to introduce me to one of his sisters, let alone five of you."

"He is far wiser than I ever credited him."

This time he snorted. "Redford is of the same opinion." He sat up and chaffed her gloved hands. She watched him, the severity of his face at odds with the boyish grin that came and went, as if fighting to exist at all. "Apparently, I am not the sort of man one introduces to one's sister."

"Does Redford have a sister?" She should pull her hands away, but she didn't. Caroline had no memory of a man ever caring for her in such a fashion. Quiet tenderness, especially in this man, was a heady brew.

"I'm not certain Redford even had parents, let alone siblings. I think he sprang into existence fully dressed, with a permanent glare of condescension on his face."

Caroline succumbed to a long, watery laugh.

Lord Debenwood released her hands and propped his fists on his thighs. "Better now? No more talk of you being a bad mother?"

"I put dancing lessons ahead of my daughter's happiness." She jumped to her feet and paced away and then back. "How should I make up for that?"

He struggled to his feet. "You had lessons as a girl. Teach her yourself."

"I couldn't possibly..." The snow flurries grew more insistent. They dusted his hair and shoulders. He appeared impervious to the cold. And she wondered. "I don't have the proper skills. Lord Debenwood, what are you doing?"

He'd snatched her into his arms and waltzed her around three times before she caught her breath. Very skillfully for a man with a badly crippled leg. And he didn't let her go, in spite of the flash of pain across his face. For all the wind and open space, Caroline found it nearly impossible to breathe. And if the glint in his eyes was any indication, he knew it. Drat him.

"One does not need skill or lessons to dance, Lady McAlasdair. One only needs a heart for grace." He brushed the snowflakes from her nose, her cheeks, her eyelashes. "Children are born greedy, evil little monsters. I know I was. Miss Lilly is a bright, loving child with an exceedingly kind heart. That does not happen by accident. As far as I am concerned, your daughter is already a great lady. Teach your daughter to dance from your heart. It has done well by her thus far."

"Th-thank you, my lord." Caroline stepped reluctantly out of his arms. "Lily is very fond of you as well."

"With time, we must hope she will outgrow her questionable taste in men." He gave her a quick bow and slowly made his way back towards his house. "Good night, Lady McAlasdair."

Caroline watched him go. Each clumsy step sent a shaft of pain beneath her breast. The only light now came from the windows overlooking his garden. Redford had placed a lamp on every window sill. The butler, indeed the viscount's entire staff, looked out for him. And Lord Debenwood had ventured out of his house, something he never did, to… apologize for trying to shoot Lily's dance instructor? Hardly. To tell Caroline he knew who she was? Not even a hint of recognition. To look out for Lily, a child to whom he owed nothing. To comfort Caroline, to whom he owed even less.

"I'm going to Hell," Caroline muttered as she pushed the door between the two gardens open and slipped inside the one behind her brother's house. "Sulphur-reeking, brimstone burning Hell."

"You may be right, Caro."

Caroline shrieked as Grace appeared out of the darkness. "What on earth are you doing out here?" She clutched her chest and rested a hand on the governess's shoulder. "It's freezing." They hurried towards the open kitchen door.

"Things may be about to heat up," Grace said once they reached the warmth of the kitchen hearth. She gave Caroline a weak and wary smile. "Rumor has it your father is coming to Town."

"Hell's front parlor." Caroline flung off her cloak and peeled off Lord Debenwood's gloves to take the mug of hot chocolate Grace offered her.

"And then some," Grace agreed. "Whose gloves are

these?"

Chapter Six

What had possessed him to follow her into the garden? Worse, he'd given her advice on how to raise her child. Rather like the local cock-bawd advising the vicar on Sunday sermons. Lucien groaned and flung an arm over his eyes. He'd never played such a mawkish fool with a woman in his life. Five years had passed since he last even spoke to a woman who wasn't his mother or in service in his household. Perhaps he'd lost the knack.

He'd come in last night and sat in front of the fire for hours, with no company save Bonaparte and an unopened bottle of brandy. He'd crawled into bed just before dawn and still he did not sleep. She was consumed with guilt for choosing the wrong dance instructor. So consumed, she'd wept. And she was the last woman he expected to shed a tear in his presence. There was a fierce beauty in her far beyond her fair face and courtesan's figure. It called to him in a way he had no desire to answer. Well... He had plenty of desire. An uncomfortable amount of desire once the cold night air hit it. He had no right. Not anymore.

Lady McAlasdair had no reason to suffer guilt. He—he had every reason, which was why he had no claim to this sudden interest in life outside his self-imposed prison.

Nothing and no one had tempted him to limp down the seventeen stone steps into his garden. Until Caroline McAlasdair and her sprite of a daughter. Every step had sent shards of pain rattling throughout his body. Even now, his bones ached from the cold and the strain of crossing his garden. Coming back to feeling after five years numbness hurt in ways he never expected nor wanted.

Why, then, did he see her face every time he closed his eyes? The roses of her cheeks touched with the glitter of her tears. Her blue eyes gazing at him, demanding he be something he'd never be, perhaps had never been. Much more of this and he'd be in tears.

He'd set his course five Decembers ago when he climbed into a racing curricle, out of his senses with liquor and arrogance. His need to prove something, he'd long since forgotten what, had cost him a crippled leg, his military career, and two people their lives. Every night his sleep, when it came at all, was plagued with visions of the men who died in battle because he was not there to ride beside them. His beautiful neighbor might have the power to give him back his life. He did not have the right to live it. No one warned a man of the cost of his actions long after the action was done. A useful damned piece of information to have.

Enough of this. Lucien flung himself into a seated position on the edge of the mattress. He'd gone to bed in the clothes he'd donned to shoot Lily's dancing master. Damn, his bad leg was fond of neither treks across the garden nor the night's cold. He pushed off the bed and muttered curses as he crossed the room. He pulled the drapes away from the French windows and immediately let them fall back into place. Apparently, he'd slept a bit. From the height of the sun in the sky, more than a bit. Someone needed to inform the sun it was December. In England.

Brandy. He needed brandy. He limped to the fireside table and reached for the bottle. The bedchamber door burst open. Lucien flung the bottle into the air and fell against the mantel, fist mashed to his chest.

"Excellent," Redford announced as he caught the flying bottle. "You haven't opened it."

"Dammit, Redford." He took a few short breaths. "Are these attacks part of some bizarre plot to force me to stop drinking?"

"My lord?"

"Give me the bottle, Redford. You enter my chambers as some French marauder, give me a heart seizure, and nearly cause me to drop some of the finest brandy ever smuggled out of France. I need a drink. I need several drinks."

"My apologies, my lord, but you cannot drink this brandy. I have promised it to Cook." The butler cast a gimlet eye on Lucien's wrinkled clothing and rumpled appearance. "Perhaps you might forgo the brandy this afternoon." He tucked the bottle under his arm and made for the door.

"Cook cannot take up drinking. I'll never have another decent meal." Lucien dropped into the armchair before the fire and scrubbed his hands over his face. He needed a shave. In December? What difference did it make?

"If you had a care for Cook you would eat the meals she prepares rather than limiting your repasts to brandy, wine, port, and whisky. My lord." Being right did not make a pontificating Redford more palatable. "She has no intention of taking up drinking."

"I have had neither food nor drink since you refused to

allow me to end that prancing pony of a dancing master." A resonant growl erupted from his stomach as if to emphasize the point.

His pestilence of a butler strode to his side and slapped a palm across Lucien's forehead. Lucien shoved the hand away. "You are not the least amusing."

"If you are not ill, I can only assume nearly killing someone in a drunken rage suits you." Redford paled. He cleared his throat. "My lord, I…"

"No matter, Redford. It is December. For both of us." Lucien often forgot this man had stayed, when many butlers of his caliber might have sought a more congenial situation. He knew Lucien for what he was—a drunk, a scoundrel, a recluse, and a murderer—and his loyalty never wavered. "If Cook has not taken up drinking, why does she need an entire bottle of my best brandy?"

"To stir up the Christmas pudding, my lord." The man moved at what amounted to a sprint for any respectable butler and attempted to leave the room.

"Stop right there." Lucien struggled to his feet. Redford froze, staring at the door as if it were his last hope of redemption. "Turn around, Redford, if you please."

"Yes, my lord?" His gaze wandered about the room and refused to land on Lucien at all.

"Cook stirred up Christmas pudding for the servants on Stir-Up Sunday. Or was there another reason for the ridiculous noise and chatter in the kitchen two Sundays past?"

"Yes, my lord." Redford ran a finger beneath his neck cloth. A sign of the Apocalypse, to be certain. "I mean, no, my lord."

"I never eat Christmas pudding. Or Christmas anything, not to put too fine a point on it. Therefore, she cannot be stirring up a Christmas pudding for me."

"Of course not, my lord. You have expressly forbidden it. Every year."

Lucien snorted. "As if any of you heed what I forbid. She will not need brandy for the pudding again until Christmas Day. Am I correct in my assumption?" As Redford was never unnerved, Lucien was enjoying this.

"This bottle is for Lady McAlasdair's Christmas pudding." The words came out in such a huff, Lucien nearly didn't catch them. When he did, the hairs on the back of his neck stood up. A singular sensation when one had been surprised by very little for a number of years.

"And I am providing a bottle of my very best brandy for her ladyship's Christmas pudding because…?"

"It is a polite gesture?" Redford looked as if he wanted to adjust his neck cloth once more, but he restrained himself. Just.

"I am known for any number of gestures, Redford." Lucien grabbed the bottle, but Redford refused to let go. "None of them polite. Especially where the most expensive French brandy available is concerned. This bottle is not leaving this house." Lucien pulled again and still Redford refused to release it.

"No, my lord, it is not. Cook has invited Miss Lily, Lady McAlasdair, and Miss Howard here to help her stir up the pudding." He sniffed. "Apparently, *Mrs. McGillicutty* does not allow foreign cooks in her kitchen."

"Foreign? Cook is from Lancashire. Which practically is Scotland. That woman has a great deal of—" It struck him.

"Lady McAlasdair is coming here? Today?"

"Almost this moment, my lord." Redford snatched the brandy loose from Lucien's limp hand. "If there is nothing else, I will take this to Cook."

"Cook? The same Cook who invited strangers into *my* home to stir up a Christmas pudding with *my* brandy."

"Strangers? It isn't as if they have not been here before, my lord."

"Yes, and not once has it been at my invitation," Lucien shouted, without understanding why. "It is bad enough she barges into my bedchamber, *through my balcony doors*, whenever she bloody well pleases. Now my servants are inviting her in to take over my kitchen. I don't invite my own mother to visit in December, why in God's name would you think I... Redford? Redford, what are you doing?" Lucien stared at the bottle of brandy his butler had shoved back into his hand.

"I will allow you to inform her, my lord." Redford marched to the door, opened it and stepped into the corridor. "You may inform Miss Lily your self-pity and drinking are more important to you than her Christmas pudding. I will not be a party to it. Good afternoon, my lord." He bowed and slammed the door. Redford *slammed* the door.

Lucien stumbled back into the fireside chair, the brandy clutched to his chest. Wonderful. Redford was put out with him. Once the butler informed Cook there would be no Christmas pudding stirred up for the ladies next door, Lucien's goose was cooked. And his meals in future would not be. The last time he'd upset Cook, she'd sent up trays of half cooked eggs and burnt bacon and some sort of gruel for his supper. He hardly ate, but he enjoyed the sights and sounds of a good meal. Worse, if Cook conspired with the McGillicutty creature, his repasts for the next six months might be haggis and cold porridge.

Lucien shuddered.

With a foul oath, he wrenched the cork from the bottle of brandy. In the time it took him to spy a glass on the desk across the room, his fingers had settled the cork home once more. He slapped the bottle onto the tea table before the fire and levered himself out of the chair. He stumbled to the wardrobe and began to rummage through the clothes therein.

"This is a bad idea," he muttered. "A very bad idea. A ridiculously bad idea." He flung a black jacket and a white linen shirt over his shoulder in the direction of the bed. "I'm going to toss Redford into the street without a character. Right after I murder him." He backed away from the wardrobe and bent over, hands propped on his knees. "Where the devil are my black trousers?" He glanced at the brandy and then at his chamber door.

"Dammit," he bellowed. "Redford."

The door popped open as if on springs. Lucien fixed his butler with a fulminating glare.

"I have told you before, my lord, my Christian name is not Dammit." The butler glided across the room and poured the pitcher of steaming water he carried into Lucien's shaving basin. "An unfortunate oversight on my mother's part, to be sure." He whipped a straight razor up and down the strop several times. "Shall we, my lord?"

"Go to the devil." Lucien collapsed into the ladder back chair Redford pulled away from the wall.

"Even for such a short trip, might I suggest a shave?"

Redford floated a towel around Lucien's neck. "My lord?"

Half an hour later, cleanly shaven, dressed in fresh clothes, and hands shaking, Lucien stood at the baize door into the kitchen. He pressed his fingertips to the worn felt.

"I need a drink," he muttered. A suspiciously butler-like hand pressed to his back.

"No, my lord. You need to go into the kitchen and greet your guests."

Lucien nearly dropped the much-debated bottle of brandy. He looked over his shoulder at the diabolically serene face of the bane of his existence. "My... I have a mother, Redford."

"Shall I summon her so *she* can give you instruction on being a good host?" The butler did him the courtesy of retreating a step. A single step.

Lucien considered his offer, but not for long. "No. I cannot send her away without a character."

"How fortunate for her."

"You, however..."

"I beg you, my lord, do not raise my hopes." With that, the man palmed the door open and nudged Lucien into the kitchen.

A whore entering church was greeted with more noise than his entrance into his own damned kitchen. Even Bonaparte stopped mid-scratch to stare at Lucien in canine incredulity. He didn't remember having so many servants. Cook, at least two kitchen maids, a pot boy. He obviously needed a larger kitchen. They stood in expectant silence, frozen in place, and looked at him as if he'd suddenly grown two heads. Perhaps if he did, one would not be pounding like an infantryman's drum.

The normally chattering Miss Lily, swathed in one of Cook's aprons, had been placed atop a high stool the better to stir the large pot on the stove. An eerily silent Cook guided her hand. The doll, Miss Debenwood, had her own stool and sported a tiny apron as well. When the child smiled and waved at him, he could do nothing save wave back. And feel like an idiot. A nauseous, decidedly shaky idiot.

"Lord Debenwood, you've brought the brandy," an amused voice announced from just outside the pantry door. "How thoughtful of you."

"I am nothing if not—" She was laughing at him. With her eyes and her gently upturned smile. Happy. Lady McAlasdair… Caroline, in a hunter green dress and a snowy white apron, with a bowl of currants and walnuts in her long, graceful hands. And he was staring at her like a love-struck schoolboy. "—thoughtful."

"Indeed, my lord?" She strolled by and plucked the bottle from his hands. "I am happy to hear it. Christmas is a time of thoughtfulness." He watched her walk away, the tantalizing sway of her hips sending all thoughts of uninvited guests and what month it was utterly out of his head.

"Did he drink half of it, Mama?"

"Miss Lily!" the governess, Miss… Howard warned from her place at the large preparation table. She tried to sound sternly horrified. And failed miserably.

"Mama said if you did offer the brandy you would probably drink half of the bottle first," Cook's golden-haired miniature assistant assured him and then promptly swept her finger over the spoon. The kitchen suddenly burst into a tumult of activity.

"How *thoughtful* of her." Lucien fought the pressing desire to grin as the lady's cheeks turned a becoming shade of pink.

In moments, the kitchen hummed with cheery activity. The preparation table was laden with spices, cloves, fruits, and sweetmeats—all being made ready to add to the pudding mixture. Lucien had a vague childhood memory of Christmas puddings past, of a much younger Cook sneaking him currants and pieces of orange. The short, round Lancashire woman's black hair had gone nearly white now. More than twenty years had passed and still she stayed. What made him think of that?

The scent of cinnamon, lemons, and fresh heather awakened him from his reverie. "You can come inside, my lord. It is your kitchen." Lady Caroline's voice at his shoulder startled and settled him all at once. He didn't like it. His entire body pulsed with needles of sensation like a limb shaken to feeling after it had fallen asleep. A cold sweat popped out between his shoulder blades. Along his spine. He stuck his hands into his pockets.

"Take care, my lady," he said. She'd come to his side so silently and stood so close, a slight dizziness washed over him. "That is a treasonous notion. This is Cook's kitchen. We are mere peasants in her kingdom."

She gave his shoulder a deliberate bump. "Some of the peasants appear to be in revolt."

He followed her gaze to where Lily, whilst Cook consulted with Miss Howard, filched a handful of biscuits cooling on a tray and divided them between Jack, his pot boy, and Bonaparte. It was difficult to discern who disposed of their ill-gotten gains quickest, Jack or Bonaparte. Both gazed on Lily with obvious adoration. Lucien chuckled and shook his head. With a seriousness only a child possessed, Lily picked up her doll and held her up to the pot, their heads bent together as if discussing the pudding.

"If Miss Debenwood asks for a taste, I shall have no choice but to ask you to send for the men from Bedlam," he said softly, unable to resist the urge to bump Lady Caroline's shoulder. It sent a shiver coursing through his body.

"If Miss Debenwood asks for a taste, they shall have to fetch us both, my lord." Merriment fairly sparkled in her voice. She brushed her fingers down his jacket sleeve. "You are looking quite civilized this morning, if it isn't dreadfully forward of me to say."

"No more forward than Redford forcing me to break my vow of sloth in order to visit my own kitchen." A bit too much information there and not well done of him at all. She did not move, but she did not reply.

Childish giggles drew their attention to the quickly diminishing tray of biscuits. Young Jack made a show of carrying a bowl of oranges towards the pantry. He stopped in front of Lucien and Lady McAlasdair and tilted his head at the bowl. She quickly scooped up the purloined biscuits resting atop the fruit and handed Lucien several before dropping the rest into the pocket of her apron. The lad scurried around the table and handed the oranges to Miss Howard, who gave both Lucien and Lady McAlasdair a *shame-on-you* shake of her head.

"You McAlasdair women are set on putting me on Cook's bad side." Lucien popped a biscuit in his mouth and then was forced to swallow it whole as Cook fixed him with a scrutinizing scowl. Lady McAlasdair began to choke on the biscuit she'd bitten into and Lucien slapped her squarely on the back. Miss Howard snorted and clapped her hand to her mouth. The two kitchen maids sat heads bowed and shoulders shaking. Lily clutched Miss Debenwood close, her mouth a little "o" and her eyes bright with joy. Lucien winked at her.

"Aren't you glad you shaved, my lord?" Redford handed Lady McAlasdair a cup of water and moved past Lucien to cast his eye on Lily's cooking efforts.

Lucien rolled his eyes.

"It isn't fair, you know." Lady McAlasdair tucked her arm through his. "You punish Redford with your penance."

"I am punishing myself. And deservedly so. Do not make me something I am not, my lady." He'd spent so much of his time cold these five years, her heat threatened to burn him alive.

"I have no illusions about you, my lord. But in punishing yourself you punish him as well."

"He could always leave." Lucien had never thought about it before, what his life might be like without Redford in it.

"And yet he has not."

"Afraid I'll dismiss him without a character." Lucien glanced at her simply to see her smile and the something in her eyes he could not define.

"He has worked for you all these years. I should think that would suffice as character enough."

Lucien let loose a bark of laughter. It hurt—his lungs, his throat, his face. What the devil? The kitchen grew silent. What were they staring at?

"Do you have a sixpence for the pudding, my lord?" Lily broke the silence and her enthusiasm set the kitchen abuzz once more.

"I don't…" Lucien reached into his waistcoat pocket and drew out a sixpence. He handed it to Lily with a flourish and a bow that made her giggle. As he rose, he caught Redford's eye. The butler inclined his head.

The Christmas pudding preparations began in earnest. The cloth was laid out on the kitchen work table and everyone gathered around to do their part. Lady McAlasdair joined Miss Howard and Lily, still perched atop her stool, and the chatter and laughter grew until it filled the room. And through it all, Lucien heard the gentle tones and sultry music of Caroline, temptation of every sort and every thing he did not want or need.

His hands no longer shook. He took a breath and then another. His face ached. He was smiling. He was swimming, nearly drowning in sensations so strange and foreign to him he doubted he'd ever experienced them in all his twenty-nine years.

"Come, my lord. It is your turn to make a wish." Lily waved him over. Lady McAlasdair held out the spoon. And the world opened and closed all together in a jumble of light and sound. How was it possible?

His home had been invaded, split wide. A diminutive blond Atlas had lifted the weight of his ill-lived life from him as if it were no more than a doll to be lifted to view a Christmas pudding. And Winterbourne's sister? What manner of woman suffered the cruelties of her father as parent and yet raised such a child? What strength of heart did it take to rise above such an upbringing and become the sort of lady who brightened every room she entered with her grace and compassion?

"Hurry, my lord. Miss Debenwood wants a turn."

Lucien started across the kitchen. The room swayed to the left. Redford should have allowed him at least one drink before he came downstairs. The toe of his boot caught on the leg of the Rumford stove and he stumbled. Into the stool on which Lily McAlasdair stood. He heard the screams and the clatter of the stool on the bricked floor. He reached out, grabbed, and caught nothing.

He'd gone mad. The screams became the screams of horses. The noise, the breaking of racing curricles against the cobblestones of Covent Garden. And the little girl, broken and bleeding amongst the flowers she tried to sell to buy her supper.

Lucien dropped to his knees and gathered Lily in his arms. He brushed her hair from her face. Her mother and the governess knelt on either side of him.

"Lily," he rasped. "Lily."

"Where is Miss Debenwood?" She sat up and patted her hand along the floor. "Mama, is Miss Debenwood hurt?"

Lucien dropped his head to his chest. Lady McAlasdair laughed and took her daughter in her arms. Miss Howard retrieved a slightly bedraggled Miss Debenwood from the kindling box where she'd landed. All around him, relieved voices rattled along as if nothing had happened at all.

"She is not hurt," Lucien whispered. He raised his head to meet Caroline's blue eyes. "She is not hurt." A look of horror crept over Caroline's face. She knew. Someone had told her what he'd done.

"Lord Debenwood?" Lily scrambled from her mother's embrace and came to stand beside him. "I'm perfectly fine. Not even a bump on the head. Miss Howard says so."

He lifted his head to find her solemn eyes upon him. "I should not have come down. You might have been killed. I might have killed you."

"Did you mean to?" she asked.

"What?" He needed to get out of this room before he embarrassed himself.

"Did you mean to knock me over?"

"Of course not."

"Are you sorry?"

"Very much."

"Will you do it again?" Her childish voice grew more solemn and determined with each question.

"Never."

She threw her arms around his neck. "Then it goes away and we never think of it again. Love makes us ever so forgetful. It forgets all the bad things and remembers all the good. And if you truly love someone, you simply must forgive them."

"I don't understand." God help him, he truly didn't.

"Mama says if you are truly sorry and truly love someone, they have to forgive you." She kissed his cheek. "And I do love you, Lord Debenwood." She stood up and brushed off Miss Debenwood's dress. "Even when you are grumpy. Is the pudding ready to put in the cupboard?" Lily and Bonaparte trotted across the kitchen to Cook's side.

Lucien pushed to his feet. His leg threatened to buckle under the strain, but he did not care. He had to leave. Now. In his haste, he knocked the stool over again. He did not breathe until he had stumbled through the baize door and made it to the foot of the stairs.

"Lord Debenwood."

Anyone but her. He did not need to see the accusation and loathing in her face.

"Lucien, wait." Caroline grabbed his arm.

It was too much. "I was happy in my solitude. I'd found peace and resolve, as much as a man like me deserves. Your daughter is changing that and I don't want it. I don't want her to visit me again. I don't want either of you back in this house." His chest hurt. His throat burned and he was shouting. Shouting at the most beautiful woman he'd ever known.

"For heaven's sake, Lily is fond of you. It was a simple kiss from a child. It signifies nothing." She gave an exasperated huff and turned to go.

Lucien's mistakes tended to be over with before he realized they were mistakes. He saw no reason to change now. He wrapped his arm around her waist and pulled her into his arms. Her squawk of protest disappeared beneath the determined onslaught of his kiss. He'd never get the chance again, and he intended to take this memory to his grave. He sank into her heat and softness, teased and tempted, devoured and caressed her lips. She laced her fingers through his hair and tugged him closer. He had to stop. Now. Or he'd never let her go. He pressed her away from him. It took a few gasps for them to catch their breaths.

What had he done?

"And that kiss, my lady. What did it signify?"

She touched her fingers to her lips. "I don't know."

"Then God help us both, because neither do I."

Chapter Seven

A night and a day, Caroline had wandered about her townhouse, rather her brother's townhouse, in a sort of stupor. Abject guilt and tumultuous wonder tended to do that to a lady. Oh, she managed her household. She and Grace organized the Christmas festivities for their little family. Lily begged to go next door to "care for" her Christmas pudding. And Caroline made excuses.

She'd lain in her bed all night and remembered every moment from the time Lord Debenwood entered the kitchen to the moment he kissed her senseless.

"And that kiss, my lady. What did it signify?"

It signified she'd never truly been kissed in her life, save by this man. A man who would despise her if he knew the truth. She'd seen his face as the stool bearing Lily fell to the floor. The fear and anguish, his eyes caught in the memory of that Christmas Eve of five years past. She didn't have to ask. She simply knew.

Of course, Lily's fall had frightened her. Her daughter had suffered more in her nine years of life than many people suffered in a lifetime. But the frail and injured Lily was no more. Last night her miracle of a daughter had done as she always did. She'd bounced up like an India rubber ball. And

Lord Debenwood, as stubborn and strong a man as she'd ever met, had cracked like an earthenware bowl.

"Caroline?" Grace came to stand at her shoulder. "Are you going to spend the entire evening staring at the rain?"

"Rain?" She drew her hand from the windowpane and shook her head. When had it started to rain? How long had she been standing at the window staring out at the square? Hours or only moments? Most likely the same amount of time she'd spent mooning like some chit just out of the schoolroom over a simple kiss. A not so simple kiss. A soul-searing kiss that had shaken her to the soles of her slippers. She raised her fingertips to lips still sensitive from the press of his.

"Caroline, what on earth is the matter?" Grace's concerned face caused Caroline to shake her head.

"Lord Debenwood. When Lily fell, you saw his face, Grace. He was horrified." They strolled back to the drawing room fireplace and settled into the chairs on either side of it. "He may not remember me, but he remembers what happened that night and it is destroying him."

"He is allowing it to do so," Grace observed. "You have allowed it to make you a better person. And a better mother. You are not responsible for his frailties."

"Frailties." Caroline snorted. "Lord Debenwood is many things. Frail is not one of them." She picked up the glass of sherry she'd abandoned earlier. "I had no choice but to become a better mother. I had Lily. And a second chance. He has had none."

"Men's frailties are not as obvious as ours, Caro. Every day we wake up is a second chance to become a better person. In five years he has done nothing to do so."

"Until Lily trespassed into his bedchamber. He cares for her. And she adores him."

"I think she is not the only one." Grace studied her with those all-too-discerning grey eyes of hers. "You care for him, and as happy as I am to see you interested in a man, I am afraid this one poses nothing but heartache. For both of you, unless you tell him the truth."

"I want to tell him, but I cannot help but wonder if it would do more harm than good. Especially as I have no intention of pursuing our friendship any further."

"Friendship?" Grace rolled her eyes and raised the decanter to offer Caroline more sherry. "I do not kiss any of my friends the way you kissed him yesterday evening."

"I didn't kiss him."

Grace raised her eyebrows.

"He kissed me. And how dare you sneak about spying on me."

"I wasn't spying on you. I was spying on him."

Caroline pulled the embroidered pillow from behind her back and threw it at the governess. Who promptly threw it back.

"What should I do, Grace? Am I a coward for not telling him the truth of that night? If he is frail, as you say, would the truth help him or hurt him?"

"Only you can decide if it is cowardice or something else that guides you." A slight tap at the door caught their attention. "Just as only you can decide how much you care for Lord Debenwood, kisses or not."

"Unfair, Miss Howard," Caroline groused. She glanced at the ormolu clock on the mantel. It was nearly ten in the evening. An unusual hour for the servants to interrupt them.

"Come in."

"Unfair is my stock and trade, Lady McAlasdair. Ask your daughter."

They turned their heads to the open parlor door. Brooks stood in the doorway, an odd and unsettled look on his face. He appeared almost afraid to enter the room. Caroline was half out of her chair at once.

"Is it Lily?"

"No, my lady." Not another word more.

"Is my father—"

"Oh, no, my lady." Had the man been a papist, he'd have crossed himself. Twice. Her father tended to produce that result. In everyone who'd ever had to misfortune to meet him.

"For God's sake, Brooks, what is it?" Trust Grace to get to the heart of the matter.

"Mrs. McGillicutty came to me," he started.

"She came to *you*?" Caroline could not help her incredulity. Her faithful Scotswoman cook despised Brooks, or "that Sassenach prig," as she called him. She'd have thought the woman would not go to Brooks were her skirts on fire and he the only source of water in ten miles.

"No one is more surprised than I, my lady. As she was not in possession of her meat cleaver, I chose to follow her and..." He clasped his hands behind his back and cleared his throat. "It is Lord Debenwood, my lady. He is... not himself."

"Where?" Caroline pushed past the butler and started towards the front door. She had no plan and no idea what was amiss. She only knew she had to find him.

"Caroline." Grace's steady voice tugged at her common sense.

Caroline turned to find Brooks indicating the stairs. The three of them climbed to the first-floor landing and hurried down the wide corridor to the floor to ceiling window overlooking the back garden. The rain flung itself at the window panes, begging for entrance or advancing like an invading army. Thunder rumbled in the distance. Lightning illuminated the view with temporary flashes of white fury. Through it all, they heard it, the incessant barking of a blur of white racing along the wall between the garden below and the one next door.

"Why is Bonaparte out of doors on a night like this?" Caroline turned, with the intention to don her cloak and rescue her daughter's loyal friend.

"He is not alone, my lady," Brooks said softly. "He came to the kitchen door to fetch help. Mrs. McGillicutty tried to bring him inside, but he refused. She followed him and…"

A bone-chilling crack rent the air. Caroline braced her hands against the window panes and stared out into the night. "Oh, dear God. Lucien." Standing in the middle of his garden, clad in a white shirt and buckskins, he stood arms outstretched, bathed in the dangerous light of the storm.

"Grace, look after Lily," she tossed over her shoulder as she picked up her skirts and sprinted for the stairs. "Brooks, go next door and rouse the house. Find Redford."

"But, my lady—"

"Find him!"

Her slippers slid along the foyer and down the corridor towards the kitchen. She slammed the door open to find Mrs. McGillicutty standing at the kitchen door, a heavy plaid clutched in her hands. Caroline took the blanket and stopped long enough to squeeze the Scotswoman's hand in thanks.

She didn't remember crossing the back garden or struggling through the door between the gardens. The icy rain beat at her in an effort to drive her back. Fury and cold and wind howled in protest of her daring to breach the storm's rage.

And Lucien.

Lucien Rollinsby stood in the center of the storm, arms outstretched and head thrown back, shouting at the sky. His clothes clung to him like skin. He had on his boots, thank God. As if that made any difference at all. Caroline planted herself in front of him.

"Are you mad? What are you doing out here, you damned fool!"

He continued to shout at the heavens. The wind tore the words away so quickly she could not make them out. Perhaps there were no words at all. Only the agonized cries of a man driven to the last edge of his pain and unable to find his way back from it. Tears began to burn her throat and then her eyes. Not now. She had no time for tears now. Caroline tried to grab his arm, to shake him, anything to bring him back from the dark abyss into which he'd flown. His skin was ice cold and his arms like stone. She shoved against his chest—once, twice, to no avail.

"Lucien," she cried. "Lucien Rollinsby, stop this!" With no idea what else to try she wrapped her arms around his waist and pressed her lips to his chest. "Stop this. You must stop now. Stop!" she cried against his skin as she shook him. Slowly, his arms fell to his sides. She looked up into his face. He stared down at her, not seeing her at all. She wrapped the plaid around his back and with an arm around his waist turned him towards his balcony steps.

Almost that moment, servants poured out of the kitchen

armed with lanterns and blankets. Some were already dressed in their nightclothes. Others had obviously thrown on their clothes in haste. Bonaparte led the way up the steps to the balcony doors into his master's bedchamber. Redford, white as a sheet, met them at the wide flung doors.

"Oh, my lady, I am so sorry. I was reading and fell fast asleep. I did not even know he'd gone out of the house. He never leaves the house." He helped her to settle Lucien into a chair before the fire. One of the maids fetched two blankets from the chest at the foot of the bed. Redford used the blanket she'd wrapped around his master to chafe and dry the man off. And still Lucien said or saw nothing and no one. The servants looked at her in expectation.

"Build up the fire," she directed one of the footmen. To the other she said, "We will need enough wood and coal to keep it going through the night if we are to prevent pneumonia." The two young men jumped at once to do her bidding.

"Cook, we need some good strong tea, some bread, and broth."

"Yes, my lady." Who knew a lady so round and no longer young might move so quickly?

"The rest of you, we need a tub and as much hot water as necessary to fill it."

Every servant's eyes stared at her in horror. One of the maids finally said, "He does not bathe in December, my lady. At least he hasn't... until this year." They all nodded in agreement.

"There you have it then. It is *still* this year, is it not?"

"Yes, my lady," they murmured as one.

"We will need towels and bath sheets as well. At once, if

you please."

A much-bedraggled Bonaparte hopped up on the bed. Caroline snatched the clean towel from the shaving stand in the corner and wrapped it around him, rubbing briskly. "Good lad," she whispered as she hugged him close. "Good lad."

Redford looked up from his work trying to warm Lucien's bluing skin.

"Apparently Bonaparte came and alerted Mrs. McGillicutty to his lordship's... presence in the garden and she alerted Mr. Brooks."

"I shall have to thank her when next I see her," Redford wrapped Lucien, eerily silent and still, in a fresh blanket and drew the wet shirt out from under it to hang on the fire screen. He knelt down and drew off his master's boots and stockings.

Lucien blinked the rain from his eyes and offered her a weak smile. "We should sell tickets, Lady McAlasdair, for Redford apologizing to your Scottish banshee will be the show of the season."

"There he is," Redford said softly as he tucked the second blanket around Lucien's legs.

A footman came in to set about filling the wood box and the coal scuttle. He built up the fire and with a bow departed on silent feet.

"Stop fussing, Redford. The lady will think I am some sort of invalid." He tried to sit up and winced as his bare foot touched the floor.

"I already think you are a lunatic, my lord," Caroline replied as she finished drying Bonaparte and placed him on the bed. "Invalid would be an improvement."

He studied her, his eyes never leaving her face. The door opened and two more footmen came in bearing a hip tub. Several more servants came in carrying buckets of steaming water.

"Take it back," Lucien ordered.

"My lord, you will catch your death," Redford pleaded.

Still the viscount's gaze never left Caroline's face. "Take it back. It is December. And I have just partaken of a rather brisk shower bath, in case you have forgotten."

The servants froze. They looked to Caroline and then to Redford. The butler dismissed them with a wave.

"You too, Redford. I assure you Lady McAlasdair is capable of putting me in my place."

"Of that I have no doubt, my lord. My lady?"

"I will be fine, Redford. Thank you. Send the food and the towels up, if you please."

"And brandy," Lucien added.

"No brandy," Caroline corrected. Redford scurried out as if his life depended on it.

"I will remind you, my lady, this is *my* house. You may take your leave as well."

"And I will remind you that is Mrs. McGillicutty's best plaid you are wearing and I braved a bloody thunderstorm to wrap it around your bedlamite *arse*."

He plucked at the blanket. "Are you certain she did not poison it?"

"She used the last of her poison on the biscuits she sent over yesterday."

He smiled and shook his head. "You are soaked to the skin, my lady. At least come and sit by the fire."

Caroline marveled at how the howling madman turned

so swiftly to the gentleman he was raised to be. Her marvel turned to guilt when she remembered the role she had played in driving this good man to such madness.

"Lord Debenwood, there is something I must tell you." She settled into the chair, her hands folded in her lap.

"Any woman who insists I come in out of the rain must call me Lucien." He rose clumsily to his feet and limped to the bed where he dislodged Bonaparte from the counterpane and dragged the thick quilted article to wrap it around Caroline before he resumed his seat. "And before you say anything, *Caroline*, there is something I am going to tell you."

"My lord... Lucien, I would rather you—"

A brief rap on the door and Redford entered with a large tray of covered dishes.

"Redford, are you losing your hearing?"

"Unfortunately not, my lord." With a brisk efficiency born of years of training and years of getting round the surly viscount, Redford organized the offerings of bread, cheese, ham, broth and a pot of stout-smelling tea on the tea table. He placed two bowls of broth, two plates, two cups and saucers, and two sets of silverware to the side of the table, bowed, and left.

Caroline and Lucien stared at the food. "You need to eat something, my lord. You are pale, thin, and will no doubt have influenza by morning."

"I will, if you will," he offered.

Why couldn't she simply tell him and allow him to throw her out of his house? It was the proper thing for her to do. He'd be angry and more than a bit hurt, but he'd know he was not at fault. He'd end his exile and get on with his life. And he'd never speak to her again.

"Well, Caroline? What's it to be. Will you risk my coming down with influenza or will you join me?" He held the teapot poised over the teacup closest to her.

"You do not play fair, Lucien Rollinsby." She picked up a plate and began to fill it.

"No, I do not, my lady. I never have, which is how I ended up in this damnable fix in the first place."

She stopped and stared at him expectantly. Perhaps this might be opening she needed. He was gazing into the fire, his earlier madness lurking in his pain-filled eyes. "Eat your broth," she ordered. He pulled a face and reached for his bowl.

They ate in companionable silence. Oh, Caroline noticed the way he glanced at the bottles of liquor on the oriental commode across the room. Each time he did, she added more black tea to his cup or another piece of bread to his plate. She told herself it was to help him, to make him eat, when it was obvious he seldom did. She dared not admit once this midnight supper was done she would tell him the truth and lose any chance to ask for more kisses, more anything from this man she had so wronged. She pushed her plate away and pulled the counterpane more closely around her.

"Lucien, I want to—"

"I have a set of pistols," he announced quietly. "For the past five years, I have loaded them every December 1st and unloaded them on Christmas Day." He struggled to his feet and propped his arm on the mantel. He stared into the flames once more. "I know there is every sort of rumor as to why I never leave this house and why I do any number of the things I do."

"You don't have to tell me this."

"I know."

Caroline held her breath. She knew what it was to have a secret and long to share it with someone, anyone who might help you bear its burden.

"Five years ago, my brother died. Consumption. I returned to England on leave to bury him and to get the estate affairs in order so I might return to my regiment. I elected to spend Christmastide in London rather than at home with my mother, who was deep in mourning. Not terribly amusing for a cavalry officer of all of four and twenty."

Caroline saw the sadness in his smile.

"Christmas Eve there was an entertainment of some sort. A great many young people in high spirits. A great deal of liquor. A great many lovely ladies to impress. And very little common sense to be found. It began to snow." He limped to the French windows and gazed out into the rainy night.

Caroline read the tension in his shoulders and down his broad, thin back. She wanted to tell him to stop. She needed to tell him she knew the story as well as he did, perhaps better. She could not.

"A wager was made. A race was declared. Only two of us were fool enough to race through London in the middle of a snowstorm." He turned and leaned against the French windows, his fists clenched at his sides. "I will not bore you with the details, Caroline. You have a brother. You know what idiots we men can be. It was dangerous and fast and exhilarating and I wanted more than anything to win."

"Lucien." Caroline wanted him to stop, but she wanted him to tell her, because she feared he might break if he did not.

"In the end, I did win." His voice was raw. His eyes bright with unshed tears. "I made the turn into Covent Garden. Lord Dickie Forsythe did not. His curricle turned over on top of him. Mine shot past his before it turned over on me. The men of the watch managed to free the horses. Forsythe was dead where he lay. I am told I was nearly so, more's the pity."

"Don't say that." Caroline's throat shredded at every word.

"Forsythe lost his life. I nearly lost my leg. And it still might have been right and fair, Lady McAlasdair. Save for a little girl selling flowers on a corner of Covent Garden on Christmas Eve in the snow." He gasped a long, agonized breath. "When they lifted the wreckage of my curricle off me, they found her, a broken tiny angel with her last three roses in her hands. I killed her, Caroline. She was only four years old, selling flowers for her supper on Christmas bloody Eve. And all that is left of her is a little white dog and a grave in St. Martin's cemetery."

Caroline gasped softly as their canine chaperone woofed at the mention of his name. Bonaparte was there that night. She had no memory of the furry witness to that awful chain of events.

"So now you know my secret. It has been five years, one more than she spent on this earth, and still I cannot bring myself to use one of those pistols. How fair is that, Caroline?" He pushed the doors open and turned his face into the rain.

Caroline stood and dragging her counterpane cape behind her she wrapped her arms around him. She rested her head on his back and felt the shaking as dry sobs wracked his body.

"Let me go, Caroline. I had made my peace. I was ready to pay my penance. Then you and your daughter invaded my life and I cannot make myself do it. I was ready to go, damn you. Let me go."

"Your life is not your own, Lucien. It is not yours to take. For when you do, you are not the one who will miss it. If your life is over, it is others who will suffer the loss. Not you. I won't let you do this. You have done enough. It is time to get on with your life."

"What can someone like you know about death, Caroline?" He turned and allowed her to pull him back into the room and wrap the counterpane about them both. "I have lived with death for five years and never doubted my decision for a moment until you came along. What could you possibly know?" He cradled her face in his hands. "You are life and joy and every wonderful thing I vowed never to want again."

"I only know this, Lucien." She rose onto her toes and kissed him. She kissed him with all the pain and guilt and passionate desire within her. The storm continued to roll outside, overtaking the city with fury and the incredible power of nature. And in this room a storm broke as well.

He fumbled with the buttons and tapes at the back of her dress. They undressed each other in a frenzy that slowed only when they could do nothing but kiss, speak their desire with lips and tongue and breaths caught on the edge of the storm. Once he was naked, she pushed him onto the bed. The last of her clothes slipped over the side of the mattress to the floor. Caroline kissed her way down his body, warming him with her lips and hands. He groaned at every touch.

She ran her hand down the length of his shaft and he

bucked wildly muttering her name. She used her fingertips, gentle kisses, and swirling licks to bring him to the point of incoherence.

"God, Caro... Please!" His words came out in an agonized rush as Lucien reached for her. He dragged her up and in one powerful move had her poised above the flesh she had hardened to the point of breaking. She braced her hand on his arms and took him in, inch by delicious inch. Her body stretched and opened impossibly as he slid into her more than ready sheath. For a moment she paused, seated to the hilt on him as he pushed into her in a short powerful rhythm.

His hands molded themselves to her breasts. Caro moaned from the sheer pleasure of his touch. She caught the rhythm and took it over as he sought her breasts with his mouth in a near frenzy. Her cries caught in her throat as he suckled her, nipped her, licked her and then suckled again. Surely everyone in the house must hear them as their moans and gasps mingled in the primal, wordless song of passion.

A long low moan shook Lucien's body as he drove into her in almost painful thrusts. Caroline felt it begin—the crest of the tide of sensation that meant she was close, so close. She gripped his shoulders and drove herself onto him, matched him thrust for thrust. So in tune were they she could feel his body tighten, felt the explosion begin in him even as it roared through her from the place they were joined. Then it was there—a cataclysm of senses, his and hers. Caroline tasted his flesh on her tongue. The heat of his carved shoulders burned her palms. The mingled scents of sweat and sex, his sandalwood, her lavender filled her head.

Above it all—the sounds of their joined flesh, their cries of joy, the loud rush of their breathing—and the overwhelming beat of their two hearts made her feel more alive than she had ever felt. Lucien collapsed onto the pillows and drew her down, still joined to him. He wrapped his arms around her as if he would never let her go. His hands moved over her in a carillon of tender caresses. He kissed her temples, her cheeks, her hair which now fell wild and free all around them.

"Caro," he murmured. "Caro, I didn't expect... you were incredible... I can't... why did you...?"

Caroline laughed and pushed her hair away from her face. She gazed up into his exhausted and somewhat amazed face. "Which of those should I answer first, Lucien?"

"I have no idea," he replied with a grin. "I would like to know what I did to deserve such a surprise, for future reference, of course."

"Did you enjoy it?" A silly question, but she wanted to hear him say the words.

"Immensely, my lady. I would very much like to enjoy it again if you will tell me what I did to provoke such an assault on my person." His eyes sparkled with what must be joy. She had never seen it in him before this moment.

"You have been a complete and utter *arse* tonight," she started.

"Oh," Lucien interrupted. "In that case, I shall have no trouble at all provoking a repeat performance."

Chapter Eight

Christmas Eve arrived too soon. For the seven days since the storm, Caroline had lived a modest version of a life she'd never dreamt possible. Lily's daily visits to care for her Christmas pudding always ended with the three of them having luncheon together. A luncheon Lucien's Cook reveled in creating and Redford watched his master eat with the same pride and concern as any worried mama. Which was good as the viscount did not eat again until after Lily was tucked into bed and Caroline slipped next door for a midnight supper and a few heavenly hours in his bed.

For seven nights, they spoke of his childhood, and hers, and everything save his confession after she'd dragged him in from the rain. And just before dawn each morning, he stood at the top of his balcony steps and watched her cross his garden and slip back inside her brother's London home. His house was both his prison and his sanctuary. And Caroline came to realize he would never leave it, save for one night a year, until he knew the truth.

There had been no visit to Lucien's house today. Lily did not understand, but the opening of gifts and the little celebration Caroline, Grace, and the servants had put on for her made up for it. Lucien had sent over another splendid doll and a picture book of dogs. His gift from Lily and Caroline lay on the hall table. She did not know if he would accept it once this night was done.

"You are going?" Grace asked from the parlor door.

Caroline drew her cloak around her and fastened it at the neck. She pulled on Lucien's gloves, the ones she foolishly tucked beneath her pillow every night. Married at fifteen, she'd had no chance to be a silly, enamored schoolgirl. For a few weeks this December, she'd done so, and her memories of this December would have to suffice.

"I have no choice, Grace." She opened the front door to reveal her brother's carriage at the ready. "I love him and I have to tell him the truth. Will you wait up for me?"

Grace hugged her tight and then pushed her away. "Of course I will."

Caroline stepped out onto the doorstep. Her brother's silly lions on either side of the door sat covered in snow. White flurries danced down the street and brushed against the doors and windows shut tight against the Christmas Eve cold.

"Caro?" Grace called from the foyer. "All may yet be well."

The trip to Covent Garden did not take long. Few carriages moved along the streets of London on Christmas Eve. For the first time in five years, Lucien had not brought his pistols. He didn't think much past that. The closer his carriage drew to the corner where his life had changed forever, the more he fought the warring thoughts between his heart and his head.

For the first time since he began this annual ritual, he

had the faintest glimmers of what might be hope. For himself. And for some sort of future. All because a little girl followed his ragamuffin dog into his bedchamber and an Amazon dressed in black came to defend her daughter. Nothing in his jaded, selfish life had prepared him for the warmth and courage and passion that was Caroline McAlasdair. Every night revealed new secrets about the lady and more, new secrets about himself. Secrets he'd never dared whisper.

He wanted to live. Something had stayed his hand year after year. Perhaps Caroline and her mischievous daughter were the answer to all his doubts and fears. He hoped so.

He hoped.

The carriage slowed and rocked to a stop. Lucien grabbed the red roses on the seat next to him and braced his hands on either side of the door his coachman held open. He winced as his bad leg hit the cobblestones. The snow was coming down more heavily now. He patted his coachman on the shoulder and limped towards the corner he knew so well.

The Garden was empty, too cold for even the toughest of tarts to ply her trade. Or perhaps they stayed away in deference to the day. He was glad for the solitude. Lucien stood on the corner and stared down the street into the night. He had but to close his eyes and the sights and sounds of that night came to life in his mind. Every year he mulled over the same guilt, the same regrets. He'd sell his soul to go back and make a different choice. The things that drove him then—grief over the loss of his brother, arrogance, resentment of the new duties of the estate that fell to him, the desire to get back to his regiment and the life he loved— none of them loomed large in his mind's eye now. Well, none loomed as large as a golden-haired beauty who'd told him his life was not his to take.

"Good evening, Lucien." Conjured out of his musings, Caroline McAlasdair took the roses from his hand and placed them on the corner curb, exactly where the little girl had braved the cold to sell flowers on a Christmas Eve five years ago.

"Caroline, what are you doing here?" He cupped her elbows and drew her close. "You are supposed to be the sensible one." He kissed her forehead. "I'm the madman who leaves his house but once a year to place flowers on a corner."

She reached up to touch his face. Her sad little smile made his heart ache. He'd seen it dozens of times since she'd invaded his bedchamber and yes, his heart. He wanted desperately to know what made her so sad when all she brought to others was happiness and joy.

"I was here that night, Lucien. The night Dickie Forsythe died." She curled her fingers in the lapels of his greatcoat, as if afraid he meant to walk away.

What had she said?

"I was at the party when the wager was made. I was newly widowed and had taken up with Dickie almost the moment I arrived in London. By the time the wager was made, we were all half seas over."

"I don't understand." He didn't. His head grew cold and empty. Ice began to seep into his veins.

"Let me tell you this, Lucien." She rested her forehead against his chest. "Please."

He managed to nod.

"Dickie was too drunk to walk, let alone drive a carriage. I put on his coat and his hat. He insisted on riding on the bench with me." She gasped and shook her head. "Everyone was so merry. It swept us away. None of us was thinking. I was the one you raced that night. I crashed Dickie's carriage and killed him whilst I was thrown clear."

"I don't remember that, Caroline. I don't understand." She was there that night, which meant she knew everything he'd confessed to her. How could she let him go on like that and not say anything? "Is that why you moved into your brother's house? To tell me you were there. To tell me you knew my darkest secret all along?" The ice crept from his veins to his heart and his veins had turned to fire.

"I had no idea you lived in London, Lucien. We have my duplicitous brother to blame. But there is more. Let me tell you the rest before I lose my courage. Please."

"What else is there, Caroline? You were there for the worst night of my life and you have kept it from me since the moment you moved your daughter, her governess, and that Scottish harridan into your brother's house. Why?"

"I want your word." She stared into his eyes. "I want your word as a gentleman you will not reveal what I am about to tell you. You will despise me, but should you reveal the truth it would hurt the one person you and I both love. I want your word."

Lily.

"You have my word," he rasped.

"They took you home and sent for a physician. Dickie's friends took him home to his mother." She pulled out of his arms and backed away, almost in fear. "The beadles took the little girl to the Foundling Hospital. I followed them. She was in a bad way and the physician there said there was little he could do for her. I lost my daughter to the same bout of cholera that took my husband and dozens of his tenants. That is why I came to London, to bury my grief and guilt."

"Your daughter...?" His head hurt. The cold had gotten to him. There was no other explanation for the madness that seized him.

"Lily Rose McAlasdair died five years ago in Scotland. No one knew because my mother-in-law and I did not tell them. Had we done so, my father would have found a way to marry me off again. Lady McAlasdair wanted to give me time to find my own husband. Then we would announce my daughter's death. But we found another way. I found another way. I took that little girl you thought you killed from the hospital. I found the finest physician in London and swore him to secrecy. A few days later we traveled to Edinburgh where the physicians are finer still. I have lived in exile for five years to keep her safe. Not even my brother knows the truth, nor does Grace. She knows about the accident. She knows I am responsible for Dickie's death. She does not know her charge is an orphaned flower girl from the streets of London who will one day be the richest lady in Scotland."

Lucien shook his head. He took a step back and his leg nearly buckled. When she moved to help him, he raised his hand to stop her. "I sent Redford to the hospital. They said she died. I sent money to have her buried in her own grave instead of a common hole. Bonaparte followed him home. He was all the little girl had left." He raised his head and took in her pale face, her trembling bottom lip. "He was all *your daughter* had left."

"I did not know. My only thought was to make her well and pray she would forget her life before that night. She did. She is Lily Rose McAlasdair now."

"She is alive. I have mourned her death for five years." He took a step towards her. "For five years I have contemplated ending my own existence over a lie."

"I didn't know, Lucien. I did not dare inquire after you or Dickie's family or anyone who was there that night. My daughter's future depended on it."

"Your daughter is dead, my lady." Rage hurt. It hurt worse than any bullet wound or saber slash. He hurt and he wanted her to hurt, whatever the cost.

"No one knows that better than I." Her face lit with an anguished rage. "I was sent away when she grew ill because my husband feared I might be carrying his heir and that was more important than my daughter having her mother. I never had the chance to comfort my dying child. I never had the chance to tell her goodbye. I have no need to be reminded of what I have lost. I live with it every day." The tears in her eyes warred with the fury in her words.

"So you took in an orphan and gave her your daughter's name."

"I did what I thought best. In a moment of pain and madness I did the unthinkable. And now my *daughter* is depending on you to keep her safe, Lord Debenwood. I have wronged you and I wronged Dickie, but she has done nothing."

"Do you really believe I would do anything to hurt Lily? I love her! And I thought—" No, he would not say it. It no longer mattered. It was all a lie and he had to get away before he said or did something he could not take back. The last time he'd done so a man had died and he had thrown away five years of his life in mourning a ghost who did not exist.

"Lucien, had I known what you were doing. Had I known

you would mourn an unknown child so..."

"You did know, Lady McAlasdair. You have known for weeks." He bent down and picked up the roses. A few petals fell to the ground, like blood drops on a field of white. His wounds did not bleed, but they were no less the deep for it. "You took me to your bed. It is a pity you did not take me into your confidence. Apparently the joke was on me."

"Lucien, please."

He handed her the flowers. "Take these to Lily. I bought them for her. You got a daughter out of my folly. I got a bad leg and five years in a prison you made. Dickie Forsythe lost his life. Happy Christmas, Caroline." He crossed the street to his carriage, stumbling and slipping in the snow as he went. He did not look back. All the hope and trust and desires for the future lay in the snow like fallen rose petals. He'd lived the last five years for this night, for his tie to a little dead girl and his duty to her memory. What did he live for now?

"Dammit, Caroline," he muttered as he banged on the ceiling of his carriage and his driver set it in motion. As they turned back towards Grosvenor Square, he saw her. She had not moved from the corner. She stood with a bundle of roses in her arms and his heart broken at her feet.

Christmas Day dawned crisp and clear. Which was far better than Lucien's state of mind at the moment. He'd spent the rest of Christmas Eve and most of the morning slumped in his chair by the fire. Somewhere around six in the morning, Redford had stopped popping into the room every half hour to check for pistols and brandy consumption. He'd found neither. Lucien wanted a brandy. Badly. He wanted clarity more. Clarity to understand how he had so badly judged Caroline's character. Perhaps she had not known about the last five years, but she'd had every opportunity since she'd arrived in London to tell him the truth, to set him free from his guilt. Why?

Bonaparte jumped down from his place on Lucien's pillow and went to scratch on the French windows. Lucien rose and pulled his quilted robe more tightly around him before he limped to let the hairy little beast outside. A few short barks at the top of the stairs and Bonaparte headed towards the door into Winterbourne's garden. Then Lucien saw them. He pressed his hand to one of the frosted panes. The icy coat did not obscure his view.

Bare and broken branches rattled like bones by the wind. A few stray flurries circled the air above the blanket of snow where the gentlest, most giving creature he'd ever known taught her daughter to dance in a frozen London garden. Miss Howard played a lively tune on a violin and called out encouragement to the dancers. Caroline had taken his advice. She walked Lily through the steps with all the laughter and enthusiasm worthy of a Christmas Day. It had to be bitterly cold out of doors. It seeped into his hand from the frozen glass. Here in his bedchamber dressed in the warmest of robes, with a roaring fire at his back, Lucien felt colder than he had in all his life. All the warmth in the world glowed in the smiles of two dancing angels in a winter's ballroom. And as always, he'd put it just out of his reach.

He tore himself away from the sight—old memories already. By his choice. He wandered around the room that had been his self-imposed prison for five years. And it had been self-imposed. Caroline lied. She'd hidden the truth of his innocence from him in the wilds of Scotland. His almost innocence. Nothing absolved him of his part in Forsythe's death and in the grievous injury he'd done the child he now knew as Lily Rose McAlasdair. Were Forsythe here, he'd plant the man a facer for allowing Caroline to drive that night. She might have been killed. And much as he wished to deny it, a world without Caroline in it was not a world he wanted to contemplate. Even if he never spoke to her or held her in his arms again.

If he believed in fairy tales, he might convince himself his selfish, drunken behavior had actually saved the nameless little girl selling flowers in the dead of winter. Who could say how her life might have played out had she not been so horribly hurt, and had Caroline not taken her in to replace the child she'd lost? She'd lied to the whole world about Lily's identity, but sometimes more good came from a lie than harm. The orphaned Covent Garden flower girl was heiress to one of the largest holdings in Scotland. And Lucien would never forgive Caroline for making it so.

He ceased his aimless perambulation and settled into the chair by the fire. Bonaparte trotted back into the room and jumped into the chair beside him. He really should send the furry pestilence back to his little mistress. Lily did not know it, but Bonaparte was actually hers. He scratched absently between those pricked up ears. A brisk knock and the creak of the door announced Redford with a breakfast tray.

"I am not particularly hungry, Redford."

"Cook sent this up for Bonaparte, my lord. If you are polite, he might share it with you." The butler placed the tray on the tea table and lifted the covers from the dishes. Bonaparte hopped onto a stool at the table, left over from tea with Miss Lily, and began to devour a bowl of kidneys and gravy.

"When he has finished his breakfast, send him next door. He will be happier with Miss Lily." Lucien took the cup of tea Redford poured him and sipped it slowly.

"That is his decision to make, my lord. Not yours."

"I did not take you into my confidence to have you side with a four-legged pest." He selected a slice of bacon and began to chew it.

"You took me into your confidence because you know I can keep a secret, whether it be yours or Lady McAlasdair's. She lied to you, my lord. But I cannot believe her intention was to do you harm."

"The road to Hell, Redford." Lucien stared at the teapot and tried to forget midnight suppers and nights laughing and loving he knew he'd never know again. Bonaparte jumped back into the chair, wiggled into a spot between Lucien's bad thigh and the arm of the chair, and sighed.

"Is a road one chooses to travel, Redford observed. "Just as he chooses to get off it and get on with his life."

"That is all, Redford. Happy Christmas." He waved a hand towards the door. Redford sniffed and turned to go.

"Bonaparte knew who she was all along. And he knew who you were too. He could have gone with Miss Lily when her ladyship took her away to those Edinburgh physicians, but he stayed. With you. He knew you were the one who hurt his mistress. You'll never make me believe he didn't, but he stayed. He forgave you. I thought you'd at least have the sense God gave a dog, my lord."

"Apparently not. She ruined my life. Or perhaps she simply ruined my reason for living. Mourning a dead girl has been my whole occupation these five years. What do I do now?"

"You know the girl now, my lord. Were she dead, do you believe her forgiveness would be any less? People do not change. Who you are in life is who you are in death. Dead or alive, this particular girl would forgive you. She would want you to live a long and happy life. A life with her and her mother in it."

"If people do not change, what hope is there for me?"

Redford stepped between Lucien and the fire. "You are a good man, my lord. No matter how bad you have tried to make yourself, that good man wins out. Bonaparte knows it. Miss Lily knows it. You cannot fool the very best judges of character. They know you. As do I. As does Lady McAlasdair. You deserve some happiness. Best get about being yourself. You're the only one you're fooling."

"Go away, Redford. And I take back my Happy Christmas." Lucien finished off his cup of tea and handed Bonaparte the rest of the bacon.

"You are alive, and sober, and eating, my lord. You cannot take that back. I can think of only one more thing you can give me. If you but have the courage to do so."

"I fear I am fresh out, Redford. Close the door behind you."

Bonaparte's soft *woof* stirred Lucien from the doze into which he'd fallen. Apparently learning one's entire life was a lie and having one's heart broken by the woman one... well, suffice it to say, he knew he had slept because the late afternoon sun now shown weakly through his open French windows.

Open? Not again.

"Happy Christmas, Lord Debenwood." Seated in the chair across from him, Miss Lily, with a smartly dressed doll in each arm, stared at him, worry furrowing her brow.

Lucien sat up and looked about, in the pitiful hope her mother had come with her, no doubt. The only thing worse than a fool was a pitiful fool. "Where is your coat, Miss Lily? You should not be here."

"Mrs. McGillicutty sent me out without it. I think she was afraid." She picked up a piece of toast and inspected the selection of jams on the tray.

"Afraid? What in God's name is she afraid of?" Lucien rose slowly and stepped towards the bed in search of a blanket or garment of some sort to wrap around her in order to send her home.

"My grandfather. He was shouting at Mama in the parlor, and Miss Howard told me to go and stay with Mrs. McGillicutty." She bounced out of her chair. "Mrs. McGillicutty told me to come and tell you to hurry your Sassenach *arse* over there. However, I don't think I am supposed to say *arse*, especially not to a viscount."

Lucien tried not to grin and then realized what Lily had said. "Your grandfather the duke?"

"Yes. Mrs. McGillicutty said to bring your pistols if you have the sense God gave you."

"Lily, you stay right here, do you understand? You and Bonaparte do not leave this room unless Redford or your mother or I tell you to, understand?"

"Yes, Lord Debenwood," she answered solemnly. "I understand." She smiled brightly. "Are you going to shoot my grandfather?"

Chapter Nine

Caroline had cried so many tears for Lucien she had none left for herself. Which was just as well. Tears were not helpful when dealing with her father. Very little short of a well-sprung carriage and a team of fast horses was helpful when dealing with His Grace.

"Did you really think you could hide away in the hills of Scotland forever and I would not find out what you were about, girl?"

"Frankly, Father I have not given it or you a great deal of thought. What is it precisely I am about?"

He prowled the parlor as if he owned it. Alex would be furious when he discovered their patriarch had entered his home. Caroline might have purchased a ticket to see such an encounter were the threat of bloodshed not certain.

"Your husband has been dead five years. It is high time I found you another." He walked around her, his eyes traveling over her as if assessing the latest offerings at Tattersal's. "You're not fresh and only one child to your credit. A girl at that, but you are still presentable enough."

"I have no intention of marrying again, least of all a man of whom you approve." Especially not when she feared her heart belonged to a man who would never forgive her.

The duke grabbed her wrist and squeezed. She stared into his face and did not move. He'd grown old since she last saw him. And she'd grown unafraid.

"You will marry where I tell you and I will manage the girl's inheritance. My sources inform me it is considerable."

She pulled her wrist free and walked to the fireplace where she picked up a poker. "You will not touch my daughter or anything that is hers, old man. Get out of my house."

He was on her in two strides. She raised the poker. He grabbed it and wrested it from her. She slapped him. The crack echoed in the high-ceilinged room. It was followed quickly by a louder and more shattering crack.

"Move away from the lady, Your Grace, or I shall be forced to shoot you."

Lucien. He'd left his sanctuary. For her. And he'd fired a pistol into her brother's ceiling.

"Who the hell are you to threaten me?"

Lucien leveled the pistol at the duke's chest. "Lucien Rollinsby, Viscount Debenwood. Your visit is over, Your Grace, unless you wish to spend Christmas in the family mausoleum." He glanced at Caroline, his eyes moving over her as if to check for wounds. "There is a mausoleum, isn't there?"

"A large one. Not as large as the one my brother built for our mother, but large enough." She gazed at him, taking in his slightly disheveled appearance and his rakish grin. Never had a knight errant looked so handsome.

"Debenwood? You're a madman. Everyone knows it. Some sort of recluse. You would not dare shoot me." The duke made a great show of drawing his snuff box from his pocket and indulging in a pinch.

"A madman is far more likely to shoot you than not." Lucien stepped closer and pressed the muzzle of the pistol to her father's chest. "I shot your granddaughter's dancing master for making her unhappy for half an hour. You have made Lady McAlasdair miserable for twenty-four years." He stared the duke down. Lucien neither moved nor blinked.

"He shot her dancing master?" The duke goggled between Lucien and Caroline.

She managed a solemn nod.

"This isn't over, girl," he growled even as he gave Lucien a wide berth. "This isn't over by half." His hurried footsteps on the marble floor, Brooks's murmured farewell, and the resounding slamming of the door finally gave Caroline leave to fold herself into a yellow chintz chair in a heap.

"You put a hole in the ceiling," she observed as she fought back tears.

"It is your brother's house. I am certain it has seen worse. He won't mind. I daresay he will be more upset I did not put a hole in His Grace."

One tear and then another trickled down her face. Lucien came to kneel beside her chair. "There is still time to remedy that, if you wish," he offered.

"My lady, are you all right?" Brooks hurried into the room. "I was in the cellar. The duke knocked young John to the floor."

"I think brandy is in order, Brooks," Lucien said briskly.

"Of course, my lord." Her brother's butler hurried to the sideboard and returned to offer a half-full glass to Lucien.

"For the lady." Lucien handed her the glass and lifted his chin, signaling her to drink.

She took several sips and coughed.

"Better now?"

Caroline nodded. "Thank you, Brooks. Please see to John and tell Miss Howard all is well. Where is Lily?"

"Under guard in my bedchamber," Lucien informed her as Brooks left the room.

"Under guard?" She handed him the glass, which he placed on a side table.

"Redford and Bonaparte. Apparently your Mrs. McGillicutty sent her to me with instructions for me to *get my Sassenach arse over here*."

"Oh, Hell's front parlor." Caroline watched as he struggled to his feet. "Lucien, I—"

"I did not know it at the time, but you saved my life when you saved hers. You didn't have to tell me. I don't know how many more Decembers I might have put down my pistols and cried craven before I finally ended myself. Thank you for that." He clasped her hand and raised it to his lips. "Goodbye, Caroline. I hope you and Lily have everything you desire in the coming year."

Caroline stared at the doorway long after his footsteps ceased to sound going back towards her kitchen. He'd come in through the door between their gardens. He'd left his house to come to her rescue. But he still had not forgiven her. And how could she blame him when she could never forgive herself?

He'd spent the night prowling his house, just as he did every Christmas. This time, however, his pistols were cleaned and packed in their case. He'd taken a long bath and donned the black velvet robe Redford insisted on laying out for him.

He'd even had a bit of Christmas dinner. The servants had allowed him a dish of their Christmas pudding as the other one had been sent over for Miss Lily and her family. He'd slept several hours and now the house was coming to life. It was Boxing Day and whilst Redford certainly had it all in hand, Lucien needed to do something. Especially as the one thing he wanted to do he could not bring himself to do at all.

He strolled into the dining room to find Redford inspecting the silver.

"Good morning, my lord. Is there something I can do for you?"

"I don't think so, Redford." He walked down the table and adjusted a spoon here, a silver salver there. Lying on the table next to Redford was the Christmas gift sent over from Winterbourne's house yesterday evening—a handsome cane with a carved silver head. Apparently, his butler intended to polish the cane head with the silver.

"Would it be easier if you still believed the little girl to be dead?"

Lucien started. Redford looked at him expectantly.

"One man's life was taken," Redford continued when Lucien remained silent. "Nothing can justify that, but the choice was his. Three lives were spared for a reason. Lady McAlasdair is living hers for that child. Is that why you are angry with her? She made a better choice, and your guilt is making you angry with her?"

"I don't know." He didn't, but Redford's questions made him uncomfortable, like wearing wool against his skin.

"Bad things happen every day, my lord. They happened to her as well. She has chosen to take the broken pieces of a bad thing and make it wonderful. That is her gift. She heals broken things with no thought to the jagged edges life has given her."

"I am one of those broken things. I know that, Redford. But I'm afraid."

"Of what?"

"That I have been broken so long not even she has the power to heal me."

"She doesn't. Until you trust her enough to put those broken pieces in her hands."

"She lied to me. She continued to lie even after she knew what it was doing to me."

"You did that to yourself, my lord, if you don't mind me saying. And trust is about forgiveness and faith. All you have to do is decide. And believe."

"Is it really that simple?"

"Love frequently is, my lord."

The light from the rising sun caught the silver dog's head of the cane Lily had given him for Christmas. Lucien reached for it. He examined the silver head, very like Bonaparte's. The cane was an exquisite work of art. The silver head expensive, the carving of the dark mahogany wood the work of a first-rate craftsman. A child, no matter how indulged, did not have the money to purchase such a gift. Caroline had taken the time to commission it long weeks before she and he had become lovers.

"Did you ever stop to think this was all part of God's plan, my lord? He's tried everything else to wake you up. If this doesn't work I don't know what will." Redford bowed, paced out into the foyer, and started up the stairs.

What did the man want of him?

Lucien followed him into the foyer. "If God wants me to

execute a plan he needs to be like Wellington and bloody well tell me," he shouted up the stairs. He gripped his new cane and started up the staircase after his butler.

Redford rounded on him. "That's what angels are for, you great dimwit. He didn't realize you'd be so thick about recognizing them." Standing in the wide corridor of the first floor, servants stopped and stared, aghast.

All the warmth in the world dancing out there in a winter's garden. All the warmth. And all the forgiveness.

"I am an idiot," Lucien muttered.

"Try not to make it a permanent condition, my lord. I doubt He can convince any others to take you on. He had to import these angels from Scotland of all places." He shuddered.

"Well for God's sake, move your *arse* and help me," Lucien leaned on his cane, the one Lily had given him, and waved his hand towards to next flight of stairs. "Help me get dressed."

It was badly done of Caroline to pack up her household, bid Brooks and her brother's other servants a fond farewell, and to make her escape the day after Christmas. She told herself it was to give them time to reach Scotland for Hogmanay. As the carriage drew away from Winterbourne's townhouse and started its slow progress away from Grosvenor Square, she admitted the truth, to herself at least.

She did not want to see Lucien again. The betrayal and anguish in his eyes when he learned what she'd done was too much for her to bear. Forced to marry one man, foolish enough to attach herself briefly to another, she'd not really known a great many men in her life. She'd met dozens.

Danced with them. Flirted with them. Kissed a few. In the space of a few weeks, she'd come to love the one man she knew she was born to love. Lily was her reward in life, one she'd never live long enough to deserve. And Lucien was destined to be her penance, one she'd never live long enough to forget.

"I don't understand why we can't stay and see Uncle Alexander." Lily clutched Miss Debenwood and peered out the carriage window. "I thought you liked Lord Debenwood, Mama. I know he likes you."

"I like him very much, sweetheart. But I did something a long time ago to hurt him. And then I lied about it. And if we stay, I will keep reminding him of the lies and the hurt." She pushed an errant curl over Lily's shoulder. "I think Lord Debenwood has been hurt enough."

"Is that why we left Bonaparte with him? So he won't hurt so much?"

Caroline smiled in spite of the burning sensation at the back of her throat.

Grace reached across and squeezed her hand.

Caroline put her arm around Lily. "That's right, dear. Bonaparte will look after him for you."

"I still don't understand."

"You aren't the only one," Grace muttered.

Caroline kicked her. The carriage lurched to one side as they made the turn out of Grosvenor Square onto the main thoroughfare through London. Lily handed Miss Debenwood to Grace and knelt on the seat to look out the rear carriage window. After a few moments, she began to wave.

"Lily, dearest, sit down." Caroline exchanged a puzzled glance with Grace. "What are you doing?"

"Waving at Lord Debenwood. He's come to see us off."

"What?"

"Good heavens."

Caroline lowered one window whilst Grace lowered the other. A light mist of snow flurries obscured her view for a moment. There in the middle of the street Lucien Rollinsby, Viscount Debenwood, ran through the snow. Ran. Not elegantly in the least. His gate painful to watch, his lean body rocking from side to side as he did so, but he was running. Running after their carriage. Grace half stood, pushed Caroline aside, and knocked on the little window behind the coachman.

"Stop the carriage," the governess ordered. "Stop at once!"

"Grace, wait. Why are you—?"

What was he doing? What was he thinking? Caroline scarcely dared hope. Perhaps he'd changed his mind about Bonaparte. What should she do? Fortunately, she had Grace to answer that question for her. She reached around Caroline and opened the door.

"Get out of the carriage, Caro. Let him see you." She practically shoved Caroline into the street.

She blinked away the snowflakes. His face. She needed to see his face. She took one step forward, then another. Grace and Lily hung out the carriage door. She wanted to run to him. She wanted to, but the lies and hurt and secrets held her back. What did she have to offer him other than more pain?

Caroline gasped.

He fell. Lucien lay sprawled in the street. He pushed himself to his knees on a cane. The silver head glinted in the feeble sunlight.

"Get up," Caroline whispered. "Get up."

He raised his head. His eyes met hers. She watched him firm his jaw. Slowly, oh so slowly, he rose to his feet. He took a step. Steadied himself. Took another. Then Caroline was running. Racing down one of the most high-in-the-instep streets in London like the hoyden she'd been five years ago, but so much wiser now.

She flung herself into his arms and nearly knocked him over again.

"Lucien, oh, Lucien, my love." Caroline kissed him until they were both out of breath. "Can you ever—"

He touched his gloved finger to her lips. "Did you mean to?"

She shook her head, breath baited in anticipation of his next question.

"Are you sorry?"

"Very much."

"Will you do it again?"

"Never."

He tightened his arms around her. "Then it goes away and we never think of it again. Love makes us ever so forgetful. It forgets all the bad things and remembers all the good. And if you truly love someone, you simply must forgive them." He touched his forehead to hers.

"And do you truly love me?" Caroline asked gazing into the face of the bravest and dearest man she'd ever known.

"Of course, I do." He brushed his lips across her brow and moved to whisper in her ear. "Shall I prove it with a kiss?"

"Yes, please."

He seized her mouth with such a kiss she believed herself in the middle of a summer's day. The snow, the wind—it all melted away against the heat and passion Lucien poured into her with his kiss.

"Don't go," he rasped when he released her lips at last. "I love you, Caroline. I don't know what I was thinking before, but it doesn't matter. All that matters is I love you, and I need you. You, and Lily, and Bonaparte, and even that tyrant Mrs. McGillicutty."

If she lived to be a hundred, Caroline would never forget his face in that moment. The clear, glorious light of love in his eyes. The fiery forgiveness of his kiss. The strength in the arms of a man who'd fought back from the hell she'd had a hand in creating to chase her through the streets of London in the snow to—

"Oh, Lucien, what are you doing? Get up, you'll do yourself a harm, my love."

With the help of his cane, he'd lowered himself onto one knee. "Lady Caroline Chastleton McAlasdair, will you do me the very great honor of becoming my wife?"

"Here, Lucien, in the middle of the street?"

"Not here, precisely. All you have to do here is say yes. And then help me up because I'm not certain I can at this point."

"Then, yes, Lucien, I'll be your wife. Now please, get up." She grasped his arm and helped him to his feet.

The carriage rumbled up beside them. Lily leapt out of the door into Lucien's outstretched arms.

"You're using my cane." She fairly beamed at him and threw her arms around his neck. He closed his eyes and held her close. Caroline's heart swelled beyond the confines of her ribs. She did not know if she'd be the best mother Lily might have had, but she had no doubt Lucien would be the best father in England.

"I take it we will not be returning to Scotland today," Grace said as they all climbed into the carriage.

"No, Miss Howard, today my ladies and I are going home." Lucien used his cane to rap on the roof. "And a good thing too. Bonaparte warned me not to dare return without you."

"Talking to Bonaparte again, are you?" Caroline teased as he laced their fingers together and raised her hand to kiss it.

"Until your brother moved you and your noisy household in next door, Bonaparte was all I had, my love. I wrote Winterbourne a most inelegant letter about it the day you

arrived."

"And now, Lord Debenwood?" Grace inquired.

"Now, I have to write him a *bloody letter* and thank him."

"Thank him for what?" Lily asked.

Lucien gazed at Caroline, that incendiary gaze, burning with the promise of days and nights of gifts, of celebration, and of love. "For the most unforgettable Christmas of my life."

About Louisa

Louisa Cornell is a retired opera singer living in LA (Lower Alabama) who cannot remember a time she wasn't writing or telling stories. Anglophile, student of Regency England, historical romance writer—she is a member of RWA, Southern Magic RWA, and the Beau Monde Chapter of RWA. Her first published work, the novella *A Perfectly Dreadful Christmas* in the anthology Christmas Revels, won the 2015 Holt Medallion for Excellence in Romance Fiction. Her first full-length Regency romance novel came out in May 2017. *Lost in Love* is the first in Cornell's Road to Forever series. Currently working on the next novel in the series, *Lost in Desire*, Louisa lives off a dirt road on five acres in the middle of nowhere with a chihuahua so bad he is banned from vet clinics in two counties, several very nice dogs, and a cat who thinks she is a Great Dane and terminates vermin with extreme prejudice.

Check in on Louisa's latest books, Regency obsessions, and adventures at
https://www.facebook.com/RegencyWriterLouisaCornell
and http://numberonelondon.net/

Our Thanks

This is the fourth in the Christmas Revels series, and each new edition has been more successful than the last. For this, we would like to thank our readers, many of whom have said they look forward to the arrival of each new collection. We do our best to offer you thoughtful stories with Christmas at their heart and hope to continue to be worthy of your interest. Do we guarantee that you will "love" each and every story? Of course not. We all have different tastes. But we *can* guarantee that we have all taken great care to present the best tale possible.

We hope you enjoyed our efforts and that they have enhanced your Christmas spirit. If you missed any of the earlier volumes of *Christmas Revels*, be sure to check them out—*Christmas Revels*, *Christmas Revels II*, and *Christmas Revels III*. Each contains totally different, but equally delightful, novellas.

Also, please consider leaving an honest review at any of the purchasing sites. This helps other readers decide if this book will meet their needs. We're glad you chose to visit with these pieces of our imaginations.

Thanks,

Kate Louisa Anna Hannah

81176919R00239

Made in the USA
Columbia, SC
17 November 2017